THE OTHER SIDE OF REALITY

BOOK THREE

THE DOOR OF DOROGON

DEDICATION

To my two eldest grandsons, Gavin and Eathan Russell, and my granddaughter and youngest grandson Kaia Grace and Ian Ryan Durham; and to all the grandchildren everywhere, young and old, whom the Living One so deeply loves.

∞————————————————————————————————————∞

This Trilogy is also dedicated to the memory and impact of Charlie Kirk whose gracious and staunch love of the truth helped so many to find the light leading to *the other side of reality*.

ABOUT THIS TRILOGY

This Trilogy is what C. S Lewis would have called "a supposal." It is a story using *likening*—comparing different aspects of reality to what it is *not* for the purpose of revealing more of what it is—to pull the reader into an other-worldly adventure from which he or she may look back on this world with an enhanced objectivity and clarity.

The haunting awareness—clear to some and vague to others— that this world is pointing beyond itself, that it is even sometimes a poor mirror giving us fleeting, tantalizing glimpses of another world, or an echo that dies away before the beauty of some majestic melody can be fully heard, often awakens us to deliciously painful longings. *The Other Side of Reality* seeks to bring the objects of these longings into sharper focus for the reader, and perhaps, for some, to awaken the experience of such longings for the first time.

These longings point to more than desire. They leave an imprint on the soul like an ocean wave leaves on a beach. The imprint testifies to the reality of the wave. When we properly contemplate the imprints left on our souls by the invisible waves often washing over us uninvited, we are startled by an involuntary spring of hope rising within us. It is a hope crying for life to have a meaning and purpose that comes from beyond this world and will outlive this world.

In this sense, this Trilogy is an attempt to give perspective: a perspective much needed in a culture where reductionism has shriveled the organ of meaning—our imaginations—by dehydrating the significance of life and everything it contains. If, *"this is only that"* is the ultimate pathway to reality, then the only possible conclusion is unrelenting despair.

But that despair, itself, raises the question: Why do we despair? Why do we hope for more? If there isn't any more, why do we long for it? Why do we pine? If we are mere accidents between two cosmic voids, why do the desires for meaning and purpose, identity and security tug so relentlessly at our souls? Are there truths beyond our senses to which this hunger and thirst point?

The Other Side of Reality, by means of a fascinating story, seeks to raise and focus these questions in the form of a *supposal*. *Suppose* someone were taken to the other side of reality and could see not only the material world but the world lying beyond and behind it. *Suppose* they were also taken out of their time and dropped into the flow of our world's first history. *Suppose* there was a critical reason for them to be there and the meaning and purpose of all future life would hang on their willingly engaging a dangerous journey, and so forth. By means of such a story, it is my belief this kind of *likening* can silhouette the answers—the *objects* for which we hunger and thirst—and resurrect the true passion of living.

I make no apologies for believing there is another side to reality and that it can be known because *Someone* is seeking to reveal it. What is more, I believe the other side of reality has a very definite character and nature; it is filled both with risk, danger and possible tragedy as well as adventure, love and possible triumph; and you will determine which it will be for you by how you engage these unseen actualities.

Welcome to *The Other Side of Reality!*

— *Gary L. Durham, June 14, 2025*

PREFACE

Dr. Gary L. Durham is a fascinating man—scholar, science buff, theologian, counselor, teacher, musician, even a bit of a daredevil. He's one of those guys who keep surprising you with new facets of his personality that you didn't know were there. He's the only man I know who writes patents for fun on his "day off" and thinks zip-lining less than 100 feet off the ground is boring. Among his many other talents, I've discovered that Gary is an incredibly creative storyteller. I'm honored to call him my friend.

The Other Side of Reality is an imaginative adventure born in Gary's heart many years ago and is finally making its way to the printed and digital page. It's the tale of a young woman who is pulled into a daring quest in which the future of humanity is at stake. The quest takes place on The Other Side of Reality, the realm in which both material and spiritual realities are seen and interacted with in ways that reveal the Creator's grand Story more clearly than most of us have ever imagined. She fights intense battles, confronts many faces of evil, learns to love and trust, and is forever changed by her encounters with *the real world* like you've never seen it. The story entertains, inspires and teaches, all with one stroke. Editing this work has been a labor of love.

Congratulations on discovering *The Other Side of Reality*. This tale will enrich your life!

— Don White, Editor

ACKNOWLEDGEMENTS

In undertaking any endeavor and bringing it to completion, I doubt any of us can fully comprehend the extent to which we owe gratitude for the contributions of others. From our first breath until our last we are continually being formed and re-formed by the influence of other people either for good or ill.

At this stage in my life, I have come to acknowledge and appreciate that whatever successes I can claim are owed more to the competent generosity of others as they have impacted my life. By sharing their knowledge, skill, friendship and gifts with me they have determined the outcome more than any autonomous efforts of my own. In deciding and executing the writing of this Trilogy, I have found it to be a journey continually highlighting and reenforcing this truth.

In one sense, in writing a supposal with historical truths interlaced and undergirding the whole novel story, with the addition of theo-philosophical and apologetic applications embedded, I was in my element. However, I soon realized my many years of academic research and theological writing had trained me to a style of writing inappropriate to the new audience I was seeking to reach. And it was the many contributions of my colleagues and friends lovingly seeking to assist me, which confirmed this realization.

They loved the story. They loved its many impacts on the worldview of the reader. Yet, they ever-so-patiently kept suggesting I needed to use a very different style of writing to communicate it.

My primary editor, Don White, was the first to suffer through seeking to redirect my writing style to one more appropriate to the content and its intended audience. To state Don is a good friend who has the patience of Job is no overstatement. His kind, yet unyielding editorial skill and work continually confronted me with the need to stop and seek to learn another way of writing.

To the extent I succeeded remains to be assessed by you the reader. To the extent attained it is due to the generous, skillful, loving and persistent help of numerous literary friends God has brought into my life.

That being said, I must express my heartfelt, though abbreviated, appreciation to the following colleagues, friends and family members:

To Joshua "Gavin" Russell, my grandson, whose brilliant, creative and imaginative mind added untold value in getting me beyond some stop points when once I took the story, begun many years before, off the shelf to be finished. Gavin, Papa will always be more grateful than you could possibly know! I will always treasure our times of reading and discussing the books on our *Man Trips*. There are many ways in which this is your story, too.

To my editorial reading group, many of which are very talented and successful authors in their own right, the Red Inklings: thank you for the many hours of reading, discussions, corrections and suggestions. To Hugh Vickery (who has two excellent books just becoming available for which the Red Inklings provided editorial feedback), Diane Rudd, Rose Arndt, Jeannine Voisinet, Rose Rohloff (whose red pen was merciless but effective), Anthony DeSantis (whom I want to congratulate on his New York Times best seller, *The Stowaway In First Class*, which the Red Inklings helped to edit), and Rick Walker.

Also, a few years back as the books were taking form, I want to thank my accountability reading circle, which at that time included Gary & Irene Merritt and Diane Rudd. They held me to the task and provided much-appreciated feedback week after week.

To my dear friend and ministry partner, Gary Merritt, whose loyal and effective ministry as Executive Pastor has enabled me to give myself more fully to the teaching and writing I am called to do.

To my general editor, Don White (mentioned above), whose skillful and creative massaging and rephrasing of my early manuscripts has made this work much more readable and attainable to a broader audience than my own academic and sometimes-verbose writing style could have accomplished.

To a good friend, who has since unexpectedly gone Home to be with our Lord, Darren Currin, who took several vacation days from his ministry at Life Church in Oklahoma City, to go through the books with me as a content editor. I will always be thankful for your contributions.

To my C. S. Lewis reading group at New Hope, which took several weeks away from our normal diet to read through some of the early material for the Trilogy. Thanks for being willing to descend from the joyous, intoxicating heights of *Jack* to the lowlands of Gary.

To several precious friends who have been willing to read the manuscripts and give sage feedback. Among them my lifelong best friend and brother, Rev. Larry Ryan, and another precious longtime friend, Dr. Steven Fletcher, and a longtime colleague and partner in ministry, Rev. Alan Scott. Also, Dr. Stan Toler, Dr. Pat and Mark McNab, and Lois Fazier (Lois read some of the first chapters written over 30 years ago when the dream of this Trilogy was first given birth). Thanks to all of you for letting me impose *my* dream on *you*.

To my wonderful New Hope family who are a constant encouragement to me and my ministry. No pastor/teacher could have a more positive atmosphere of love and support in which to serve.

To Tony and Judy DeSantis, Gary and Jan Motley and Larry and Gayla Ryan for making unsolicited financial investments in seeing this dream become reality. Your generosity has been a blessed confirmation for me to finish strong.

To my precious, loving and supportive family. My son-in-law, David, my daughter, Janet, my grandsons, Gavin and Ethan (and Gavin's new wife Kayla), for your example of sacrificial ministry and commitment to excellence as missionaries in Tanzania, Africa and now in the counseling ministry here in the states after your return. To my son, Ryan, who has served many years in ministry as Worship Pastor, many of which has been here at New Hope, and his wife, Colleen. Thanks for being such dedicated, loving parents to my two grandchildren, Kaia Grace and Ian Ryan. Ryan, your creative gift of music and composition shared in both worship settings and through your albums, is a constant source of inspiration. Every week you lead in creating a Spirit-anointed atmosphere of worship in which I can preach and teach.

To my dearest friend and loving wife, Sheryl, who has been my partner in many different ministry assignments from missionary, pastor, teacher, counselor, musician, etc. Your own mastery of music and your use of it to serve our Lord and even teach hundreds of students is beyond expression. Several years ago, the Living One used Sheryl to confirm I was indeed to finish this project. Sheryl, you are God's gift of so much beauty and grace to me and our family. I am indeed blessed to journey this life with you!

Above all others, my thanks goes to the Living One, Himself, King Jesus, who kept stimulating and sanctifying my imagination and efforts to His purpose through the long and sometime-tedious hours of writing, rewriting, editing and revising. All the while, His Presence never left my side, giving me direction and clarity and the self-control I needed to keep this hyperactive Type-A personality focused on such a long task.

Repeatedly I have looked back after writing a chapter and realized He had written something through me I could never have conceived of on my own. All the good is from Him. All the flaws are from me.

I have grown as I have struggled to find new ways of communicating the old, unchangeable, ever-new realities of His beauty and glory. And in those months of emersion, I really did have the privilege of being sometimes on *The Other Side of Reality!*

— **Gary L. Durham, June 14, 2025**

TABLE OF CONTENTS

Map of
Severed Lands

The Great Chasm

Beast of Paranoia

f EL

Thanatos' Domain

ateau

Nekus Canyon

Rock Bridge

Altar

ellicose's
Domain

Valley

Lavon's Savanna

The
Garden

Dorogon Ridge

Mist Forest

Ruins of Dorogon Castle

Mist Mountain

Hill of Voices

Tree Bridge

Dry Stream Bed

IMPORTANT NAMES AND MEANINGS

Diakrina (Dia-KREE-na): The prefix, Dia, is to be pronounced Anglicized as in, *Diaphragm*

Strateia (Strah-TEE-ah—Anglicized from the true Greek pronunciation, Strah-TAY-ah): Warfare, to make war, a great host or army, thus as applied to one person: A Great Warrior

Anomos Poneros (AH-no-mos Po-NAY-ros)

Heylel (Hay-LEL): Morning Star; one who shines brightly

Scepter Of Kabod (Kah-BAHD)

Kingdom Of Parad (Paw-RAHD)

Tuphoo (Too-FAH-oh)

Thanatos (THAN-ah-tos): Fallen angel of death, lord over the realms of the dead

Nekus (Neh-koos): The canyon of Thanatos, which name means corpse

BOOK THREE
THE QUEST REVEALED

Chapter One

THE BATTLE FOR RESURRECTION

With the Living One's last words still ringing in her ears ("LOOK IMMEDIATELY FOR MY FOOTPRINTS! DANGER IS ON YOU!"), Diakrina landed in a crouched position with both hands on the handle of her sword. Its blade was still engulfed in the tornado of Light from the Lantern of Logos. As everything came more into focus, she was able to confirm to herself she was standing in the large courtyard in front of Thanatos' Temple of Death. All was not quite dark as the pale, greenish light, she had encountered before, was radiating from the Temple complex out over the entire courtyard.

The light illuminated everything up to about hundred feet in the air. Above that, it faded slowly into a dome of inky darkness, which felt as if it pressed down like a heavy lid.

Diakrina found herself wanting to cover her ears as the roar of the falls had instantly crescendoed to its full incomprehensible roar as the light deposited her in the courtyard. It felt more like the crashing of hundreds of ocean waves every second than it did waves of sound in the air. She was once again completely engulfed in a thunderous silence. Nothing whatever could be heard but the falls of Nekus and that sound was too big to hear; it deafened instead of defined.

It was painful.

Her first inclination was to confirm her orientation in the courtyard so she could start immediately toward the descending stairs. She looked up from her crouched position and located the large obelisks halfway between her and the Temple. These were to her left, as she had landed facing the east canyon wall. From this orientation she knew the stairs would be to her right.

Diakrina pivoted on the balls of her feet in the direction of the stairs and rose slowly in the pounding surf of sound. At first, she found it hard to keep her equilibrium under the constant hammer-like blows rolling over her. She had fully intended to run immediately toward the staircase, but as she was rising and steadying herself, out of the corner of her eye, she caught a glimpse of a crimson footprint to her left.

It was pointed in the direction of the canyon wall to the east, not in the direction of the stairs. There was a split second of bewilderment as her resolution to run straight for the staircase was temporarily frozen as her mind tried to sort out what to do next.

She turned her head to stare at the footprint and then saw a second glowing footprint appear one stride beyond the first. It was in that instant the memory of the other part she had last heard before being dropped to this ledge came rushing back, "LOOK IMMEDIATELY FOR MY FOOTPRINTS."

Diakrina didn't understand why she needed to run toward the canyon wall instead of the staircase. But she now knew better than to question.

She pivoted left and began running in the direction the footprints were leading. The glowing footprints always stayed two steps ahead of her even though she was running as fast as her legs could carry her. In fact, the length between the footprints seemed to indicate a running stride. It struck Diakrina she was being urged to hurry!

The reason for this haste was not long in manifesting itself. A large dark shadow flicked past, from left to right, on the rock in front of Diakrina as she was running. When she glanced upward, she saw the unmistakable form of a flying Nekros circling back to her right to come around on her backside. Immediately Diakrina knew this was no ordinary Nekros: it was ten times the size of those she had battled on the crystal stairs between the Porticos and the Castle. Its size made it seem more like a dragon than anything else to which she could compare it.

Diakrina didn't slow down to look but rather doubled her efforts as she continued running toward the canyon wall pursuing the glowing footprints. Yet, she couldn't keep herself from constantly glancing upward trying to keep track of the huge flying beast. She quickly realized she had more to worry about than just the one large creature. For descending out of the canopy of dark sky, above the greenish glow being cast over the whole courtyard by the temple, were several more of the giant Nekros circling toward her.

A cold panic began rising inside Diakrina. All she could do was trust to her Guide. She ran as fast as her legs would carry her.

In the dull greenish light, she was suddenly surprised by the appearance of large, house-size boulders in front of her. In fact, if she had not been faithfully following exactly where the footprints were leading, she likely would have run face-first into one of them. As it was, she found she had been led right into a narrow opening between two large stones.

It was none too soon. She had no sooner entered the narrow opening than rock and debris rained down on top of her. She heard nothing—for you must remember no sound could be heard in this place of continuous thunder—but she felt the two boulders on either side of her shudder from the impact of the great beast which had just missed her as she entered the opening.

In fact, as she raised her shield over her head to deflect the falling stones, she was knocked to the ground by a large talon slashing down into the opening from overhead. The Nekros had reached toward her with his long legs as he hit the top of the boulders. Fortunately for Diakrina, her fall had put her just beyond the reach of the beast's grasp. It slashed at her several more times just failing to reach her by inches.

Diakrina rolled over onto her back in time to see the large talon probing the air above her. She was sure she screamed as the large, curved claws came within inches several times. But of course, it was like a silent scream failing to become audible as it was drowned in the ocean of sound coming from Nekus.

Diakrina wasn't sure what to do next. She was afraid to rise for fear of coming within reach of the terrible talons. But she clearly couldn't just lie where she was as the beast continued to claw at the opening between the boulders and rain rock down on her, which likely meant it was tearing a wider breach at the top so it could reach deeper into the gap.

Diakrina turned onto to her right side and held the shield up over her head with her left arm. With her sword still in her outstretched right hand she began crawling deeper into the opening between the boulders. The fury of the beast above her only increased as it tore relentlessly at the top of the stones sending a constant rain of dirt and rock down on her. And every few seconds her shield would be slammed down onto her body by the force of the large claws slashing frantically at her.

Not knowing what else to do, and not having time or presence of mind to look for the footprints, Diakrina kept crawling deeper into the passage between the great boulders. She could see the red glowing eyes from the Nekros as it would push its head down into the opening to follow her movements and then, lifting its head out, would slash violently down at her.

She had crawled only about twenty feet when she realized the Nekros was no longer slashing at her. She peeked out from under her shield and could just tell by the slight contrast between the blackness in the passage and the dull, greenish light coming from the gap above, that the space between the boulders had considerably narrowed. It was now too small for the Nekros to continue reaching through. However, she could see the beast following her movements with its large glowing red eyes as it continued to stalk her along the narrowing space between the rocks.

Realizing the Nekros could no longer slash at her, Diakrina scrambled to her feet and retreated even farther into the boulders. She had not gone far when the opening above disappeared as the boulders came together completely at the top. She was now actually in something like a narrow cave.

With the rock and debris no longer falling on her, Diakrina lowered her shield and, using the swirling rainbow of Light coming from around the blade of her sword, paused to look around her. Ahead of her was a solid wall of rock. It was clearly another large boulder. At its face, the passage turned both left and right. It seemed obvious to her she should turn right since this was the direction of the staircase she was trying to reach.

Diakrina turned down the right-hand passage. It opened at the top between the boulders on either side of her so there was once again enough of a gap overhead to allow a small amount of light to come from above. She had not gone far before there was a pile of smaller boulders on the floor of the passage requiring her to climb over. She had taken only a couple of steps up the boulder pile when a small pebble fell from above and landed on her shoulder. She looked up and realized the gap between the boulders had widened and the Nekros had located her.

Because she was now closer to the top it was fortunate the Nekros had dislodged the pebble and alerted her. For the moment she looked up the talons of the Nekros lashed downward toward her. She saw it too late. She was too high to avoid it altogether. She ducked her head under her shield and struck blindly with her sword over her head.

Her sword did not so much strike as it was struck. Diakrina was tumbled backwards down the rock pile. As she was falling, her desperate struggle to locate the Nekros resulted in her seeing two things happening above her. First, cartwheeling through the air above her was a portion of the Nekros' appendage. At the same time the face of the Nekros, which had been pushed down into the gap between the boulders, was obviously in the contortions of a scream, which Diakrina could see but not hear.

Then the crimson light from her sword, and the rainbow of light from the swirling Lantern, together shot through the gap above her, where the Nekros' head was protruding downward. The wounded Nekros seemed to literally explode as his head vaporized right before Diakrina. The demise of the Nekros and Diakrina's tumble down to the original level of the passage, put her out of danger for a few seconds. She lay on the tunnel floor looking in astonishment at her sword with the rainbow of solid, swirling Light all around it. "Wow!" was all her mind could manage.

Though she had a good portion of the breath knocked out of her, she struggled to her feet and began retreating down the passage to where she had taken the turn. Here the passage was completely covered and she felt secure enough from the other Nekros to stop and try to gain her breath.

As she stood there panting, she looked to her left down the original passage she had first crawled down. While the part of the passage closest to her was covered and dark, the farther part of the passage was dimly lit by the gap between the boulders. The greenish light was just strong enough Diakrina realized something was moving toward her from the far end of the passage!

Diakrina froze, staring hard in the dim light trying to make out the moving form by piecing together the patchwork of subtle movements which were detectable here and there. Whatever it was, it was large. Not as large as a Nekros: they were too big to fit into the passage. Its movement was unusual. It didn't seem to be flying or walking. What could it …?

Panic flooded Diakrina. It was slithering … like a serpent. Not more than 50-feet from her, red, unblinking eyes glided into view. Diakrina's heart was in her mouth. For some reason—likely the pure terror of wanting to retreat—she swiftly whirled 270 degrees around to her right and ran several steps down the passage from which she had just come. She would have to risk getting past any Nekros as she scrambled over the rock pile.

But again, out of the corner of her eye, as she was spinning around to retreat, she saw a glowing footprint pointing down the other passageway which went left toward the Temple and away from the stairs.

It was then Diakrina realized she had likely put herself in this predicament by once again forgetting to look for the footprints. She had wasted time taking the wrong turn and having to retrace her steps. But there was no time to scold herself now. She quickly reversed direction hoping she had time to get to the opposite passage before the serpent arrived at the intersection.

It was going to be close. She was now, like never before, watching intently for the footprints, which were her only sense of hope and help. She bolted across the intersection of the passageways and saw the serpent, the size of a small train, was only twenty feet away and closing fast. In her panic she never gave a thought to what she had just seen the sword accomplish as the Nekros had touched it. All her panic-saturated-body could do was run.

And run she did. With all her might she bolted down the passage and was relieved to see the crimson footprints leading the way. The narrow path between the boulders made a quick turn to the right and continued for about thirty feet and then made another sharp turn to the right. Now she was at least headed back toward the staircase.

Though she could hear nothing due to the thunder of the falls, Diakrina could somehow sense the slithering scales of the serpent gliding over the rocks of the passage behind her, coming ever nearer. It made the back of her neck crawl with a burning sensation feeling also like a kind of tremor of dread. But she dare not take time to look back. She could only hope all the sharp turns would slow the serpent's progress.

The footprints then turned down a side passage back to the left again—toward the canyon wall. Then after about five long strides, turned her back to the right once more. Diakrina was beginning to realize she was in a kind of maze winding between large house-size boulders. While much of this maze was narrow, and the top of the gaps between the boulders small enough to keep the Nekros out, it was still wide enough for the serpent to continue its' pursuit.

But that was about to change. Once again, the glowing footprints led Diakrina, still running at breakneck speed, to make a sharp right turn into a very narrow passage. It was so narrow Diakrina had to hold her left arm straight out in front of her so the shield would turn sideways and fit through the passageway. She also needed to turn her shoulders somewhat to make them narrow enough to pass. Obviously, this was because she chose to hold her right arm back behind her with the blade of the sword pointed back at the approaching serpent. Even with all this, she was still scraping and bruising her elbows and knees as they chafed on the boulders to either side.

Then the passage became even narrower. It began to close in very tight at the top so that Diakrina could no longer stand and run. She had to stoop in a very awkward position while still trying to keep her body slightly turned sideways. This slowed her progress so much she could no longer keep from looking back for fear the serpent was right on her.

It was! And it was so big it seemed to fill the whole available space in the passageway behind Diakrina. Its' large Anaconda-like body and wide head, fitted with glowing red eyes and flicking tongue, was so close Diakrina could have touched it with the tip of her sword if she had reached a foot or two behind her. But its progress was also greatly slowed due to the way the passage squeezed in on it.

Diakrina would have wondered if she were not headed for a dead end if it had not been for the continual presence of the glowing footprints, which were clearly leading her. She pushed and scraped forward as fast as she could with complete disregard for the scuffing her skin was taking. The serpent twisted and curled up and down the narrow cut trying to find the widest places through, until its' long body was contorted and entwined all up and down the narrow corridor.

Diakrina then came to a place where she could no longer go forward without getting down on her hands and knees and crawling. Since the footprints continued, she darted into the small tunnel on all fours. She had not gone more than ten feet like this when it suddenly opened back up enabling her to stand fully upright.

She jumped to her feet and turned with her shield and sword at the ready: she was sure the vile serpent would come through onto her. But to her surprise it couldn't. The tunnel was too small, and the serpent was trapped in the narrow passageway trying to fold back on itself and retreat to another route.

Diakrina wasted no time watching its contortions. She turned and ran down the narrow corridor up ahead following the glowing footprints. They turned again to the left and continued for some time in a passageway nearly covered yet was large enough for Diakrina to run with her shield and sword in their proper positions.

Then the passage came to a sudden end. Diakrina came up against a wall of rock rising high into the air. It was part of the canyon wall at the place where it curved back west toward the staircase.

The footprints turned to the right and disappeared. Diakrina pushed up close to the rock wall and then realized there was enough room between the wall and the last boulder to slide sideways along the wall with her sword in front and her left arm and shield behind.

The breach along the wall—between what turned out to be a long line of boulders—continued for about 100 yards and took Diakrina several minutes to negotiate. Then, abruptly, the boulders came to an end while the canyon wall continued. The last boulder lay at an angle away from the canyon wall which made for a wider opening. The pale green light shining in where the boulders ceased made the end of the breach seem like the mouth of a cave.

Diakrina crept to the opening. She peered up into the greenish canopy of light which covered the whole area of the falls and the temple courtyard. She was searching the black sky above for any hint of the giant Nekros.

They would surely be looking for her. She wondered if they actually would be expecting her to head for the staircase. After all, they were one-way stairs, and she doubted the beast would anticipate anyone trying to use them to leave the courtyard.

Diakrina looked for the footprints once again. There were two—a left and right—side by side at the opening, evidently indicating she should stand here and size up the situation and wait to be led.

As she peered out west over the southern end of the courtyard, she could see the place where the staircase opened onto the ledge. It was about 70-yards away. The area between was a very open space which ran along the place where the canyon wall curved back west toward the stairs. When it reached it, it turned sharply back south with the staircase at its very edge. This edge formed part of the ledge which ran along the river and was above where the waters of the river plunged over Nekus Falls.

She was afraid to stay where she was very long. She was constantly looking behind her to see if the accursed serpent had dislodged itself and was slithering toward her. Yet, at the same time, she was in no hurry to fight the giant Nekros. If they were to see her too soon, she might not make it across the large open area between her and the staircase.

Diakrina looked intently at the faintly glowing footprints. As she stood there anxious about what to do and when to do it, someone began speaking to her in her thoughts.

"Look at your sword Diakrina. Remember it is encased in the Light from the Lantern of Logos. It is this infinite Light which will take you through the nine-barriers. Get your sword out in front of you to lead you and then charge across the open area as fast as your legs will carry you. Don't stop to look to the right or to the left—nor to look up or look down. Focus on the landing of the staircase and think of nothing else except reaching it and passing through its first barrier without a single hesitation."

There was a very pregnant pause and then she heard very distinctly, "If anything gets in the way, slay it with the sword without delay. The Light will engulf you and protect you. But it will destroy anything else it touches."

Diakrina looked up and stared at the landing in front of the staircase across the large open area. Then she looked back down at the slightly glowing crimson footprints in front of her. She knew the moment had come. She waited like a sprinter coiled for the starting gun. She pulled her shield close, checking to make sure the crystal container with the Atheon was secured behind her on her left side. She then gripped her sword.

Suddenly the footprints began racing across the expanse. Diakrina swallowed hard and gave chase. She ran for about 20-yards without incident. But then, a dark shadow flashed on the ground ahead of her and she knew a Nekros had spotted her and was circling overhead.

The race was on!

Almost exactly like a four-hundred-meter sprinter in full stride

Diakrina ran straight for the landing without heeding anything else. Two Nekros began circling her. The first suddenly dived straight at her, talons fully extended. Diakrina ducked and rolled just as the grasping claws slashed at her. She rolled back onto her feet without even pausing and again hit full stride.

The second Nekros was hovering in the air low and made several attempts to grasp Diakrina. Each time she stutter-stepped or cut hard around the slashing appendages. It stalked her for several yards thrusting its talons down into the ground all around her, sending dirt and rock like missiles through the air, in a frantic attempt to get its vise-like grip on her.

And while Diakrina was darting and dodging this second Nekros, the first one circled around between Diakrina and the landing of the staircase and settled down like a huge dinosaur between her and the opening. Obviously, it had surmised her goal and was determined to prevent her from reaching it.

Diakrina had been told not to stop. She had been told to slay whatever came between her and her goal. This she was determined to do. Yet … at the same time … it seemed so impossible. The mountain of creature was simply too big for her to attack. And the closer she came to it the more foolish her hope of being able to fight seemed.

All of this was tumbling through her mind while at the same moment the fierce countenance of the red-eyed beast was turning hatefully upon her. Just the look of it would have sent her screaming in the other direction if she had not once again looked down and seen the crimson footprints leading her stride for stride straight at the beast.

Diakrina bit her lip and gathered all her resolve. She ran headlong into the Nekros with her Light encased sword pointed straight at the highest point on its body she could reach, which was its' underbelly. When her sword touched the skin of the creature there was a huge explosion of Light. Shafts of Light went everywhere except in Diakrina's direction. She was instantly encased in a protective sphere of radiance.

Thousands of shafts of Light, harder than the most tempered steel, shot out like hundred-foot daggers. The beast in front of

Diakrina was shredded into small smoking pieces of flesh. The pieces soared into the air and then rained down onto the courtyard floor. She didn't have time to check what happened to the other Nekros, but the shafts of light were so many, and so far-reaching, Diakrina had no doubt it met the same fate as it was only a few feet above her.

And while all this was happening Diakrina was still running. She jumped and dodged through the pieces of falling Nekros and kept her eyes on her goal: the top of the staircase.

She transversed through most of the falling pieces and realized she was now only about twenty yards from her goal. "Almost there!" she said to herself.

Then something struck at her heel from behind and caused Diakrina to almost fall. It took all her effort to keep from sprawling face-first onto the ground in front of her. As she was flailing at the air, she turned her head enough to see what she had previously feared: the giant serpent had caught up to her.

Everything seemed to be in slow motion as Diakrina's senses were now engaging every millisecond at hyper speed while she was trying to keep her balance. She could see the serpent pulling its head back to her left to make another strike. If she fell now, it would be on top of her. For some reason, at that moment, she remembered the formerly impenetrable walls of the stairway. They had been hard as steel and were almost impossible to see due to their near transparency. Would she be able to get through the first one quickly enough?

Somehow, she managed to keep her feet under her and continue running. The landing of the stairway was only a few steps away. But there was no stopping the strike of the serpent. She could feel the inevitable attack coming toward her left side.

Diakrina swung her shield backward toward the serpent while at the same moment she flung herself, sword-first, toward the spot where the first barrier should be. There was nothing for it but to grip the sword handle with all her might and hope.

The head of the serpent hit her shield hard. In fact, the strike of the large reptile slammed the shield into her left side and accelerated her body—which was in midair—toward the wall. It was all she could do to keep the sword pointed straight out in front of her; yet somehow, she did.

The swirling rainbow of Light around the sword blade hit the barrier. Instantly every color you could imagine, and then some you could not, burst all through the clear substance.

Diakrina's body hit the barrier; and at the same moment the head and body of the serpent hit it as well. To Diakrina the barrier was like hitting a really dry, thick wall of Jell-O, not steel. It flexed and distorted but still held her fast for just a few milliseconds as only the sword actually pierced the wall.

However, to the serpent the barrier was like solid steel and marble. In fact, there was so much difference in the way the wall reacted with Diakrina and the serpent, for a second she was depressed into the wall like a person hitting a trampoline while the serpent's coils were splattered against the original position of the wall several feet behind Diakrina. This put her several feet beyond its coils.

At the very millisecond she reached the full extent of her depression into the clear, flexing crystal of the wall, out from the sword came a blaze of golden Light and heat again. It flashed all through the translucent substance and immediately Diakrina felt her body pass into the thick barrier. She held tightly to the grip of the sword, which seemed to be pulling her through the substance of the wall. At the same time, the golden Light which saturated the wall caused the flesh of the serpent to noticeable shrivel and darken as it was instantly burned. The snake went manic as it endeavored to withdraw its coils from of the wall, for smoke had instantly burst from its flesh.

Diakrina literally fell out of the first barrier and onto the first step beyond it. It was the first time any one of these barriers had seemed a welcome obstruction. And the more of them she could put between herself and the serpent, all the better.

Besides, Diakrina was in no mood to stop between these tomb-like walls. So she pushed the sword immediately into the next barrier and watched the burst of colors explode into the substance. Again, this was followed by a blaze of golden Light and heat, which allowed her to push into the substance of the wall and then feel the sword actually pulling her through as the tornado like movement of the Light of Logos around her sword seemed to be moving drill-like through the wall.

In like manner Diakrina pushed through each barrier in turn until there was only one left. As she passed through each barrier it became progressively darker except for the Light display going on from the sword and the Lantern each time she pierced a wall.

By the time Diakrina stood in front of the last barrier, it was completely black and only the sword and Lantern gave her any illumination. Somehow, even though the translucent walls seemed to be clear, they did not allow any light to pass through them and the greenish glow radiating from the Temple of Death, was now completely extinguished.

Diakrina paused as she faced the final barrier, which was part of the large stone gate at the entrance to the stairs. She remembered a long ascent back to the Altar lay ahead in the inky darkness of Nekus Canyon. She had no idea if there were any surviving Nekros still hunting her, and if there were, if they could fly to this side of the barriers in the canyon.

She felt sure the serpent could not come through the nine barriers, and since it could not fly, she doubted it could get around the barriers by going out over the river. But of course, this said nothing about whether there were other serpents or creatures to be contended with.

Yet, even with all these questions, there was a new boldness in Diakrina. For the second time she had seen the Light from the Lantern of Logos make her sword like a laser-bomb shredding anything she might encounter.

She paused for only a second. But in that second, she found herself looking for the footprints. Though she could see nothing else beyond the last barrier, somehow, visible beyond it—at the level of what had to be the rock below the final step down—she could see two crimson footprints about five-feet away. It was as if someone were standing and waiting for her beyond the barrier.

She thrust her sword into the final barrier and then pushed through amidst the brilliant display of Light and color.

Diakrina was shocked. She stepped out, not into inky darkness, but into bright sunshine.

It was not night in Nekus Canyon on this side of the final barrier. The whole canyon was filled with the blaze of a midday sun. What is more, she instantly felt the warmth of the sun and again realized how bitterly cold she had been on the other side of the nine walls. She had taken little notice of the cold before; only because she was running for her life from the moment her feet hit the stone of the courtyard floor.

Diakrina stood panting and blinking in the blazing sun for several minutes while she covered her eyes partly with her shield. She needed to catch her breath after the long dash and battle. Finally, her eyes adjusted enough to the daylight she could lower the shield and take in her surroundings.

It was the first time Diakrina had actually seen Nekus Canyon. To her right, near the very bank of the river, was the tall, square stone pillar reaching high into the air with its many carvings on its four sides. Its twin, on her left, was stretched straight out in front of her on the ground. It lay in front of the staircase entrance where it had fallen. The roar from the falls still echoed all through the canyon and a damp mist rising from the falls filled the air.

The river was wide, about three hundred yards, by Diakrina's estimation. It was flowing toward the falls down a long slope up against the west canyon wall to her right. The volume of water was so great and deep it was rolling with large deep swells instead of tumbling as it swept by at a terrible speed.

The great height of the canyon walls was ominous. They made you feel like you were being pressed and channeled, like the river, toward some predetermined destiny. This feeling was given direction by the descent of the upper canyon toward the falls and the thunderous sound of the falls coming from just behind her to her right.

Diakrina could now see there was a narrow bridge of rock which extended out away from the entrance to the staircase along the riverbank. On the left of this narrow bridge of rock it dropped away into a great pit which filled the vast area from there to the eastern wall of the canyon, which was about five hundred yards away. This pit ran all along the left side of the narrow rock-bridge until it reached the east side of the staircase Diakrina had just come down. There the pit turned back toward the eastern canyon wall forming the backside of the ledge from which the staircase descended. As the pit arched back away from the stairs it turned sharply north again and made a deep crevasse between this end of the ledge and the wall of the canyon which seemed to run a long way north toward the Temple of Death until it almost severed the ledge and the temple from the canyon wall.

Out in front of Diakrina the rock-bridge continued alongside the river until it reached the place where the great pit ended. There, it joined to the floor of the upper canyon descending toward Diakrina from the South. This floor of the upper canyon fell away abruptly into the great pit everywhere except where it joined to the rock-bridge and where, to the right of the rock-bridge, the river flowed. Diakrina could see the face of this abrupt cliff from where she stood. She realized it was this ledge from which she had nearly fallen when she panicked in the darkness the night she was passing through Nekus.

It was clear to Diakrina she would need to retrace the steps she had taken that night. This meant walking along the riverbank up the rock-bridge until she reached the upper descending canyon floor. Then she would angle left and make her way back to the southeast as she climbed up the steep ascent that led back to the mouth of the canyon and the great Altar. The Altar was along the eastern canyon wall. It was there Strateia said he would be waiting for her.

Just the thought this climb out of the canyon would soon take her beyond the thunder of the falls where other sounds could be heard again brought Diakrina to herself and caused her to take her first steps toward the rock-bridge. However, she paused for a moment as the rainbow of Light, which had been around her sword ever since Strateia had instructed her to use it, lifted from the blade of the sword and floated slowly back to her breast and then sank deep into her torso. A sense of secure peace flooded over Diakrina, and she closed her eyes and took a long deep breath. After a couple more slow, deep breaths she could feel her jangled nerves relax in every part of her body. She was ready for the climb.

The rock-bridge ascended slightly as it rose to meet the upper canyon floor. Diakrina, still ever alert to the possibility of encountering other forms of danger, kept her sword in her hand and her shield pulled close to her left side as she set out in a slow but determined jog up its length. Getting to the Altar was all she could think about now.

Chapter Two

THE FRAGRANT ATTACK

As Diakrina made her way across the rock-bridge toward the upper canyon area, every step away from the gates of Thanatos seemed to be the lifting of some dark heavy burden from off her body. The result was Diakrina began to jog faster the farther she went, even though she was climbing upward and the trembling in the rock-bridge from the thunder of the falls still had to be reckoned with.

When she reached the upper canyon floor she turned left and retraced her steps, as well as she could remember from her blind descend, along the cliff which dropped into the great pit now to her left. She made her way through large boulders and kept the east canyon wall in front of her as she transversed the width of the canyon while also climbing up its length toward the south.

Once she had gone about a hundred yards up the canyon, the effect of the canyon floor between her and Nekus Falls soon began blocking its' direct roar. She was once again in a kind of sound shadow, which caused the direct sound waves to pass over her head and resonate back at her from high off the canyon walls. This lowered the decibels of the roar considerably and was an instant relief to Diakrina.

What is more, the greater the distance she put between her and Nekus Falls, the less she could feel the trembling of the canyon floor coming through her feet. The higher she climbed the more she felt as if she were indeed rising out of a very haunted and condemned space. As the roar continually lessened it seemed as if the canyon was losing its' grip on her and reluctantly scrutinizing her escape.

In spite of herself, she kept looking behind to insure there was nothing pursuing either on the ground or in the sky. In about forty-five minutes she could see the canyon was starting to level out and it mouth lay not too far ahead.

Diakrina remembered the Altar, where she had escaped the pursuing beasts and committed the flaming torch in trust to the Altar, was over against the east wall of the canyon to her left. So she continued to transverse the canyon width as she made her way toward its mouth.

She wound her way through another boulder field. As she came through between two large house-size stones, she spotted the ledge in the canyon wall up ahead where the Altar was carved into its sides. She quickened her pace and headed straight toward the ledge.

When she reached it, she was surprised to find the ledge was not as easy to get on top of, as it had been the night she was saturated with adrenalin and fear as the two beasts chased her in the darkness. It took her a couple of tries. She had to finally back up and get a run at it, before she succeeded.

When she did, she immediately rose and started ascending the white marble-like steps reaching from there to the top of the Altar. And there, smiling like a welcoming brother, was Strateia seated on the raised stone at its very center.

"Welcome back to life, Little One," he said with an enthusiastic smile.

Strateia then rose, and when he did, Diakrina could see on the other side of him was a collection of fruit and nuts—that he had already hulled—laying along with a crystal-like canteen full of water. He strode toward her and placed one large arm around her shoulders.

"This is no small achievement, Diakrina. Your quest has literally been resurrected from the grave."

Diakrina welcomed his strong embrace of assurance. She was glad to see the great warrior again. Yet, she realized, as never before, she had not been alone while she was absent from Strateia. She had been accompanied and led every single step.

It was then she glanced down to the surface of the Great Altar. There, just starting to fade, were two crimson footprints. She had been delivered back into Strateia's trust.

Strateia followed her gaze and then smiled. "Yes, Little One, you were never alone."

Diakrina forget herself and turned and hugged the lower torso of the great warrior, for that is all the higher she could reach. Strateia seemed not the least offended by her display of gratitude and simply placed his large hand on top of her head and stroked her hair for a few seconds.

"Come, Little One," he suddenly said, turning toward the pile of fruit and nuts. "I think some nourishment and rest are in order. These are the best I could find here in the Severed Lands, but I think you will find them enjoyable."

Strateia then looked upward toward the sky. "I didn't dare try to return to the Garden for food. There is far too much activity all around us. Anomos' troops are looking everywhere for you … and me," he added. Then looking down at Diakrina again, "It will not be long before word from Thanatos' realms about your escape through the barriers will reach Anomos. And by that time we need to be on the move toward Lord Mazzaroth. But I think we have enough time for you to eat and catch your breath."

Diakrina sheathed her sword for the first time in hours as she moved to the pile of food and sat down on the far side of it. She lay down her shield, pulled the strap of the crystal container over her head and placed the Atheos to her left side. Strateia sat down in the same place from which he had previously risen with the food between them.

"While you eat, I need to inform you of our plans."

Diakrina nodded her acknowledgement for she already had a mouthful of peach and couldn't easily speak.

"There are few places where Anomos' hordes are not looking for us. The time has come when you will not be able to avoid contact with his warriors. We are going to ask Lord Mazzaroth to help us. If he and his men are willing to create a diversion, we may be able to find our way over the mountain through the Mist Forest."

Diakrina looked up suddenly when Strateia mentioned the Mist Forest.

"Strateia, I really had hoped we could avoid any further contact with that place. I still find the memory of that night in the cave very difficult."

"I do not doubt it, Diakrina. Yet it will likely to be necessary to challenge the Mist again. We cannot, in our present circumstances, allow fear to keep us from the best possible course. Anomos needs no added advantage. And giving in to fear always gives him one. In fact, driving straight at fear is almost always the best course in these matters. It is the last thing Anomos expects—just as he did not anticipate you would be sent back through Nekus Canyon. He does not easily entertain the idea of a resurrection.

"What is more Diakrina, you need to remember how the Living One turned what you experienced in that cave for good. In the end you have been made freer and stronger. You will not be as helpless as you were before."

Diakrina gave this last statement some thought and then stopped between bites to respond.

"Yes, I see that. And perhaps I actually need to face the Mist again. But I still can't find any pleasure in the thought."

"Nor should you!" interjected Strateia. "Dealing with evil is always like having to cope with seasickness: one never grows to like it. But part of our strength, Diakrina, is we do not merely do what we like. We do what we know needs to be done. This is one of the ways sanity has the advantage over evil."

As usual, Strateia's point was a ray of insight to Diakrina. She continued eating until she had finished the fruit and then she gave a sigh. Then sliding off the stone lid of the Altar down onto the floor, so she could use it to rest her back against, she continued munching on the nuts.

As she sat there, she caught the most delicious scent. Immediately she knew what it was. She turned around to her left and pulled the crystal container toward her. There, shining as bright as ever, was the Immortal Fruit. As Diakrina pulled the container into her lap, she was hit in the head by a wonderful, but deadly sensation. She had had little time to think about the Atheos. She had kept it hidden under her shield to protect it from those trying to steal it or from those who did not need to know of its existence.

Here in her lap, the golden fruit seemed to almost reach through the crystal enclosure toward her. She was mesmerized by it. She sat staring at it for several moments. Then, before she realized what she had done, she lifted the container to her face and took in a long, deep breath.

She shouldn't have.

A passion strong and coercive flooded her every sensation. Her eyes widened in ardent obsession. She was instantly in the very grip of a supernatural desire. Everything in her wanted to extract the fruit and consume it instantly. Before she realized what she had done she turned around onto her knees and began smashing the container again and again onto the surface of the raised stone in an attempt to shatter it.

Strateia instantly understood what was happening and grabbed Diakrina by both hands and riveted them in place. Diakrina screamed and struggled with all her might. Strateia took hold of the crystal container with the Atheos in it and pulled it away from Diakrina while he continued to hold her at bay with his other hand. He tossed the container onto the other side of the raised stone about six feet from Diakrina and then continued to patiently hold her until she began to come to herself.

When she did, she immediately stopped screaming and struggling as her eyes focused again and she looked straight into Strateia's face. He was looking at her rather sternly, but there was no anger in his countenance. He took her face in his hands and pulled her close and blew a breath of air over her nose and mouth. Immediately Diakrina's head cleared, and she came to herself.

"What did I just do, Strateia?" asked Diakrina as bewilderment flushed over her face.

"You got too close, Little One."

Diakrina blinked her eyes a couple of times as Strateia slowly released his grip on her face. She looked across the raised stone to the crystal container lying on the marble-like surface.

"I don't understand, Strateia. It has never had such a powerful effect on me before."

"Diakrina, if you remember, I warned you the Immortal Fruit would begin to saturate the container. And in doing so it would then become a greater and greater danger to you. What is more, by being enclosed all this time, the fragrance from the Fruit has become concentrated. It has begun to seep through as the crystal has become fully saturated. When you breathed in at the surface of the crystal you were hit with a double dose of its essence."

"It is a wonder I didn't break the container, Strateia."

"There is no chance of that. The crystal container is made of a substance which comes from Infinite Light. It is far too dense to be shattered. In fact, its molecular structure is such that every blow or force exerted against it is incorporated into its material strength and only makes it more resistant. No one can remove the Immortal Fruit from the container but you or the Living One. And He will not remove it unless you give Him permission. He has placed it in your trust. He will not revoke that trust unless you misuse it.

"And remember, Diakrina, even for you the Atheos can only be removed by willfully unlocking the seal intentionally: recanting the covenant word by uttering the inscription backwards."

"If this is true, Strateia, isn't the Atheos already secure? Why, then, do we need to take it back to the Garden?"

Because, as you have just experienced, even the fragrance from this Fruit is too much for your race in your present state. And this container cannot lock in its fragrance. If this container, which will continue to now be saturated with the Fruit until the Fruit is removed from it, were to remain in the world, it would be a terrible source of evil among men. Wars would be fought, blood would flow deep, as obsessed men would launch terrible slaughter against one another to obtain it. And those who did obtain it would be driven mad by its constant enticements which could never be satisfied as the crystal container would keep it ever visible and fragrant, and also, forever out of reach. No, Diakrina, we will finish the quest. Too much hangs in the balances for far too many people."

Strateia's logical prediction was a very sobering insight. It chilled Diakrina to the core and made her realize how necessary it was for her to continue the quest. But could she?

"How am I to carry the container now it is so saturated with the Fruit's fragrance?" questioned Diakrina. "You saw what it did to me just now."

"You must ask the Living One to help you remember the vision He gave you concerning what it would be like to live immortally severed. Through this revelation, and with His help, you can gain control over your response to the Fruit. You can train your responses to consider the fragrance an evil—as it really is to you at present—so you abhor it while it remains in the Severed Lands."

"But it isn't really horrible, Strateia. It is beautiful and desirable beyond words. How can I ever train myself to see it as being ugly and dangerous?"

"You can because, in this present circumstance, that is exactly what it is! You must learn to see things according to their effect and consequence, Diakrina, not merely according to their appearance and power to give momentary pleasure. It is like the good and beauty of sex. When it is engaged in the wrong way and at the wrong time and perhaps with the wrong person, what is good can become deadly. But if you wait until the right time and place—in marriage—it will deliver its glorious gifts without harm or regret.

To you, right now, this fruit is like a deadly serpent hidden in a beautiful bouquet. Its beauty and fragrance are the bouquet. Its effect is the deadly serpent. You have been shown its hidden danger. Teach yourself to abhor the flowers you know are nothing but a lure to the serpent's deadly bite.

"What is more, Diakrina, do not worry you will never again be able to love Immortal Fruit. One day you will be where no Immortal Fruit will ever again be deadly. And such knowledge will make the

Fruit even more fulfilling, if that is possible.

"But in the meantime, you should not allow the crystal container too close to your face. Keep it primarily behind you and under your shield. Respect its power and with the Living One's help you can control your response to it."

Strateia then stepped over the raised stone area and picked up the crystal container. He walked back to Diakrina and sat it down by her shield. Then picking up the shield, he placed it over the container.

"Use the shield. It can help you control yourself. What is more, from now on the Living One is going to cause the Shield to put a containing aura—force—around the Atheos. This will lock the fragrance within the aura as long as you keep it under the shield. This is so we can enter the land of men without it attracting too much attention. You need only obey and keep it under the shield, and you will have complete control over its appeal. Do you understand?"

"Yes, Strateia," answered Diakrina, who was relieved to have this new source of help from the shield.

Then pausing and looking down at her, Strateia added, "You have enough time for a short nap. I think it would do you good. The sun will be setting soon, and then we must go. We will have to travel in the darkness to avoid detection."

Diakrina lay her head back on the stone and dozed off almost immediately. Strateia allowed her to sleep for about an hour before waking her.

"It is time, Little One. The sun is low in the sky. We must go now."

As Diakrina was picking up her things she was extra careful as she lifted the shield. But there it was. The scent radiated toward her as the shield was lifted off.

Again, it was maddening. But she was ready. With each hint of the fragrance Diakrina attempted to attach a very specific terrifying memory from her vision to the Atheos: The one that came forcefully into her mind was the moment when the Diakrina of the vision heard her doom being pronounced as the realization of her eternal confinement in the total isolation of the outer darkness was washing over her like a horrible black cloud. To this Diakrina would also add the memory of the dark, rolling black rings which the Serpents of Paranoia spit at her: the sticky, cold panic which you could not wash off no matter how hard she tried. In her mind she worked hard to attach these horror-filled moments to that very specific fragrance so she would never encounter it without these mental associations.

Yet, she knew this would not be enough if she did not receive help. "I know you are with me, Living One," she found herself saying, "Please give me help and strength to always see the truth about the Atheos. Don't let me forget."

She lifted the strap over her head carefully and positioned the crystal container behind her so the shield on her left arm was in front of it. As she was doing so, she found she had to continually keep alert and consciously keep the associations in her mind. Otherwise, the fragrance would slowly put her under its spell. And if she were not careful to keep the shield down over it, the container would not be inside the aura and the fragrance would begin to fill her head. It was both maddening and frustrating at the same time. She realized she needed to develop a military-like habit in the way she carried it.

Strateia knew the burden she was now carrying. He walked up to her and placed his hand on her shoulder.

"You will win, Little One. You will grow stronger."

Strateia then motioned for her to follow him, and they began descending the stairs of the Great Altar as the last rays of the sun were sinking over the western mountains.

Chapter Three

BELLICOSE

The shadows were long as Strateia and Diakrina walked up the path toward the river to the place they had camped for a short while before Diakrina entered Nekus on that former moonless night. Diakrina could not help remembering how she had run down this descent toward the Altar in absolute terror. How grateful she was to be striding behind an eight-foot warrior and friend.

When they came up over the rise which Strateia had disappeared beyond that night to obtain the fish, Diakrina could see Nekus River far ahead of them. It made a sweeping turn toward them on their right as it headed toward the canyon mouth. Strateia stopped for a moment to allow Diakrina to catch up.

"We will turn to the southwest here and angle toward the river. When we reach it, we will need to follow it for several miles. The river then turns back west and passes through a canyon which heads in the direction of the southern end of the Great Meadow.

"When we reach the canyon mouth where the river exits, we will begin to ascend a large plateau which follows the river on its west bank. This plateau will rise very rapidly into the mountains which form the canyon through which the river cuts. When we reach the top of the plateau, there is a place above the river where a natural rock bridge—about five hundred feet above the river—crosses over the river where it cuts through the plateau.

"The rock bridge will take us high above the opposite bank of the river to the northern part of the plateau and the mountain range going north and west from there. We will turn back west again and hike over and around several peaks on the top of the plateau. From there we will then come down into a high valley where Lord Mazzaroth and his people live.

"Diakrina, we will both have to use our swords, and you your shield, for light to find our way. If we make good time, we should obtain the descent, which leads down into Lord Mazzaroth's valley, just before sunrise.

"However, this whole region, up to the rock bridge, is the haunt of Bellicose. He is a fallen archegos—a captain of the host—of immense size and power in Anomos' service. He fashions himself a god of war: thus his name, Bellicose, which means, warlike. Before he fell with Anomos he was of the same order of being as you met in the Guardian of the Gate in the Garden."

"Do you mean," interrupted Diakrina, "like the Guardian that stood taller than the three-hundred-foot-high gates and was composed of living flames?"

"Yes, Diakrina, the same. Bellicose no longer burns with golden white flames as you observed in the Guardian. Bellicose burns with angry red flames mixed with the pale greenish flames of putrefaction. He is the angry blood-red blaze of war which spreads suffering and death. We must do everything we can to avoid him.

"One reason for making this journey at night is to put him at a disadvantage. His blazing red and green flames, and his immense size, will make him easy to spot for miles. Our first task is to locate him and then determine how best to circumvent him. You can be sure Bellicose has been alerted to be looking for us. He will be on the prowl. All of Anomos' archegos will be on alert." Then with a look of determined realization on his face, Strateia added, "Tonight we will surely be in need of the Living One's help. Come!"

Strateia turned slightly to their left and began striding toward the river at an angle to its near bank. The river was some four hundred yards west of them, and it took several minutes to reach it hiking through rock-filled terrain by this approach. When finally they came to the river, they turned to their left, fully south, and followed its bank for about an hour.

As the sun had now fully set, it was very dark for about twenty minutes. This made it necessary for them to use their swords to pick their way through the rocks and boulders. But then the moon broke the eastern sky behind them and the whole terrain exploded in a relief of pale light with long tortured shadows across the rugged landscape.

It was a near full moon. As the sky was clear, without a cloud, the soft light awakened the whole panorama of mountains and valleys lying before them. It seemed to Diakrina as if a whole new world had materialized out ahead of them. It was torturous and dreamy all at the same time. The pale light of the moon bathed everything in thousands of silhouettes of contrast.

But this was no night for admiring landscapes. Strateia's resolute pace kept Diakrina focused, and in a slow trot just to keep near him. They soon came to the place where the river began turning fully west. They turned right and followed it. Immediately they began climbing at a very steep grade up a long plateau as the river fell away to their right and a canyon began to form.

Strateia was considerate of Diakrina and would occasionally stop and wait for her to catch up and give her a moment to rest. Unlike him, Diakrina could not jog up this steep ascent without some reprieve. Yet, she was shocked she was not really short of breath. As yet, she gave this little thought, though later she would learn the reason why.

After about an hour and forty-five minutes of climbing they reached a place where the plateau seemed to level out. From there it continued as a rugged ridge all along the canyon and the river below. At the height of this plateau Diakrina could see the moonlit top of its northern extent on the other side of the canyon. And when she looked toward the west, she could see the moonlight illuminating the far reaches of the canyon ahead of them. There seemed to be two sheer, deep sides that formed the canyon on the distant horizon.

What is more, she could just make out a large tower of rock which rose from the plateau near the edge of the canyon on their side. From this tower an arch of rock rose into the sky and transversed the canyon and made connection to the far side. It was far enough away it would take them several hours to reach, but at least she now had some idea of their destination.

As it turned out, they had climbed up to a high summit on the plateau which had made it possible for Diakrina to see so far ahead. But as they continued Diakrina almost immediately lost sight of the rock bridge. This is because as they continued, they had to transverse small valleys of rocks and boulders on top of the plateau. These shallow descents and re-ascents would happen several times as they made their way in the direction of the rock bridge.

As they came up out of a depression and topped a long ridge falling away again into another depression—one somewhat larger than any of the previous ones—Strateia suddenly stopped and quickly stepped behind a boulder as he reached out his arm behind him and took Diakrina with him.

"Quiet, Little One. Don't move."

Strateia then leaned out from the boulder to take another look. He slowly pulled his head back and turned toward Diakrina.

"Put your sword in its sheath so there is no light."

Then Strateia did the same with his sword. He then slid behind Diakrina and pulled part of his robe of light around her and her shield. Then, as Diakrina had never seen him do, he somehow made the light of his robe go out. It transformed into a perfect camouflage. It blended perfectly with the rock around them. He then pressed Diakrina up against the backside of the boulder, so his large body and robe fully covered her.

He had no sooner done so, than Diakrina, who could still see along the boulder out from under Strateia's robe, saw red and greenish light begin to dance on all the surfaces beyond the boulder.

Strateia whispered ever so quietly down toward her, " It's Bellicose. Don't move and don't say anything until I tell you that you can."

Diakrina very quickly began to feel waves of heat radiating through the air from the direction of the dancing red and green light.

She immediately remembered the heat coming from the large black gates in the Garden where the Guardian stood just beyond them. However, simultaneous with the waves of heat came something she had not experienced at the Garden gates: a strong, acrid stench filled the air. Mixed with the heat it was like an acid stinging her nose and making her eyes instantly begin to water. It was most uncomfortable.

The dancing red and green light continued to get stronger and so did the heat and terrible smell. Diakrina was glad she was covered by Strateia's robe as it deflected much of the heat. Otherwise, she was sure it would have been intolerable.

Then she saw him. He was about two hundred feet north of them, along the very edge of the canyon, and headed up over the ridge they were on—headed back east in the direction from which they had just come. The moment he was actually visible to Diakrina the heat from the being hit her directly in the face through the slit through which she was looking—which was formed between Strateia's robe and the boulder. It was like a large heat lamp had been turned on within three or four inches of her face. She pushed back hard against Strateia in an effort to get her face behind the folds of his robe. She was rewarded with immediate relief from the direct, searing rays, but still found it extremely uncomfortable to breathe, as the air seemed to be nearly on fire.

It was then she realized she could see the great flaming creature by looking through the material of Strateia's robe. In fact, she could see him better, as he was too bright—and the heat far too intense—for her to look at him directly.

What Diakrina could now discern looking through the folds of the robe was this flaming being was an incredible mixture of angry red flames and ghastly dancing pale green flames having the effect of radiating putrefaction. These flames licked at the air from greenish and red cracks in a dark skin—if you could call it skin—which looked more like slightly cooling lava than anything else she could compare it with.

Diakrina couldn't help associating the stinging in her eyes and the stink in her nose with the ghastly pale green flames. It seemed the acrid stench was being beamed straight at her, not floating through the air like odors normally do. The foul stink was caustic like acid and the angry heat from the red flames seemed to burn it into everything around the creature.

His features were very different from what she had seen regarding the Guardian of the Gate. The Guardian had also been very difficult to look at directly. But he had been much further away and there was none of the acidic, stinging stench. What Diakrina had been able to discern of the Guardian was a countenance of moving symmetry: a kind of stern and powerful glory. It was terrifying beauty; yet, somehow, pure and reassuring.

But the countenance of this creature was distorted, chaotic angry flames of hate-filled pride. There was never a single, clear feature or expression on his countenance. Rather there seemed to be a moving, stampeding collision of menacing and inconceivably evil expressions at war with each other for supremacy. His face was like a bloody battlefield where many different bitter, angry countenances were slaughtering each other.

Diakrina stared at him in astonishment. She had never seen anything so terrifyingly evil. Here was militant malevolence, encroaching wickedness and scorching horror all in one.

She was suddenly seized with a terrible resolve to not meet this creature. No wonder Strateia had determined it was best they do everything possible to slip past him undetected. His great height and mass filled the horizon and cast deep shadows behind every feature of the near landscape. Every blade of grass, every tree or shrub was vaporized if the flames of his body touched them. Every rock was scorched black where his feet tread.

Amazingly, the landscape did not catch fire around or behind the creature. As best Diakrina could determine, this was due to the instant vaporization of everything combustible. There was nothing left to propagate a fire to other untouched plants once the flames from the creature contacted something. Every living thing was turned to ash. All earth or rock was scorched black and left smoking and simmering as if near a liquid state.

Bellicose continued past them for about a hundred yards. But then, unaccountably, he stopped and turned and began surveying the whole landscape behind him. This he did for several minutes as if trying to find something or someone. It was then one of Diakrina's most horror-filled moments took place. Bellicose spoke.

"I SENSE YOUR PRESENCE FEEBLE HUMAN!" bellowed a deafening voice seeming to shake the whole plateau and make the canyon below roll with thunder. "I CAN'T FIND YOU BECAUSE YOU ARE BEING HELPED, NO DOUBT, BY ONE OF MY FORMER BROTHERS. BUT I KNOW YOU ARE HERE! I CAN SENSE THE SUBTLE FRAGRANCE OF THAT FRUIT."

Evidently this being's powers of detection were such the shield did not completely keep the fragrance of the Atheos from being detected by him. Diakrina felt the firm press of Strateia's body slightly increase as a way of steadying and reassuring her. She was grateful for it: it pulled her back from the very threshold of wanting to scream. Bellicose's voice made every organ in her body vibrate in a sickening resonance with the rumble of his words. It was devastating.

There was a long, terrible silence as the creature continued to move his continually distorting countenance searchingly over the landscape. His gaze radiated hatred and murder. He was looking for something to conquer and spew his venom over; he desired someone to dominate and subject to his will.

As the silence—horrifyingly pregnant with terrible possibilities—stubbornly settled like a suffocating, unrelenting presence, the blazing heat from the stationary creature began to make the very air too hot to breathe. Diakrina needed to breathe. But she found she dreaded the stinging pain of every blistering gasp. Also, her eyes were now watering and burning and she could no longer look at anything. She felt her very blood was near boiling. And the stench was crushing.

"Will it ever end!" she was screaming in her frantic thoughts. "It has to end!"

And just when she was sure she was at the very conclusion of her sanity and ability to control herself—struggling fiercely just to keep conscious—Bellicose suddenly turned and continued down the plateau to the east.

With his every step, the searing, blistering atmosphere lifted slightly. Diakrina blinked repeatedly trying to clear the hot putrefaction from her eyes. And all the while Strateia communicated his stern command she not yet move by using the press of his body.

Bellicose was so tall, it evidently took several minutes for his flaming head to disappear down over the rim of the next small canyon atop the plateau. So Strateia held Diakrina in firm suspension until he knew they could move without being detected.

Without warning he flung his robe aside and whispered to Diakrina, "Quick! Follow me!" With that he slid around the north end of the boulder they had been behind and quickly led Diakrina down into a maze of boulders descending into the small mountaintop canyon ahead of them.

Nothing was said as he hurried her down into the bottom of the hollow and then up the other side toward the western end of the plateau and the rock bridge. There were no stops for breathers and Diakrina didn't need them: she was too full of adrenalin to even feel the strain of the furious pace.

What was more, the air became cool and fresh again the farther they distanced themselves from the foul Bellicose. This in itself was enough to pull Diakrina continually forward.

But for Strateia there was another reason not to speak or rest: they were far from being out of danger. He knew Bellicose would soon come back. He would be intent on keeping a constant eye on the rock bridge as it was the one place he could be sure they would show up if they were in his domain. Strateia knew he had to get Diakrina over the rock bridge in short order before Bellicose circled back around on them.

When they reached the top of the ridge ahead of them, Diakrina could see by the moonlight they were not far from the tower of rock supporting the bridge on this side of the canyon. Soon, Strateia slowed the pace and pulled up short behind some boulders at the foot of the tower of rock. When Diakrina came panting up behind him and stopped, Strateia pushed her gently past him, farther behind the boulder. He then turned and began looking out from behind the edge of the great stone at the sky.

"What is it, Strateia?" asked Diakrina with a slight tremble in her voice which she could not eliminate though she was trying very hard to do so.

"We must keep an eye as to Bellicose's location. He will be back this way ... and soon."

Diakrina stepped behind Strateia and peered out at the sky in the direction he was looking. Far on the southeastern horizon she could see a reddish and greenish glow. It seemed to be reflecting off the atmosphere above Bellicose. What became instantly clear to her was Bellicose had made a large circle back to the south and was now headed back west as he was circling back toward the area of the rock bridge.

"We haven't much time, Little One. We must be over the bridge before he gets back to this area. We don't have time for you to climb this tower of rock."

With that Strateia turned and picked her up and before she knew what was happening, they were rising to the top of the tower. When they landed on the top of the tower of rock, Strateia put her down immediately.

"Why don't you just take us across the canyon, Strateia? I don't understand."

"And I don't have time to explain it to you. Come!"

Strateia led her around some piles of stone and then across the top of the tower. When they got to the far side of the tower, where it was joined to the rock bridge, they had to climb down about twenty feet to the top of the bridge. From there the huge rock bridge arched slightly upward out toward the center of the canyon. It was about as wide as a football field. Except for the occasional pile of stones, it was mostly smooth rock all across its top to the far side of the canyon.

Strateia stopped Diakrina as they finished their descent down onto the bridge. "Catch your breath for a moment while I check on Bellicose's whereabouts." With that he flew upward back to the top of the tower. Almost without pause he swiftly descend back to Diakrina's side.

"Secure everything, and get prepared to run, Diakrina. He is coming over the horizon. And we must be on the other side and hidden before he gets to where he can see the bridge."

Diakrina checked the crystal container, secured her sword and shield and checked to make sure the page from the book was safely inside the folds of her garment.

"I will come behind you, Diakrina, staying between you and Bellicose just in case. Run, Diakrina! Run now!"

Diakrina took a deep breath and began running across the great open arch of the bridge. The bright moonlight made the top of the bridge adequately illuminated so she could plot her course without difficulty. She ran like a sprinter at the peak of the race just before they lean for the finish line. She could hear Strateia behind her.

"Don't slow down, Little One," he said in a loud whisper. "Run!"

And run she did. She didn't know she had such speed in her. Some kind of strength and coordination previously alien to her seemed to be flowing into her arms and legs. She was as light on her feet as a gazelle and felt she could hardly be moving much slower or less gracefully than that amazing animal.

And yet, it seemed the other side of the bridge and canyon would never come. It stretched out into the moonlight much farther than she had expected.

Then she saw the silhouette of some boulders ahead of her and realized she was only about fifty feet from the other side. But at almost the same moment her shadow appeared out in front of her elongated toward the boulders. All around her shadow was the pale reddish and greenish dancing glow of Bellicose's light.

"To the right of the boulder, Diakrina. Then duck to the left behind it!" came Strateia's strong whisper almost in her ear.

A surge of adrenaline hit Diakrina's whole body. She charged forward aiming for the right side of the large boulder ahead. When she reached it, she never slowed down but continued with her left hand and shield stretched out slightly behind her so she could touch the side of the boulder as she passed down it. When she realized she was past it, she darted left and fell to the ground behind the stone.

Just as she was falling to the ground the area beyond the shadow of the stone lit up with blazing red and green light. And instantly Diakrina could detect the acrid stench of putrefaction: not strong but definite. Strateia was so close to her they both seemed to dart behind the boulder at the same moment: her to the ground, he still on his feet whirling to look back around the corner to see if they had been detected.

Bellicose was still approaching but was actually quite some distance from the tower of rock on the far side of the canyon. His great height had caused the light from the top of his head to burst over the tower and onto them just as they were ducking behind the stone to be safe from his gaze.

When Bellicose was actually close enough to see over the tower, they were already behind the boulder. He came closer with several of his massive steps and stood looking over the canyon and the rock bridge. He seemed to be inspecting its every feature for several minutes. Strateia watched him and continued to keep Diakrina on her knees by putting his hand on her head with a gentle pressure. This fixed her to the spot where she had crawled up behind him.

Even with the creature on the other side of the canyon, the air became hot and once again Diakrina's eyes began to burn and tear up from the searing stench. After about three minutes of scanning the bridge, Bellicose turned back east again and began his circle once more. He was clearly still on the search. They had, amazingly, managed to get through undetected.

After about five minutes, Bellicose was far enough away Strateia turned around and allowed Diakrina to stand.

"Close, Little One," he said with a serious smile. "Close."

By now Diakrina had had time to find her breath and the sense of immediate relief flooding her filled her with questions being held at bay by the previous danger and activity.

"Did Bellicose really detect the fragrance of the Atheos, Strateia?"

"I don't think so. And I don't think he actually discerned your presence. He was likely lying. He was merely seeing if he could flush something out by evoking fear. He reasoned if you were hiding in the boulders, such a tactic might cause you to reveal yourself."

"He was not far from wrong! If it had not been for you, it might have worked."

"But it didn't, Little One. Come! We must put some distance between this place and us before he circles back around."

And with that, they were off at a fast jog.

Chapter Four

THE NIGHT JOURNEY

As Diakrina and Strateia headed west-northwest over the top of the mountain plateau, small clouds began to form in the sky. They were not large or many. Yet, they were moving slowly across the night sky. This resulted in the bright, full moon being covered ever so often. When this happened the terrain ahead of them would lose its deep, shadow-punctuated features and it would be necessary for Strateia and Diakrina to pull their swords and rely almost totally on the light each provided.

Yet, they did not lessen their pace. Strateia seemed determined to arrive in what he had called, "the valley of Lord Mazzaroth," before sunrise. While the pace was grueling by our standards—and Diakrina was sure when she first came through the Door of the Rose she could never have endured it with as little rest as Strateia was now allowing her—she found herself able to push herself much further than she ever had before.

Her time in the Severed Lands had certainly hardened her physically. Yet, there had to be more to it than this. This was the first time she had been forced to run over rough, steep terrain for several hours. She should have been winded and gasping for breath. But she wasn't. "Why?" Diakrina found herself asking.

This question only grew as the night's run over the mountaintops continued. Diakrina was beginning to notice she was actually feeling very energized from this long marathon.

At the next rest stop, where Strateia stopped to look upward at the stars and refine their heading, Diakrina took the opportunity to see if Strateia could give her any reason for her newfound stamina.

"Strateia, I have never been able to run like this before. And certainly, I could never have run like this over this kind of challenging terrain. Yet, I feel great. In fact," she added after a short thoughtful pause, "I am pretty sure this run would have been at the limits of endurance of the greatest athletes in my time. Is there some reason why I am not tired and winded?"

"Yes, Little One, there is a logical reason," said Strateia turning from his sky calculations toward her. "Remember, I told you when you came through the Door of the Rose, you were not only brought to the other side of reality—in order that you might directly perceive the spiritual realm as well as the physical—but you were also pulled back along time. You are no longer on the earth as you have known it. This is the antediluvian world. It is very different from the earth as you have experienced it.

"One of the great differences is the earth in its present form—in this time where we now stand—is around 12% smaller in diameter. Your scientist will ultimately discover this fact and come to realize that the earth in your day has a larger diameter than in the past due to tectonic ruptures and movement allowing it to expland.

"However, the mass of the earth is the same. The effect of this same mass being within a smaller diameter, which results in less surface, is it yields a higher atmospheric pressure. Here the atmospheric pressure, at sea level, is slightly more than twice that of your time: close to 30 lbs. per square inch. This increased pressure results in a triple oxygen saturation level of your blood. Add to this the fact there is greater vegetation coverage on the earth, which results in a slightly higher oxygen level, and you can understand your new found endurance.

"Diakrina, do you remember how quickly you healed at the Spring of Longings?"

"Yes. But didn't you tell me it had to do with the healing properties of the water?"

"And so it did. But it was also due to this greater atmospheric density and higher oxygen levels. You are living in an earth-sized hyperbaric chamber as compared to your time. And as you know, hyperbaric research in your time is being used to speed up healing and is showing great promise in healing stubborn wounds and certain medical conditions."

"Is this why the people of this age live so much longer than we do in my day?"

"It is part of the reason. There are several other factors. For example, the magnetic field of the earth is much stronger now. It is about 5 gauss of pulsing, non-alternating field. It is only about 0.5 gauss in your age. This loss of magnetic field is a loss of health-sustaining energy to the cells of the body energized by this earth-field. The stronger magnetic field also reduces the amount of radiation reaching the earth's surface by rejecting more of the Solar winds. The weaker field of your day allows more harmful radiation to reach you.

"Another factor is due to the stronger magnetic field of the earth at this point in its history, it forms a lattice of frozen water-vapor. This creates a frozen vapor about twenty miles above the earth encircling the globe. This structure—frozen from water vapor—is very light and superconductive. It, therefore, rides on the magnetic field of the earth, which keeps it suspended in place. It is just thick enough to filter much of the harmful radiation coming at the earth. This causes, along with the greater atmospheric pressure—and slightly higher CO_2 levels—the larger vegetation you have seen here."

"Is this the water that is going to fall in the time of Noah?"

"No, Diakrina. There is not enough of it to cause a large flood, let alone a worldwide flood. It is frozen water vapor. The quantity is far too small to cause anything like that.

"What is more, if that much water were above the earth as unfrozen vapor, its changing to a liquid form and falling to earth would create an exothermic reaction completely burning up the earth's surface and atmosphere.

"While this canopy does fall during the flood, its transformation from a frozen state to a liquid state creates an endothermic effect and the result will be an instant deep freeze on the earth's surface at the poles and in many other areas. This is why mammoths were found in your time which had been so instantly frozen, the flowers and vegetation in their mouths were still undecayed and their flesh was still edible when they were first thawed. One of the American presidents, just before you were born, actually tasted a steak cut and cooked from one such mammoth.

"The water that will cause the flood will come from what the Great Book calls, "the fountains of the deep." There are large, underground water reservoirs which are the size of seas and oceans. They will collapse and cave-in due to tectonic activity. These caved in areas will become the great oceans and seas of your time. The tsunamic effect of the crust of the earth collapsing into these great reservoirs will cause the whole surface of the earth to be inundated."

All this talk about the Deluge got Diakrina to thinking of other questions she had always wondered about. Before she realized what she had done, she blurted one of them out.

"Why are there large creatures, like dinosaurs, now, but none in my time? Is it due to this lack of harmful radiation?"

"No. Even though this lack of harmful radiation gives them a longer life, and therefore they can reach larger sizes, it is not the primary reason. It is the greater air pressure and oxygen levels, Diakrina. Large dinosaurs have lungs which can only adequately oxygenate their bodies in this double atmospheric pressure. Most of your scientists will say little about this due to their evolutionary myth-religion, which this fact would not be favorable to. But they have actual data from the fossils which shows most of the larger dinosaurs could not live in the single atmospheric pressure of your world. Their lung-to-body-mass ratio is too small. They became extinct in your time because after the Deluge, with the breaking up of the earth surface, the earth's slow expansion in diameter began. This resulted in lower and lower atmospheric pressure. This doomed the large dinosaurs to extinction."

Diakrina found this all quite interesting. But Strateia suddenly ended their conversation with a wave for her to follow him as he began a warrior's cross-country trot in the direction of the new heading he had determined.

They ran over very rugged terrain of mostly great slabs of rock. Many were over half a mile long, which descended and re-ascended in altitude constantly. These slabs were covered with large house-size boulders. These boulders they had to either climb over or navigate through.

You must remember all of this landscape was actually on top of a very large plateau seeming to continue for miles in all directions. This terrain, isolated by its uplift, gave Diakrina the sensation of a smaller, exalted world which betrayed its boundaries—where the plateau fell away—because the point at where the horizon met the sky was always too close and too low down for a full earth vista. It had the effect of making the star-filled sky seem too large.

After traveling in this starry-sky-dominated world for over an hour, Strateia abruptly stopped. When Diakrina caught up to him and came to stand beside him, she realized there was a long, vast shadow in front of them stretching out to their left and right. Far in the distance Diakrina could see what looked like the tops of hills which formed the far side of a valley. This was because the moonlight, which was low in the sky by now, illuminated only the upper portion of its slopes. They were obviously standing on the edge of a great depression in the plateau.

"Below lies the land of Lord Mazzaroth. We have made good time. We will pause here and wait for the sunrise."

Strateia walked over to a rock to his right and hoisted himself upon it into a seated position facing the valley. It was a little too high for Diakrina. But there was one not far to Strateia's left which was much shorter; so, she made use of it.

Diakrina lay down her shield and immediately this resulted in the crystal container being uncovered. The fragrance from the Immortal Fruit came powerfully up into her head. Diakrina shook her head slightly and quickly took the strap of the container off over her head so she could place the container on the rock beside her underneath the shield. When she had managed to complete this she took in a deep breath and gave a long exhale. Strateia, who was watching all this, stood back up.

"It is good you use the shield in this manner. It is creating the barrier between you and the Atheos which I told you about. It is keeping the fragrance contained."

"Yes, and I am glad it does," responded Diakrina. "I'm not sure how well I would do without the shield's protection."

Strateia looked at her for a second and then said, "I'll be back in a moment. Wait here." And with that, he was gone.

He returned in about ten minutes. He was carrying an arm full of long slender grass blades which he had harvested into a sheave. He sat down on the rock again and laid the bundle of grass blades down beside him. He then began pulling out the blades and started weaving them together, clearly with the intent of making something.

Strateia looked up from his weaving and seeing the question marks in Diakrina's face as she watched him, nodded toward the shield under which was the crystal container.

"We need to make some kind of cover for that container so anyone who sees it will not be able to look inside it. The shield will help contain the fragrance to a large degree, if you keep the container under it. But it will not completely contain the essence of the Atheos. Those around you are going to be influenced by it and detect its presence to some extent. It might help if we can make the crystal container look a little more common and less likely to contain anything of real value."

After working very skillfully for several minutes, Strateia then motioned toward the shield and said, "Hand me the container."

Diakrina lifted the shield and tried to keep it somewhat between her and the Atheos as she picked it up to hand to Strateia. But the fragrance still hit her in the head with a delicious magnetism.

Strateia took the container quickly and placed it in his lap. He then began weaving the grass around the container so it looked like a mere grass tote bag. He did not stop when he had enclosed the crystal, but continued seamlessly making a strap woven around the strap attached to the container. Diakrina noticed the grass tote bag looked like it had a flap on the side opening over the top. However, as she had watched how Strateia had woven it, she knew this was a skillful illusion. There actually was no way to look inside it, as it was totally sealed. The woven bag would have to be cut off to get at the container inside.

The speed at which Strateia could execute this task was amazing to see. What is more, the artistry of his weaving would have made the most skilled weaver jealous.

When Strateia finished, he stood up and walked over to where Diakrina was seated. He lifted the shield and placed the finished product under it.

"There, that will help. But you must be very careful to keep this under your shield as much as possible."

"I will, Strateia."

Strateia returned to his seat and again looked out over the valley. They sat there taking in the calm of the pre-dawn hours. Somewhere in the distance Diakrina heard a whippoorwill's song and it made her think of her grandfather's farm.

"Diakrina," said Strateia presently, "the men you are about to meet are very long-lived by your standards, as I have already told you. Lord Mazzaroth is 750 years old by your reckoning. His father, known to you as Adam, is 880 years old. Their appearance to you will be quite astonishing. So, it is my intent to prepare you, somewhat, to meet them without being too overwhelmed."

"You speak as if they are hardly to be recognized as humans by me, Strateia. Could they really be that different?"

"Yes. And when we come into Lord Mazzaroth's lands you will need to interact with them for I will not do so."

"What do you mean, Strateia? Will they be able to see you and realize you are with me?"

"Yes. Their perception of the realms of cause—the spiritual realm, as you call it—is still somewhat functional. In a fashion they will see me, and they can hear me if I speak to them. But they will not expect me to speak to them or to communicate with them in any way. However, it is good they can be aware of my presence. If they were not, they might not give you any more attention than a small child. And they certainly would not invite you to a meeting with Lord Mazzaroth or listen to anything you asked of them. Yet, because they will discern I walk with you, they will give you an audience."

"Why will they not expect you to speak to them, Strateia?"

"Lord Mazzaroth has taught his people what his father taught him concerning the warriors of the Living One. They know we only communicate with those to whom we are sent. I will only speak to them if the Living One directs me to do so. They are aware of this fact. They realize they are forbidden to try to communicate with me unless I first invite their correspondence."

"In other words, I have to do all the talking!" quipped Diakrina in mock frustration.

"Something you do very well, indeed!" snapped back Strateia playfully.

It would be good to remind you ever since Strateia had given Diakrina the ability to understand and speak the ancient language, most of their conversations had been by means of it. But, like bilingual people will often do, they mixed it with English and sometimes this would result in a momentary transition back to English lasting for several minutes.

But for Diakrina, at least, the power of the ancient language—what she came to refer to as, Antediluvian—was like a magnet. Unconsciously, it had become her new linguistic home. This, of course was important. She was about to enter a society where the only language spoken in all the earth was this, Antediluvian.

As they sat in the calm of the star-punctuated canopy, Diakrina looked down into the darkness of the valley below. She was trying to see if she could possibly discern any of its features. To her amazement she caught what looked like the flicker of light in various places: as if modern city lights were occasionally showing through the trees by the stirring of the branches by the breeze.

"Strateia, are those lights below?" Then pointing down toward several of them, "There, flickering through what must be trees?"

"Yes, Little One, those are lights."

"Are they campfires or torches?" asked Diakrina.

"No, it is illumination by means of their technology."

"Technology?" said Diakrina as if the word had been misused by Strateia and was out of place.

"Yes, Diakrina," responded Strateia in parrot-like fashion, "tech-no-lo-gy."

For a moment Diakrina sat there with a look of utter perplexity on her face. Until that moment she had not realized she had a very preconceived idea of the society she was about to enter. She had unconsciously assumed it would be … well … primitive. Certainly, her discussions with Strateia had removed any idea of mankind in this time being savage—like grunting cave men. Yet, unknowingly, she had replaced it with a kind of noble savage idea. And this conception did not include things like science and technology except, perhaps, on the most rudimentary level.

"I see you have unfounded assumptions hindering your acceptance of this fact," said Strateia.

Diakrina was about to protest the, "unfounded assumptions" part, but then she thought better of it. What she actually said was, "Well … I … uh … guess so."

Strateia smiled at her and seemed to be enjoying this moment of stumbling self-awareness in Diakrina.

"You, and those of your time, Diakrina, are very full of such assumptions. And what is more, you are often led astray by these assumptions without the slightest awareness.

"Diakrina, in this valley below us, many of the theories about early man which unconsciously control your conception, will be demolished. Unfortunately for you, the historical skepticism of your time, and its resulting revisionism, has made you moderns—as you call yourselves—very ignorant and self-deluded about such things. What has been unconsciously assumed—which is an imposed context on your thinking caused by this skepticism—will, here, be dragged kicking and screaming into the light of reality. And the intensity of this unrelenting reality will vaporize these notions and expose them for the illusions which they are."

Diakrina was still opened-mouthed and speechless: staring unblinkingly into Strateia's face all during this short clarification. Even after he finished, it took her several seconds to find her voice.

When she did find it, she simply furrowed her forehead and said with the breathy exhale of a deep sigh, "Wow! … Never thought one word, placed in a new context, could expose how invalid, and unexamined, my whole framework of understanding can be."

Diakrina then pointed again to the lights randomly being exposed by the stirring of the treetops below, "You mean to tell me, those are electric lights?"

Strateia smiled at her and then answered. "Once again, your lack of context has caused you to jump to a conclusion not quite accurate. You assume if these are some form of artificial lighting, they should be the same technology as you are familiar with: electrical lighting. While in the very broadest manner of speaking we would have to say electricity is certainly involved, in a more specific and accurate description we could not call these electric lights.

"The lights below are not produced by the resistance of current in resistive wire, as in incandesce lighting, nor by the exciting of gas molecules through conducting a current through it, nor even by light emitting diodes. It is a form of induction, but not an induction that results in current and heat in an element like metal. It is the use of magnetic fields to induce a resonant frequency in the atoms of a clear crystalline structure. This resonance has a self-genesis component to it related to the crystal's structure and mass. The result is direct electromagnetic radiation in the optic range from the mass of the crystal.

"Also, they have a technology for producing light by the application of magnetic resonance to water in a somewhat different manner. This creates a sphere of light within a mass of water.

"But how do these ancient men understand and use such advanced science?" interrupted Diakrina. "It took centuries of scientific discoveries to lead to the development of our forms of electrical lighting."

"Well," answered Strateia, "you must again remember ancient, from your point of view, does not mean primitive in the sense of lacking the ability to produce science and technology. Your ancestors in the valley below are far superior to mankind in your day in both biological perfection and in intellectual capability. What it took an Einstein or a Tesla a lifetime of scientific investigation to discover, the men in the valley below understand innately.

"Remember, Diakrina, as I shared with you before, things did not start out noncomplex and then evolve to complexity. Everything starts with the Perfect One. He is the Source of all that is. And when he created your kind, they were at their zenith in this age, as to physical life and intellectual ability.

"What is more, each of the people of this age live several centuries. Not only is the normal level of intelligence among them what you would call super-genius by the standards of your day, but also they live long enough to accumulate much knowledge as an individual and as an unbroken society. There is not the loss of knowledge due to lack of handoff between the generations. One man can continue to learn for seven or eight centuries at four or five times your intellectual rate of acquisition."

"No wonder they can be so advanced," interjected Diakrina.

"But there is another reason, which it is important for you to understand, as well," added Strateia. "Your ancestors below, do science from a fuller perception of reality than those of your time are capable. They not only have firsthand history of what the world was like before the great severing took place between men and the Living One, they still have a greater residual perception of the dimension of cause: the spiritual realm.

"In regard to the spiritual world they are like men who see dimly: men only partially blind. And to speak by way of analogy to physical perception, they still have retained some of their other means of perceiving the spiritual realm directly, much like a person who has lost part of their eyesight but still has their sense of hearing, touch, taste and smell.

"The people of your time are like men who have lost all their sight, all their hearing, all their sense of touch and taste, as regards the spiritual world. They still have something analogous to the sense of smell regarding the spiritual realm. And while this troubles them with the realization there is more to reality than they can otherwise perceive, mostly your people suppress what little perception does come through this residual spiritual sense.

"What is more, because it is very vague, they are easily led astray concerning spiritual reality by any attempts they make to engage their vague perception. This is due to so few being willing to submit to the Living One's authority and guidance, which could guard them from delusion. But as it is, Anomos' soldiers play deadly games with the ignorance of those who think they can understand the spiritual realm on their own."

"Do you refer to those who regard themselves as psychics and those who do paranormal research?" asked Diakrina.

"Yes. Many of them do have a heightened retention of sensitivity to detect the spiritual realm. But they do not have anywhere near enough to be accurate. This results in the evil servants of Anomos deluding them and puffing them up with pride concerning their supposed insights. When in reality they are almost always mistaken. It gives many of Anomos' minions much sadistic delight.

"But the point of this is the people of this time do their science of the physical world within the framework and recognition of the reality of the spiritual realm from which it came. In fact, even your modern science was birthed mostly by men who had such a spiritual framework within to work and discover because they were followers of the Living One or had been deeply impacted by a worldview nurtured by those who were His followers.

"However, due to these men's greater direct perception of the spiritual realm, they better understand the physical laws of the material world. This is because the material realm came out of the spiritual realm and is constantly sustained by it, and is best correlated and understood by means of it. They are able to make direct correlations of physical laws which you can correlate, if at all, only by very indirect and laborious processes which are limited to physical perception and investigation.

"To illustrate: It is as if two physical laws are sometimes

uncorrelated in your perception because one of those laws is hidden beyond some great wall your material senses cannot reach past. However, the men of this time can see beyond that wall and find simple what for you is often a difficult enigma.

"To extend the illustration further: It may be someone of your time ultimately travels all the way around the earth, so to speak, to see what lies on the other side of the wall. If he goes for the express purpose of examining what is there and correlating it to what relates to it on the other side of the wall, which he has already seen, he may indeed make the connection. But in a sense, he had to go around the world to get next door. And when he gets there, he must correlate the two laws abstractly in his mind without any direct perception of both."

"This is all rather overwhelming, Strateia. It occurs to me you are preparing me to walk into a very advanced civilization. But if this is true—and I do not doubt you—how is it very little of this science has survived to my time?"

"You will remember, Diakrina, as I told you before, the scientist of your day are increasingly having to admit the evidence points to advanced civilizations in your past. Recall I told you they tend to dismiss this evidence or accept it as inexplicable. But increasingly they are resorting to concocting silly myths about aliens coming to this planet and giving ancient men technology.

"Of course they have no evidence for this. They simply assert the fact of the technology itself points to such a conclusion. But this is only because they have already rejected more plausible explanations—for which much of the raw material and historical validation are already in the Sacred Book which they ignore."

"The primary reason all this knowledge will disappear, along with the civilization it presently produces, is the time of judgment by water will bury this world completely. There will be little recognizable human artifacts from this period in history as much of the surface of the present earth will be turned upside down and buried.

"Also, the technology you will see—and you will only see a small part of it—is so perfectly integrated with the natural world around us it often looks more natural than man-made. This is due to a superior technology able to go beyond elementary levels of energy extraction which rely on the lower forms of energy expression, such as, for example, heat."

Diakrina couldn't help but think how silly all this would sound in the university classrooms of her school. And it was just that imposed sense of incredulity, due to ignorance and misinformation, making her now pity the actual silliness of her own time.

"It dawns on me we, in my day, are like kindergarteners who imagine themselves all grown up, when in fact, we know next to nothing about the real world."

"Speaking of dawning …" Strateia turned and pointed to the horizon behind them.

Diakrina turned and immediately discerned the faint predawn glow preceding a sunrise.

"It is time we begin our descent into Lord Mazzaroth's land," said Strateia unseating himself and turning again to look at the eastern sky. "The sunrise is only minutes away and we should be on our way by then."

Diakrina took one last look down into the still dark valley. She knew in a few hours it would no longer be an unknown place to her. And she, unlike any others of her time, would be allowed to interact with the most ancient of mankind.

This would indeed be a day to remember.

Chapter Five

THE LAND OF MEN

Diakrina lifted the shield and prepared herself for the unavoidable effect of the Ātheos. How hard it was not to look forward to it! But of course, that is exactly what she could not let herself do. Instead, she fixed the two scenes of judgment and utter paranoia in her mind and placed the now camouflaged crystal container over her shoulder and swung it to her back as quickly as possible.

When she finally had everything in place, Strateia gave her an approving up and down glance. He then said to her, "There will be times when I need to speak to you in the presence of others what I do not intend for them to hear. When this is needed, I will speak to you like this … in this tone of voice. The voice Strateia used had a tint of a silver tone in it Diakrina always detected when He gave a battle cry. But it was now soft and gentle. This is a voice only you will be able to hear. Do you understand?"

"Yes, Strateia. This will be a comfort. I am sure I will need your direction constantly."

"It will not be my direction. It will be the direction of the Living One which I will relay to you."

Then nodding toward the valley rim he began picking a path downward between the boulders.

Diakrina fell in behind Strateia and took note his stride was much slower and relaxed than it had been all through the night. They had not gone far down the rim until they came to a path angling toward them, from the north, down the face of the rim. Where they met the path, it did a sharp turn as it folded back under itself and continued down the rim returning to the north.

They were almost immediately in trees. If it had not been for the daylight spreading across the sky, it would have been very dark indeed. But even though they were in the shadow of the plateau above and behind them, and therefore received little direct light from the sun rising in the east, there was enough light to make the path discernible.

Strateia and Diakrina followed the path as it angled downward into the valley across the face of the valley's rim. Every so often it would fold back under itself and continue the steep descent in the opposite direction.

After about thirty minutes of following this switchback, the rim they were descending became noticeably less steep and the path stopped switch-backing north and south and instead turned straight west down into the valley.

Here the trees that composed the forest became increasingly larger. By the time they had gone another two hundred yards the angle of descent was very gentle, and the trees became what Diakrina could only label as, gigantic.

They were like the enormous trees seen as she and Strateia were making their way into the Great Meadow. In the predawn light the massive trees seemed like titans standing over and around them. Each dominated several acres of land. And once again Diakrina began to be aware of a kind of observing sentience, which she could not help attributing to the presence of the trees.

Suddenly, sunlight hit the tops of the giants as the dawn rose high enough to angle down into the valley and illuminate the topmost branches. All around Strateia and Diakrina birds erupted in a chattering symphony of song. And as if on cue, it seemed each tree came alive with hopping, fluttering birds, multicolored butterflies, buzzing bees and scampering squirrels. All around their base rabbits poked their heads out, chipmunks began their foraging, and a family of red fox yawned and stretched at the mouth of their den, which was dug under one of the tree's enormous roots.

Life was everywhere. If Strateia had allowed it, Diakrina would have sat down at the nearest clearing and soaked in this amazing rhythm of life. Yet she knew such leisure was no longer on the agenda. Instead, she did her best to keep pace while also looking around at the activity in and under each canopy of life.

Diakrina was roused back to their purpose by the voice of Strateia.

"Diakrina, look up ahead."

Diakrina walked up beside Strateia who had stopped in the middle of the path. He was pointing up ahead to a place where sunlight was streaming down across the path. This was because there was a gap in the forest. And dominating the area where the path continued into the sunlight was a large stone arch. The arch was at the beginning of a stone bridge, which arced upward in the sunlight as it reached across a fast-flowing river. And standing on the bridge looking in their direction was a young man dressed as a warrior.

Instantly, Diakrina forgot about everything else. It was clear the young soldier had already spotted them and was giving them his full attention. He was dressed in a tunic appearing to be made of some kind of bright blue material. Around his waist was a large leather belt on which hung a dagger in front, just to the left of his middle. On his left side hung a scabbard made of some kind of bluish metal very shiny. From its top a sword handle of polished gold protruded. On his left arm he had a small round shield made from the same kind of bluish metal as the scabbard. It had some kind of gold symbol engraved into it.

He was wearing no helmet, which allowed Diakrina to see he had a full head of light, almost golden, brown hair long enough to rest on his shoulders. He had a close-cut beard and mustache framing a highly chiseled face of very handsome features. But what shocked Diakrina most was that even from this distance she could tell he was about the size of Strateia. He was like no man she had ever seen before.

"He belongs to the sons of Lord Mazzaroth," said Strateia. "The gold emblem on his shield is that of the house of Mazzaroth."

Then turning to her, Strateia said, "Diakrina, you must immediately introduce yourself and request to be taken to Lord Mazzaroth. He will ask you to what family you belong. You are simply to answer you have been sent by the Living One and have no family affiliation. Then state your mission is urgent and can be revealed to only Lord Mazzaroth himself."

"Will he be friendly?" asked Diakrina, as she was starting to realize what a large, powerful and imposing person she was about to approach.

"He is no one to trifle with, to be sure. He is one of the princes of Lord Mazzaroth's immediate family. But he is a man of honor. You should be in no danger. Besides," added Strateia, "I will be right beside you. He will not be allowed to harm you. What is more, he can see me nearly as well as you can. He will recognize I belong to the Living One's Host. Lord Mazzaroth's house is taught to give us honorable heed."

The young warrior had turned fully toward them and was standing with his feet planted somewhat apart in a relaxed, yet alert stance. By this he was telegraphing to them he knew of their presence and was waiting for their response.

Diakrina took a deep breath and let it out slowly. "Ok, here we go."

She began walking toward the young warrior trying to look relaxed, yet intentional. The closer she came, the more the young man eyed her curiously. And, despite herself, the more an expression of amazement washed over and mingled with the business-like countenance she was trying to maintain.

When finally she stopped about six feet away from him, looking up into his down turned face, she had quite forgotten, for the moment, what to say or do. What is more, he too now had a look of inquisitive wonder on his own face.

Diakrina's mouth was slightly open and her eyes wide. And for a few seconds both stood looking at each other like strangers from different planets meeting for the first time. Finally, the youth glanced up to his left at Strateia who was standing to Diakrina's right and slightly back of her. He eyed him for a moment and then looked back down at Diakrina and raised one eyebrow as if to say, "Well …"

Diakrina came to herself and immediately began trying to remember what she was supposed to be saying.

"I am Diakrina. I request to be taken to speak with Lord Mazzaroth."

As she spoke, both of his eyebrows raised slightly and a look of unalarmed shock came over his face.

"You are the size of a child, but you do not speak as a child." Then remembering himself he continued. "You request to be taken before Lord Mazzaroth. May I ask to what family you owe your allegiance?"

"I have been sent by the Living One. I have no family affiliation."

The young warrior—for so he appeared to Diakrina—stepped slightly toward Diakrina and to her left side as he walked somewhat behind her in a half-circle as if sizing her up.

"Can you explain to me the nature of your mission and what you wish to speak with Lord Mazzaroth concerning?"

"I can only say that my mission is urgent and can only be revealed to Lord Mazzaroth, himself."

Once again, the young warrior looked up at Strateia and studied him carefully. Then he walked back around in front of Diakrina.

"Well, you seem harmless enough. And it is clear you are accompanied by one of the Living One's warriors. I will extend my shield over you and bring you into my trust so you can be taken to Lord Mazzaroth."

These words were no sooner out of his mouth than Diakrina heard a swishing sound over her head and then a thud. What had happened was Strateia had suddenly leaped from behind her toward the young warrior and grasped at the air just in front of his chest. The thud was the sound of his hand grasping a large arrow, about the size of a small spear, by its shank and stopping its point only inches from the warrior's chest.

Before Diakrina could fully take in what had just happened, a loud battle cry came from several voices behind them. When she turned, she saw a number of warriors, about eight in all, rushing from behind trees to the left of the path. They were dressed in dark grey tunics with dull black shields and were holding coal-black swords which looked more like oversize machetes made from a single piece of metal than anything else Diakrina could compare them to.

They were huge men. All but one of them was larger than Strateia or the young warrior. They towered at least twelve to fifteen feet in height and all of these large warriors had very bushy, red beards and long stringy red hair streaming down over their shoulders and down their backs.

The one about the same size as Strateia and the young warrior, was not running toward them but had stepped out from behind a tree and was reloading his bow with another arrow.

This is when everything became really crazy. Strateia and the young warrior both pulled their swords and met the charging mob of giants. Strateia was of course the swiftest and he met the first two giants leading the charge with a swift crosscut of his sword that went right through the torsos of both of them, cutting them each in half. The young soldier met the third man and cut the man's legs out from under him by side-stepping him and swing his sword through the man's knees from the backside. As the man fell helplessly backward toward the warrior's feet, he then ran him through the chest with a quick thrust.

Another giant, right behind this one, would have run the young warrior through if it had not been for Strateia getting there first and removing the attackers head with a frontal blow to his thick neck. Strateia's blow had such force it not only stopped the giant's charging thrust, but also sent his whole body flying backwards.

The young warrior met another of the black clad attackers and a loud report of metal on metal sounded as each warrior's swings and thrusts were blocked by the counter of the adversaries. While all this was going on, two black-clad combatants, which had been at the back of the charge, pushed passed Strateia and the young warrior.

They were clearly headed straight for Diakrina.

Diakrina had hardly moved for the few seconds all this was transpiring for she was wide-eyed and stunned into motionlessness. She was overwhelmed at the speed at which everyone was moving. These giant men moved like cats … just as Strateia had describe the movement of the Nephilim.

The sight of the two giant men charging at her with extended swords shocked her out of her trance. However, she still was not sure what she should do.

As Strateia was just finishing the swing beheading the one soldier, he had caught sight of the two charging toward Diakrina.

"Run, Diakrina! Run for the bridge!" he shouted with his strong, silver battle cry cutting through all the ear-shattering reports of the swords.

However, Diakrina, having come to herself at the same moment, had already started pulling her sword and had taken a fighting stance with her shield held in front of her. It was too late to run. One of the black-clad warriors, moving faster than the other, was almost on her.

It was at that very moment Strateia heard the twang of the bow as the bowman let loose another arrow at the young warrior. The young warrior was locked in deadly combat with one of the giants and had his back to the bowman. Strateia shot through the air, caught the large, spear-like arrow by its shaft and then, without the slightest hesitation, turned in the air and threw the arrow straight at the giant about to reach Diakrina.

The arrow went through the back of the giant's neck into his spine. His arms flew outward and upward, and he froze in his tracks. The black-clad warrior behind the one pierced by the arrow slammed into him and sent him sprawling forward toward Diakrina. The great bulk of his head hit Diakrina's shield and knocked her backwards. Somehow, however, she managed to keep her feet. Fortunately, the warrior which had slammed into the back of the other, then stumbled over his comrade's legs and fell forward over his body and hit with a thud face down on the ground to Diakrina's immediate left.

Before she hardly knew what she had done, Diakrina jumped astraddle of his head and rammed the blade of her sword down into the back of his neck at the spine. The giant's arms went stiff with an outward motion and then he slowly began to go limp.

Meanwhile, Strateia had turned his attention toward the bowman. But he had turned and run back into the forest and Strateia let him go, as he no longer posed a threat.

Then a loud growling exhale was heard as the young warrior's sword found its mark and the last of the seven giant warriors fell dead. There was an immediate silence broken only by Diakrina's heavy breathing.

The young warrior pulled his sword from his dead combatant and turned to survey everything. When he saw Diakrina, who was still straddling the dead warrior, pulling her sword out of his neck, his eyes widened.

He walked back toward the bridge and up to Diakrina—who had gotten clear of the two bodies—taking a long look at her and the two giants felled at her feet. One had an arrow in his neck and the other she had just pulled her sword out of. He then turned and looked back at Strateia.

"I don't know who you are, Diakrina, but I am glad you are accompanied."

Then he looked down at Diakrina's sword.

"You carry a sword of crimson light, like the guardian. And evidently you are not as harmless as you look." With this last statement he glanced in the direction of the slain giant Diakrina had just stepped away from.

Diakrina didn't say anything as she was still trying to take in what had just unfolded. Strateia walked up to her.

"That was one of Anomos' search parties. We got here none too soon."

Then turning to the young warrior Strateia spoke to him.

"You extended your shield over us just before the attack. The Living One asks you to honor your pledge and protect Diakrina's life and mission from the schemes of Anomos."

The young warrior eyed Strateia carefully.

"I will keep my pledge. Yet, I see I have involved my Father's house in something of a very serious nature."

Then turning again to Diakrina, the young warrior looked down at one of the slain giants.

"These are Nephilim warriors in league with the house of Cain. The man, the one which ran away, the archer, was Tubal-Cain, a sixth-generation son of Cain. He was their leader. I recognized him immediately. If they are in league with Anomos for the purpose of capturing or killing you, then you must be embroiled in something with grave implications."

Diakrina looked at Strateia who nodded a subtle affirmation. Then looking back to the young warrior, "I confess that I am. It is a matter of serious importance for all mankind. But I can divulge nothing more until I stand in the presence of Lord Mazzaroth. These are my instructions."

Once again, the thoughtful warrior sized her and Strateia up with his eyes. Then with a sense of resolve he changed his manner.

"Then, I guess we should finish our introduction which was so rudely interrupted. I am Jared, the fifth from Adam among the firstborn sons. My father is Mahalalel, son of Kenan, who is the son of Enosh, who is the son of Seth, who is known among us as Lord Mazzaroth. He is the son of our great father, Adam, who still walks among us as our true head. He is the son of El.

"I am the father of Enoch, who is the father of Methuselah, who has yet to greet a son. I am in my three hundred and seventieth year."

When Jared said he was in his three hundred and seventieth year, you could have pushed Diakrina over with a feather. In her mind she had been referring to him as the, young warrior, for, indeed, he looked like a young man in his early twenties in the prime of his powers. However, now she realized she was in the presence of the oldest man she had ever met.

Jared noticed the wonder on her face.

"Have I said something which raises a question for you?"

Diakrina came to herself and realized instantly she had no way of making him understand how his statement of age had affected her. He knew nothing of the short-lived times from which she came that made what was a normal statement of everyday fact for him so amazing to her.

"No. Please excuse me." Then changing the subject, "Shouldn't we be going somewhere more protected?"

"Perhaps you are right."

Jared turned and began walking over the bridge.

"Come," he said. "I will send a detail of men to prepare these bodies to be sent back to the sons of Cain. I will take you to Lord Mazzaroth."

Diakrina fell in beside Strateia as they both followed after Jared.

"Strateia," she whispered, "that man is nearly four hundred years old. Yet, he hasn't even the hint of age on him. He looks like a young man, still."

Strateia smiled at her and whispered back, "Much more time than that has passed since my creation. Do I look old to you?"

There was no hint of vanity in this question. It was clearly rhetorical and for Diakrina's benefit—to contextualize her statement so it was severed from her modern-world perspective.

"Of course not!" retorted Diakrina.

Then nodding toward Jared, Strateia said, "Wait until you meet the true patriarchs among them."

"You mean Adam and Lord Mazzaroth?"

"Yes."

"Why is Adam not the ruler among them instead of his son?" asked Diakrina.

"He is the honored head. And in that sense still rules. But he has given active rule over to his firstborn. But make no mistake. He never speaks without being heard and obeyed."

When they came up to the top of the arch in the bridge, Diakrina could see the river came from the north down the valley. The sunrise was full by now and the morning was bright and clear. The massive trees, which reached over four hundred feet into the air and branching out so their great tops created an unbroken canopy, beginning about hundred and thirty feet up and filling the sky from there up to their tops, made it impossible to see up the valley for any distance.

However, what you might call the first signs of civilization, other than the bridge, could now be seen. For at the base of the bridge a wide walkway, paved in large stones, each about 20 feet square, and laid in progressing pattern so the center stone always led the two outside stones, began and turned to the right. It stretched north into the forest as far as Diakrina could see into it.

They descended the bridge and turned to follow the stone walkway. Because it was three square stones wide at all points, the walkway was about sixty feet across. Diakrina immediately could see the stones were highly smoothed and polished. Their edges were so straight, and so perfectly set together, but for the visual change in each stone's unique color and grain, you would likely have been unable to see it as anything but a single stone in the shape of the walkway. However, the change of color and grain in the stones made the sharp line merging their edges very distinct.

Diakrina couldn't resist stooping to run her fingers over one of the joints between two stones. She could not feel the joint with her fingers. It was too perfect to be detected tactilely. She was convinced the edge of a knife would not have been deflected in anyway if you ran it across the joint. How two pieces of stone could be so perfectly cut and joined was beyond Diakrina's comprehension.

Jared eyed her curiously as she explored the surface of the stone pavement but said nothing to her. When she rose, he turned and led along the wide, stone boulevard in the direction of the forest.

As yet they had seen no other humans. But just then a group of ten soldiers, all dressed like Jared, came striding toward them out of the shadow of the trees. They were busy talking among themselves and good-natured laughter interjected itself occasionally into their playful banter.

When those at the head of the group saw Jared with Diakrina and Strateia following him, they all became silent and stopped and waited for their approach. However, Jared stopped some distance still away from them and asked Diakrina if she would wait where she was for a moment. He then continued toward the group of men.

When he reached them, each man stood up straight and nodded his head forward in a kind of salute of honor. Jared paused and released them all from their salute with a quick nod of his own. They gathered around him as he began speaking to them, presumably about Diakrina and Strateia and the battle having just taken place only moments before.

Diakrina was so taken with watching these men. All were nearly eight feet tall, all seemed perfectly proportioned and all were as handsome as mythical Greek gods. She realized it would be useless to try to determine the age of any of them. But it seemed quite clear Jared was likely the senior among them. But of course this might not have been due to age, but rather some system of family ranking or military structure which Diakrina had no recourse to.

After several minutes, seven of the men formed a group heading Diakrina and Strateia's way. However, they only greeted them with a nod of the head and continued past them toward the bridge. It seemed clear they were on their way to deal with the bodies of the slain.

Three men stayed with Jared and now accompanied him as he returned to Diakrina and Strateia. As they approached, Jared turned toward those with him and introduced them.

"Diakrina, these are three men of my family. This is Tiras, my brother." A golden-headed young man (Diakrina could think of them in no other way than, young men) nodded at Diakrina. Diakrina nodded in return.

"This is Ashur. He is the son of my father by a different mother."

Ashur had coal-black hair, thick and flowing, down to his shoulders. He nodded to Diakrina, and she acknowledged him.

"This," pointing to the third, "is my son, Enoch."

A young man with very bright eyes, which seemed to dance with intelligence, stepped forward and nodded to Diakrina.

"Enoch, Tiras and Ashur," continued Jared, "this is Diakrina who has come to us on a mission from the Living One. As you can see, she is accompanied."

All three men looked in Strateia's direction, but none made any attempt to acknowledge him other than with this glance. And it was clear they expected no response from Strateia.

Tiras spoke to Diakrina. "Please express our thanks to your guardian for saving Jared's life."

Diakrina was about to respond when she heard Strateia speaking in that silver tone which he had said only she would be able to hear.

"Remind Tiras he is to give his thanks personally to the Living One."

"I am sure," began Diakrina in response to Tiras, "the Living One would be glad to hear your thanksgiving personally."

Tiras' eyebrows lifted slightly as a look of being both reminded and corrected came over his face. It resolved into a pleasant smile as he nodded his head in polite acknowledgement.

"We will now take you to Lord Mazzaroth without delay," said Jared.

He then turned to Tiras and said, "Hurry ahead and inform the Fathers of everything I have told you."

Tiras turned and began running gracefully down the paved road toward the forest and disappeared into the trees.

Jared then turned in the same direction and began leading down the very center of the stone pavement into the great trees. Diakrina and Strateia fell in behind him and Enoch and Ashur brought up the rear.

Diakrina overhead Enoch say quietly to Ashur, "She is the size of a child, but she does not speak like one."

Once they entered the trees everything began to change.

Nothing could have prepared Diakrina for a city of the kind beginning to unfold around her in the trees. This was not a city with trees in it. It was trees with a city in it: but what a city.

You must remember these trees were gigantic oaks, elms and old-world style poplars. Their great trunks were greater in diameter than the giant red wood named, General Sherman in California. In many cases they rose over a hundred feet before the first limb extended outward. But above this, their great limbs extended out and upward in amazing mass and thickness, which reached to heights of over four hundred feet. Each tree dominated several acres of ground under its canopy. And the height of the area under each tree to the bottom of the canopy was tall enough to contain a ten-story building with ease.

At first the stone pavement extended straight into the forest only. But it soon began to branch out, not like roads or spokes of a wheel, but like spreading, connected patios filling spaces between the trunks of the great trees. And here and there beautiful stone structures began to appear, rising several stories under the canopy. Some of these structures had great extensions bridging over to the trunks of the trees and connecting to large-railed balconies encircling a tree.

But the further they journeyed into the city the more complex and intricate its structures became. You would see what looked like a ten-story stone building of great size. It would be built like a great high-rise but with intricate features planned into its shape and surface. But the great surprise was as you looked upward toward its top you would see the great canopy of a tree spreading out from the very center of the structure. These structures actually made one of the great trees the central constituent of the whole building.

It seemed instead of cutting down the large trees to make room for a city, they had used the trees creatively as the very skeleton of the city itself and had built their structures in harmony with them. Diakrina could not be sure, but it seemed many of these buildings had several more stories rising up into the canopies among the branches using this same method, in some instances, and building between large branches in others.

Everywhere there were creative and beautiful interconnecting walkways and stairways in the sky between the buildings and even among the different pinnacles of the upper parts of buildings. These seemed to be built to be flexible so they could move with the trees in a wind or perhaps to accommodate growth. And here and there Diakrina could see men and women and children beginning to move about in the morning light.

Soon they began to encounter people walking among the trees and on the main boulevard, which still continued straight ahead into the forest. The city was coming to life with the day. All the men were of similar height and build. But when Diakrina saw a young woman walking toward her for the first time she was stunned.

Diakrina couldn't help but stare. Here, walking toward her, dressed in what looked like something we would call a sari, made of beautiful white silky looking material, was a woman of perfect form and beauty as would seldom ever be seen in our world today. She would have made people stare on any street in our times. But what seemed so incredible to Diakrina was this utterly beautiful woman was around seven feet tall.

To hear she was this tall would immediately make someone, who had not seen her, think no matter how beautiful she may have been, such height would have been a detractor. Not only was it not a detractor, somehow, it enhanced her every physical feature. You could not have wished her to be even a millimeter shorter than she was.

To Diakrina she was like a walking piece of incredible art: almost too perfect to actually be alive. She later determined what made her so remarkable was her great size was not accompanied by any distortion or disproportion of features as is often seen in women who have grown to unusual size. Diakrina, despite herself, simply stopped in the road and watched her approach.

As it turned out, most of the people did not give Diakrina much notice until they got close enough to take notice of how she was dressed. In their eyes she was simply the size of a young child of eight or nine years. But as they would get closer, Diakrina's unusual dress—children were not seen with glowing shields and swords—would attract their attention.

The woman would have walked past Diakrina without taking much notice of her at all—for it seemed it was an unwritten rule among them that a woman did not engage men with her eyes when walking past, and Diakrina was among men—if it had not been for Diakrina actually stopping in the middle of the boulevard and standing staring as the men walked on ahead of her.

When the woman glanced at her out of the corner of her eye, she started to look back down again, but then a look of curiosity came over her countenance. She too stopped in the middle of the stone pavement looking down at Diakrina who was slowly walking up to her.

The woman started to speak, "Child, why are you dressed …" but never finished her sentence. She obviously could not contextualize what she was seeing.

This brought Diakrina to herself. "Please excuse me, madam, I am sorry for staring." Then, in spite of herself she added, "You are incredibly beautiful."

For some reason this did not seem to mean much to the lady and she only continued to smile a crooked, somewhat bewildered smile at Diakrina.

"Come, Diakrina!" It was the silver voice of Strateia which none could hear but her.

Diakrina turned toward the men and noticed for the first time they had all stopped to wait on her. She gave a smiling nod to the woman and hurried off toward them.

They continued for about a half a mile into the forest-city and the structures never ceased to be creative and new in their design. But soon Diakrina could see they were coming to a great open space in the bottom of the valley, which was stretching out ahead of them. The closer they came to the open area the more the canopy opened, and the blue of the sky took its place.

When they reached the place where the open space began, Diakrina could now see it was a great bowl-shaped area where hundreds of gardens were located on either side of the paved road. Already the fields were full of workers who were planting and tilling.

Diakrina also noticed the river, which they had crossed earlier—they had been walking toward its upstream source—was now visible off to their right. It curved south back across the center of the open area and its source retreated to the far west side of the valley, to their left, and then up a hillside which began to rise in the far end of the valley. Because of the fall in elevation the river was moving very fast at this point but was too deep to create much white water. Rather it roiled and swirled down its course.

Where the river intersected the stone boulevard at the center of the great open area, there was another large arched bridge stretching across to the river's far bank. And dominating the whole area beyond the river was a massive structure; unlike anything Diakrina had ever seen. In what appeared to be the structure's center, it was built around a great tree like all the other structures she had seen previously. But such a tree Diakrina could never have imagined. It dwarfed every other tree or structure.

Diakrina estimated it rose over twelve-hundred-feet at its pinnacle. Its trunk, she learned later, was over ninety-five feet in diameter. This tree was more like a great redwood tree in form, for it had limbs only the last hundred feet of its top. Yet, otherwise, it was nothing like a redwood tree because the leaves were more like those of a very large maple tree and its limbs extended out much farther in all directions in ratio to that of a redwood tree.

However, just as astonishing was the great structure built around its base. It was a pyramid of such a scale as to be more than double the size of the Great Pyramid in present day Egypt. It came to a complete point at the top on its front side, which was one of its four sloping sides. It seemed the great tree rose out of, and interrupted the slope, on the backside of the pyramid, which was opposite to where they were standing. The pinnacle of the pyramid rose to nearly eight hundred plus feet. This left about four hundred feet of the great tree still towering beyond the already massive structure.

It was a breath-taking sight. The casing stones of the pyramid were of a white marble, which had obviously been polished to a near mirror-like sheen. It was dazzling in the morning sun. The front of the pyramid, unlike the Great Pyramid of Giza, had a structure serving as an entrance. It came out about two hundred yards from the structure like a great portico. It had four rows of columns, two on each side, and between them a large, grand entrance proceeded toward the pyramid.

The columns rose around three hundred feet in the air and were topped by a very thick, flat roof which had decorative writing of some kind all around its face, both front and sides. The whole structure of the portico, like the pyramid, was also covered in polished white marble, which reflected the rays of the sun.

Jared led them to the bridge, and they all began the ascent of its arched pathway over the river. At the top of the bridge Jared stopped and waited until all were gathered near him. Then he pointed to the pyramid and said in a very formal and reverent manner, "Behold! The Pyramid of the Tree."

Immediately, Diakrina realized there was an intended play on a word in this title. She had, of course, not taken notice of it until now, because she had so little experience with their language and her knowledge of it was a continually unfolding gift. But when she heard Jared say, "Behold! The Pyramid of the Tree," the unfolding gift of knowledge of this language made her immediately aware that in their tongue the word for tree was also the word for, promise. What she heard Jared say was, "Behold! The Pyramid of the Tree/Promise!" or she could have equally heard it as, "Behold! The Pyramid of the Promise/ Tree."

Later Diakrina would understand the word promise was the deeper, intended meaning, but the word tree was not to be disassociated with this meaning, as the idea of a tree was also the idea of a promise in their language—a kind of word picture of an idea.

Jared continued. "This is the meeting place of the great counsel ruling our people, the Sons of El. It is here, Diakrina, you will be brought before Lord Mazzaroth and the Ruling Council of Elders. By now they will have received my message sent by Tiras. We will be expected."

Jared then turned and began walking down the arch of the bridge and began leading them toward the Pyramid of The Promise, which was still over five hundred yards away.

"Jared, may I ask how your word for tree, came to also mean promise?" asked Diakrina.

Like any of us who use a language and seldom think of the source of its meaning, Jared paused for a very short moment of recollection as if the question had somewhat surprised him. But then, obviously remembering he began, "It is rooted in the content of the Great Promise given Lord Mazzaroth's father and mother at the gates of the Garden. The promise is of one who will come who will destroy the power of Anomos over us, curing us from the power of the great curse and once again giving us access to the Tree of Life and its immortal fruit. This hope of once again being given the right to, The Tree, is the content of, The Promise. So the idea of The Promise has become entangled and bound in our hearts and minds with The Tree to which it points. When we think of the Tree of Life we think of The Promise. What is more, our great Father, Adam, says the Living One has indicated to him—he knows not how—that a tree will somehow be involved in the fulfillment of this great promise."

When they reached the beginning of the portico, which led to the pyramid, Diakrina discovered it had three steps running all the way around it. And like the Great Portico of Sapient Castle these steps were not of ordinary size. They were each about a three-foot rise, which placed the floor of the portico about 9 feet above the ground.

As they approached the great steps, Jared, Strateia, Enoch and Ashur, all mounted them and walked up them as one normally walks up steps. For Diakrina, however, it meant climbing on top of each step like getting on top of a table. This she did without too much loss of dignity as she was now much more agile than she had been outside Sapient Castle.

The long corridor, flanked on either side by the two rows of massive columns, was incredibly beautiful. Each column seemed to be made of a single cut of white marble, which had subtle swirls of blue, crimson and green, and had been polished until its surface was almost like porcelain. Diakrina could not imagine how 300-foot columns could be cut as one piece and then moved into place. They were far more massive than anything even the largest modern cranes could have lifted.

What is more, each column stood on a pedestal proving to be made of solid, hammered gold with the most intricate workmanship carved into it. The capitals crowning each column seemed to be made of the same gold workmanship.

This raised all kinds of questions in Diakrina's mind. One thing was clear: She was not among savage, primitive (in the sense of lacking technology) mankind. It was while these thoughts were dominating her thinking Diakrina caught sight of workmen who seemed to be doing finish work on the left side of the portico. When she positioned herself to get a better look through the columns at what they were doing, she was shocked to see a massive piece of stone literally hovering in midair with some kind of platform under it seeming to be made of a metal structure filled with crystal-like material. The crystal material was glowing with a cool blue color and Diakrina took note there was a slight humming sound coming from some kind of resonance taking place in the crystal-like material. Perhaps it was this hum that had first attracted her attention, though she was not conscious of it at the time.

Jared took notice Diakrina had stopped following and was slowly walking in the direction of the workmen. Strateia was following her. Jared sensed what she was doing and patiently waited while she continued her investigation.

"How are they lifting that massive stone, Strateia?" asked Diakrina. "There are no cables or ropes. Nor would cables and ropes be enough if they had them to lift such a stone."

"It is by a principle which you might call, Earth-Field Levitation," answered Strateia. "As I told you, the field of the earth in this time is ten times stronger than it is in your time. They have developed a means of redirecting the flux from the earth's magnetic field into a very small space. Like a hundred trillion small wires the lines of flux are pulled together from all over the horizon and redirected so that they pass through this lifting platform. This results in a stretching of the flux lines into a tensioned state. This causes a lifting force.

"If you could see them—the flux lines, as you call them— you would see they are coming from the north from a wide area of the landscape and bundling down until they all pass through the platform. They then pass through it and begin spreading out again over the landscape of the valley as far as you can see in all directions to the south.

The Sons of El have developed a cold plasma energy source by which they are able to generate the incredible gathering and controlling magnetic flux fields which pull the earth's field into interaction with the device. I will not attempt to explain this cold plasma energy to you, as it is quite profound in its theory and application. Let it suffice to say it is capable of creating extremely powerful magnetic fields. It produces these fields by tapping into the magnetic energy holding matter together by means of an organized and harmonious method."

"Are you saying this energy is atomic?" ask Diakrina turning fully toward Strateia.

"Yes and no," answered Strateia. "Yes, in it is power coming from the atomic structure of matter. No, in that it is nothing like the destructive atomic methods your generation uses to release power from the atom. This is a harvesting of energy by the ordered conversion of matter. The methods of your age are actually quite primitive (in the sense of, unsophisticated) as compared to this technology.

"There is one other source of energy they utilize. It has to do with what many of your scientist now refer to as the quantum field. The older scientist of the 19th and 20th centuries, like Michael Faraday and Nicoli Tesla would have used the term, ether. It is the energy field filling the whole universe.

"If you manage to create a kind of frequency-generated zero-point, it causes the energy to flow through any device interacting with this zero-point. It flows as radiant-based energy not electron-based energy. Its characteristics are unique and the energy available to be harvested in this way is endless, as long as the universe continues to exist. This energy source and those learning how to harvest it have been suppressed in your time. But here there is no suppression so they can go beyond the primitive energy sources your cultures rely on."

It did seem strange to hear the modern science of her day referred to as primitive in comparison to technology, which was actually the most primitive—ancient—science in the world. No one back at Durham University she attended would ever believe this!

Jared waited patiently but soon caught Diakrina's eye and indicated they must go. "We dare not keep Lord Mazzaroth and the Elders waiting. It would not be honoring," he said as they fell in behind him again.

When finally they had traveled the full length of the great corridor, they came to the entrance proper to the Pyramid of The Promise. The entranceway itself was a very wide and tall rectangle cut into the sloping side of the pyramid. It was at least 100 feet tall, and it led into a large open area, which proved to be the only room in the Pyramid. This great room was the shape of a pyramid itself and was only smaller than the outside of the Pyramid by the difference of the thickness of the stones composed it.

What astonished Diakrina was the inside was not dark. There

was light coming from every surface on the inside—almost as if it all were phosphorescent. This light had no color of its own and left the surface of every wall its natural color; not causing it to appear to be glowing. Yet, somehow, you could discern light was indeed filling the space of the pyramid by emanating from the sloping walls.

Diakrina observed in the back of the great room the massive trunk of the tree could be seen as it ascended from the floor up though the back slope of the pyramid. There was a wide aisle passing between two large structures proving to be the backside of something like an amphitheater with seats arching around toward the back of the pyramid away from them. By looking down the wide aisle between them Diakrina could see there was a very large, raised platform in front of the trunk of the great tree. In the center was something like a large throne chair. At this point she could not be sure if there were more than one of these chairs as she could only see the middle where the aisle allowed a view of what was beyond the seating structures.

Jared led Diakrina and Strateia, with Enoch and Ashur following, toward the aisle. It took a few moments to cover the great distance up to where the aisle between the seating began. The area they transversed was so large over four football fields could have fit into it with room left over.

As they approached the entrance to the aisle, which was lined with rows of burning torches on either side, Jared paused; and so did everyone with him. He pulled a small horn made of some kind of animal horn from a leather pouch on his belt. He then blew from it a strong and melodic signal of two tones with the second tone jumping a full octave. He repeated this several times and then announced, "Jared, the son of Mahalalel, requests entrance to the Hall of Elders of the Sons of El."

There was a short silence and then a horn was heard to sound within the Hall echoing Jared's melodic request. Then a very resonant voice which seemed to fill the whole pyramid said, "You are welcome, Jared, son of Mahalalel. Enter the Hall of Elders of the Sons of El as is your right."

Jared motioned for them to follow him into the aisle between the two large stone amphitheater structures. Diakrina knew she was about to be the center of attention before men of great knowledge and wisdom. She swallowed hard and tried to compose her thoughts.

Chapter Six

THE HALL OF ELDERS OF THE SONS OF EL

Jared led them to the point where the mouth of the aisle emptied into a great hall. He paused again and said, "I have with me one over whom I have placed my shield. She is accompanied by a servant of the Living One."

A chorus of deep, resonant voices instantly responded in unison—they seemed to almost sing—"HIS NAME IS FOREVER BLESSED!"

The same deep, resonant voice, which had spoken to grant them entrance, spoke again. "If you have extended your shield over this one, we too extend our shield. She may enter without fear."

Diakrina could now see the one who spoke. He was standing on the steps in front of the great central chair. To say he was impressive is a vast understatement. His voice conveyed an inexplicable sense of towering and unique character and force of personality. There was eloquence, smoothness, in the timbre of his voice that astonished you. It was both beautiful and frightening at once. His words were like being caressed by thunder and being made instantly aware of a hidden power. Yet, balancing this terror was the communication of a calm and wise kindness, which was irresistibly magnetic. Something of this man's soul haunted—in a gracious sense—the very atmosphere where his voice was heard.

Like the others Diakrina had met, he was tall and god-like in form. He had a golden brown, well-trimmed beard two inches short of touching his collarbone. There was a small, golden crown on his head. It rested on a head already crowned with thick, flowing hair long enough to just break and rest on his shoulders.

His face was stunning. At first Diakrina could only stare and wonder what this stunning quality actually was. Then it hit her: his face had a sense of age and maturity about it without having a single wrinkle other than those which any twenty-year-old might have to reveal lines of expression. He was an ageless elder. He was a man of mature years, a father—even a grandfather—while remaining still in his physical prime.

Diakrina would not have called him a young man—that would never do!—there was a sense of antiquity about him. But he was in no way an old man to the eyes. Yet, she knew he was much older than any man she had ever seen before. In fact, he was seven hundred years of age!

This was Lord Mazzaroth, Seth, the son of Adam. He focused his steely grey-blue eyes on her, which were full of kindness but no vain sentimentalisms. Then he spoke again.

"I am informed your name is Diakrina. I am also informed you have been sent to us by the Living One."

He then looked straight at Strateia. "It is clear you are well validated by the Living One's warrior. What is more, we all pause to give thanks to the Living One for the aid Jared received."

With that the whole assembly of men rose to their feet and lifted their hands toward the roof of the great pyramid and in a chorus of perfect musical unison they said,

"THANKS TO ELOHIM, THE LIVING ONE, WHOSE GREAT POWER AND GREAT PROMISE IS OUR CERTAIN HOPE!"

The room shook with the resonance of their voices. Diakrina found herself somewhat embarrassed when it was finished that she had not joined in the proclamation of gratitude. But of course, she had no way of knowing what to expect or what was expected of her in these proceedings.

The whole assembly sat down again, and Lord Mazzaroth turned and walked up the steps to the great chair and seated himself. Diakrina noticed to his right there was another impressive chair, though somewhat smaller, which was empty. He motioned for Jared to lead Diakrina and Strateia to the center of the half circle in front of the great platform. This he did.

It became unusually silent in the great hall. Then Lord Mazzaroth spoke.

"Diakrina, Tiran, by means of Jared, has informed us of the attempt by the sons of men to capture you. It seems clear you are entangled in something of significance. For it is reasonable to conclude Anomos is the one who desires your capture."

He paused for a moment to allow Diakrina to respond. She found no words but nodded her head in acknowledgement of his assessment being accurate.

"We have extended our shield over you and, therefore, you have involved us in this affair. If we are to continue to extend our shield over you, it is necessary for you to share with us the nature of your mission. For direct conflict with Anomos is no small matter. As you may know the fallen elohim—the 200—which he leads, have given birth the Nephilim, a hybrid race of fallen gods and fallen mankind. They pose much danger in their strength and fierce hatred for us. They are under Anomos' control and in his service."

Diakrina realized she must speak and looked over at Strateia for help. He spoke to her in the silver voice which only she could hear.

"You must insist on a private audience with Lord Mazzaroth and those known as his High Council. Even there, danger may lurk, but it will give us more time and delay the spies which are here in this room."

It shook Diakrina to think of there being spies in this place where such noble men stood. Yet, she knew too much to doubt Strateia. So, she turned to answer Lord Mazzaroth who was waiting patiently for he could see Strateia was speaking to her, though he could not hear his voice.

"Lord Mazzaroth, I have been instructed to seek a private audience with you and your High Council before I make known my mission. I assure you my revelations to you will justify the request."

There was a rumble of discontent swepting over the half-circle of men seated behind her. Immediately, a man behind Diakrina stood. Lord Mazzaroth raised his head to acknowledge him and then said, "Hared, son of Kenahman, you wish to speak?"

"Yes, Lord Mazzaroth."

The man then left his place in the circular seating and came into the half circle in front of the large platform. He walked up to Diakrina's right, opposite the side Strateia was standing on, and Jared, who was standing there, took two steps to the right to make room for him. He then addressed Lord Mazzaroth.

"My Lord, there is much mischief in the air. Many of us are disturbed at what we have heard concerning this detachment, led by Tubal-Cain, as we have learned. This is the kind of conflict that can result in much spilling of blood. If indeed this is the case, it seems to many of us the wisdom of the full body of Elders should be consulted. I request, therefore, that you consider denying this request to meet only with you and the High Council."

Lord Mazzaroth nodded an acknowledgement to Hared for the point he had made. He then looked again at Diakrina.

"It is clear to us you have been instructed to ask for this private audience," and here he glanced at Strateia. "Yet, Hared, son of Kenahman has made a valid request. Tubal-Cain would not risk invading our territory without urgency being laid upon him. And if we are to risk the possibility of engaging Anomos, the Nephilim and the sons of Cain who are in league with him, it is a matter for all the Elders of the Sons of El to consider."

Here he paused for a moment and studied Diakrina with a keen eye. Then continuing, "However, the weight of your request, coming as it does with instructions from a warrior of the Living One, is not without strong claims to being granted regardless of the Elder's desires."

Hared stepped forward a half step as a way of requesting

permission to speak again. Lord Mazzaroth nodded his approval.

"Should the Elders not first examine the credentials of this Diakrina? After all, deception is not beyond possibility."

"Do you doubt the High Council's ability to carry out such an examination?" responded Lord Mazzaroth.

"No, my Lord. I was not impugning the ability of the High Council. Rather …"

But Hared never got to say more for Lord Mazzaroth held up his hand in a manner making it clear Hared was not to continue.

"Then we would violate logic to consider that a reason to refuse her request."

Suddenly, a collective inhale was heard all around the hall. At first Diakrina thought it was in response to Lord Mazzaroth's mild rebuke of Hared. But that proved not to be the case.

For from Lord Mazzaroth's right, from the far side of the great platform, came a man striding out from behind the great tree. At the sight of him everyone in the hall stood and then descended to one knee and bowed their heads. Lord Mazzaroth stood, and turning toward the advancing man, bowed his head in a salute of honor.

Then, as if on cue, in perfect unison, the whole body spoke together.

"WELCOME, OUR FATHER, SON OF EL. YOU HONOR US WITH YOUR PRESENCE."

∞——∞

Diakrina says she will never be able to express the sensation coming over her when she realized the identity of this man. But how could she have not known. If she had thought Lord Mazzaroth magnetic and overwhelming, all that was now eclipsed.

Striding to the center of the platform and approaching Lord Mazzaroth—who still kept his head bowed in honor—was a walking piece of poetry. Diakrina now had a new definition for the word, perfect; and for that matter, many other words like glorious, magnificent, splendid, marvelous, superior, excellent and superlative.

Without a thought, not even realizing she had decided to do it, she sank to one knee and bowed her head while still trying to peek glances at him (for she could hardly bear not to gaze at him). He walked up to Lord Mazzaroth and took him by the shoulders with both hands—he was a head taller than Lord Mazzaroth—and kissed him on the top of his bowed head.

"The blessings of the Living One be on you, my son."

His voice was music. Everything she had felt and experienced in the voice of Lord Mazzaroth was amplified in this voice. One could almost imagine an echo of the voice of the Living One, Himself, could be heard through him. Here was the son of no common Father!

Lord Mazzaroth then lifted his head and embraced his father with a smile of clear delight. He then stepped aside and motioned for his father to take the greater, central chair. This he did. Lord Mazzaroth then seated himself in the slightly smaller chair to the right of the center chair.

Once they were seated, the Elders all rose, bowed their heads in a kind of salute, and then seated themselves.

"I am honored to have such children to give me respect even in the deformity of my fallenness. I greet you, my sons."

"WE GREET YOU, OUR GREAT FATHER."

Diakrina had lifted her head but still did not have the presence of mind to rise. As she looked up and formed the name, in her mind, "Adam, the son of El," she could not contextualize his statement about deformity. In her mind, no one so magnificent could be in any degree deformed. This was humanity in all its possible splendor, as far as she was concerned. But it also crossed her mind how Strateia had taught her the Intruder—Anomos—who appeared incredibly glorious, was actually very deformed as compared with his former state.

It always astonished her that at that moment something inside of her rose up like anger. When she could take account of herself, she realized she was angry. She was angry that this near god—this walking, breathing paragon of excellence and living art—had been so slandered by the ignorance of the people of her time as a grunting caveman. The stunning, almost otherworldly prowess-of-existing (as she termed it) of this father of mankind, made such ignorant caricatures seem like a kind of blasphemy. (And she had no doubt Anomos was behind it and indeed intended it to be a blasphemy against the image of the Living One which this man so clearly possessed.) She was offended and ashamed of her own times. "How could we get it so terribly wrong?"

"Diakrina, you may rise," Adam said addressing her directly and with the kindness of a father. Then turning to his son, Lord Mazzaroth, he said for all to hear, "Only a few moments ago I was given a vision by the Living One. He has taken me into His confidence as regards this matter."

Then turning to Diakrina and lifting his hand toward her he said, "Diakrina is my daughter, though many years removed. And it is by the kindness, power and wisdom of the Living One she is able to stand before us."

Then turning to the Elders he questioned, "What is the great curse burdening us?"

In unison the whole assembly answered like a class doing their catechism,

"WE ARE SEVERED FROM RELATIONSHIP WITH THE LIVING ONE AND FROM THE TREE OF LIFE BECAUSE WE HAVE TURNED INWARD IN SELF-ALLEGIANCE AND SELF-DEPENDENCE. SIN CROUCHES AT OUR DOOR CONTINUALLY AND WE ARE BURDENED TO CONTINUALLY CONQUER IT AND YET ARE ENSLAVED."

"And what is our hope?" continued Adam.

"IT IS THE GRAND PROMISE:
'I WILL PUT GREAT HOSTILITY BETWEEN YOU AND THE WOMAN,
AND ALSO BETWEEN YOUR SEED AND HER SEED;
HER SEED WILL CRUSH YOUR HEAD,
AND YOU WILL (WHILE BEING CRUSHED) STRIKE AND BRUISE HIS

HEEL.'"

"You have spoken well, my sons. Now hear my words. A second curse threatens us. It is infinitely greater than the first, for it can have no promise of remedy. The details, I will not divulge, for I too, like my daughter, have been so instructed."

Then turning to Lord Mazzaroth he said, "My son, it would be wise to give her the audience with the High Council she seeks."

Lord Mazzaroth stood and turned toward his father and bowed his head in a salute of honor. "It will be as you have said, my Father."

With that, all the Elders stood to their feet and spoke as one.

"WE HEAR AND OBEY THE WORD OF OUR GREAT FATHER, THE SON OF EL."

Adam stood. The Elders fell to one knee and bowed their heads in a salute of honor to him. Then Diakrina heard him say under his breath to Lord Mazzaroth, "I will meet you and the High Council in the Inner Room. Do not delay. The matter is urgent."

And with a smile and a nod at Diakrina, the most splendid flesh and blood being Diakrina had ever seen, walked away in the direction he had come and disappeared.

Chapter Seven

THE INNER ROOM

Diakrina turned toward Strateia and noticed immediately he was looking very intently in the direction of the assembled Elders who were now rising to dismiss themselves. She followed his gaze and saw Hared, and three others were moving quickly to exit the Great Hall. They seemed to be intent on getting somewhere fast.

When Strateia saw Diakrina had taken note of the attention he was giving to these men and their almost frantic exit, he gave a subtle nod and glanced in their direction and said, "If I am not mistaken, there go the traitors to inform Anomos' minions. Time will be short. You must stress urgency on the High Counsel. I believe you have the support of their great father, so do not be timid."

Jared came over to her and motioned for her to follow. He walked up the steps of the large platform and fell in behind Lord Mazzaroth who was proceeding to follow the route his father had taken. She noted several men who had been seated in the center all fell in behind them and were following. Diakrina took these to be the Elders of the High Counsel.

The platform was so wide it extended beyond the ninety-foot trunk of the great tree about seventy-five feet on both sides. They walked around to the left of its trunk and Diakrina could see they were being taken to a large area beyond the place where the tree extended upward through the backside of the Great Pyramid.

When they had fully circumvented the massive tree, there were steps descending back to the common level and they were emptied out into an area under the sloping structure of the backside of the Great Pyramid. Several hundred feet, in the direction toward where the Great Pyramid's sloping side met the floor, there was a massive stone table. It was in the shape of a perfect equilateral triangle with its pinnacle pointed toward the tree and its base running parallel with the place where the pyramid's sloping side met the floor.

In the area where the table stood you could not actually see the place where the pyramid joined the floor for there was a fifty-foot-high wall rising on the far side of the table about thirty feet beyond it. Diakrina estimated each side of this massive stone table was one hundred and forty feet long.

There were only two great stone chairs on the far side, set perfectly centered. On the two sloping sides toward the pinnacle, which pointed toward the great tree, there were thirty-five stone chairs per side—resulting in seventy chairs in all. Therefore, the total number of chairs, with the two on the backside of the table, was seventy-two.

At the pinnacle of the table—the nearest portion to them as they approached—was a backless stone bench wide enough for at least two people. This, Diakrina was to learn, would be her place: the designated place for those coming before the High Council. The lack of a back to the bench somehow symbolized that those who were seated here were not seated with authority in the High Council.

Adam and Lord Mazzaroth made their way toward the two large stone chairs on the far side of the table. Jared took Diakrina to the bench and told her to stand in front of the bench at the point of the great table and to be seated only after the Elders of the High Council had all been seated. Strateia took his place behind Diakrina and the bench and stood towering over her, facing the two great stone chairs at the far side of the table.

Jared then went around to their left and made his way to the seat fourth from the far end, nearest the front of the table. Diakrina would later learn this left side of the table, which was at the right hand of those seated in the two great stone chairs, was the place where the order of authority descended from Adam and Lord Mazzaroth. In the first chair, at the very corner was Enosh, the son of Lord Mazzaroth—Seth—which was Jared's great grandfather. Next to Enosh, Kenan, his son and Jared's grandfather. And seated next to Kenan, Mahulalel, his son, and Jared's father. The fourth seat was Jared's. Next to him, in the fifth seat, was Enoch, Jared's son. And in the sixth seat, she was to learn, was Methuselah, who was just old enough he had only been admitted to the High Council three years earlier. (He was only 143 years old!)

Diakrina had to assume this ended the direct descent of the firstborns, as Methuselah—she would confirm later—had not yet had a son, as he would be 187 years old before his firstborn son would be born. This meant other family lines, which were from second born and third born sons continued around the great stone table until it reached the last seat on the far-right side, near the head.

All the Elders waited until everyone was in his place. Then Adam and Lord Mazzaroth took their seats. This released the seventy Elders of the High Council to be seated. Diakrina then seated herself. Only Strateia remained standing.

Lord Mazzaroth's Father stood. Every head around the table bowed in a salute.

"I confessed to the whole body of Elders of the Sons of El, I was given a vision by El, Himself. He has informed me a second curse is planned by Anomos. It would be greater than the first, for it has no cure. It too comes by means of fruit from a tree: but not fruit from the Forbidden Tree. No, this evil seems even more beautiful and desirable. It harnesses a greater beauty to be twisted for a greater and more powerful deception. This fruit is from the Tree of Immortality."

When Adam made this last statement, you could hear a common gasp in the great room. Enosh, seated in the first chair of the Elders, immediately stood to be recognized.

"Yes, my son, Enosh, you may speak," said Adam.

"My father," began Enosh, "you call this a second curse—a greater curse with no cure—yet, do we not live in the hope of the promise of once again being given access to the Tree of Immortality?

How can what is our great hope and desire be a curse to us? Why must we now reject what we pray daily for El to give us?"

Adam lifted his hand and nodded at Enosh. He sat down to await his answer.

"You will remember El banished us from the Tree of Immortality to protect us. If we were to partake of its fruit in our present state, it would make our state permanent and unalterable. El's great love for us is seen in this forbidding. He plans to bring us back into the Great Dance of Life and to destroy Anomos and his perversions. He will give mankind immorality.

"El has determined to rescue us from the grip of Anomos and his evil slavery. This is the meaning of the Great Promise when it says, 'HER SEED WILL CRUSH YOUR HEAD'. The power of Anomos, the Great Serpent, is in his head—the poison of lies coming from his mouth. He has planned a very great evil for mankind, greater than the first, to forever alienate us from the Living One and keep us for his eternal slaves.

"When your great mother and I ate from the Forbidden Tree, we severed ourselves, and therefore, all our children, from the unconquerable life of the Living One which had poured through us unhindered up to that time. The Fruit from the Tree of Immortality cannot restore this lost access and relationship. The power of the Immortal Fruit is in its ability to sustain forever what already exist. Therefore, what once would have been good for us has become a curse. It would confirm us forever as subjects in Anomos' doomed kingdom of Parad now that we have become partakers of the Tree of Independence—the Tree of Self-Allegiance.

"If the Living One is to rescue us, it means He must give us more than mere immortality. Something must be done, which is beyond my power to understand—it is not yet fully revealed—which will allow us to be justified before Him while at the same time condemning the evil enslaving us. It must be a great act which will acquit us justly, so El's justice remains: He cannot—will not—compromise His justice or holiness while reaching toward us with His love."

Then he paused for a moment as if to focus everyone's attention as he added, in a manner clearly intended as a reminder of something obvious, "Of course, there can be no true love that is unjust. It would be a contradiction to its own nature: it could not exist."

Adam then paused again, searching for the right words, as if these insights were known to him but had never actually been expressed before.

"El will remain just in how He brings us Home. Then He can truly destroy Anomos' perverse challenge and slander. Only then can we be truly secure.

"I cannot understand how this can be done, but I trust His Promise to send one who can and will do it. In some great deed, which we cannot now imagine, and by virtue of some great standing which it is hard to imagine a man could obtain, this one will both cancel the curse over us and crush the Great Serpent's head. Some masterstroke will end evil's claim over, not only us, but also the whole of creation.

"This is what Anomos hopes to make impossible. He hopes for a future mankind beyond the power of the Promise. Perhaps even beyond the power of this great one promised to us. He seeks to produce a line of immortals immortally severed from true Life, like himself. And such human immortals would give him fearful power to subjugate the material realm to the kingdom of Parad. Those who would eat of this fruit would be a new order of fallen immortal creature: one both spiritual and material and one capable of procreation. The Living One has made it clear to me this must not be allowed to happen. It would be worse than the offspring created by the rebellious elohim who took Cain's human women and procreated the Nephilim—the evil giants. For though they have immortal fathers, the Nephilim are mortal as to the materiality they have from their mothers. They have bodies that can die. We have our selves caused many of them to die in combat."

Then with a look of such royal determination it caused Diakrina's eyes to widen, Adam looked around at the faces of each of his sons and said in a voice of utter authority, "Once again we face the question of whether to eat or not to eat. THIS TIME, WE WILL NOT EAT!"

Adam then turned to look at Diakrina across the great expanse of the stone table.

"My daughter, show them the proof of Anomos' scheme."

Diakrina understood by this she was to bring the crystal container, with the Immortal Fruit, out from under her shield and put it on display before the Elders of the High Council. She wanted to ask Strateia if she should obey, but she could not imagine disobeying this command from her Great Parent.

"Do as he asks, Diakrina," she heard Strateia say in his silver voice which she knew none but her could hear. "It is necessary. But you must warn them of its effect and charge each man to control himself."

Diakrina stood.

"My father, I will do as you request. However, I must warn everyone here of the power of this Fruit to overwhelm the will through the passion it produces to possess it: the effect is beyond description. Each of you must determine to control yourself with all your sanity and resolve. The power of this Fruit to drive one mad with desire is exceedingly great."

Diakrina then took hold of her shield and pulled it from her arm and laid it on the bench beside her. She then took hold of the strap of the crystal container and pulled it over her head and lifted the crystal container onto the surface of the table.

Immediately, the fragrance from the Fruit hit her in the face with terrible delight. She pushed back a little from the point of the table in an attempt to put some distance between her and the Atheos. The effect of the Fruit on those seated immediately to Diakrina's right and left was also instantaneous.

Strateia reached over Diakrina and took the container. With only his hands he tore a seam in the covering he had previous woven and removed it. Then he lay the container on the table in front of her.

Suddenly, the elder seated to Diakrina's immediate right gave a gasp and his eyes went wide with astonishment. With hardly a pause he immediately reached for the container. His hands had no sooner lifted it toward him than the man next to him pushed hard at him and grabbed the container from him. Before he could gain full possession, the man just beyond him grabbed at it also as the first man tried to reclaim it. This resulted in an immediate tug of war with six hands all clenching hard around the crystal.

If this had been allowed to continue, Diakrina had no doubt it would have turned the whole High Council meeting into a battlefield. However, before it could go further, with the skill of a surgeon, Strateia slapped the side of his sword blade softly and repeatedly across the arms of the three combatants. Their arms went up in the air and so did the container.

Strateia caught it. He quickly set it back in front of Diakrina on its side. Then picking up her shield from the bench beside her, he placed it over the container on top of the stone table.

The man closest to Diakrina, still under its spell, lunged toward the shield to lift it and grab at the container. But a blast of golden light coming from the shield hit the man in the chest. It sent him flying through the air over the bench and behind the chair he had been seated in. He hit the floor with a thud but was otherwise unharmed.

While all this was going on, Adam and Lord Mazzaroth had both jumped to their feet. "Order! Order!" both were shouting. Everything went suddenly still.

Strateia, moving his sword slowly back and forth over Diakrina's head, kept the men on either side of her at bay. Slowly, sanity returned to their eyes. After a few moments they all sat down somewhat sheepish.

Both Adam and Lord Mazzaroth stood with their eyes dilated in shock at what had just transpired. Diakrina had, by this time, composed herself.

"My fathers, if I may speak?" she requested.

Lord Mazzaroth, still standing along with his father, nodded his approval.

"As you can see, there is great danger here. I cannot stress how urgent it is you help me immediately."

There was a pregnant silence as each elder looked back and forth around the whole stone table.

Adam spoke.

"You shall have all the help we can give."

He then sat down and left Lord Mazzaroth standing alone.

"What is it you need us to do, Diakrina?" asked Lord Mazzaroth.

Diakrina didn't know how to answer. But to her relief Strateia spoke to her in his voice she knew none but her could hear.

"Tell Lord Mazzaroth, the warrior, Strateia, sent from the Living One, will answer this question if given permission to speak."

Diakrina cleared her throat.

"Lord Mazzaroth, if you will give permission, Strateia, the warrior of the Living One who accompanies me, will address the Council concerning your question."

"Let it be so," responded Lord Mazzaroth. He then sat down.

Strateia walked around the bench, and Diakrina moved to one side so he could stand at the very point of the great stone table. Then in a voice both calming and commanding, Strateia addressed the High Counsel.

"Sons of El, it is of the utmost importance Diakrina, with the help of her shield and sword, be allowed to carry this Immortal Fruit back to the Garden. To do this, she must pass through the Mist Forest to the great Tree Bridge spanning the Great Chasm. Though none of you can cross it, by being a daughter of Adam, who has lived beyond the fulfillment of the Great Promise, there is every chance Diakrina will be able to succeed.

"However, Anomos has sent out many armed units to capture her and the Atheos—which is the Immortal Fruit—to keep her from reaching the Bridge. If she is to succeed, three things must be done. First, I ask you provide eight units of soldiers, 16 soldiers each, to work with us. They should be your very best and most trusted.

"Second, seven of these units must be sent out ahead of us in a very wide arc to discover and intercept Anomos' forces wherever they may be between here and the Bridge. The eighth unit is to travel with Diakrina and myself as her protectors.

"Diakrina and I, and the eight units, will travel first, north from here. Then we will turn back east for a short distance until we are far enough east to be nearly at the backside of the western mountains of Nekus, which border the western side of the canyon. We will then turn back south and make our way along this range until we come to a cut, which I know, that will take us through the mountains to the mouth of Nekus. From there we will make our way south toward the Mist Forest.

"Third, you should assemble all your fighting men not part of these eight units. Leave at least 20% of them to guard your city and your families. Send the main body on a determined march down toward the west, beyond the western ridge of your valley, through the western mountains and into the Great Meadow. Once you reach it, turn back south and keep traveling south until you encounter the great arch of the Nekus River on the Great Meadow's southern border. Cross it. Then turning east, make straight toward the Mist Forest. By this means you will avoid Bellicose who is already on the prowl in the highlands.

"When you reach the edge of the Mist Forest, take your army into the Forest and travel southeast toward the top of the mountain at its center. Be careful of ambush. But make your way openly toward the top of the mountain where it rises above the Forest—we want you observed. There take up positions on the high ground overlooking the Forest.

"Do not try to hide your presence from Anomos—though I doubt you could. Rather, we want his forces to think Diakrina is with you while we take a different route to the Mist Forest and enter it at its northern-most end. To further give the impression Diakrina is with you, you should take a young girl and dress her as Diakrina, with a shield and sword, and put her on horseback to ride with you.

"We must move quickly with these preparations. Already, four men from among your greater body of Elders, who have married the daughters of the son of Cain, and are in sympathy with Anomos and his scheme, have reported this meeting is taking place. You cannot avoid involvement now. The die is cast."

With that said, Strateia turned and stepped back behind the bench.

Lord Mazzaroth rose to his feet. He looked around the stone table at every face. Then taking a deep breath he addressed the Elders.

"We cannot consider shrinking from our duty: and our duty this has clearly become. The hope of all future generations turns on what we now do. This is our fight. We fight for our return to our place—and our future children's place—in the Great Dance. It is my determination we must declare war on the sons of Cain who are joined to Anomos and his forces."

Then looking around at each man, "Do I have the agreement of the High Council of the Sons of El?"

Jared stood to be recognized. Lord Mazzaroth nodded his permission.

"My Lord Mazzaroth, already, as this council knows, I have encountered one of these units of Anomos, which was led by Tubal-Cain, himself. He had the Nephilim with him. I suspect Anomos will use every resource he can mobilize, including the Giant Nekros. The sooner we move the better. I move for the approval of your ruling by the High Council of the Sons of El."

"You have heard the voice of Jared. What do you say, sons of El?" asked Lord Mazzaroth.

The whole council stood to their feet. Each man's sword was in his hand and raised to the sky.

"Amen!" they shouted. "It shall be war!"

Then with one voice and a thrust of their swords toward the sky, they shouted together so the very walls echoed like thunder, "FOR THE SAKE OF THE PROMISE!"

Chapter Eight

THE AMBUSH

The unity of the High Council seemed absolute. Yet, one could only hope it was true. However, it was clear this unity was less than absolute in the greater counsel of the Sons of El. For it was obvious to Diakrina Strateia's assessment concerning Hared and the three leaving so rapidly with him was likely correct. They were traitors in league with Anomos and the Sons of Men.

However, all around her the resolve among the Sons of El to organize themselves for battle seemed total. The speed with which everyone moved, the naturalness of their almost perfect organization, made Diakrina suspect these early men possessed some complex capacity for organization and interdependence, which later generations of men only dimly could display. By the time Strateia and Diakrina, in the company of Jared, reached the great portico, there were units already forming just beyond it. And it was clear the declaration of war by the High Council was already common knowledge.

Each unit, as Strateia had requested, was composed of sixteen soldiers. Each soldier held a reign to a stallion standing over twenty hands tall at the withers. These horses' conformation was like that of racing quarter horses: powerful hindquarters, broad chests rippling with muscle, long legs large boned yet nimble, with flaring nostrils and beautiful Arabian-like conformation to their heads.

And they acted like fiery, highbred Arabian horses: they each were prancing slightly and trembling visibly with excited anticipation as the last of their riding gear was being cinched tight. These great horses, snorting with excitement and tossing their heads in the air, were a beautiful sight.

However, it suddenly struck Diakrina as odd that men capable of such technology, as she had earlier seen, were using horses and strapping on swords and loading quivers with arrows for large thick bows. She turned toward Strateia and held him up a few slow steps in order to put some distance between themselves and Jared.

"Strateia, do they not use their technology to create weapons more advanced than swords, or spears or bows and arrows?"

"No, Diakrina. They have not yet learned the art of mass killing. Each soldier considers warfare to be an act of face-to-face engagement. The bow is the closest they come to killing-at a distance. Yet, they primarily use the bow at close range, except in engagements of large forces."

Jared walked among the men and their horses. He was clearly one of the key commanders of these warriors. He took charge of the hundred and twenty-eight men chosen for the eight units of sixteen men each and began giving orders.

Out beyond where these units were fitting their horses with battle gear, Diakrina could see on the other side of the bridge a larger force of men gathering. Diakrina was not sure, but she estimated they numbered somewhere between a thousand and twelve hundred warriors. They were mostly on foot. But there was a small cavalry of about a hundred.

She also noticed among them there was a young woman, which they had taken pains to dress in a close approximation of her own attire. The young woman, Diakrina would later learn, was a girl of only twelve years of age. Her name was Lilcah.

Evidently, because the larger force had to cover more territory, it was not long before Diakrina heard several horns sound on the far side of the river. The assembled soldiers and cavalry fell into a marching line, composed of four abreast. They were clearly moving out first.

However, when the command to set out was sounded, Diakrina, who by now was giving the activities across the river her full attention, was shocked to see they did not set out in a march.

The cavalry took the lead at a slow gallop and the warriors fell in behind them running with long, graceful strides. In a matter of minutes Diakrina could see them ascending a wide path rising over the western rim of the valley. They never slackened their pace, and they were soon out of sight as they disappeared into the forest.

"Strateia, how long will they travel at that pace?"

"All day and well into the night. They will take no breaks as each warrior has his own water supply with him and will drink in stride. They also have fruit in their side packs and will eat once or twice without pause."

"What about the horses?"

"They will need nothing until tonight. They are of greater stamina and strength than the horses of your time. They could gallop for two days and nights without harm. However, they would, by that time, need water, if not food."

"Is it the thicker atmosphere that makes it possible for these men to run so fast and long?"

"Yes. But also, it is the perfection of their physical anatomy. They have not yet undergone the thousands of years of degeneration befalling your race since the Great Deluge."

By the blast of a horn Diakrina's attention was brought back to the eight units surrounding her. The units formed themselves immediately and stood at attention.

"The captains of the units will assemble before me," ordered Jared.

Eight captains came forward and stood in a semicircle in front of Jared and bowed their heads in a salute. Jared then shared with them what they were to share with their units concerning their purpose and the plan of execution. This included a brief description of the reason for the declaration of war. The Atheos was not mentioned, but the threat of a greater curse was divulged.

He then gave detailed instructions to them about the large arcing route they would take, first, north, then east, then south to arrive at the Mist Forest. All this was communicated in such a precise manner only about five or six sentences in all were used.

When Jared had finished, Diakrina was shocked to hear the captains, all in unison, quote back to Jared every word he had said to them, without error. When they finished, Jared, obviously satisfied, dismissed seven of the units but ordered the captain of the eighth unit to remain with him.

Jared then ordered the two horses, which obviously had been saddled for Diakrina and Strateia, be brought forward.

"I trust you know something of riding," said Jared as he turned toward Diakrina.

Diakrina was relived this was indeed something she knew how to do.

"Actually, I do. My Father's family has an estate where they keep riding horses. I have grown up on horseback."

From the confused look on his face, Diakrina's mention of an "estate" and "keeping riding horses," which were both strange phrases to Jared, obviously didn't make any sense to him. However, he did not pursue it. He simply handed Diakrina a single rein, or what she had taken to be a rein before she actually had it in her hand. It was actually more like a lead rope attached to a halter-like bridal on the horse's head. It was then she realized there was no bit in the horse's mouth and the rein or rope simply attached at the bottom front just like a halter.

It was then Diakrina discovered there was no leather in the reign or halter-like bridal. Nor was the saddle made of leather. Rather, the rein and bridal seemed to be made of a finely woven rope, likely from some kind of plant fiber. The saddle, which was not much more than a very thick pad—which she was relived to see did have very simple stirrups—was also made of some kind of woven plant fiber. It seemed to be woven into a flat, thick rope, which was then coiled round and round itself, and then sewn together, so it formed something slightly thicker than a saddle pad.

She was about to ask if she needed to finish the horse's outfitting by putting on its bridal. But before she spoke, she glanced at the other horses all around her, and for the first time realized none of the horses had a bit in its mouth. Each soldier stood holding his horse by a single rein, as well. This realization left her with an open mouth yet not knowing what to say.

It was Strateia that came to her rescue. He walked over to her and took the single rein out of her hand and then placed his other hand on the horse's nose petting it with affirmation.

"Riding these horses will be quite different for you, Diakrina. First, this is a lot more horse than you have ever mounted. But you should not be concerned. You will discover it is more compliant with your every command than the horses of your time. However, you will need to understand how to communicate with it.

"First, you notice there is no bit," said Strateia putting his hand under the horse's chin and turning its head slightly. "It is not needed. These animals do not resist human direction like the horses of your time and they are very intelligent. They will often anticipate your desires. That will be important to you if we end up in battle.

"Also, there is only one rein, which is primarily used to communicate with your horse while you are dismounted," said Strateia as he handed the rein back to Diakrina. "The one exception is that you do use it to communicate a slow down or stop command in the same way you are accustom to doing: by simply pulling gently back on the rein for slow down and a little harder for stop. As you can see, this only pulls the nose of the horse backward and it understands the meaning of this pressure as a slow down or stop command."

"But how do I give direction for turning with only one rein?" interrupted Diakrina.

"You don't. Direction is not communicated by means of the rein. You simply use knee pressure. To direct your horse to the right, simply press in slightly with your left knee. The horse is trained to turn away from the pressure. To go left, press in with you right knee.

"However, do not be too aggressive with the pressure. The harder you press the sharper and more quickly the horse will turn. It may take you some practice, but you will soon learn the right amount of pressure to apply by trial and error."

Diakrina's former confidence was leveled a bit. Yet Strateia's reassurances the horse would be very cooperative helped her to relax. However, when Jared gave the order for all to mount, Diakrina realized she had another immediate problem. The horse was far too tall for her to climb on its back. It was over twenty hands tall at the withers: that is about eighty inches or six feet, eight inches tall. She could only touch the top of the saddle by standing on her tiptoes.

Also, the stirrups were far too high off the ground for her to get a foot in. What is more, there was not even a saddle horn, like on a western saddle, which she could jump and grab hold of to pull herself up.

Strateia had obviously foreseen this problem and had simply stepped back to see how she would handle the issue. As Diakrina tested to see if she could get hold of the saddle in some way that would give her a handhold, Strateia watched with a bemused look on his face.

Out of the corner of her eye, Diakrina caught his expression. She gave a frustrated glare at Strateia with a lifting of her eyebrows which said, "Ok! Are you going to do anything to help or not?" She was grateful her horse was between her and Jared so he could not see the facial dialogue she and Strateia were exchanging.

Finally, after several seconds of amusement, Strateia walked over to her horse and gave a quiet command, "Down." Immediately the horse bowed its nose to the ground and stretched its right front leg out in front of it and curled its left front leg up and back, so the bottom of its left hoof was turned up. This brought the horse's back down several feet and Strateia pointed to the upturned hoof and indicated Diakrina should use it like a step. At the same time Strateia reached up to the top of the saddle, right where a saddle horn would be if the saddle had had one, and pulled a loop of rope, attached there, over to the left so it was just visible to Diakrina.

Diakrina checked her shield, sword, the crystal container with the Atheos within, and even felt through her dress just above her belt, to make sure the page she had taken from the glowing book as she was leaving the realms of Thanatos the first time, was still folded and securely in place. Then she stood on her tiptoes with the single rein in her left hand and took hold of the saddle loop. Then stepping onto the hoof of the horse's left front leg, she stepped up, and with the help of the loop, was able to pull herself on top the horse into a riding position.

Tell your horse to rise, Diakrina, with the word, 'Up.'"

Diakrina said firmly, "Up," and the horse rose to his full height.

When she and the horse were both fully upright, all she could say was, "Wow!" She had never looked down from the back of a horse from such a height.

She quickly realized the material out of which the saddle was woven was the proper combination of soft and firm. She was pleasantly surprised at how comfortable the saddle actually was. Strateia made a couple of quick adjustments to the stirrups so they were at the proper height for Diakrina. He then walked over to his horse, and taking hold of the saddle loop and lifting his foot into the stirrup in the normal manner, mounted his horse.

Jared, who had been mounted on his horse for some time and was watching the whole procedure, smiled at Diakrina's obvious delight with her mount.

"We call your horse, Phos," said Jared. "For he is very fleet of foot."

Then pointing to Strateia's horse he said to Diakrina, "His mount we call, Phulasso. It is a word that means, to guard, to watch, to be aware. This is because Phulasso has very good eyes and ears. He seems to be aware of every movement and every sound long before anyone else. He is like having an extra guard on duty in the camp at night.

Jared then said to Diakrina, "We will do the first day's riding with all units very close together. Nonetheless, us three, with the eighth unit, will follow the other seven."

Jared then turned toward the mounted warriors, and taking out his horn, gave a signal composed of one long blast, two staccato and another long blast. The captains each shouted, "Forward!" and their respective units set out, one after the other, with each unit in four rows of four riders each.

As the unit designated to be with them set out, two rows of four warriors each, took the lead. Then Jared motioned for Diakrina and Strateia to ride with him. Diakrina urged her horse forward and began trying to guide him with the pressure of her knees. At first, she was pushing far too hard and, even though the horse seemed to know he was to stay with Jared and Strateia's horses, he clearly was somewhat confused and moving his head from side to side as if wondering if he should turn more sharply than the other horses.

However, Diakrina determined trusting the horse to do the right things was the better way to proceed in the beginning and she simply relaxed and allowed the horse to keep stride with the other two horses as they all fell in behind the first eight warriors. Then the remaining eight warriors came behind forming two rows.

Because the first of their journey was toward the north, they circled around the right side of the Great Pyramid and headed farther up the valley with the descending river now on their far left. There was a constant, slight rise to the valley in this direction with a kind of rolling, grassland terrain.

The horses were immediately urged into a slow gallop and the whole company of eight units, with about a hundred yards between each unit, settled into a steady rhythm for about half-an-hour. They soon came to a rise, over which an intersecting valley from the east— from their right—entered the valley they were in. They turned to the east and began following it. It too gained elevation as it stretched out in front of them.

This valley too seemed to be quite wide. But it was soon clear it was quickly becoming filled with stands of trees encroaching down from the hillsides. Without stopping, Jared gave a couple of short blasts on his horn and the whole company altered their formation.

Three units fanned out to the left and began riding in swerving patterns through and around the various stands of trees. The spaces around these stands were still quite large and it was not hard for them to find ever-connecting paths. These three units spread themselves so they were exploring about seventy-five yards of area to the left of

Diakrina's unit.

Three units fanned out to the right and did the same. A seventh unit continued to lead the way at the center of the valley about a hundred yards ahead of the unit surrounding Jared, Diakrina and Strateia. In this way it was clear the seven other units where riding point—a very wide point—ahead of their unit in order to detect any possible ambush.

Diakrina also noticed the units farthest to the left or right slowed up slightly, so while they were furthest away to the sides, they were closer to them as to their forward position—the ones most to the left and right riding almost even with them. This meant they were not too far away to respond if they needed to return to them quickly. The result was a kind of long arc of warriors, in the shape of a curved shield, sweeping the valley out in front of them.

This formation worked for about twenty minutes of galloping time. Soon, however, the valley began to narrow considerably and the trees to either side became more closely set. Jared gave another blast on his horn and the units reorganized themselves into a much narrower V-shape with the point out in front and with the backward wings of the V sweeping back until the riders on the back of either wing were almost even with Diakrina's unit.

The constant rise of this valley soon lifted them up until they were no longer in a valley. Instead, they were coming to the top of a large hill which was very rounded and open. When finally they were coming to its topmost point, Jared gave three short, disconnected blasts on his horn and all the units began slowing down and came to a stop at the hill's zenith.

When all the units were together at the top of the hill, Diakrina could see the terrain was about to change drastically. She surmised they were now atop of the northern most end of the mountainous plateau she and Strateia had crossed the night before. Where they had crossed was many miles to the south along the plateau's torturous top. But straight ahead of them to the east, dropping away from the hilltop, was a deep gorge descending toward a dark valley. This dark valley seemed to run north and south up against some very rugged mountains, which were on its far eastern side.

Strateia pulled his horse up beside Diakrina and pointed beyond this distant mountain range. "Diakrina, if you look carefully toward the top of that range as far as you can see to the northeast"— which was to the left and slightly forward of the direction they had been traveling—"you can detect a cut coming through those mountains from east to the west. The eastern end of this cut connects up with Nekus Canyon. It is the valley you came westward through out of Nekus and where you had to pass the Beast of Paranoia at its western most point. From there you traveled west, up north of where we are here, and continued down to the Spring of Longings.

Diakrina then looked straight ahead to the east again. "Then on the backside of those rugged mountains is Nekus Canyon, correct?"

"Yes," answered Strateia. "And the valley on this side of those mountains, to which we are about to descend through this deep cut in front of us, runs north and south. Its northern end intersects with the area just this side of where you passed the beast. But its southern end runs along this range until the mountains encounter Nekus River, coming from the southwest. The river cuts through this range forming the eastern side of the valley and then enters Nekus Canyon where you entered it. It is there we will cut through, almost to the spot where we built the fire that night. Before we reach it, however, we will turn south into the intersecting valley and make our way back down it along the way you and I traveled up when we were headed toward Nekus after we came out of the cave. Before we get to the cave we will turn southeast and begin ascending the mountainous area on which lies the Mist Forest. It rises over the cave area."

Then Strateia turned and looked down the long cut of narrow valley which lay straight out in front of them toward the east. "It will be necessary to travel down this narrow gorge to get to this first valley. I confess, I have deep concerns."

Jared came riding up to Diakrina and Strateia. "Diakrina, we will take only a short break to allow three of the units to ride out ahead of us. If you wish to dismount and stretch your legs for a moment, you can do so. But do not go far. It is imperative we get down through this narrow gorge before night fall."

Jared then glanced at Strateia. Strateia said nothing but he did look him in the face and nod in affirmation.

Diakrina and Strateia dismounted. Diakrina was eager to walk a little and stretch her legs. Strateia suggested they walk north along the top of the ridge as the ridge rose slightly in that direction. This would allow them to keep an eye on Jared and the others by simply looking back from their higher vantage point toward where their horses were nibbling some grass.

They strolled at a moderate pace, always going up a slight incline. They had not gone far when Strateia stopped abruptly and began looking back to the west, in the direction from which they had been riding for the past hour or so. From his body language Diakrina could immediately tell he had heard something that concerned him.

Suddenly he grabbed Diakrina's arm and while beginning to pull her toward some trees just to the west of their position said, "Quick, come with me!"

There was urgency in his voice and Diakrina made no delay in running along with Strateia. No sooner had they run in among, and under, some large trees than Diakrina heard a sound like the wings of a glider rushing over them and turning south toward Jared and the other warriors. Then came the sound of large wings beating the air in a slow, rhythmical fashion.

As she stole a glance upward a large shadow passed overhead. There was no mistaking it. It was a giant Nekros.

Next the air was shattered by a piercing scream as Diakrina could see the Nekros diving down onto a group of warriors standing together holding their horses. Men and horses scattered in all directions. Yet, one warrior, and one horse were too slow.

At the lowest point of his dive the Nekros snatched up the man in his left talon and his horse with his right. Two more screams were heard as instantly, from the opposite direction—from the south— two more Nekros came diving out of the sky toward the retreating warriors. However, by this time, Jared and several other warriors, who had been sitting only a few yards away, had jumped to their feet pulling their swords.

Jared shouted for archers. Within seconds over thirty men

pulled their bows and arrows filled the air as the second and third Nekros plunged into the men. Both creatures were pierced all over by arrows. Both creatures gave an ear-shattering scream and leaped high into the air by flapping their wings downward as if trying to swat the arrows away.

Meanwhile, the first Nekros, carrying both the man and the horse, had turned sharply east toward the descending canyon and could be seen flinging both toward a cliff face with such force it was clear neither man nor horse survived. As it threw them into the cliff face, it did so turning back toward the battle going on between the warriors and the other two Nekros.

Even though the two Nekros were riddled with arrows from the first volley, they descended down on the warriors again, slashing at them with deadly talons. They seemed more irritated than harmed. Warriors were hurled in all directions. However, by this time, around another fifty warriors responded with a volley of arrows. These were a little better aimed.

Arrow after arrow found its mark, hitting the Nekros in their head. A bundle of arrows found their home in the head of each beast. The two creatures both screamed and pounded the air backwards with their wings so hard, they flipped upside-down and began crashing to the ground, while the warriors near where they were falling ran for cover.

By this time the third Nekros, seeing its two companions clearly killed, had decided to retreat. It quickly arched back toward the southeast and started flying in the direction of the Mist Forest before the warriors could recover and fit any more arrows to their bows.

Diakrina's eyes were wide while all this was happening and she pushed up close to Strateia. Then, instantly, he vanished. Out of the corner of her eyes she saw only a streak of light blast into the sky in the direction of the retreating Nekros. It was both white and crimson light. Immediately, she knew it was Strateia pursuing the Nekros with his sword in hand.

The Nekros' speed was no match for Strateia. In less than a second the beast blew into a million pieces, as if a missile had hit it. Nekros rained down all over the hills to the south of the descending canyon wall.

Then, almost as if he had never left her side, Strateia was standing back beside her. Diakrina blinked, and then finding her voice, said, "Wow! That was fast!"

Strateia motioned for her to follow him as he headed toward the warriors. When they reached them, Jared and several others were already starting to take account of the injured. As it turned out, besides about nine men being cut and bruised considerably—none too seriously—everyone else had escaped injury. Except, of course, the one soldier and horse which the first Nekros had thrown up against the cliffs.

Jared went to the head of the gorge and sounded a recall signal for the units that had left earlier. He was sure they had seen the Nekros and were already headed back up the gorge. But He wanted to assure them they were right to continue their return.

Several men went to find their comrade. As it turned out, his name was Paddan. They brought his body, which must have been severely mangled, back up the hill wrapped in white blankets, which several men had pulled from among their supplies packed on their horses.

When Jared saw Strateia and Diakrina standing there, he walked up to Diakrina. "I am relieved you are safe. It all happened so fast I had concerns one of them might have snatched you. But since none of them got away, I quickly assumed you must be fine."

Then looking at Strateia, he turned again to Diakrina. Thanks to the Living One the first Nekros did not escape. If it had, our position would have been immediately reported to Anomos and his hordes."

Diakrina was surprised when Strateia spoke to Jared. "What you say is true. However, when those Nekros do not return this evening from their search, Anomos will become suspicious and will send out others to follow up. It is important we move out quickly."

Jared looked at Strateia and then said to Diakrina, "Your guardian is right, of course. We will have to move out as soon as we have made arrangements for Paddan."

As Jared started to turn away, Strateia spoke again.

"Jared, from this point forward, the Living One has given permission for you to speak directly with me, and me to you. However, this permission is granted only to you."

"Thank you, Strateia. I am grateful. Your interaction and advise is greatly valued and desired."

Jared then turned and made his way toward his men who were gathered around their fallen friend.

While Paddan's body was being prepared for some kind of ceremony, Diakrina and Strateia walked toward the west a little, and then back somewhat to the north where the two Nekros had fallen. The closer they got to the vile beasts the more Diakrina was astonished at their massive size. They had large bodies with even larger wings. They had a long neck which terminated with a serpent-like head. However, the head was different from that of a serpent's in that it had a mouth filled with large tyrannosaurus-like teeth which were punctuated by four great curving fangs: two rising from the front corners of the lower jaw and two descending from the upper corners of the mouth.

Strateia walked around the first beast until he had found its head. Then, as if to ensure its demise, he took out his sword. With one large stroke he cut its serpent-like head off. He then did the same with the second.

They walked back to the warriors, who were still making arrangements to honor their fallen companion. Diakrina could sense something very important for the men was about to take place.

What Diakrina watched unfold next made a deep impression on her. Several men took time to cut up another white blanket and use its pieces like rope to wrap and secure the other blankets around Paddan's body. Then they carefully lay him on a large stone in the center of a grassy area at the top of the hill. Jared took out his horn and gave a signal for the men to assemble.

Once each soldier, with his horse, was in place within his assembled unit, Jared nodded at the captain of Paddan's unit, first. The captain and his men formed a line with each warrior proceeding to file up to and past Paddan's body. Each soldier, in turn, placed his right hand on Paddan's wrapped head and said, "The Living One receive you and redeem you according to His promise."

All the other units did the same with each man bestowing the same blessing. But throughout this whole time of ceremony, Diakrina was shocked to see how deeply and openly each warrior seemed to be grieving. These men—these eight-foot warriors—whose physical strength and size would strike terror into the hearts of any modern day army, all freely expressed their sorrow in a dignified, yet unrestrained, way. Tears freely coursed down each face as the blessing was bestowed.

There was no stoic suppression of their sorrow. It was as if they had not learned any such pretensions nor would allow any such sham. They were full of sorrow. Their sorrow for their friend and colleague was nothing to be ashamed of. In fact, to be ashamed of it would have been to insult his memory and worth.

They were, it seemed to Diakrina, almost totally self-forgetful in the expression of their grief and respect. Yet, they each possessed such sanity and strength, nothing which lacked dignity or honor came forth. Not because it was being stifled—it was not there to be stifled. Rather they were unconsciously noble even while being totally unrestrained in their show of brother-love.

Diakrina found herself quietly weeping along with them. She finally took note they were—once having paid their respects— forming a large circle around the grassy area with Paddan's body in the center.

When the last soldier—which was Jared—had bestowed his blessing, the whole circle of warriors, each standing near his fellow to either side, locked arms. Then a deep and melodious humming began, which with the force of the hundred and twenty-seven men left, with their eight captains and Jared, made the very ground seem to rumble.

The humming began to trace out a dark and haunting melody of mourning. Yet, it soon began to blend into intricate harmonies deepening the melody until the very pathos tore at your soul. It built and built in ever-deeper chords of pain and grief. Yet, soon, Diakrina noticed, it began to ascend in both pitch and mood.

The hum began to be mixed with triumphant sounding, ahs. The harmonies continued to become more and more intricate and beautiful. Every voice and pitch-change moved in a slow, stately and deliberate manner. Yet the continual growth of the harmonies, and the ever, subtly increasing crescendo, gave the effect the whole melodic piece was accelerating in rhythm toward some yet unrealized climax.

Diakrina, who was a highly trained musician and vocalist herself, came to realize she was hearing a moving harmonic tapestry of unimaginable beauty which was lost in antiquity as far as her times were concerned. The harmonic structures became so complex they filled every possible tonal area. She was not even sure modern men possessed such elevated harmonic capabilities.

Then, as if to find more room to grow, their song slowly evolved into two quite distinct themes each with its own melodic structures winding around its own distinct melody. Yet, to her utter amazement, out of the two distinct melodies came a third. It was a third song, which no one was actually singing. It found its existence in the essence of the relationship of the other two melodies. The harmonies of each had certain components which merged to create this third melody.

This third melody began to engulf the whole symphony of sound as if, now that it existed, it became supreme and began to envelop the other two. Yet, it was nothing but the other two! The two independent melodies could always be heard and focused on if you chose. Yet, constantly growing and engulfing everything was this third, beautiful, transcending theme, which seemed to be soaring over it all. It lifted and lifted until Diakrina felt as if she would physically be pulled into the sky.

No orchestra on earth could have produced these sounds. It rose like a tsunami in an ocean of utter beauty, which seemed to tower over them like a canyon wall of untamed sound. Diakrina felt as if her spirit was being pulled right out of her toward the sky, while, her body, which was still earth-bound due to gravity, seemed to tremble at some unseen tether.

Then suddenly, as if the tether broke and something lifted

skyward on quiet wings, the music vaporized into utter silence. And instantly, intuitively, Diakrina knew she had musically experienced the release of this warrior's spirit. She could almost see him rising to meet the Living One.

The silence lasted for several minutes as each warrior looked heavenward. Then Jared walked to the center beside Paddan's body and called four warriors together, which Diakrina learned later, were his brothers. They were given the assignment of taking his body home.

These warriors cut branches from trees and made a drag cot, not unlike what you might have seen depicted in movies as those used by American Indians to move the wounded or the aged from place to place. They mounted the two poles of the cot to either side of one of their horses when it was completed.

Paddan's body was then placed on the drag cot, and properly secured with some of the white strips of blanket. Then all the units formed two lines facing each other, with enough room between for the detail of warriors with the body to pass among them as they stood at attention.

They headed west back down the valley which they all had come up only hours before. When finally they were out of sight, Jared gave orders for the captains to assemble before him. He gave them orders and then dismissed them to take charge of their units. Immediately, three of the units began galloping into the gorge.

Jared walked over to Strateia and Diakrina and motioned for them to come near.

"I believe we have enough time to get through this narrow ravine before night fall. I would prefer to camp tonight at its eastern mouth where it intersects the valley below. We will need to ride hard. Four units will go out ahead of us. Then the three of us will take our place in the middle of the unit assigned to you in the same manner as before. Then the other four units will bring up the rear."

Then walking a little toward his horse, he paused and turned back toward them and said, "I fear tonight will be our last rest for quite some time." Then mounting his horse he sounded his horn.

Strateia mounted Phulasso. Diakrina commanded Phos to kneel with the word, "Down." She mounted and then let him rise. Both she and Strateia took their place in the formation which began descending into the gorge at full gallop.

Chapter Nine

RETREAT

The gorge was very steep. There was something of a trail winding serpentine-like down its center. At best it was wide enough for two horses to travel abreast. But there were many points at which they had to reorganize themselves into single file as they rode.

To Diakrina's constant amazement, the agility of the horses and the riders made it possible for all this to be accomplished at what would have been considered break-neck speed in her family's rides. While Diakrina had already become more at home with the new method of giving direction to Phos by means of the pressure of her knees, to be sure, up to this time she had mostly depended on Phos to pick the best way through as he seemed to innately know what to do.

In this gorge, however, it required her to make decisions at times about the proper way forward as regarding her and Phos' position. Did the terrain at some narrow spot require she take the lead as she, Strateia and Jared approached it at a gallop, or was it proper for her to slow up slightly and follow them through or fall in between them? It was clear each rider was expected to make the decision best accommodating the least adjustment for all and the greatest economy of movement for the horses.

The method of guiding the horses by the horse turning away from the rider's leg pressure proved to be quite efficient as it tended to make the rider and the horse lean and move together. What is more, Diakrina found she could detect Phos' inclination as they approached a point of adjustment; she seldom found it necessary to do little more than validate him.

However, the energetic pace of the descent made it necessary to be constantly alert as the need for adjustments came at her rather quickly. The occasions for some rather masterful riding were constantly present. The almost otherworldly quickness and agility of the horses made what would be—on horses of our time—certain collisions, only opportunities for quick, graceful solutions. This gave Diakrina the feeling she was involved in a kind of impromptu artistry which unfolded in a friendly, cooperative game amid their very serious descent.

By the time this providence-orchestrated gallop had been in process for over an hour, the horses and the riders were moving like there was a single mind giving direction to every decision—they were a well-oiled-machine, if you please. Out of the synergism of their combined actions materialized a dynamic, living reality flowing over the terrain in solemn fun.

But don't misunderstand. All this fun was a surplus. It was not the thing itself and no one forgot the dangerous nature of their mission nor became less alert to it. In fact, there was a sense in which the natural flow of easy, skillful cooperation, which took on a life of its own—becoming almost automatic without being predetermined— freed each of them to give even fuller attention to being alert to their surroundings.

The other amazing thing to Diakrina was how aware she was this orchestrated synergism was not merely between the humans. The horses were clearly drawn up into it—almost as equals. They gave to this dance what they alone could give—their strength, speed and agility—while the humans gave what they could give—the more comprehensive awareness and direction needed for the whole company: the reason for the romp and the destination to be gained. If horses can know something akin to delight, Diakrina felt sure these mounts were experiencing it.

After about two hours it was clear they had lost a lot of altitude. The descent finally became less steep, and the gorge became less deep and widened out and began to reach toward a more open, sloping area making them seem to be swooping down onto the valley out in front of them. The far side of the valley in front and below them, which formed the mountains laying between them and Nekus canyon, wasn't far away. This is because the valley below, which ran perpendicular to their descent, was narrow.

In fact, the closer they came to the bottom of the slope, which was emptying them into the valley, the narrower the valley seem to become. This effect was because the mountains out in front of them seem to be rising higher and higher with their descent.

Diakrina could also make out a small stream running along the valley up against the base of the mountains. It was clearly flowing south where, as she remembered, it made a sharp turn east and joined the Nekus River at the very place where the Nekus River cut through these mountains toward Nekus Canyon.

The area of their descent was now wide enough Jared sounded an adjustment for the riders. They reorganized into the wider arcing formation they had used earlier in the day. This brought many of the following units thundering past them to take their place in the leading formation.

They had only traveled this way for about ten minutes when it became clear they were coming close to the valley floor. You could see far enough down the slope toward the approaching valley to see the first units had already reached the bottom and were spreading out to the right and left to check the low cliffs to either side for any sign of the enemy.

When they all reach the valley floor, the first units, which had gone to the left—north up the valley—had by this time started their return gallop. Jared slowed their unit up slightly to allow these units to pass in front of them and follow the other units which already had gone south. Then Jared, Strateia and Diakrina came in behind them.

As they turned down the valley, they had not gone far before the shadows of the bluffs to their right, which they had just descended through by means of the gorge, began to cast darkness over them as the sun was now low enough in the west to be blocked by these cliff's nearness. Immediately Diakrina detected coolness in the air—it prophesied the coming night.

After traveling about ten minutes south, not far ahead, there was a large stand of trees coming into view on the east side of the canyon. These trees lay along and between them and the stream. It was a small forest covering about twenty acres. Jared sounded a command on his horn and the horses and riders ahead of them turned slightly left and made for the stand of trees.

Two units rode into the trees and two units rode out around the stand of trees to the left and two rode past the trees and out around then to the right. This left the seventh and eighth units with Jared, Strateia and Diakrina.

They pulled up short of the trees and the eighth unit pulled up tight to the three of them. The seventh unit rode behind them and turned and stationed itself looking back down the valley in the direction from which they had just come. They waited about five minutes while the units explored every part of the forest. The two units within the forest spread out and rode straight through the forest's middle while the two units on each side turned and rode straight in toward the middle from either side.

When the two middle units had made their way completely through to the stream and had encountered the four units coming from the sides as they did so, one of the captains of one of the units sounded the, "All clear". Jared gave the order for their remaining units to proceed into the forest.

It was obvious the first order of business was to set up a perimeter all around their location. This was done by setting up five campfire areas: One in the very center of the forest, one on the stream facing the mountains to the east, one on either side of the forest to the north and south and the last, where they had entered the forest, facing the west side of the valley.

The warriors were so organized and efficient, in less than twenty minutes all five camps had roaring fires and the horses had all been organized into open areas near each camp where there was plenty of grass. Every warrior took his horse's gear off and then led him to the stream for water after he had cooled down.

The fifth camp, in the center, was where Diakrina and Strateia were assigned with the eighth unit camping with them—or rather, all around them. Every other camp, except the one by the stream and the mountains which only had one unit, had two units camping in their quadrant: one on either side of their fire. Each man, in each unit, took his turn at guard, which meant he walked the area between his campfire and the corner of the forest on his side. In this way the whole perimeter of the forest was covered. On the backside, near the stream, the single unit camping there divided and spread its camp along the stream to either side of the fire.

Diakrina was able to get the saddle off Phos, by undoing the cinch on the left side and then pulling the saddle off with it. There was no need to take off the bridle as it was not really a bridle, but a kind of harness and there was no bit to be removed from the horse's mouth. She led Phos to the stream to get water. After she returned with him, she unhooked the rein from the harness and released Phos with the other horses to graze through the night.

Strateia also took care of Phulasso and released him with the other horses near their camp. When Diakrina finally came into the campsite around the central fire, there was the smell of roasting grains. Grain, fruit, nuts and vegetables all began to appear out of saddle compartments. And Diakrina was to learn, upon examination of her own saddle, which she had brought into the campsite, it too had compartments supplied with various mixtures of grains and nuts and some other compartments with different kinds of fruit and vegetables.

Diakrina laid her sword beside her saddle. Then she quickly took the crystal container strap from over her head and shoulder and placed it near her saddle. Immediately she laid the shield over the top of it. However, even this calculated quick movement was not enough to keep the potent scent of the Atheos from reaching her. Clearly the fragrance was increasingly soaking through the crystal.

The strength of its intoxicating aroma was painful to resist. Diakrina found herself, almost unconsciously, reaching toward the shield to lift it again. However, she caught herself just as her hand touched the shield's surface. She closed her eyes and began purposely forcing herself to recall all the terrible images she had associated with this seductive bouquet. Even with all these terrifying memories tumbling through her head, the force of the struggle to lift her hand from the shield's surface made her body tremble from head to foot.

When finally she managed to lift her hand from the surface, she stood slowly and backed away, able at last to take a much-needed deep breath (she had unconsciously been holding her breath to keep from having to engage the scent of the Atheos).

Diakrina quickly spun on her heels and began to engage her very pleasant surroundings again to help get her mind off the Āthēos. The fire was inviting but it did seem strange to her there was no scent of roasting meat, like venison or fish or some kind of fowl. She began looking around to see if anyone was preparing to provide some such fare.

Strateia walked up to her and pulled her aside—on noticing her taking note of the fare—and cautioned her to not mention cooking or eating meat of any kind, as this was completely unknown to these antediluvians. They would consider such an idea barbaric.

As it turned out most of the food was consumed in its natural state—raw. Only the grains were lightly roasted or soaked in warm water to soften them for eating. But even some of the grains were simply crushed with flat stones so as to crack them open and were eaten like we might eat popcorn.

What Diakrina soon discovered was how hungry she was and how delicious these grains, nuts, fruits and vegetables truly were. They seem to possess deeper flavors than the food of her time. Yet, she couldn't help thinking how nice a hunk of fire-roasted venison or a couple of game birds would smell and taste every time the smoke from the fire brought that charcoal aroma she had always associated with cooking meat at a campfire. However, the fare was good. She easily contented herself munching away on the various delicacies.

The evening settled into a pleasant rhythm as men pulled up logs or their saddles to use as seats near the fire as the temperature was becoming cooler a few hours after sundown. The hum of pleasant banter and quiet laughter—for all knew too much noise would be dangerous—gave Diakrina a sense of family among these towering warriors.

After she had finished eating the primary portion of her dinner, Diakrina noticed Jared and Strateia were leaning against a large fallen tree together and talking. Jared was still eating but Strateia was only talking and listening. Diakrina picked up some blackberries she was munching like a dessert and made her way over next to them.

As she approached, Strateia was in the middle of saying, " … and of course, we cannot avoid engaging the forces of Anomos. The key is to engage them on our terms. That is where your forces, which are headed to the top of the mountain in the middle of the Mist Forest, come in.

"First, they must make it to the mountaintop before Anomos can stop them. Second, we need Anomos to think Diakrina is with this larger force. Anomos will turn loose his forces on your army in an attempt to take the girl they think is Diakrina. While they are engaged with your other men we will attempt to get Diakrina through the Mist Forest by flanking around the backside of his forces to the north of the mountain. If we succeed it should be only a matter of getting well on our way to the Tree Bridge before Anomos discovers his error."

Just then, one of the captains whose unit was camped at the front southwest corner came running into the camp and quickly approached Jared.

"We have trouble coming, sir," he said as he gave a quick salute with a nod of his head. "Far down the canyon to the south something very large is coming north toward us. We see flames glowing against the sky."

"Can you tell if the flames are from torches?" asked Jared.

"Can't be sure, sir. However, what is strange is the glow is a mixture of angry red and some kind of sickly green. We are only seeing the flames indirectly for the most part. But occasionally we get a small direct ray of light through a gap in the forest foliage. It's dreadful, sir. There is some kind of terrible foul stench … something acidic and stinging to the eyes that comes with the light. It hits you like a beam, not like an odor. It … it … is radiating, burning stench of some kind."

Instantly, Strateia vanished so quickly it was as if he had simply ceased to exist. Jared's face went pale and Diakrina could read on his countenance what he was thinking. But before he could speak, Strateia reappeared as instantly has he had disappeared.

"It is Bellicose. He is about a thirty-minute gallop south of us, coming up the canyon," said Strateia to Jared. "We have been betrayed. There must have been more spies which stayed behind to watch which way we left from your valley. They have calculated our likely path and informed Anomos.

"It appears the encounter with the Nekros may not have been inadvertent. There is little time. If Bellicose finds us, none of you will survive. Don't sound the alarm on your horn, as he is sure to hear it: for it will echo down the canyon. We must quickly and quietly retreat back north up this canyon."

"But where to?" questioned Jared with immediate concern.

"I'm not sure, but you can't stay here. To do so is certain death," answered Strateia with urgency in his voice.

"Captains!" said Jared to the reporting captain and the captain of Diakrina's unit, who had joined their huddle by now as he had seen the other captain come running to Jared. "Quickly send runners to all the camps and order the men to ready their mounts with absolute haste. Sound no alarms. Use only voice commands. Tell them it is a matter of life and death!

"You inform those units out front," Jared said to the first captain. "You," he said to the remaining captain, "have your men inform the others."

The first captain disappeared into the forest to the west, and the captain of the immediate unit began shouting orders to his men, three of which ran to the east to inform the units on the back side corners and the unit along the river.

Food was dropped to the ground. Saddles and gear grabbed up in full running stride. Calls to the horses were shouted and immediately the sound of hooves galloping through the forest in all directions could be heard.

Diakrina called, "Phos!" but the horse evidently had already understood—somehow—all horses were to run to their riders. The words were hardly out of her mouth when Phos and Phulasso came crashing into the clearing of their camp with several of the other horses.

"Diakrina, grab your things! Quickly!" shouted Strateia.

Diakrina ran to her saddle and strapped on her sword. Without thinking she bent over and grabbed the shield. The scent of the Atheos hit her like a hammer blow in the face. She immediately leaned backward trying to pull away—it almost seemed like she was trying to pull loose from some sticky, oversized spider's web.

Seeing her dilemma, Strateia caught her up by the shoulders and lifted her into the air and deposited her several feet away from the crystal container. He then reached down, picked up the crystal container, and lifted it high in the air with his right hand.

"Put your shield on your left arm!"

Diakrina obeyed immediately.

Strateia then shoved the Atheos under the shield and pulled the strap out around the shield and over Diakrina's shoulder and head.

Strateia, knowing it would be too long a process for Diakrina to put a saddle on Phos—because of the horse's great height—picked up both saddles, one in each hand. He met the two horses head on as they were trotting side by side as they reached them. With a single motion Strateia swung both saddles in a wide arc around the outside of each horse's neck landing the saddles perfectly into place onto their backs.

Diakrina reached under Phos and pulled the saddle girth under him and toward her and began cinching the saddle down. Strateia did the same for Phulasso. But before Diakrina could order Phos to kneel so she could mount, Strateia, from behind her, put his hand under her arms and lifted her skyward and landed her astraddle Phos' back. He then mounted and ordered Diakrina to fall in behind him.

Jared was mounted and began shouting orders to his captain. There was no time to share a plan of any kind. This was an all-out-retreat and Jared would take the lead. His captains were to bring their units in behind him as quickly as possible.

They thundered through the forest toward the west and came out into the canyon. The two front units were mounted and assembled on either corner. Jared, and the captain of the unit with Strateia and Diakrina, thundered past them shouting for them to fall in.

It was at that moment the stinging stench hit Diakrina in the face. It was not very strong yet. But it was unavoidable. She looked south and could see a red and green glow flickering against the sky. The men in the two units assembled out front had already pulled the neck of their tunics up over their faces in an attempt to suppress the acidic stink.

Diakrina saw Jared shake his head and immediately pull his tunic up over his face to just under his eyes. She did the same with her collar. Jared urged his horse forward and turned north up the canyon. The powerful steed under him lunged and thundered up the valley with all the other horses giving chase.

Fortunately, there was a full moon which gave enough light to somewhat see the canyon ahead. However, the horses seemed to have better vision than the men and it became necessary to give them their heads in many instances as they seemed to understand better the way forward than their riders. Somehow, they also seemed to sense the urgency.

Diakrina saw Strateia ride up beside Jared, and as Phos was immediately on Phulasso's heels, she could hear him shout to him, "The gorge we came down is just ahead to the left. Do NOT turn up it! It is very likely Bellicose will take that route to arc back toward his own territory. We need to get north of the gorge and find some place to hide. All we can do is hope he turns left up the gorge to the top of the ridge."

Jared shouted back, "I understand!"

Then it seemed something came to him. He shouted back to Strateia, "There is another gorge turning right—back to the east—about a two minute gallop beyond this first gorge. If we can reach it in time, there is a large overhanging cavern about a minute's gallop up it to the east. It is our best chance!"

"Good! Make for the cavern!" shouted back Strateia.

Strateia then handed the rein of Phulasso to Jared and said, "I'll meet you there! Keep Diakrina with you!"

Then turning to Diakrina, "I'll be back soon. Stay with Jared at all cost!" And suddenly, Phulasso was rider-less.

They were not going at a mere gallop: they were in a dead run. It did not take two minutes to reach the second gorge. Jared turned right and continued up it, as did Diakrina. The units all followed close behind and the sound of the horses' thundering hooves and heavy breathing was deafening as they were immediately channeled into a narrow canyon with very high rock walls on both sides.

Jared began slowing up and shouting for his captains to do the same. The orders could be heard echoing down the thundering ranks following behind as each soldier repeated Jared's order.

Then, without warning, Jared turned a hard right into a smaller canyon branching off. Not more than fifty yards up it, it came to a dead-end at a very large overhanging cliff. This was the entrance to the large cavern.

It was dark in the cavern ahead of them, but Jared simply slowed his mount to a trot and continued into the shadows. Diakrina followed and it took several seconds before she could begin to see anything.

As they got deeper into the cavern, by looking backward to where the overhang began, Diakrina could see the silhouette of the units coming in the cavern backlighted against the moonlight flooding down outside the opening. The riders farther behind, yet approaching from the outside, were still illuminated by the moonlight.

While she could see little of the immediate area around her, the sound of the horses breathing and their hooves echoing off the cavern roof and walls made it clear to Diakrina the cavern was large and wide. It was clearly large enough for all the units to get under and recede back into its depths several hundred feet.

Diakrina began noticing the damp smell common to underground places as they proceeded farther in. Jared then shouted an order for all the men to dismount and begin walking their mounts farther into the cavern behind him.

After about a minute of traveling down a slight sloping incline—so the wide opening of the overhang behind them now seemed to lie uphill from them—they fanned out under the cavern roof. The roof seemed to be about fifty feet high. Jared ordered all the units to organize themselves into lines facing the moonlight shining at the entrance. It was a large opening about a hundred yards wide and the units formed themselves between it and where Jared and Diakrina stood deeper in the cavern.

Each man held the rein of his horse and turned the horse to face the moonlight. Soon the breathing of the horses calmed down and the space around them became very quiet but for the occasional cough or clearing of the throat by someone, or the short snort of one of the mounts. Every eye was riveted to the long strand of moonlight flooding in the opening.

Diakrina pulled her sword out of its sheath and the soft crimson glow cast a warm light around her and Jared so the floor and roof of the immediate area of the cavern became visible.

For several minutes nothing changed. Then, Diakrina saw Strateia appear just outside the cavern. He pulled his sword and strode into the cavern weaving his way through the ranks as they parted to allow him to pass.

Diakrina could hear him whispering something to each captain as he passed him. But it was not until he whispered to the last captain before reaching her and Jared she heard what he said.

"When you hear an order to turn, have all your men turn their backs to the cavern opening and pull their tunics over their heads. Warn them to make as little sound as possible no matter how hot or acidic it becomes. Turn the horses' heads to the rear of the cavern and do your best to control them. If too much noise is made, all will die!"

Strateia then approached Diakrina and Jared.

"Bellicose has not turned up the other gorge to the west, as yet. For some reason he is continuing toward the western branch of Nekus canyon where Diakrina came out of it. He will pass by this gorge any minute."

Jared shot a glance at Diakrina and said, "You have been in and out of Nekus?"

All she could do was look back at him in the dim light and shake her head, yes.

He seemed stunned.

Then Strateia whispered to Jared, "Begin a whispering order to be passed outward to all, to turn their mounts and themselves and cover their heads now!"

Jared gave the order, and it was fanned out through the cavern in a quiet, repeated whisper.

Strateia took Diakrina by the shoulders and moved her deeper into the cavern and stood her next to a boulder near them. He whispered to her, "There is room behind this boulder for you to stand," he said. "Get behind it and do not come out until I tell you. And above all, keep the Atheos covered up under your shield. We cannot risk Bellicose detecting its scent."

No sooner had he spoken than the light coming from the mouth of the cavern tripled in intensity and there was a reflection of angry red and pale green flames on everything outside the cavern. Strateia nudged Diakrina toward the backside of the boulder.

Bellicose was not outside the cavern. He was still in the original valley just passing the entrance to the gorge that turned right— east—off of it. And even though they were around another right turn, and inside the cavern, the heat and acrid stench filled everything. The boulders outside the cavern began to steam and all the trees and grass were instantly vaporized.

Even though the warriors never said a word, you could hear a subtle groan as the horrible, radiating putrefaction enveloped everything and everyone. The heat was terrifying.

While each warrior had his tunic pulled over his head, he was, at the same time trying to keep control of his horse. They held the rein short with one hand and put their other hand on their horse's nose to reassure it. The horses still pranced up and down and clearly were on the verge of panic.

Diakrina realized Bellicose was not as close as he had been to her and Strateia the first time—if he had been the men and horses could not have survived. Yet, she still wondered at the warrior's ability to endure it.

It was clear the source of the burning radiation was still moving north as the angle of the red and green rays continued to change. He would soon be even with the mouth of the gorge that turned right off of the main canyon. All they could hope was he passed quickly and continued north.

But that was not to be. As Bellicose came even with the mouth of the gorge, the intensity of the heat and acrid stench became unbearable. But worst of all, he stopped! The warriors were doing everything they could do to control their mounts, but things were starting to get out of hand. The horses were starting to rear, throwing and shaking their heads. And in spite of themselves the warriors began to cough and gag.

Strateia could see things were getting serious. The noise level was increasing, and the cavern would act like a megaphone directing the noise straight toward Bellicose.

Strateia ran like lightening through the men to the very front of their ranks. Then he did something which Diakrina could hardly believe. He turned facing the troops and took hold of his robe of light with both his hands. He then threw his hands outward as if casting a net to each side—no, more like unfurling two massive wings! His robe of light unfurred out from him to the left and to the right and toward the ceiling of the cavern. Instantly there was a wall of white that filled the whole of the cavern just in front of all the men. Then slowly its color began to change until it matched the color of the rock of the cavern except it remained somewhat translucent.

Immediately, the heat and stench diminished greatly. The horses began to calm down and the men stopped coughing and gagging. But it soon became obvious Strateia had surmised what was about to happen next and realized the lives of all the warriors and Diakrina were at stake.

Bellicose had heard something. This is why he had stopped. He was turning up the gorge. The wall of light—the robe of Strateia—continued in place, translucent enough to those in the cavern looking out beyond the shadows to see the changes in the angles of the blistering light. But now, the terrible radiation began to grow in intensity. It was clear Bellicose was moving toward the intersection that turned and led to the cavern mouth.

Even with Strateia's protection in place the temperature was soaring upward. The acrid stench was not directly hitting them; yet it was infesting every breath they took; making their lungs burn and their eyes water uncontrollably.

Once again, the horses began pawing the ground. Yet, somehow, the warriors kept them all quiet by the control of their reassuring touch.

While Diakrina was watching all this from behind the boulder, she began to have a kind of panic rise in her. Could Strateia keep them all safe and undetected? Would the camouflage of his garment of light be enough to fool Bellicose into thinking the cavern was shallow and empty?

When suddenly the surface of the boulders just outside the cavern opening erupted into exploding laminated sheets of rock, which took about an inch of surface off each boulder due to it being instantly expanded by intense heat—and the rock underneath, which was left, began to glow cherry red within a second—everyone knew Bellicose had reached the passage which led to the cavern: he was only fifty-yards away. But the worst was yet to come.

Within seconds the surface of the cavern opening began to glow red. Then the heat began to spread inward along the roof above and along the rock walls on the side. It was clear within a few more seconds the heat would propagate through the rock until it was beyond the barrier Strateia was forming: the cavern was about to become an oven in which they would all be baked alive like loaves of bread!

Diakrina heard Strateia shout in that silver voice which none could hear but her. Yet, he was not calling to her. Instead, she heard him shout, "LIVING ONE, STRENGTHEN ME!"

Instantly Strateia began to glow as if the power coming from his body had quadrupled. His wings of light, which were forming the protective wall of light, seemed to be pushing into the cavern walls and roof. Of course, no one could look beyond the surface to see what was happening, but you could tell his wings were moving outward.

When the glowing red heat had spread through the boulders until it reached the place where Strateia's wings intersected the rock, the heat stopped spreading inward. Instead, it began to spread toward Strateia along the wings of light. His wings were acting as if they were rock at the back of the cavern: which must have given the illusion to anyone who might look in from the outside, that the cavern was shallow and the back of it was where Strateia stood.

Within a few more seconds the blazing lasers of light just outside the cavern became too strong to look at directly. The furious countenance of distorted, chaotic angry flames of hate-filled pride—that hideous face without clear features or expressions, but rather a moving, stampeding collision of hundreds of menacing and inconceivably evil expressions all at war with each other for supremacy: that face which was like a bloody battlefield where bitter, angry countenances were all slaughtering each other—came descending from the sky and peering into the cavern opening. Bellicose was on his knees searching the cavern interior.

Every warrior had his back to the horrifying obscenity—which was fortunate. Diakrina, who was looking out from behind the boulder, turned away and found herself on the ground in a squatting position with her back up against the boulder: what is more she was doing her best not to begin screaming uncontrollably.

If she had opened her eyes—which she did not, for she was trying to shut out the intense angry red and putrid green rays now flooded the cavern—she might have seen what was about to happen. But she didn't.

Before she could realize what was happening in the midst of this terrifying circumstance—that already had every sense of her body pounding in sensory-overload—something black and leather-like went over her head. Two vise grip-like appendages, one on either arm, just below the shoulders, took hold of her and lifted her in the air. Instinctively, she tried to swing her sword, which was still in her hand. But immediately a third appendage caught her wrist in a grip so forceful it made her cry out in pain.

She didn't drop the sword, but it was clear her attackers feared it enough they had been prepared to make sure she could not use it. When she opened her eyes she could see just enough through the opening at the bottom of the bag over her head to see two very large and snarled faces meet her frantic gaze. In short order she was lifted into the air, before she could see more, and laid down on something which was much like a blanket made of leather-like material. She was then rolled up like a tamale.

Everything went black and she could feel ropes being tightened around her and the rolled up constraint. Her frantic struggles—which looked like those of a helpless fish lying on a riverbank—did nothing.

"Move the sword! Cut through the constraints!" she found her mind screaming. But Her arms had been pinned to her side as they rolled her up: she could not move her sword at all.

Her feet were then lifted as they took hold of the roll and began dragging her deeper into the cavern. Panic went all through her. All she could do now was scream, "Strateia! Strateia!"

Chapter Ten

THE ENTRANCE TO PARAD

I'm not sure we can understand the astonishment overtaking the mind of Strateia—for he instantly was aware something was happening to Diakrina. Yet, none of us know enough about his kind to know how they respond to such dilemmas. And a dilemma it was—a very orchestrated dilemma.

Strateia was the only thing standing between Jared and his men and certain destruction. He could not move. If he moved, they would be vaporized.

Diakrina told me she had questioned Strateia about his response at a later time—or as she had put it to him, "What were your feelings at the moment I was being kidnapped?" At first, he only looked at her as if trying to comprehend the meaning of her question. Then, as if he had downloaded the right response, he began trying to redirect her attempts to understand in the right direction.

"I certainly had feelings at that moment, Diakrina. Yet, if you want to understand my response you should not question me about my feelings as they were not the dominant issue."

"What do you mean, Strateia?" responded Diakrina, feeling a little hurt by his response. "I know you care, so how could feelings not … ," but her voice trailed off as she couldn't find words that could embody her meaning, nor that would stand up to the look of correction flushing across Strateia's face, prophesying that what he was about to say would make her attempts to finish the question unnecessary.

"The fact of caring and feelings are not as entangled in our nature as they are in yours since your race has descended into Anomos' realms. My caring and my feelings were both a reality. Yet my caring produces in me a very different response which turns away from feeling. That response is to seek the direction of the Living One. His direction is the key to my proper reaction, which is the key to my caring finding a way to help someone like you. How I feel is not anything which can help you in such a moment, one way or the other. You don't need me to feel but to act."

Seeing Diakrina's puzzled expression, Strateia tried to explain further.

"I realize this seems rather mechanical and detached to you, Diakrina. That is because you are imagining you could only respond in this way by being somewhat detached from the circumstance emotionally. It is not so for my kind. We are free to put our feelings to one side—without denying them or diminishing them—because we care: it is our caring which demands they be set aside.

"In fact, unlike your kind, we have not come under the confusion confounding caring with feelings, so as to consider them to be identical: they are not. While caring deeply for someone and what is happening to them will always produce feelings—for they are a product of a caring heart—feelings are not caring itself."

Diakrina's face still looked like the waves of the sea in a storm. So, Strateia continued.

"For example, Diakrina, have you ever seen or heard of cases where people who cared deeply were so incapacitated by their feelings in the middle of a crisis they could not respond in any meaningful or helpful manner?"

"Sure, Strateia," she responded, being lifted a little out of her fog.

"And you have also seen panicked mothers or distraught fathers actually cause so much confusion it becomes impossible for others to help an injured or endangered child until they are taken out of the way."

Diakrina nodded.

"You have also seen those who have spent years training themselves to respond to such emergencies with calm and clear thinking and actions. They are the ones who can make a difference and are needed in such cases.

"While it often takes a certain temperament and years of disciplined training for your kind to learn to put feeling to the side so that they can truly care—by responding like they need to in such moments—it is natural to our nature to do so. While I am aware of how I feel, I am more aware—because I care—of needing to seek immediate direction so I can respond appropriately.

"For you fallen humans—whose basic nature has been twisted inward toward your self—the domination of feelings can be too much about your, self; how you are being affected by what is happening to someone you care about. This can result in making you useless to the one in need."

While Diakrina could not fully understand, it did satisfy her questions as to Strateia's personal responses. Yet, in the moment when Diakrina was being abducted, Strateia could make no response to save Diakrina. He and Jared and the whole army had been outmaneuvered.

The spies had done their work. They must have been aware of Jared's knowledge of the cavern. Together with Anomos and his minions they had hatched the plan to send out the Nekros to confirm their location. Even though the Nekros never returned, their demise confirmed the eight units were in the area.

Anomos then calculated the units would be able to make it into the valley, by means of the gorge, by nightfall. And the obvious place to camp in the valley after they turned south, would be the small twenty-acre forest they had used: Anomos knew Antediluvians are always comfortable in among trees and they would also provide the cover a secret force would desire.

Once they understood these things, all that remained was for them to devise some plan by which they could force the eight units,

Jared, Strateia and Diakrina, to flee up the valley north needing a place to hide. The cavern—they had obviously reasoned—would almost be Jared's only choice if he was to get his troops somewhere in time to save them.

By using Bellicose they also had a way to paralyze Strateia. If he were consumed with protecting the men, he would not be able to respond to Diakrina's personal protection. The key was to get access to her while Strateia was fully occupied.

This they did by betting on the cavern. They knew there was a back way into the cavern through an old underground streambed. The streambed emptied into a small canyon about two hundred yards away. They positioned the men in the cavern ahead of time. All they had to do was wait for the moment when Strateia's predictable response to save the warriors of the Sons of El from Bellicose would have him fully committed to a course of action he could no longer control or relinquish.

The warriors of Anomos would hide in the back streambed just beyond the cavern. This would put them in place to strike from the shadows at the appropriate moment. And, as they had hoped, Strateia had put Diakrina at the back of the cavern. He had placed himself and the warriors between what he considered the only danger at the moment.

The plan had worked flawlessly in regard to capturing Diakrina. Anomos had also told Bellicose, it was learned later, to destroy all the warriors of the Sons of El in the eight units. However, that part of his plan did not succeed.

As it turned out, Strateia was more than equal to the task of protecting the men. Bellicose could not get through to destroy them. But neither could Strateia do anything to engage him and drive him away without removing his protection. A single second of unprotected exposure to Bellicose and it would have been all over for Jared and his troops.

Strateia clearly received orders to stay in place. He was to keep the men safe at all cost.

Bellicose continued to hover his grotesque face in front of

the cavern opening and the men and horses continued to struggle with each other and fought to breathe without choking. Jared told Diakrina later, Strateia's power to shield them seemed to only increase as his robe of light became brighter and brighter from the fierce heat.

Soon, however, it was clear to Jared the brightness was not all from the heat. There was golden light within Strateia's robe constantly increasing every moment. Now that Strateia realized he did not need camouflage to hide the men, he determined to take a different strategy. This golden light began flooding the whole cavern. And as it did, it filled the atmosphere with something so dense it drove the heat from Bellicose out of the air around the men. A coolness came over the whole cavern and every warrior described the sensation as being protected in the middle of a great furnace—for example, like the three Hebrew men in the middle of the great furnace of Nebuchadnezzar. (Of course, they knew nothing of this story as it would take place thousands of years after their time.)

This standoff between Bellicose and Strateia continued for over forty-five minutes: time enough for Diakrina's captors to drag her through the underground labyrinth and out into the other small canyon. She was somewhat bruised from the dragging; but not too badly as the leather-like material she was rolled into was quite thick and provided some protection from the harsh treatment of her captors. They clearly cared for nothing but putting some quick distance between themselves and Strateia before the situation could change.

They had Diakrina out of the underground streamed in about twenty minutes from her time of capture. Where they brought her out, in the small canyon, she immediately could hear horses and coarse voices shouting commands. She was quickly thrown up to someone on a horse and then was laid, face down, across the horse's withers in front of the rider.

Commands were shouted and she could hear horses begin thundering away. The horse and rider she was with jumped to action and fell in behind them. Then she heard a large number of horses join in from behind.

They thundered down narrow winding canyons. Diakrina

could tell this by the constant echo of the hooves of the horses and the curses of the men as they seemed to be constantly fighting each other for position. She was clearly going to have bruised ribs before they got to their destination—wherever that might be.

Meanwhile, back at the cavern, Strateia and Bellicose were still engaged in a kind of invisible battle of light—golden, cool light blazing against red angry and putrid green, acidic light. And every moment Strateia's manifestation of light became increasingly greater. Clearly it was no longer filling only the cavern. It was pushing outward against Bellicose who was kneeling in the small passage that led to the cavern entrance. The golden light was starting to fill the small gorge.

Suddenly, there was an ear shattering—and cavern shaking— explosion outside coming from Strateia's wings. Bellicose gave a terrible roar and his face retreated out of sight of the cavern opening. The golden light flooded the small gorge leading to the cavern and Bellicose retreated in short order. The light overwhelmed him and began smothering his angry, acidic flames. He could not abide its presence nor its effect on him. He had had enough. He left immediately and retreated to the valley. He then turned south toward his own territory.

But the damage was done. By the time he was far enough away for Strateia to unfurl his robe without fear of harming the men, Diakrina was long gone.

"Jared!" shouted Strateia, "Organize your men quickly!"

Jared took up his horn and gave the assemble call, which echoed in the cavern like a train horn. Then Jared mounted and rode through the men to the cavern mouth to where Strateia stood. He jumped from his horse holding the single rein and fell to one knee in front of Strateia.

"Thank you, servant of the Living One! We owe you our lives."

All the men fell to one knee and shouted in unison, "Amen!"

"Give your thanks to the Living One! It is His power, alone, that saved you," said Strateia. He then turned his back on the men and fell to one knee himself. And then in a shout that rolled out of the cavern like a battle cry, the voice of Strateia and all the men shouted together:

"ALL PRAISE TO HIM WHO HAS FOREVER LIVED, AND DOES LIVE, AND WILL LIVE WITHOUT END!"

Rising immediately after, Strateia said to Jared as he helped lift him to his feet. "The Living One accepts your thanks and asks you give yourselves to helping to recover Diakrina and her trust of the Atheos she bears."

"We are yours to command," answered Jared.

∞——————————————————————————————————————∞

Diakrina had come to realize she could do nothing but wait to be untied and released. And she was sure that would not happen until they reached some destination.

The ride was frantic, and she became convinced they were trying to reach somewhere before Strateia might be able to locate them and work his vengeance. Suddenly, they dropped sharply and began riding down a steep incline. They seemed to be going into some kind of very large sinkhole.

After about a minute they bottomed out and made a sharp turn to the right. Immediately Diakrina knew they were going underground again. The echo of the hard surfaces were all around her and the horses continued to ride in a straight line down a gradual, but never relenting, incline seeming to be taking them deep into the earth.

However, this was no small streambed. The characteristics of the echoes made it clear it was a large tunnel: likely several hundred feet in diameter or more. Down, down they rode at a fast trot for over ten minutes. The floor beneath them was solid rock. This was clear from the sound of the horses' hooves against it and the hard jarring Diakrina was taking from the horse's rough trot.

Then finally they leveled out. After riding a little farther, she heard a coarse, dark voice command the unit to come to a halt.

Without warning the rider carrying her lifted her up and threw her to someone. Whoever it was, caught her, and immediately threw her over his shoulder like a large sack of chicken feed. She heard someone with him say, "This way!" and he began taking her somewhere at a fast stride.

As he walked, Diakrina could hear the loud clanging of metal. She knew instantly she had heard something like it before. But she was too nervous and frightened to give it any more thought.

She was carried, as best she could tell, deeper in the same direction they had been going all the time they were descending the large, long tunnel. It was only now, with all the horses' hooves silent, Diakrina began to notice the sound of tools, like picks and shovels, working in the tunnel all around and in the direction from which they had come.

She heard a very sinister and chilling voice speak from somewhere in front of them, and somewhat above them. "Stop! Unbind her. She is to be taken before the Emperor, without delay!"

Without warning she was dropped to the rock-hard floor and the cords untied. She was then roughly unrolled from her leather-like confines by someone pulling and lifting on the blanket so as to cause her to be lifted slightly and unrolled in a spinning fashion and spilled out on the rough granite floor.

Diakrina had been in almost total darkness for quite some time. The first thing she saw was a blaze of green—sickly green—light coming from everywhere. It took several minutes before she could get her eyes adjusted enough to see anything. They were anguished moments, as she still had never seen any of her captors or her surroundings and desperately desired to do so.

When finally her eyes began to adjust to the light and to focus, there was a tall warrior standing over her who was clearly not human. He had a helmet that was a simple bullet shape made of some cold, gray material. There was an armored vest covering his whole upper torso, except for his arms, because it was sleeveless. At the shoulders, on top, there were two great spikes on each side of the vest, which protruded upward and outward over the arms. He had a great black chain around his waist and from it there hung slightly smaller black chains cut into lengths, which reached to just above his knees. These were attached all the way around so as to form a steel (though Diakrina was never sure it was steel, but something much harder) loin skirt. He was holding a sword, which had a blade glowing, greenish, and he was pointing the sword straight at Diakrina's head.

It was this moment Diakrina realized she was still holding her sword in her hand. That is where it had been when she was captured, and they had rolled her up with it still in the fist of her right hand. Her first thought was to take the man's lower legs off with a quick swing. But that is when she noticed on his shins there was something like shin-guards strapped in place by chains at the top under his knees and at the bottom over his ankles. On his feet he had metal looking shoes with two great horns coming out of the toe of each. This gave her a start of memory, and also made her wonder how effective her swing would be against the armor, though she had seen the sword cut through solid stone.

Before she could execute her thought to swing, she felt a foot step down on her right wrist. Another tall warrior, standing behind her head, had immobilized her sword arm anticipating her likely reaction.

"I would consider turning loose of that sword, if I were you," snarled the first warrior in a deep, cruel voice, which sound felt to Diakrina like a splash of cold water in the face. "It is only going to get you into pain if you insist on holding onto it." And with that, the two warriors began howling with laughter.

It was sadistic laughter; filled with perverted passions. Yet, there was also some kind of fearful pride in it. They still feared the sword. Their laughter was a kind of pride-filled camouflage for their fear. It was also full of manic relief: they had her in their power.

Just as quickly as they began howling this mad laughter, they stopped. The warrior behind Diakrina repeated the demand; "Turn it loose, NOW!" and he stepped down hard on her wrist.

Diakrina screamed in pain. But at the same moment she screamed, a cry to the Living One rose up in her spirit and mind and she ended up turning the scream into a cry, "LIVING ONE, HELP ME KEEP MY VOW TO NOT RELINQUISH MY SWORD!"

Crimson light flooded the cavern. The two warriors snarled a howl of discomfort and retreated about ten feet from Diakrina.

Diakrina jumped to her feet and began circling in a fighting couched position with the sword out in front and her shield held in front on her left arm. The black clad warriors stayed at bay with their left forearms held up to protect their eyes from the crimson light coming from her sword.

It was only now she could see them both. They were covered all over with black scaly patches on their body. It looked like the beginnings of some kind of skin tumors. She knew she had seen them both before, but under the stress of the moment she could not recall where.

"Back off!" came a loud command. It was that same dark, sinister voice she had heard ordering them to release her from her bonds. The voice came from deeper in the tunnel and was located somewhat higher up.

The two warriors backed up for several more feet and left Diakrina standing by herself. It was only then she dared to turn and look in the direction of the chilling voice.

What she saw was a large portico with nine large steps all along its front. It also had nine large gothic-like columns which fronted some kind of temple-like structure rising high in the air. And standing in front of the center column was someone she had also seen before. Him she instantly recognized, which also resolved her memory issues concerning the other two.

It was the Monk! Hairesis, she had heard his two companions call him at the Porticos outside Sapient Castle. The other two were Desmos—the one in the chain armor—and the other was Sarx.

The Monk was unchanged in his appearance. He was just as she had seen him the first time. He still looked like a fifteenth century monk in his attire: A simple black skullcap, a grey, almost black robe and a great chain, much the same size as that of Desmos', attached around his waist. The waist chain, as you may remember, had various kinds of symbols hanging from it which all looked very much like pagan religious symbols. Around his neck he still wore, on a decorative chain, the so-called, peace symbol. And in his hand was the small black book, which had the pale greenish glow coming from the edge of the pages, where you might expect to see gold or silver gilding on such a book.

Just the sight of this cold creature made Diakrina's heart panic. There was something evil beyond description about him. His steady, calculating manner was more frightening than the wild, impulsive manner of the other two. He exerted some kind of predetermined control. He was out maneuvering you, thinking evil plans you could not guess—which your mind was not able to even entertain—but which he always kept covered under a cold veneer keeping you from knowing even his next gesture, let alone his next word or action.

It was quiet for several seconds. Diakrina stayed at alert but really had no idea what to do next. In the silence the background sound of the pickaxes and shovels became the dominant noise. When the Monk broke the aging silence, he spoke to Desmos and Sarx.

"I will handle this. This doesn't call for your methods." The other two snorted a kind of disgust but they obeyed all the same.

The Monk began to walk slowing down the large steps toward Diakrina. As he did so, he began muttering some kind of incantations almost under his breath, yet still slightly audible, which he was reading from his black book. It was in some strange language which Diakrina could make nothing of—and the understanding of it did not begin to come to her, as it so often did while she was on the other side of reality, when she heard languages unknown to her.

A kind of greenish aura began to glow out around the Monk. As he came closer it seemed this aura kept him from being affected by the direct rays of the crimson light from the sword. Strateia taught her later what the Monk was doing was to claim his right, as a creature of free will, to refuse the entrance of anything into the aura of his existence as long as the time of freedom remained. He was renouncing all light and declaring his total alliance with darkness.

Slowly you could see the crimson light bend around his greenish aura and not enter it. Strateia explained the Living One, for now, will not remove a beings personal moral freedom, as concerns themselves. They can reject truth and light. There will be a day when they will have to face the consequences for having done so, because for all moral being's freedom is limited and time bound. It will only be renewed in those who have used it as the Creator intended.

For the moment, Hairesis was able to keep crimson light at bay as regards himself. He continued down the stairs until he was within about five feet of Diakrina. He did not stop, but simply began walking out around her at this distance, still chanting. Immediately, Diakrina felt like she was in some kind of bubble. All sound from the pickaxes and shovels faded. Inside this bubble she could hear nothing but the Monk's droning voice. His words were like a drug. Immediately she began to become dizzy and the whole of the environment around her began to spin.

Diakrina fought with all her might to keep her balance. Yet, it took less than ten seconds—a single circle by the Monk—and she lost her balance and fell to the granite floor still trying to hold up her shield and sword.

Then everything began to spin so fast she could see nothing. It was like being on a very fast merry-go-round and the whole of reality seemed to blur together.

Suddenly, it all stopped. She was standing in total darkness and could see only the Monk, who was also standing in the featureless night surrounded by his greenish aura. Everything was silent and all the environment around her seemed to have disappeared.

It was then he lowered his book and the green glow from its pages illuminated the granite floor. There, in a heap, was Diakrina: unconscious and still clutching her sword.

Yet, here she was, standing in the darkness with the Monk. And in her right hand, somehow, she still held the crimson sword.

Then he stopped chanting and looked straight at her.

"Welcome to the entrance to Parad. You will appear before the Emperor now," came the Monk's slowly metered voice.

The temple reappeared in its place. The door at the center of the temple began to glow and it opened suddenly, casting light over them both. The light source was a longways off in the darkness beyond the door. At the same moment the light hit Diakrina, the darkness became a tunnel pulling her toward the door.

Instantly, the Monk disappeared as she was pulled past him at great speed and around the center column and through the temple door. She heard a sound like a train going through a tunnel and then a long, doppler effected, whooshing sound. Diakrina was being drawn toward the light at an ever-accelerating velocity for several seconds. She was in total shock. Yet, there was nothing she could do about any of it.

Then, as quickly as it had begun, it stopped.

As if having her eyes opened to a totally new reality, Diakrina found herself high in the air flying over an incredibly beautiful, green landscape of trees and fields covered with glorious spreads of flowers. And everywhere there was the sound of majestic music.

Chapter Eleven

THE KINGDOM OF PARAD

If Diakrina had any distinct thoughts while she was being pulled toward the light, she cannot recall them now. However, she was conscious of being filled with an attitude which she had embraced even while she stood there in front of the Monk: She fully expected to meet Anomos. And she was bracing herself for something very unpleasant.

Though she had seen a representation of him in the Great Dance as the Intruder and realized he could appear beautiful and even glorious, she also knew he was the ultimate source of evil. The Monk, which she had just encountered again, looked rather harmless in his basic appearance. But the moment you got beyond the first impression, you encountered evil chilling you to the bone. She was prepared to meet something on the same order only more disturbing.

But at the end of the crescendo of the whooshing sound filling everything as she was pulled toward the light, there was a sense of passing right into the light and out the other side. The other side proved to be another world: a breathtakingly beautiful world. And she was flying over it.

She tried to tell herself it was not real. But she couldn't. She tried to tell herself she was dreaming. But it would not do.

This was the opposite of a dream. Everything was so distinct and real it made all earthly experience seem like shadows and fading vapors by comparison. Other than the few moments she had been in sight of The City and in the Presence of the Living One, this was the most astonishing, beautiful world she had ever seen.

Below her was countryside. It was green, lush, vivid and earthlike. It could have been earth except it was clearly too perfect. It was like the Garden in many ways. Yet, it was different in some way she could not comprehend.

Everything about the countryside she was flying over seemed to pull at her like the pull of a longed-for childhood home just being remembered. It was like some part of her—some part of her deep within—remembered this place. It seemed to welcome her. Some kind of rejoicing seemed to awaken within her. She indeed felt like she had come home and found it to be more beautiful than any fairytale could imagine it.

What overwhelmed this realization was the constant vivid something continually rebuking any attempt to doubt the reality of what she was seeing. This was like a fairytale more real than any earthly reality she had ever experienced. This was a beautiful, incredible dream world, except she knew—somehow—it wasn't a dream. It was reality with the radiance of myth on it, yet she knew, beyond any certainty she had ever experienced, this place was no myth.

Diakrina found once again time seemed hard to determine. She is not sure how long she flew over this beautiful world. Time, in this place, was more complex than the linear time we experience on earth. And its other aspects, which were so real to her at that moment, she claims are hopelessly difficult to describe to someone who has not experienced it.

The landscape was filled with life. There were flocks of songbirds everywhere. They were singing the most beautiful melodies. There were butterflies of inexplicable colors and patterns flying by the thousands over the countryside below her. They were flying in lazy formations over blossoming flowers and buds on trees opening to them as they flew near. Each one seemed to shock the eyes. They were a river of life and color moving through the air like poetry.

What is more, she did not simply see such beauty. It seemed seeing and hearing were somehow connected. She heard beauty when she looked at it. And she saw beauty when she heard it. Seeing and hearing were not separate in this place. Yet they were still distinct. She could attend to seeing or hearing separately. But she was always aware hearing was accompanying the seeing and seeing was accompanying the hearing.

And all of it was combined with feeling. There was almost a sense of touching whatever she saw or heard. All things were connected, yet somehow still distinct and themselves. She could not look at or listen to anything without becoming a part of it in some sense. Yet, she was still distinct from it—and it from her—in some mysterious and important way.

When finally Diakrina realized someone was flying beside her, to her left, she also realized at the same moment, this someone had been there for several minutes—or maybe hours. It seemed to be a young boy. She knew this by how she felt about him, which feelings she realized she had been having long before she was clearly conscious of his presence. His presence seemed so natural, once she realized he was there. It seemed normal she had not taken specific notice of him until now.

They flew along together for quite some time. When she did turn her head from the beauties all around her and below her to look at him, she saw a young man, likely close to her age, who was dressed in a simple white tunic. It was a very natural looking material like you might expect to find a peasant wearing. Yet, it was clearly very clean and soft—she could feel the tunic, somewhat, as she looked at it—and it was something the wealthiest of earth would have sought to be seen wearing.

His tunic, though white, seemed to have every color of the rainbow in it as if your eyes could detect the fact white light was actually made up of all other waveforms of light—and therefore, every other possible color. He and his tunic both had that overwhelming, super-vivid aliveness everything else in the surroundings seemed to possess.

The young man smiled at her. His smile communicated

something so powerful and filled with love—not romantic love, nor any other kind of earthly love, but a love that, while it still contained them all, surpassed them and focused on greater things—it made Diakrina's heart jump inside her. He communicated some kind of love that seemed higher and more genuine and purer than any she had known among humans. Only what she had felt in the presence of the Living One could surpass it. For nothing could compare with that Love.

She felt really alive and full of joy just in seeing his countenance. She continued to look at him and neither of them felt any bashfulness or self-consciousness about looking straight at each other. They studied each other's face and eyes without any objection coming from the other's gaze.

Then, without using words—much like Revelation had spoken to her in Nekus Canyon—he spoke to her. His wordless words went through her like a wind. What he said seemed so true and welcoming. And it seemed, by its very expression, to claim to be true in a way eliminating the possibility of it being a passing fantasy or something to be doubted.

What she heard in her mind—and she instantly knew she was hearing his thoughts—translates into earthly language something like this:

"You are welcomed by the Emperor. He is filled with joy over you. He cannot wait to receive you. There is nothing to fear. You will soon learn all your troubles have passed. The time for laying down all weapons has truly come."

Diakrina was flooded by his message with a vast and crazy sensation of relief. Yet, at the same moment his mention of "weapons" jolted her. At that moment she looked down and realized she still had the shield on her left arm and the strap of the crystal container was still over her shoulder. And in her right hand she was still holding tightly to the crimson sword. This caused a question to pass quickly through her mind: "Could this fact—the sword in her right hand—be why the young man was flying on her left?"

She had no sooner had this thought than she heard the young man reply back to her. It was in a very serene manner and showed no hint of being troubled or of accusing her.

"You are correct concerning why I am to your left. We dislike weapons here. They are so unnecessary and out of place."

For just a moment Diakrina felt a sense of shame for carrying the crimson sword. But then she looked straight at it and the crimson light from the blade, which was softly glowing, seemed to shake her out of that attitude. She remembered the crimson sword was her version of the Sword of the Living One. She would never be ashamed of carrying it. If He thought such a weapon necessary, so would she.

This was the first moment in which she sensed something seemed wrong or didn't fit. Yet, before she could think more of it, the young man said to her. "You are so loved here. Look ahead. We are coming to the throne of the Emperor. He is eager to welcome you."

Diakrina looked straight ahead and saw large puffy clouds. They were billowing up and out from a central place against a deep blue sky. And all around the clouds—immeasurably higher and wider— there was a great orb of colors like a rainbow. And in this orb were shimmering beings who were arcing across the sky.

These beings left long colorful streams behind them like a stream you might see behind a jetliner flying at very high altitude. The difference was these streams were filled with sparkling colors of every possible description.

There was a hum of sound coming from all around in the orb of the rainbow. Diakrina wondered if this sound, which as they got closer began to seem somewhat like chanting, was coming from these beings. All these beings were winged. And it seemed to Diakrina the beating of their wings was producing the chanting she was hearing.

She could make no sense of what they were chanting. It was beautiful to the ear, yet it caused no meaning in her mind. She felt these beings were somehow expressing joy. And the closer the two of them came to the clouds, the more palpable and almost material the chanting became—like rain drops hitting your skin which dissipated without making you wet.

They drew near to the billowing clouds and began entering. For several minutes they flew inward toward the center of the clouds.

Then, suddenly, they came out of the clouds into an immense void, which was completely dark. It felt like it was infinite in size, yet it was not frightening but comforting.

Even though it was in one sense pitch black in the void, it was not a threatening darkness. It seemed to enfold you. And somehow—as strange as it sounds—the void was also brimming over with light. This light was everywhere but it did not remove the darkness. It was a light co-existing with darkness. It had a very strange effect on Diakrina.

It soon became clear to Diakrina she and the boy were to continue to fly toward the center of the void. As they did so, they seemed to become enveloped in darkness so the effect on Diakrina was like traveling through space with no stars visible.

Soon, however, there was something like a dawning up ahead. They were coming over the surface of a dark sphere which was very large, like a landscape below them. And coming over the horizon of the dark sphere was a point of light. The closer they came the larger it became.

Diakrina could see it was a large sea of something reflective, like water or glass. And in the center of it was a large glass-like structure, hard and clear, with steps running all around it. On the top of the structure was a large throne with a back reaching high into the darkness above it. The back of the throne became a spiral of glass seeming to be made to hold something on its top. However, the closer they came the more obvious it was there was nothing being held by the spiral.

There were stairs that ascended the spiral and the entrance to them was to the right of the throne chair: at its front. And seated in the chair was a being who was surrounded in light. In his hand he held a golden scepter which had a large stone at its top. The stone was blacker than coal. It was so dark it seemed to be a substance repelling light with absolute resistance.

"You are expected," said the boy. "The Emperor is on his throne to welcome you."

They flew to the glass-like surface of a large sea. This sea of glass or crystal contained the spiraled throne on the top of a large platform—a platform which was perfectly circular. Many steps ascended the circle on all sides. They touched their feet to the surface as lightly as a cat's tread when stalking game.

Then the young boy immediately knelt down on both knees with his back straight and with his head bowed. Diakrina was at a loss as to what she should do.

She was aware she was in Parad. So, she had no inclination to kneel. Yet, there was an incredible sense of beauty and welcome all around her making her feel as if she were committing some kind of ungrateful act of unkindness by not offering some kind of tribute.

The throne rose high above them, and she felt a warmth and love seeming to radiate from the being on its top. Nothing was said, at first, but she felt a sense of open acceptance. She was saturated in a sense of joy.

This feeling soon caused her to form a question of inquiry. She did not need to speak. The question had only formed in her mind when, instantly, an answer was given, which seemed like an explosion of light, color, love and beauty blowing through Diakrina like a crashing wave. If her question had been formed into language, it would have been something like: "Why am I here?"

The answers given were so comprehensive it is hard to explain. A panorama of answers came flooding toward Diakrina, which were like seeing a hundred movies in a single second. She was told she had come to learn the truth about the Kingdom of Parad. She was informed she did not yet know the reality of this Kingdom—this was accompanied by long tours of some of the most beautiful places she could imagine—and that once she did know what Parad was truly like, she would change her mind about her quest.

It was here, in Parad—the unfolding pictures told her—she would find the real beauty of existing. Her true potential would be unlocked in this place where the beauty of every self was allowed to unfold unhindered. There was no law here—law was not needed. She could do nothing wrong as there was no wrong.

While the answers that came at her from the throne were not

exactly in language, as we know it, the "voice" of this being was warm. As strange as it may seem, it was personal and caring. He seemed to understand humans and he was inviting Diakrina to find a place in his kingdom where she could unlock her inner most self in safety and amazement. Diakrina felt not only warmth, compassion and pathos, but also even irony and humor as well.

"You are welcome, Diakrina. There is a place for you in Parad."

She felt so overwhelmed by a sense of acceptance and joy in the presence of this welcoming being it was all she could do to try and remember the things she had been told of the evil residing in this kingdom. The voice spoke again.

"I know you have doubts caused by the slander against this kingdom. But now you will see for yourself it is all untrue. This is not a kingdom of evil. In reality evil, as you call it, is only a necessary, temporary state refining all things until they can come to their true perfection of self-expression. Some take the short path, others the long path. But in the end, all find the perfection of Parad through the power of its policy of total personal freedom. Self-discovery is the endless journey.

"Forget about evil," continued the voice. "It is a myth concocted by the enemies of Parad. They show you the process with its admitted struggles. Then they claim this is its final result. However, the rest of the story is none of those struggles are wasted. The second fall of Nekus is an endless becoming—the removal of all hindrances to the journey inward—an ever-approaching zenith which is already possessed: for it lies within."

While much being said, clearly contradicted what Diakrina believed to be true, one can hardly believe the passion carrying the wordless words—the sense of a trembling excitement causing her to feel adventure tugging to free itself from some unseen tether. It made it all seem so real. Something in the very atmosphere made you want to believe it was true.

More questions began to form in her mind. The moment they formed the same thing happened. They were immediately answered with such comprehensive information, in her earthly state she could never have processed, let alone, comprehended the profound knowledge being communicated to her. Yet, here, it was so easy. She could understand in a moment what it would have taken a lifetime of research and disciplined study to absorb in her former existence.

Finally, Diakrina looked at her sword which was slowly pulsing crimson. Immediately a question dominated her mind: "Are you telling me the Living One has lied to me?"

Immediately, an overwhelming pathos—pity—was radiating toward her coming from the being on the throne above her. It engulfed her and seemed to lovingly embrace her. It seemed to be saying—without actually saying it—he was indeed sorry she had been so misinformed: sorry she found it necessary to ask such questions.

Then she heard, "We would make no such accusations here. He is allowed to have his reality and to interpret things as he chooses. Here our freedom is extended even to those we disagree with. We only wish he would extend the same courtesy to us. In time, however, we are convinced even he will come to see the Kingdom of Parad is what should be embraced. When that time comes, we will welcome all those who have learned from their long journey the truth which we already possess."

Diakrina couldn't help asking, "What truth?"

The answer was a long explosion of information. The best she could translate it was it had something to do with a deeper truth—the truth of the great becoming—arising out of a necessary forbidding making possible some great deed which gave an opportunity to create what never existed before.

Immediately Diakrina began to remember parts of the story Strateia had told her about Heylel, who became Anomos. How he had sung at the beginning of the great falling about a deeper possible magic of freedom where the creature unlocks his full potential through a forbidden act; in this case, climbing the Spiral's stairs and seizing the Kabod. Strateia said he had sung:

"Look within, and find the key,
For the Living One longs for this to be;

As He planted the seed beyond the Great Sea
And timed the unfolding from antiquity.

"Look within, He placed it there;
He wants you to find it and choose to dare
To actualize the great deed with care:
Did He not, Himself, create the Spiral's circuiting stairs?"

When Diakrina came again to herself, she couldn't help asking, "So, you are saying, at least, the Living One is mistaken, isn't that so?"

The only answer she received was, "Look around you. What have you seen in my kingdom? Is it beauty and peace? Or is it what you expected?" All these questions were accompanied by quick reviews of all the beauty she had seen on her flight over Parad.

Diakrina had to admit Parad was not what she had expected. It was breathtakingly beautiful and peaceful. It was anything but what she had anticipated. It was more like what most people imagine as Heaven than anything else she could think of.

"Diakrina," came the voiceless voice, "You can help make the peace and reality of Parad sure. Parad needs to be opened to your kind in new ways. It needs to spread this deeper freedom to mankind more fully. We need to unlock mankind's greatest potential. If your kind can be made immortal from the start, their pathway to knowledge, their journey through what you call evil, will be shorter. As immortals they can live long enough to evolve through the many necessary stages until they unlock their true potential and come to peace here in Parad.

"You, Diakrina, have been welcomed here to enact a great deed. You can unlock the true divinity of humanity, allowing it to ascend the heights and take its place among the immortals. And in performing it, you will become a great immortal queen."

Diakrina's head was swimming. She became suddenly aware as the one on the throne above her spoke he had ceased to merely communicate with the wordless words. He was now singing—at least that is the closest human equivalent to it. It was more beautiful than human singing and the music was hypnotic and haunting.

Diakrina was enveloped in joy and a dream. She could see and hear and feel the very things he was singing about coming to past. A dream full of wonder and glory began weaving around her mind and heart. It seemed to be saying Parad—the severed kingdom—was severed from all constraints. It would rise to new heights and create new realities. Mankind was being invited to become part of its ever-evolving promise. The deeper magic, the deeper truth, was its great secret, its ultimate glory. And only Parad birthed and nurtured this great secret of endless evolution—forever rising above and transcending one's previous self.

Then she heard the voice sing a pleading appeal:

"Put down your sword and embrace the peace.
Here all your people can find what they seek.
Lay down the quest and take up our dream.
The hopes of the ages are more than they seem.
Deep in the self lies a seed of new humanity.
Within Parad it will find a new sanity.
Unlock the door, don't fail to pass through.
On its far side lies joys that sparkle like dew—
An unending evolution forever coming true."

The young man who had been with Diakrina this whole time, and had been kneeling on the sea of glass, rose to his feet slowly as the song came to an end. He walked up to Diakrina and placed a hand on her shoulder. The gentle pressure of his hand made it clear he was asking her to come with him somewhere.

He pointed to her left. Far away on the sea of glass was a pile of something. Diakrina could not quite make out what composed the pile. Yet, it was clear he wished for her to walk toward the objects.

Diakrina could think of no reason she should not do so, so she turned toward the piled objects and began walking that direction. As she did, hauntingly beautiful music—heart-pleading strings and soul-penetrating woodwinds and spirit-lifting sounds which no earthly instruments could replicate—began to quietly fill the air. With every step it grew slightly louder. And in the heart-rending beauty of unearthly melodies, she began to hear a whispering voice singing. Subtly and hypnotically, she heard over and over:

"Peace ... Peace ... Peace.
Learn resistance no more.
Peace ... Peace ... Peace.
All swords become distant lore.
Peace ... Peace ... Peace.
Embrace what freedom is for.
Peace ... Peace ... Peace.
Parad will make your heart soar."

Over and over these lyrics were both whispered and sung. And the pleading strains of the music gave them a pathos tearing at Diakrina's heart producing a terrible longing. Something rose up inside her and cried for it all to be true.

It made her walk with the young man toward the objects on the sea of glass seem like a ceremonial march toward some unseen altar as a very serious act of worship. It seemed as if an aisle was being formed between invisible beings gathered on either side of them. They were being escorted, as it were, up some long royal approach to some very important moment and place.

This caused the longings descending on Diakrina to intensify. As these longings rose and lifted within her and began to fill her, she then heard something else replace the former words and soar on the wings of the pleading melody.

A heaven beyond Heaven;
A god beyond God.
That which was low rising beyond;
A new order of existence that dances on the dawn,
Remakes creation:
An alternative song.

And then, right in front of her was the pile—of swords.

∞——∞

While all this crescendo of excitement and awe-filled anticipation rose within and around Diakrina, there was something else happening at the same time in the background of her consciousness. It was not until she stood looking at the pile of swords at her feet she began consciously engaging it and realizing it had been there all along.

Deep inside her something was violated—this seemed to her the best word. Something was protesting loudly. It was like a screaming conscience too long ignored. When she actually began to give it audience—which took no small effort, as the awe-filled anticipation being imposed on her was persistent and insistent, stubbornly adamant and demanding—she realized the protest was a very deep and troubled revulsion which was beyond expression.

Yet its meaning was unmistakable. It seemed to be a combination of the ideas conveyed by the word, "lie" and the word, "blaspheme" and the word "sacrilege." Yet, it was more than these. It was also a kind of courageous horror at witnessing a terrible injustice and a deep cry of outrage. Something hideous was being masked. Something beautiful was being hijacked and used to cover something twisted and despicable.

Diakrina said later the best word picture she could come up with to communicate the passionate horror and outrage of this protest coming from deep within her would be like the horror and outrage of watching someone fill a pit with hundreds of writhing, venomous serpents and then covering it with a fragile trap door on which was placed a sandbox with wonderful toys inside. Obviously placed there to attract delighted children from a nearby park to run and jump inside.

The contrast between these two very different perspectives, both of which were overwhelming in exactly opposite ways—one ecstatic worship and trembling anticipation of some great and beautiful moment, the other like witnessing the horrible ax-murders of a schoolroom full of children—paralyzed Diakrina.

It was in this state Diakrina came to stand in front of the large pile of swords. They were of every imaginable shape and kind. Yet, many of them looked very much like her sword. They were piled together in no particular order: like an army of conquered soldiers had all filed past and cast their weapons down under compulsion. There had to be several hundred of them. The young man, who was still on her left, warmly smiled at her as he placed his right hand softly on her shoulder and then held out his left hand, with the palm up, toward the pile of swords.

"Your moment has come," he said softly. "Peace is yours." Then he paused and looked into Diakrina's eyes with what seemed to be the deepest of noble affections.

"How I envy you, Diakrina. You will cast down your sword forever and seize the ultimate place of honor for your race. And you will be the greatest ruler among them. You will live as queen among immortals in the kingdom of Parad. All this beauty will become the possession of mankind," (and as he spoke of beauty a million glorious scenes flooded through Diakrina's mind in a single second, yet she was able to comprehend and marvel at each one).

The youth continued. "Parad will extend itself, through you and your people, to rule the whole material creation. The great secret— the deeper freedom—which you will now embrace will be a quantum leap into a constant unfolding and validating of, the way of the self."

Here his eyes shown with mesmerized intoxication as he said, "Deep within you, in the most impenetrable darkness, lies a treasure. It is yet unseen. However, immortality will cause it to endlessly unfold like a never aging flower never ceasing to bloom."

The wordless voice of the youth rose in great swells of oratory which was perfectly in sync with the awe-filled music which continued all around them and lifted his every expression on wings of longing. Each expression was like a stab of painful joy in Diakrina's heart. It was also like a terrible, burning fear—a fear mankind's true potential and glory would never be realized if she did not act now. However, this fear was being doused by a cataract of hope-empowered joy: the long desired and justly deserved honor and vindication due to mankind could be greeted. Its shining potential illuminated some far horizon by its very approach.

Then the youth's voice reached its pinnacle. With admirable, unrestrained commitment, which poured from him in triumphal tones of realization, he shouted to both Diakrina and the sky, "The power is within you! You will save the universe! You will become a goddess through whom all that is material will be cured. Evil will grow up. It will evolve to find its true purpose. Parad will rule!"

Diakrina was undone. Her arms went limp at her side as he was prophesying to the sky. She looked up into the young man's face just as he was shouting, "Parad will rule!" … and that is when she saw it.

It was only a slight gleam in his eye—and it lasted only a millisecond—yet it was absolutely unmistakable. There was a flash of greenish, arrogant radiance breaking through from his eyes and upon his face. It was as if she had seen someone—something—other than the young man for a millisecond. Yet, it was so quick, so fleeting, she instantly felt she must be mistaken. As her eyes fixed skeptically on him for the few seconds following this quick flash of utter contrast, again she could see nothing but the handsome and joy-filled boy with dancing eyes.

And the power of his enraptured delight might have caused her to think no more of it if it had not been for the shuddering witness rising inside her. Once again a sense of utter violation and disgrace, a sense of outrage and severely offended integrity, boiled over from deep within her. As it did, it must have so impacted her she could no longer hide its effect. For instantly a look of both shock and anger flooded the countenance of the young man.

Now you must remember all I have described in the last few paragraphs happened with the span of a few seconds. Diakrina's arms were still at her side having surrendered to the awe of the great crescendo pouring from the music and the young man. Yet her mind and countenance were, however, overwhelmed by the objection exploding within her.

Instantly she knew what she should have known all along. This was all a deception! In a flash she rehearsed it all: Of course, evil could not evolve into peaceful goodness. And what were those lines in that song?... A heaven beyond Heaven? … A god beyond God? … Pure blasphemy! This was Parad's bid to enslave mankind and the cosmos forever. It was their attempt to get her to willingly give up the immortal fruit.

Then it hit her. The glorious being on the glass throne was Anomos—the fallen Heylel. Yet, who was this beside her? She had no sooner conceived this question than there was an explosion of greenish light in front of her. A bolt of pale green light hit her limp, right hand with near shattering force. Her sword was knocked from her hand and spun through the air like a propeller to the far side of the pile of swords. Diakrina screamed, "NO!" and grasped at the air. But it was too late. The sword was out of sight.

At the same moment her right hand was struck, the explosion of green light transformed the young man. There standing with a snarling smile of glee, was the Monk.

Diakrina's only thought—even as shocked as she was in that moment—was to retrieve her sword. But before she could move the Monk was already at work. He waved his greenish, glowing book in the air and began a stirring motion. Immediately the pile of swords began to stir and tumble like they were in a large industrial dryer as they rose into the air. The hundreds of swords were scrambled together and dropped again to the glass surface with a crash. Any thought of running to the other side of the pile and easily finding her sword was now hopelessly undone.

The Monk now turned his gaze upon Diakrina. Gone was the young man of joy. Gone was the quiet and joy-filled countenance. Diakrina was looking into the eyes of pure evil. She knew, as she had never known before, how utterly foolish was any idea evil could ever become anything but what it is—a horrifying, deceptive and dangerous defrauding impostor: a cunning parasite and vicious serpent.

The Monk held out his book toward Diakrina and began to mutter incoherent phrases: a kind of sinister babbling. Instantly, Diakrina felt a sickening weakness descend on her. She was immediately too weak to stand and began sinking to the glass surface.

Yet, deep within, the same outraged integrity rose up. She gathered all her reserves of strength and gave a great pleading cry, "Living One! Help!"

The forgotten shield at her side exploded in every direction with flames of white, gold and blue. The Monk was hurled backwards through the air and landed on his back with a thud some fifty feet away. All around Diakrina was a flaming orb of light which encased her.

The Monk jumped to his feet and began running toward the glass throne. There was a vast explosion of greenish light from the being sitting on the throne and Diakrina heard a voice roaring so cold and bloodless it chilled her to the very depths of her being.

"How dare you run to me in your failure!" Once again, the Monk was hurled through the air. This time he was thrown far to the other side of Diakrina. The whole glass sea shook with the explosion of greenish light.

But Diakrina had only one thing on her mind. She was running to the pile of swords. She began throwing swords behind her in an attempt to dig through the pile until she found her own sword.

"There it is!" she thought. She picked it up. But it was not her sword. It looked like it, but it clearly did not fit her hand. Suddenly Diakrina saw a crimson glow coming from deep within the pile.

"That has to be my sword!" she thought. Yet as she began digging as quickly, yet carefully as possible—remember, swords are very sharp—the monk who still could not approach her due to the orb of the shield holding him at bay, opened his book and began chanting. At the same time, from a distance, he waved his hand at the pile of swords. Instantly, all the swords began glowing with a red glow. The crimson glow of Diakrina's sword disappeared as all the blades became awash with red light.

Diakrina screamed in rage and kept digging toward the place from where she thought the crimson light had been coming. Yet she ended up picking up sword after sword thinking she had found her sword, only to discover it was not true.

The Monk began circling the orb of light in which Diakrina was protected. He began to laugh hysterically as he watched Diakrina frantically digging through the pile of swords.

"One sword is as good as another, my dear," he snarled. Then he roared with manic laughter. "Why worry about finding your original sword. Any sword will do. Besides," he continued in a dark and suddenly sober tone, "no sword is going to save you!"

Diakrina kept digging.

The Monk began his manic laughter again.

"I can't tell one from the other!" Diakrina began screaming to no one in particular. She was in panicked frustration. She began grabbing swords, and as quick as she had confirmed it was not her own, she would throw it behind her back. Soon swords were clattering on the glass sea in all directions.

The more frantic she became the more the Monk roared with evil glee. Then he stopped his laughter and began reading from his book again. Diakrina continued to dig into the pile of swords. Surely, she would soon find it. There couldn't be too many more.

It was then she looked up at the remaining pile in front of her. She blinked her eyes for a moment and stopped digging. "Were there still that many swords in the pile?" she asked herself. Then she saw what was happening.

As the monk mumbled from the pages of his book, swords were materializing in the pile. Hundreds of new swords were beginning to appear. And every sword was a near perfect replica of Diakrina's sword.

Diakrina jumped to her feet and roared at the Monk to stop. But he paid her no mind. He just kept mumbling from the pages of his book and swords kept piling up until the pile was now bigger than it had been before she had thrown hundreds of the swords behind her.

"It is hopeless, my dear," mocked the Monk. "Give me the Immortal Fruit and I will let you find your sword and leave."

"No!" screamed Diakrina, turning on him. "You shall not have it!"

"I don't think you are in a place to deny me, young lady," scolded the Monk. "You are under our law here. And the Emperor has the right to all things within his realm. You will surrender it."

"Never!" shot back Diakrina.

She then turned back to the ever-growing pile of swords. Her eyes lifted to its summit in despair.

"Living One, I can't do this. How am I to regain my sword?"

It is then she heard a very beautiful and clear voice—His voice.

"Hear Me, Diakrina.
My Word is living and active.
It is sharper than any human made double-edged sword.
It penetrates even to dividing soul and spirit,
Joints and marrow;
It discerns the thoughts and attitudes of the heart.
Nothing in all creation is hidden from My sight.
Everything is uncovered and laid bare before My eyes.
And all will have to give an account to Me.
My word is a sword in your mouth not only in your hand.
Ask that the truth be made plain.
Command your sword to proclaim its allegiance."

Immediately, there came into her mind what she must do. Diakrina turned toward the muttering Monk and addressed him.

"Your Emperor is the father of lies. You utter lies when you open your mouth. You cannot keep the truth captive with lies. In the end truth will stand. Lies will vanish."

The Monk paused in his muttering and stared hard at her. Then as if to counter what she had said he began muttering with greater intensity.

"You are not the only one who can speak. I have the Living One's word in my mouth. It is a sword of truth discerning the true from the false. By His truth, I cast down your lies and illusions."

Diakrina then turned toward the growing pile of swords and shouted. "In the Name of the Living One, I command every sword of truth to display its allegiance to the Living One! And I command it to destroy every lie that seeks to conceal it!"

Within the pile of swords there was a rustling. Suddenly crimson light burst from within the pile of swords. Immediately every sword in the pile began to melt like a mist before a desert sun. A greenish fog began floating toward the sky. When the whole pile had all vaporized, there, standing on its handle with the blade pointed in an upward salute to the Living One, was Diakrina's sword.

The face of the Monk went pale as Diakrina walked over and picked up the sword and lifted it in a high salute to the sky and shouted, "The Name of the Living One, who is the Truth, is victorious forever!"

She heard a scream from the Monk and a roar of rage from the glass throne. But before she could hear or see anything else, she was suddenly pulled into the air at blinding speed.

She passed back over the glorious landscapes she had flown over before, only much faster. Her speed continued to increase until all was a blur in the world below her.

Suddenly, she was in a dark tunnel. There was a roar like an advancing locomotive within the tunnel. Diakrina held tightly to her sword and its crimson light blazed out in front of her within the darkness.

Then she saw the door of the temple she had passed through, only from the inside this time. Beyond it she could see someone lying on the hard stone of the cavern. There were large creatures standing around looking down at … her.

Then in a flash, all went dark.

The next thing Diakrina remembered was her ribs hurt and the stone beneath her was very cold.

Chapter Twelve

ALMOST CHECKMATE

Diakrina learned later the whole time she had been gone, the shield had protected her body. As soon as she lay physically unconscious on the stone floor of the cavern, Desmos and Sarx had attempted to reach under the shield and take the crystal container. Yet every time they had tried to lift the shield, either with their hands or even with the tip of their swords, the shield would blast them backwards to the ground with an explosion of white, gold and blue light.

Just the touch of that light to these creatures was like burning, searing acid. They would scream in pain and explode with vile curses.

They even tried to move Diakrina's body so her position would cause her to uncover the crystal container from under the shield. Yet every time they tried to touch her body, the sword would explode with crimson light with the same results.

Now don't ask me how the sword and the shield could be both with Diakrina in the material realm and also with her in the purely spiritual world she had been in for those four hours. Diakrina said it had something to do with a kind of incarnation: both the sword and the shield had a spiritual essence that had taken on physical properties.

As she said to me, "It seems when I was given my own version of the Sword of the Living One, it became a sword a human soul could use. As the words of the Living One have been given physical structure and expression through human instruments in the Great Book, so the sword, which is dense spiritual reality, was incarnated as a physical sword when it was given to me. It was made a sword which an embodied being could interact with and use in both the spiritual and physical realms."

In the same way, her shield, which was a physical embodiment of her trust in the Living One—her faith, which is spiritual in essence—had this same incarnate characteristic. Therefore, as she could be in the spiritual realm and in the physical realm at both one and the same time, so could these two weapons. They were both spiritual and material.

Diakrina told me she believed she and her body were never actually parted as both were still connected by the silver cord. This had been the second such experience, which Revelation had warned her about in Nekus Canyon. While her spiritual perception and person was active in the spiritual realm, it was not absent—as we think of absent—from her physical body.

"Mankind is a living soul," she said, "the union of both spirit and body. Only death, which is an abnormality—and was never intended—severs them. I was not dead. And as spiritual reality is super—beyond—natural and is therefore not limited by the four dimensions of space and time in the same way the physical body is, it can exercise perception and actions transcending the physical body— at least in the body's present form."

Because of the sword and shield, Desmos and Sarx, with several of their other companions, had been working at their attempts to get at the Atheos for about four hours—the whole time Diakrina was in Parad—with no success. By the time she became conscious again within her aching body, they had exhausted all their ideas and were standing around her arguing about what to do next.

Diakrina took note her sword was still in her hand and the shield was still on her left arm. She also took note she was aching all over—mostly in her ribs—from the rough ride she had endured on her stomach slung over the rider's lap.

She lay there for several minutes not moving but simply

listening to the arguments and curses coming from her captors. Then a burst of greenish light came flooding out of the door of the temple. Out walked Hairesis. The moment Diakrina's eyes fell on his countenance she could see he was in a rage. Likely he had been severely dealt with for his failures in Parad and had been sent with orders to get the Immortal Fruit at all costs—or else!

Diakrina knew she needed to get to her feet. But she was still groggy. She finally did manage to struggle to her feet—in the manner of a slightly inebriated woman—just before the Monk had descended the stairs and crossed the distance between them.

When he finally came striding up, his eyes were wild with a red, glowing rage. Desmos and Sarx took one look at him and stepped backward—clearly fearful. He fastened his eyes upon Diakrina, and a cold shiver began crawling up her spine.

"You think you have won," he said in a hissing, breathy voice pushed through clenched teeth. "NOT SO!" he screamed. Then he doubled up both his fists—for his book was now tucked under his belt and his hands were empty—and his arms went straight down and stiff at his side. He began to tremble with intense fury as his eyes dilated so wide he looked utterly insane.

"We have your body under our control. You will give us the container with the Immortal Fruit, or we will kill you." Then turning to Desmos and Sarx, "Back up, both of you, if you do not wish to be destroyed."

Diakrina did her best to strike a fighting stance toward the Monk so as to be ready for whatever he had in mind. But she could hardly have imagined what began to happen next.

The Monk took his greenish, glowing book from his belt and opened it slowly to the very back of the book, while never taking his eyes off Diakrina. This time he turned the pages of the book toward Diakrina and held the book out in front of his face with his arms fully extended.

Slowly the pages of the book began to glow with sickening green light. Out from the pages of the book something began to materialize. Diakrina watched with terror-filled eyes as the head of a very large, bright green serpent pushed out from the pages. It had red glowing eyes which stared unblinkingly straight into Diakrina's eyes. She instantly had an overwhelming desire to close her eyes and break the serpent's gaze: but she couldn't. No matter how hard she tried, her eyes were glued to the hypnotic glow coming from the vertical slits of the serpent's red pupils.

Slowly and steadily the large reptile continued to emerge from the book. While its hideous body began looping toward the stone floor as it emerged, its head never lowered. Instead, its head moved, ever so slowly, toward Diakrina, while its body continued to slither out of the book and pour onto the floor. Diakrina tried to vent her fear by shouting at the monster only to discover she couldn't. She frantically tried to close her eyes or turn her head, but to no avail.

Diakrina tried to call for help. She could not speak. She tried to lift her sword toward the vile viper. Her arm would not move. Her whole body had become rigid and entranced while her mind, still nimble and active, watched helplessly as the head of the serpent moved closer and closer to her face. Inside she was screaming. Outside she was helplessly frozen.

The eyes of the serpent were perfectly on a level with her own. As its huge body continued to coil out of the pages of the book its head came within a foot of Diakrina's face and paused. Its eyes were hideous. But try as she might, Diakrina was frozen eye to eye with the viper.

Then it slowly dropped its jaw. A greenish vapor began to pour out of its gaping mouth, and it was then blown slowly into Diakrina's face. An acrid stench, like that she had remembered coming from Bellicose, filled her whole body. Again, she wanted to scream, yet she could not move or make a sound.

Then it happened. The serpent began controlling her body. She watched as her arms began to move. It was like watching someone else move. It was as if she were not capable of even feeling what her body was doing. Both her sword arm, and her left arm with the shield on it, went limp to her side.

Inside she was shouting, "NO! THIS CANNOT HAPPEN! THIS CANNOT HAPPEN!" But it did happen while her body continued to slowly and obediently obey what was obviously the serpent's will. Diakrina began an internal struggle feeling like it would tear her apart. The veins on her face were standing out until they looked as if they would pop. Sweat, in this cold place, poured from her body's every pore. She was mad with rage and frantic to get her sword arm back under her control, but her body would not obey her.

A hissing, sinister voice came from the serpent as it began to speak.

"You will drop your sword."

She heard her sword drop to the stone floor of the cavern as the serpent continued to hold her gaze. She was its prisoner within her own body. She could do nothing to keep her body from obeying it.

"Give her one of our swords," it hissed.

Hairesis looked at Desmos and nodded his head toward Diakrina. Desmos, who was to the front-right of Diakrina some distance away, took a sword from one of the human soldiers near him and moved in a wide arch to her right and came up somewhat behind her.

"Place it in her hand," hissed the serpent.

Diakrina watched as her right arm extended slightly and her hand turned up to receive the sword handle. There was nothing she could do to stop any of it. Desmos placed a sword with a pulsing green blade in her extended hand. It was rather large for her; yet she could only tell this by what she could see of it, as her hand could feel nothing of the sword.

Then she watched in horror as her right arm began bending at the elbow and raising the blade of the sword toward her own throat. When the sharp edge of the sword blade touched her neck, her arm stopped.

"You will now release your hold on the shield," hissed the serpent.

Her left hand relaxed and she turned loose of the shield handle. The strap of the shield slid down her arm and the shield clattered to the cavern floor.

"Now, reach over your head and remove the strap of the container from your shoulder," instructed the serpent.

Diakrina fought to find some way to gain control of her left arm. But it was to no avail. She watched as her left hand reached for the strap of the crystal container, which was on her right shoulder, in order to lift it over her head.

Yet before her hand could move there was an explosion of flying bodies as soldiers, to Diakrina's right, were thrown into the air in all directions. Desmos and Sarx were also thrown to the cavern floor and their swords were ripped from their sheaths and thrown cartwheeling toward the temple pillars.

And there, with two others like himself, stood Strateia. The two like him had their swords at the throat of Desmos and Sarx while each stepped down on the head of one of them with his right foot. Their blades were pulsing crimson and caused the two vile warriors to stiffen with obvious fear; they were afraid to even flinch.

Strateia stood with the point of his sword only inches from Hairesis' throat. The Monk stiffened and his eyes went wide, yet he held his position with both hands holding tightly to the book he was extending toward Diakrina.

At the same moment, Diakrina heard the clash of steel behind her as horses came thundering into the cavern. There were screams indicating the soldiers who had captured her and carried her here— which had been standing all around at a distance watching her ordeal with the serpent and Hairesis unfold—were being struck down as Jared's warriors rode mercilessly through them. Within moments, Jared and his men were in control of the whole scene. They encircled Diakrina, the serpent and Hairesis, and Strateia who had his sword at Hairesis' throat, while Desmos and Sarx were immobilized with a foot and blade from one of the other two warriors.

As the last of the clashes ended, Diakrina heard the Monk quickly utter something in a strange dialect. Almost instantly the serpent, without its head moving, quickly coiled its large body around Diakrina like a massive boa constrictor.

"Recall your nekro-vapor and release her, now!" shouted

Strateia.

"Not so fast, my warrior friend," snarled the Monk as he continued to hold out the glowing book toward Diakrina. "She is under my control. I have already given the command for the nekro-vapor to cause her to slit her own throat if you as much as touch me with that blade. I am the only one, now, who can stop it from killing her. And even if you send me to the Abyss by thrusting your blade through me, the nekro-vapor will finish its work before you can stop it."

Obviously, what the Monk said must have been true. For Strateia did not move. For several seconds everyone frozen in place and no one said anything. Then the Monk spoke again.

"If you want to save the girl, you will have to give me the Immortal Fruit. For I will not spare her unless you vow to put it safely in my possession."

The cold, cruel certainty communicated in the Monks voice left no doubt he meant exactly what he said. It was likely he would rather be sent to the Abyss for the remainder of time than face his emperor without the Fruit.

Strateia's sword did not move. And the Monk continued to stare at him wide-eyed. The serpent continued to hold Diakrina's gaze and to coil its body even more tightly around her.

Then Diakrina heard the voice of Strateia—his silver voice, which only she could hear.

"Diakrina, it is the will of the Living One that you be kept alive. Your quest is not finished. However, we must relinquish the Atheos to them for now. This is the Living One's will, but he asks you to agree and consent. My advice is, of course, to consent. There really is no other way. You can answer me in your thoughts. I will hear you."

"But how will we ever get it back," was what came flooding into her mind. "Is there no other way?"

"No. Not at the moment. This is almost checkmate. However, you need to remember they cannot open the container. The Atheos will be safe inside it for now. They do not yet understand this. If they did, they would never give you up. So, by saving you, we will keep the

Atheos from being fully available to them and there will yet be hope to finish the quest. Do you understand?"

"Yes. But if they understood I alone can open it, then they would not kill me, right?"

"You do not understand the rage, arrogance, and insanity of evil. We cannot trust them to act rationally under these conditions if this fact were made known to them. Evil will do all the harm it can when it is clear it can no longer win. Do you understand, Diakrina?"

"Yes."

"Then do you consent?"

"Y … Yes," came her hesitant reply.

There was a short pause and then Strateia spoke to Hairesis.

"Recall your nekro-vapor and release Diakrina to my care, and I vow to you, in the Name of the Living One, I will hand over the crystal container to you."

Diakrina saw the Monk's eyes narrow in delighted relief as a look of sinister triumph slowly spread over his twisted face.

"I agree, as I know the Living One will hold you to your vow." Then he added under his breath, "Which is one of His weaknesses we can always count on."

Strateia's eyes flashed crimson fire. "It will only be a matter of time before you will learn His perfect integrity is no weakness. It is rather the certainty of your eternal doom!"

The Monk's face quickly drained a little of its defiance. Yet just as quickly a cold determined look replaced it and he answered, "Well, we haven't time to indulge this little discussion, have we?"

He then paused for a moment and looked Strateia up and down as if to check for any other course of action. Slowly he lowered his book and the serpent began uncoiling from Diakrina's body. Then, just as it had slithered out of the book's open pages, it began to reverse itself and retreat backwards into the book.

When finally the eyes and head of the serpent began to pull back from Diakrina's face, she felt the sensations of her body starting to return. When the head retreated into the book's pages, and the Monk snapped it shut between his two palms, Diakrina was able to move her eyes freely once again and her body became her possession once more. She dropped her arm and released the sword to clang to the stone floor.

Strateia lowered his sword slightly and the Monk took a step away from him as if to get out of reach of it. He then turned to Diakrina and said, "I'll take that Fruit, now."

Diakrina looked to Strateia, who nodded slowly at her to relinquish the crystal container. She slowly lifted the strap over her head and then held the container out toward the Monk by means of it. The Monk smiled a twisted smile and reached out and grasped the strap. He had no sooner done so than there was a flash of greenish light which left nothing but a greenish vapor filling the air. He and the crystal container, with the Immortal Fruit inside, vanished.

Diakrina quickly knelt and retrieved her sword and shield. Strateia turned to Jared and motioned for him to come. Jared came striding toward Strateia as Diakrina quickly moved to Strateia's side.

"Get her out of here and guard her with your life," he whispered. "It will not take them long to realize they cannot open the crystal container without her. You and your men head for the Mist Forest to join up with your other men who are there on the mountain. We"— here he glanced toward his two companion warriors, each of whom had a foot still on the head of either Desmos or Sarx, with a sword pointed only inches from their faces—"will keep these two enemy warriors pinned here until you are well out of reach. Then I will catch up to you."

Then Strateia turned to Diakrina and put a hand on her shoulder as he looked down into her eyes.

"Do not fret Little One. The quest is not lost. It has simply taken an unforeseen detour. Go with Jared and do as he says. I will be with you shortly."

Then turning again to Jared, he said, "Ride like the wind, my friend. Time is short!"

Diakrina's horse, Phos, had been brought along with the

warriors and she was quickly lifted onto his back. Jared then mounted his horse and gave the order to ride. The first few units took the lead with Jared and his unit surrounding Diakrina and the other units coming behind.

The horses were immediately urged into a full gallop and the warriors and their horses thundered back up the cavern incline. Soon they were out of the cavern and back up the sides of the sinkhole.

They set out on a full reversal of their previous course, but of course, by-passed the overhang leading into the cavern. They galloped into the small valley and turned south again and rode hard in the direction of the Mist Forest.

The sun was just starting to escort the stars from the sky as the night was now over. By the time they reached the small, forested area where they had camped, Phulasso, who had been rider-less to this point, suddenly had a rider: Strateia.

Jared nodded to him and Diakrina smiled with relief. But she was very troubled about the loss of the Atheos. And it made her smile somewhat strained.

Strateia knew what her strained smile meant. He smiled back at her with a confident smile mixed with a firm set of his jaw, revealing his uninterrupted engagement of the task at hand. Clearly, he had an ability Diakrina could only wish for: to put what had happened behind and look ahead to what must be done.

To Strateia there could be no regret. Only the situation at hand, and properly engaging it, mattered to him. Once again, even as they rode, and the sunlight began to cast long shadows from the rim of the valley on their left, Diakrina found herself looking over at Strateia, who was riding next to her, with a sense of utter amazement. He was so, otherworldly—so different—yet, in a wonderful and comforting way.

They raced past the forested campsite and continued down the valley. In about an hour they came to a place where the small river to their left turned slightly to the left—east—as it emptied into a break in the rim of the valley. There it joined a river coming from the southwest, somewhat to their right, which crossed in front of them as it turned east to pass through the break in the canyon wall.

This was the Nekus River. Diakrina recognized the spot though she had not been on this side of the river the night Strateia and she had been here. They had followed its far shore to the southwest until the river turned west into the canyon that passed through Bellicose's territory. They had climbed the plateau and ultimately crossed the river high above on the rock bridge as they ran from Bellicose's gaze.

But there was no rock bridge down here. And in order to get to the valley leading into Nekus Canyon, so they could pass back down it away from Nekus Canyon, they would have to ford the river here and pass through the cut in the valley wall on the far side so they could then turn south again.

The water of the river was deep and swift. The river was very wide. Diakrina could not image how they were going to get to the other shore. But she was no Antediluvian. And though she was riding an antediluvian horse, and knew it was far superior to any horse she had ever ridden, she still could not yet appreciate the full difference.

To her surprise, Jared sounded some short blast on his horn and the units leading the way turned and headed southwest, upriver, along the shore of the Nekus for several hundred yards in the area where it was beginning to turn toward the east. This was evidently to get them a little above the swifter, rolling water emerging as the river headed southeast toward the canyon.

When the lead captain found a place he obviously considered a good crossing point, he gave a signal on his horn and, without slowing at all, turned his horse into the river. The horse gave a great leap and landed in the water, swimming very fast toward the opposite shore. Despite the horse's speed the swiftness of the current began carrying the horse and rider downstream very fast.

The other warriors turned their horses into the river and soon the river was full of warriors and horses swimming hard toward the far shore while being carried swiftly toward the canyon. When Diakrina reached the river's edge Phos never hesitated. She grabbed at his main and held on for dear life as he gave a great leap from the shore into the water. Diakrina was clearly giving no direction to Phos but knew she didn't need to. He would follow Jared's horse without fail.

Diakrina was stunned at how fast the horses could swim once she was actually experiencing it. Yet it did not keep her from wondering if they could reach the far shore soon enough to avoid getting caught in the rapids leading into Nekus. And just the thought of the terrible waterfall lying not too far downstream from where the river entered the canyon—and the even more horrifying the one beyond it; the silent, endless waterfall—made Diakrina shudder despite being preoccupied with holding tightly to Phos.

She need not have worried. The horses carried them to the far shore with distance to spare. And without even a pause, each rider came ashore with his horse lunging through the water as his hooves touched bottom, and breaking back into a full gallop. The stamina of these horses was amazing.

As they passed through the cut, they rose over the rise where, on the other side, Strateia and Diakrina had camped the night she entered Nekus. They galloped over the hill and turned south again toward the Mist Forest and the mouth of the cavern she and Strateia had come out of after passing through the mountain on which the Mist Forest was located.

The horses retraced the ground much faster than they had covered it on foot. That evening now seemed so far in the distant past to Diakrina. It was only about half an hour until Jared sounded a signal for them to begin slowing down.

When they came to a place where a path seemed to turn to the left and disappeared up into the forest covering the mountain, Jared gave a signal for all the units to come to a halt. This they did and gathered at the head of the trail organized by units in a circle.

Jared, Strateia and Diakrina rode into the circle as the units from behind closed the circle in. Then Jared turned to Strateia.

"Do you have instructions for us?"

"Yes. The goal now is to get Diakrina to the Tree Bridge before she can be captured. If they capture her, they will find a way to make her open the crystal container. At all costs, this cannot happen!

"This trail, as you know, leads up the mountain on the near side of the Mist Forest. It skirts its western edge, bending back to the east all the time as you climb up to the mountaintop in the south. We will travel this trail together until we are almost to the top. At that point the forest is still quite heavy, and it will be hard for Anomos' Nekros to keep track of us.

"Just before we come to the area where the mountain's top comes out of the forest and rises to the natural fortification of the cliffs—where I trust your other warriors are already entrenched—two units will break off from the others taking Diakrina with them. We will stay in the thick cover of the forest and try to keep from being spotted.

"It is important Anomos and his warriors, who are not far behind us, think we are still with you and headed for the mountaintop to seek reinforcements. We need them to follow you all the way to your other warriors. However, our two units will be cutting straight through the Mist Forest—he will consider this unlikely for us to do—so we can go around the far side of the mountain low down on its slopes. We will then ride through the forest down its backside toward the area of the Tree Bridge."

"Your men who join up with the other warriors are to engage Anomos' troops when he arrives at the base of the mountaintop. You are to fight as if you are protecting Diakrina. In fact, you will be, by keeping his warriors engaged with you while we make for the Tree Bridge.

"Just before we get within a mile of the bridge, as we will be coming toward it from the northwest, there is a large meadow that must be crossed. Before this meadow, in the trees, there is a large ruin at the top of a hill that ends with a cliff face, called Dorogon. It over looks this meadow, facing toward the Tree Bridge. Here the two units can set up defensive positions and wait.

"Even though we will be in sight of the Tree Bridge from the top of this hill, we cannot risk the final push for the bridge until we have the whole army to help us. Anomos already has several units stationed guarding the approach to the bridge.

"If we succeed in making him believe Diakrina is with you on the mountaintop, he will, by this time, likely have determined to send units around to the other side of the mountaintop in order to trap you and set a siege. Once we have our defenses in place at Dorogon, I will come to you and give the signal to abandon the mountaintop and pour straight down the backside. Hopefully we can do this before any of his troops can circumvent the mountaintop and get into position behind you.

"This downhill retreat will give you speed and will allow your men to get some distance between you and Anomos' troops before they make it over the mountaintop. You are to head downward through the forest toward the meadow at full speed. We will wait at the northwest edge of the meadow in the ruins of Dorogon until you are close enough to fan out from us toward the Tree Bridge and become a ring of resistance all along the southwestern line of our path to the bridge.

"A third of your army is to proceed straight toward the Tree Bridge as you come down the mountain in order to draw out Anomos' units there. With this much of the army you should be able to make short work of them and then turn and help complete the wall of protection giving us guarded access to the bridge. Only then will we make our charge to gain the bridge."

Jared nodded his approval and immediately appointed the captain of the third unit to take charge of the remaining units when he and his unit, and the lead unit, separated from them. There was no need to repeat what Strateia had said for he had spoken out loud so all the warriors could hear.

Diakrina was troubled. The quest seemed to be reduced now to only getting her out of the reach of Anomos. There was no talk of recovering the Atheos. Surely, they must find a way to get it back. She wanted to ask Strateia about this, but there was presently no time for such questions and answers.

Then Strateia spoke to the warriors once more.

"I must warn all of you to keep your focus on this quest with a warrior's fighting resolve. Do not entertain fears of failure or of the enemy. Most of all do not entertain fears of the unknowns in the Mist Forest, which will be, at first, to your left, and then later, as you come down the backside of the mountain, all around you. The Mist needs time and focus to work its evil illusions and get its claws into you. Give it neither or it will claim you! If you dwell on fears, it will use them to distort your perception and generate your demise.

"This is especially important for those of you in the two units that will be with us as we cut through the Mist Forest. You must exercise courageous focus and resolve. Do not give attention to any of the illusions with which the Mist will attack. It acquires the power to give seeming reality to its illusions from your fear. Fear is ultimately a choice. Don't give in to it. Keep riding. Keep focused. Trust your horse's senses as they will be unaffected by the illusions the Mist is weaving.

"If anyone succumbs to the Mist, do not—I REPEAT—do not try to rescue them! It will only result in fighting shadows and you yourself will likely be overwhelmed. The result would be total disorganization of the units. You help each other best by keeping focused on the quest and each other and shouting encouragements. But do not play the Mist's game and try to fight the Mist to rescue one another.

"Unfortunately, in this situation, the only one who can free someone under the Mist's delusions is the warrior himself. Each of you must accept the courage and the strength from beyond—which the Living One will give to you if you seek it—to win the battle within: For it is there the stronghold of fear must be toppled."

Then Strateia stood up high in his stirrups and raised his voice slightly to add urgency to what he was about to say next.

"This quest to get Diakrina to the Tree Bridge must succeed. For if it fails, all hope for the Promise will be ripped from your future children. You alone, and your immediate offspring, could be saved: and that likely by death.

"If Anomos is able to create a race of evil immortals, he will use them to exterminate you. Your future generations will never come to exist. The promised Seed will never come. We must succeed!"

Jared raised a sword to the sky, as did all the others. "Sons of El, we will not fail!" he shouted. And then in unison all the men responded, "FOR THE SAKE OF THE PROMISE!"

Their shout had hardly died out when the scream of a Nekros echoed from the sky above them, then the scream of a second and then a third. Jared shouted, "Up the trail into the forest for cover!"

He then turned to Diakrina and Strateia shouting, "Follow me!" as he urged his horse into a dead run right behind the first unit of warriors.

Diakrina and Strateia did the same and all the other units came charging behind. Even though the Nekros dove toward them, fortunately they were into the forest in short order. The trees were large and completely overhanging the trail and thus gave good overhead protection from the Nekros, which ended up crashing into some of the treetops and raining down an avalanche of large limbs.

However, the agility of the horses came through and all the units were able to jump or dodge all the falling debris and make it deeper into the cover of the trees where the Nekros lost track of them due to the canopy being much too thick and formidable.

Clearly, the race was on.

Chapter Thirteen

NEKRO-MIST

As the units thundered into the forest the great canopy of trees blocked the direct light of the sun. The forest was composed of the very large, rough barked trees rising hundreds of feet into the air. The upper foliage was so dense only indirect light could reach them.

It took several minutes for Diakrina's eyes to fully adjust before she felt she could actually see far enough ahead to have some sense as to where the trail was going. Phos and the other horses, however, seemed to have little difficulty. The units galloped at breakneck speed through the winding maze of trails.

Almost immediately the trail began to have a rather steep, continual incline. They were clearly climbing the lower slopes of the mountain. Not far into the gallop Diakrina began to notice the trees becoming covered with the Spanish Moss-like hanging plants she had seen while climbing toward Sapient Castle. In the dim light this gave the whole forest a troubling and ominous look.

Yet, even more troubling, she soon became aware a mist was rolling toward them in the trees to their left. Once again there was the strange sight of a mist working its way uphill. (The forest to their left dropped away somewhat as the rise of the mountain was not only ahead of them, but also slightly to their right.) This mist was using the serpentine pattern of folding back on itself which Diakrina had witnessed when she encountered the Mist the first time. Instantly Diakrina knew this was no ordinary mist. This was, the Mist!

In spite of her resolve, a chill came over her at the very thought of this cold, bloodless obscenity. She shook her head and focused on the trail and Jared's horse just ahead of her. The less she looked at the Mist, and thought about its snaking, rolling presence the better.

Then they began making a wide arc slightly to the left for several hundred yards as the steepness of the trail leveled out for a short way. That is when Diakrina saw it. Up ahead of them, rolling across the trail, was a thick cloud. They were going to ride straight into the Mist.

Jared gave a signal of short blasts on his horn. It was a command for everyone to pull up closer to the rider in front of them. As it turned out, this meant a rider pulled his horse's head slightly to one side—say the right side—of the hindquarters of the horse in front of him. The rider behind him would then pull his horse up until his horse's head was slightly to the left of the hindquarters the horse ahead—and so on through the ranks.

This was done without slowing the pace. Its purpose was to make sure the units could stay coordinated when the visibility diminished.

And diminish it did! They hit the Mist, and the level of illumination became like dusk before sunset. Diakrina cringed with unpleasant memories. For at the same time they entered the Mist a cold stinging sensation hit her in the face. Very quickly her whole body began to chill.

Jared was forced to sound a signal to slow the pace. This was to ensure the captain of the lead unit could see far enough ahead to make decisions about the path forward.

Then she noticed it: "It was a presence." That is how Diakrina described it. The immediate sensation was of something—someone—being all around you—almost wrapped around you. Your flesh began to crawl with the sense of being touched all over: some invisible, cold, clammy thing. For Diakrina it was all too familiar.

The thickness of the Mist made it necessary for the units to slow their horses to a walk. They simply could not see far enough ahead to move any faster. Strateia came up beside Diakrina and placed a warm hand on her shoulder. He clearly understood what she was experiencing: a kind of terrible déjà vu. His strong, warm hand was reassuring in this cold, dark atmosphere.

Strateia then said to Jared, who was just ahead of them, "The trail will quickly begin to rise up ahead. It is possible we will get above this mist again."

"Understood," answered Jared.

On the heels of his response another voice spoke. It seemed to come from everywhere around them. It was a breathy, hissing voice. It was cold, hateful and taunting.

"Wherever you go, we will come.
Run! But speed will never give birth to enough distance."

If screaming a denial could have helped, Diakrina would have responded. Everything in her wanted to do so. (And likely, so did every warrior.) Yet she knew it would be useless. Still it was hard to let its proud taunts go unanswered. The very atmosphere, right up to your face, seemed filled with an arrogance sporting everyone's silence as surrender. It was a noiseless sneer provking you to respond, if you dared.

However, Diakrina knew from experience what it desired was to be engaged. To lure the focus on to its self so it could work its devilish, twisted illusions. She determined to give it no satisfaction.

Strateia pulled past Diakrina and up beside Jared.

"I will go to the front and lead with my sword. I can blaze a hole in front allowing us to move faster until we climb up above this foe."

He then pulled his sword, and crimson light caused the Mist all around him to recoil for several yards in all directions. Strateia galloped up ahead and Diakrina could see the Mist parting as he rode forward. Then, as it closed behind him, as he continued to the front of the units, the crimson light could only be subtly detected.

Jared gave a command on his horn, which meant to follow at the pace set and keep the ranks up tight and close. Almost immediately the horses were back to a slow gallop.

But the Mist was not finished. As they moved back into a gallop each began to hear that same hissing voice whispering in their ear. It seemed so close to you each of them felt as it they were the one being single out to be hissed at—though later they all confirmed it was happening to all of them at the same time.

Where do you think you are going?
There is no help up ahead.
I have already devoured your army.
Look around you in the trees and you will see.

Diakrina knew better than to look. Yet for some reason, she did. There in the whirling Mist she saw the forms of dead men hanging by ropes from limbs or impaled on branches. It was ghastly. The Mist was up to its tricks again.

Then she began to smell a terrible odor. It was the smell of rotting corpses. Even though she was trying not to look at the tortured bodies in the limbs of the trees, she could not escape the stench. It was horrifying.

Immediately she turned her head away and purposely fixed her eyes on the back of Jared's head while saying to herself repeatedly, "It's not true! It's not true!" Yet the hissing, whispering voice, which she could not pull her ears away from—it was like a buzzing mosquito in her ear canal she could not disengage—kept chanting the same things over and over in a slightly different order.

There is no help up ahead.
I have already devoured your army.
Look around you in the trees and you will see.
Where do you think you are going?

Then again it would say,

Look around you in the trees and you will see.

I have already devoured your army.
Where do you think you are going?
There is no help up ahead.

This different order, this scrambling of the same assertions, had the effect of highjacking your attention. It fixed it against their will on what the Mist was saying. They were almost afraid not to listen in case it didn't merely chant the same things and added something different which they needed to be on their guard against. But the constant scrambling was just a ploy. It was a way of causing you to listen closely to the same fear-generating rants repeatedly.

Once again Diakrina could feel a damp, depressive sense of hopelessness attempting to wrap itself around her. Fear was trying to coil around her like a python. What if these images in the trees were real? Could the Mist have killed all the army, or perhaps, even a major portion of it?

Diakrina found herself holding the end of the single rein in one hand and using both her hands to cover her ears. But the effect quickly reminded her this was not the answer. As before, it was like sticking her head in a large fifty-five gallon drum. It made the voice resonate and roll around in her head.

Diakrina began a countering, resisting chant in her mind, "I cannot hear you. I cannot hear you. I cannot hear you," over and over. While she was doing this she also heard a warrior behind her groan a loud, "Shut up!" Yet, other than this one loss of nerve, she never heard another single response from any of the warriors.

To her relief they began to climb back up the mountain as the trail turned again to the right. They were soon riding out above the Mist. The relief from the stinging cold, the hissing voice and the nauseating stench was instantaneous. Strateia put his sword away and slowed down until he was back riding close behind Diakrina. The captain of the first unit resumed his post leading the gallop.

"Strateia," Diakrina asked in a nervous voice, "were those bodies in the trees real?"

"No, Little One. Only two warriors were lost to the army as

it marched through here. And there is yet a possibility they will be recovered or find their way out of the Mist Forest before it claims them."

"This gave Diakrina a momentary surge of hope. If more than fifteen-hundred men came up this mountain and only two were overcome, then it was possible to resist this cold serpent and beat it at its game.

They now gained altitude quickly. The strength of the horses was pushed to the limits to keep the pace as quickly as Jared and Strateia demanded. And all the while, Diakrina couldn't help occasionally looking over her shoulder to confirm the Mist was not overtaking them.

Within another forty-five minutes of hard riding, they came to where the steep rise leveled out. The trail turned almost straight south. The trees were still above them, but they were starting to thin out up ahead.

Jared sounded a command for everyone to come to a halt. As they were stopping, Diakrina caught sight of the reason. Up ahead, not more than a hundred yards or so, the trees ceased, and the trail began winding up through boulders on a very steep rise toward the summit. This was likely where Strateia intended for the front two units to separate from the others and continue east around the base of this summit, keeping well beneath the forest canopy.

Here there was an open space among the trees straddling the trail. It was large enough for all the units to gather in a circle around Jared, Strateia and Diakrina. As soon as all the warriors were in place, Strateia spoke.

"This is where the first two units will separate and head around the base of the mountaintop toward the ruins of Dorogon." Then turning to Jared, "By now your army has heard your commands on the horn and knows of your approach to the base of this summit. You should signal the army to have every warrior string his bow and prepare to give your six units cover as they make their way up the summit. I have no doubt the Nekros will appear as soon as you are in the open without the cover of the canopy.

"While the Nekros will not risk trying to attack the army directly—as the archers would bring them down—they will try to pick off the men while they are trying to scale the peak. So, it is imperative the army move close enough to the top of the north face of the peak, so their archers are in range to provide cover."

Jared nodded his agreement and turned to the captain of the third unit.

"Captain Arioch, you are in charge of the six units. We will be ready to leave once you have the units ready to take the summit. When you are ready, sound the command for the army above to provide you with cover. Give Captain Moreh five minutes to get the men in place. Then, without delay, give the command to make for the top."

"Meanwhile," added Strateia, "while their attention is on you and the warriors, we will start for Dorogon."

"Understood, sir," answered Arioch, as he whirled his horse around and began for the base of the summit so he could assess the best formation for organizing the advance. Within minutes he returned and began giving orders regarding the formations. The units organized themselves quickly. Meanwhile, Jared and the captain of the first unit, whose name was Kedar, led Diakrina, along with Strateia, slightly out into the trees east of the trail.

The forest to the east dropped away down an embankment before it leveled out again. It was clear from the tops of the trees to the east it then began a slight rise as it circumscribed the base of the summit. (The trail they were on was, at this point, on a small ridge which stretched south to join the summit.) When they had found a place promising for descending into the woods, they gathered to await Captain Arioch's signal.

Within a few moments Arioch's horn sounded a series of commands. After a few seconds they were answered from the top of the mountain. Diakrina sat on Phos looking out over the trees below where they were about to descend. In just a few moments, after Captain Aroich had given Captain Moreh the prescribed five minutes to get the army in place, they would gallop down this hill into the Mist Forest and begin their race for the ruins Strateia had called Dorogon, while the other six units fought their way to the mountaintop.

At the same time Diakrina heard Arioch's horn sound the charge for the summit, Jared nodded at Captain Kedar to move out. It was then Diakrina took one last look over the forest before urging Phos forward.

Her eyes widened. Slithering through the trees below was the serpentine Mist.

Chapter Fourteen

ATTACK OF THE NEKRO-MIST

As the horses lunged into action down the slope toward the forest below, Strateia, who had also seen the slithering Mist begin working its way through the trees, urged Phulasso forward to overtake Captain Kedar. He drew his sword and took the point. To Diakrina, Strateia looked like he was leading a battle charge into the Mist at the head of the two units.

When Strateia reached the bottom of the slope and galloped into the trees, he hit the Mist almost immediately. The crimson rays of his sword caused the Mist to recoil in every direction away from him. Some of the Mist was vaporized when the rays from his blade hit it. You could see a remnant of floating steam in the air where the Mist had been.

As before, there was the stinging, wet cold hitting each of them in the face as the Mist surrounded them. Even though Strateia was making a cleared trail through the forest where the Mist was vaporized or had been forced to recoil, there was still enough of the cold vapor remaining to emulate a bitter cold day.

What is more, for those in the second unit, the Mist closed back on them before they could reach the temporary, ever-advancing Mist-free path Strateia was creating. This made visibility a major issue as they could only partially discern the rays from the crimson sword but could not see much of anything else.

Earlier, when they had been on the trail, it had been possible to merely follow the crimson light ahead and keep pace by following the path. However, here in the forest, where there was no set path, and Strateia was constantly weaving and dodging to find a way forward, it became nearly impossible for the second unit to keep up. They could not see limbs in time to dodge them or discern the forms of trees which were immediately in front of them.

Diakrina was at the back of the first unit where she was riding next to Jared. They were riding at the place where the ever-advancing clearing Strateia was making through the Mist was starting to close again. Jared and Diakrina became aware the gap between themselves and the second unit was growing ever greater.

The captain of this unit, whose name was Jaros, was forced to sound a signal on his horn calling for the pace to be slowed. The two units were quickly being separated and that was unacceptable.

Strateia slowed up and, turning in his saddle, called back to Diakrina.

"Diakrina, take out your sword and do as I do. Your light will part the Mist for the unit behind you."

Diakrina immediately wondered to herself why she had not thought to do this on her own. She later concluded her earlier experience in the cave with the Mist had so deeply impacted her she was too preoccupied with its presence to be properly engaged in what needed to be done.

She immediately pulled her sword. The crimson blade pushed back the Mist for ten yards in all directions. Strateia turned forward again and reset the pace. The result was the unit bringing up the rear was now riding within the clearing generated by Diakrina's sword as the pace was fast enough for them to utilize the clearing before the Mist could recoil.

The mountaintop was to their right. It soon became evident there would be several streams coming down the mountain. As these streams crossed their path they would have to be forded.

This seldom yielded to a straightforward solution as the streams often coursed down deep cuts in the mountainside. This made it necessary for them to navigate large boulders, crumbling rockslides and slippery, wet, left-sloping inclines which took them over smooth slabs of stone. This not only slowed the pace considerably but also resulted in several slides or short tumbles of a horse and rider. However, the warriors were so agile, as were their horses, the rider would immediately make a flying dismount in the uphill direction allowing his horse to utilize the terrain below him to regain his feet.

Once or twice, this resulted in a horse and rider sliding far enough downhill to the left they disappeared into the Mist. However, all knew not to try to render aid by pursuing them into the rolling cloud. In every case, the horse and rider were able to regain their feet and rejoin their unit without much delay.

They came upon an area where several of these streams where pouring down the mountain through deep cuts. This made it necessary for them to slow down and pick their way down and then back up the opposite side of these stream-filled ravines. It was here, where they slowed to make the crossings, they caught the sound of battle behind them up the mountain. They could hear screams of Nekros. There were various commands discernable as the commander of the forces atop the mountain shouted orders to the archers.

Diakrina found herself praying for the men in the other six units. She hoped the Living One would help them to prevail without much loss of life. From the sound of it there were several Nekros engaging them. The creatures were not only trying to destroy them, but they were also trying to slow them up so Anomos' warriors—which could not be too far behind—could catch up before they made good the mountaintop.

Then they heard a great crash. Something large obviously fell into the treetops close to where the warriors were ascending. It seemed the archers had eliminated at least one Nekros from the skies. While everyone glanced back over their shoulder toward the southwest, there was no time to stop and listen.

Once they navigated the streams, they were off again picking their way through the forest. From here they were starting to skirt the mountaintop's lower slopes. It was now possible to turn somewhat southeast, which pointed them in the direction of the Tree Bridge.

However, there was still some climbing to do as the lower reaches of the mountain stretched out as a sloping ridge for several miles toward the northwest. It was this ridge they would have to ride over. Riding down its other side is where they would find the ruins on the hill Strateia had called Dorogon.

As they were riding southeast and about to begin ascending the sides of the ridge crossing in front of them, in the east—in the area below them and to their left—they began to hear very loud, high-pitched sounds. At first everyone assumed it was the Mist up to its usual tricks. And as it turned out, this was not totally untrue. But they were about to find they had more than the Mist to deal with.

When Strateia heard these high-pitched sounds he immediately, without slowing his horse, handed the rein of Phulasso to Captain Kedar and told him to slow up until he returned—this is because they would momentarily be without the benefits of the crimson light from his sword. He then vanished. He couldn't have been gone more than ten seconds when he suddenly reappeared, remounted on Phulasso.

"Quick, we need to find a defensive position, now!" shouted Strateia.

He then pointed to the right where a portion of the mountain dropped off above them, creating a fifty-foot-high cliff. He turned Phulasso toward it, and without waiting for the captain to give any commands, shouted, "Follow me! Now! There is no time to lose!" And with that Strateia began leading a retreat toward the base of the cliff. No questions were asked. The urgency in Strateia's voice said all.

At the base of the cliff there were rock formations spreading out in a shallow, outward arching, horseshoe shape from the center of the cliff in both directions. When they were within a few yards of the cliff, Strateia, who had clearly taken command for the moment, directed the two captains and Jared to create a defensive line across the mouth of the horseshoe by deploying both units in an arching line.

Jared, quickly understanding the intent of this tactic, took hold of the left side of Phos' bridle with his right hand and galloped toward the central area beneath the cliff with Diakrina in tow. There he and

Diakrina dismounted just in time to hear Strateia shout to all the warriors.

"Arm yourselves with bows and arrows." This the warriors immediately began doing even while Strateia continued. "Large serpents are coming. Some are false—the product of the Mist. But mixed in with these phantom serpents are real ones. This is going to be very confusing and dangerous—for it will be very hard to determine which are false and which are real.

"The only safe strategy is to shoot at every serpent you see. It is the only way to engage the real ones, which will be using the Mist-generated serpents as decoys in which to mingle. Be prepared to use your sword as well. For in the confusion some will likely break through and it will become necessary to engage them by hand."

No sooner had Strateia's commands been given than ten to twelve sets of red, glowing, unblinking eyes appeared in the Mist. The eyes were some twenty feet in the air. They were just out in front of the line the warriors had formed. Right behind each set of eyes was a large serpent head beginning to slowly advance toward them.

"Shoot now!" came Strateia's command. And with tremendous skill and speed the warriors in unison let go a volley of arrows. Many clearly struck the mark and the writhing body of several large snakes—instantly in death throes—began coiling out of the Mist in every direction. This created the need for the warriors to duck and leap trying to avoid their large twisting coils. Some of the warriors simply could not get out of the way and were knocked violently to the ground and steamrolled by the bodies of the serpents.

But all this was the least of their problems. For while the warriors had all shot at the heads of serpents—both real and false—each being about twenty feet in the air, unseen were three or four real serpents advancing slightly behind the others. They were coming in low, slithering at ground level.

What turned the attention of the warriors to these low approaching serpents was the writhing, twisting bodies of the dying serpents, which had been struck with arrows, began colliding with the serpents advancing closer to the ground. This had two beneficial results: it caused the warriors to become aware of these other advancing serpents and it also hindered the serpents enough it gave the warriors time to refit another volley.

One viper, on the left side of the defensive wall, was too close to be stopped. And before any arrow could be shot, he struck at two warriors who were fighting side by side. A warrior was skewered through on one of the serpent's fangs. The other was able to swing down with his sword with a blocking motion on the serpent's other fang in time to deflect it. Yet the head of the serpent recoiled sideways as it passed him and sent him flying through the air up against a part of the cliff wall. This motion of the serpent also dislodged the warrior it had just killed from its fang and sent his body crashing onto several other warriors.

The immediate problem was this serpent was now through the defenses. It was inside the wall of warriors and not far from Jared and Diakrina, which is exactly where it immediately headed. Yet it was not fast enough to reach them before Strateia moved swiftly between Jared and Diakrina to block its path.

The serpent recoiled for a moment preparing a strike. When it did strike its speed was no match for Strateia. Before the head of the serpent could get halfway toward him, he had leaped to the right. When the serpent's head and body reached the full extent of its strike—which put its fangs only feet from Jared and Diakrina—Strateia's sword found its mark. The head of the serpent was severed from its body. And while the head fell gaping to the ground, the body recoiled in a fit of spasms that tied the serpent into writhing knots.

The result was its twisting coils knocked down warriors in all directions. This meant there had to be a quick scramble to reform the defenses. As the men were attempting to close ranks, it became clear another serpent on the far right had managed to penetrate the defenses undetected in the confusion.

It was fortunate Diakrina had her sword in her hand and was ready. For Jared was on her left, with his back to her, as he had positioned himself between her and the first advancing serpent. He, nor Strateia, realized what was happening behind them.

What Diakrina saw was two serpents coming fast. There was no way to know if both were real or not. But she was certain at least one of them was no phantom. For what had caused her to turn and take notice was hearing a commotion behind her and to the right. The serpent, or serpents, had crashed through several warriors, sending them sprawling in all directions.

There was no time to cry for help. They were too close for that. But which one should she engage? If one was false and the other real and she engaged the wrong one, the other would overcome her. If they both were real she was in a lot of trouble!

While Diakrina was gripping her sword and staring in fearful confusion at the two advancing horrors, suddenly everything seemed to go into slow motion. As it did the sound of the battle around her also seemed to be muffled and recede as if at a great distance. Then she heard it.

A firm, peaceful and golden voice spoke: "THE SERPENT STRIKING AT YOU WILL BE THE FALSE ONE. FOR THE REAL SERPENT INTENDS TO CAPTURE YOU IN ITS JAWS. THEY WANT YOU ALIVE. PAY NO ATTENTION TO THE STRIKING SERPENT BUT GIVE ALL YOUR ATTENTION TO THE OTHER."

As everything seemed for those few moments to be moving in slow motion—though it makes much more sense to say that Diakrina and her awareness had been so accelerated everything around her, which was moving at normal speed, seemed to be slowed down in comparison—Diakrina took note the serpent on the right was raising up into a striking position while the other, on the left, was lowering its head and twisting its gaping mouth over so the roof of its mouth was advancing on her left and its lower jaw advancing to her right.

The serpent raised into the striking position suddenly struck forward to engage her first, before the jaws of the actual serpent reached her. It seemed so odd to Diakrina she had time to take notice of all this and think to herself, "That serpent on the right is the phantom and it is striking first in order to get me to engage it instead of the other serpent, which is the real threat."

She turned her full attention to the serpent on the left. Right before its head thrust forward the head of the phantom struck. But Diakrina gave it no notice. It was only later she remembered as the phantom reached her the rays of the sword vaporized it. She remembered this by recalling the cold mist splashing across the right side of her face and body.

Right behind the strike of the phantom came the jaws of the real serpent. Diakrina was ready to defend herself. She was determined to cut through the roof of its mouth as it lunged at her. But before she could strike at it, the serpent had miscalculated its lunge and the front side of one of its fangs hit her. It sent her stumbling backwards away from the serpent's mouth. However, the serpent kept coming forward in order to engulf her. But she was able to keep her feet enough to regain her balance. The result was as the fangs rushed past her, she was still facing the top of the serpent's mouth with her sword over her head ready to strike.

And strike she did—straight down into the serpent's upper mouth! She bore down with all the strength of her body into the sword. The crimson sword did not fail her. It cut through the serpent right behind its fangs. And the flesh of the viper presented little resistance to it.

The result was the whole of the snake's upper mouth, with its fangs and nose, were cut clean away. When the snake's mouth snapped shut it had no roof to its mouth to close on Diakrina.

The recoil of the snake's head to the left, away from Diakrina's sword, caused its lower, inside jaw to hit her in the back, just as she was finishing her stroke. This sent her cartwheeling in the same direction the snake's severed nose and fangs had gone. This nearly resulted in Diakrina being pierced through by one of the severed fangs as she flew up in the air and missed coming down on a fang's point only by inches. However, she did miss it and fell onto the roof of the serpent's severed mouth and slid to a stop between its two upright sabers.

By this time Jared had seen what was transpiring. He ran toward the serpent and landed a terrible blow at the underside of its throat, which cut part way through its mass and evidently severed its spinal cord. While the head went limp, it was still attached to the rest of the body, which like all the other dying serpents began writhing and rolling so it pulled the head of the viper into the air half severed and flopping back and forth.

In the meantime, the other warriors had gotten off several more volleys of arrows at serpents true and false. And the result was all the real serpents had been finished. And when the Mist realized the actual serpents were defeated, the counterfeit ones dissolved into the featureless cloud all around them.

Strateia, however, was not satisfied and flew into the Mist and disappeared. There was a momentary sound of battle and then the sound of a serpent's body could be heard thrashing about in the forest. When he reappeared, it was clear the battle was over for the moment.

"I was sure there would be at least one serpent in reserve," said Strateia. "If it had been able to return to Anomos, its return without the others would have signaled it had been involved in a conflict and would have tipped our hand. As it is, let us hope the return of none of them will cause Anomos to assume they encountered nothing on their patrol through the Mist Forest."

"But won't the Mist reach Anomos and his warriors and inform them?" asked Diakrina.

"Fortunately, the Mist has been too preoccupied with catching us on its own with the aid of the serpents, which it knew were coming. It wanted the credit for Diakrina's capture for itself to gain power in Parad. But you are right the Mist will have no recourse now but to attempt to catch up to Anomos and inform him. We must hope his troops are high enough up the mountainside, above the tree line, in pursuit of the others, the Mist will not be able to climb to him in time to inform him before we reach Dorogon."

Then Strateia turned to Jared. "You may leave four warriors behind to prepare the body of your lost warrior to be brought to us at Dorogon, where you may there release him to the Living One before you take him home with you. But the others must leave with us now. No matter how well things go, we haven't much time left."

"Understood," answered Jared.

He then instructed Captain Jaros, to whose unit the fallen warrior belonged, to make the necessary arrangements quickly. This was done and then Jared sounded the command for all the units to remount and move out. Only four of the other warriors stayed behind to wrap and prepare the body of their brother to be moved. They were also from Captain Jaros' unit, and this meant his unit of sixteen was now down to eleven soldiers until the others rejoined them at Dorogon.

Chapter Fifteen

DECENT TO DOROGON

Once again Strateia took the lead. And once again Diakrina used her sword to clear the way for Captain Jaros. The Mist was still all around them in the forest. But as they began to ride up the ridge, they soon rode out above it.

The forest still surrounded them, but the trees were not as thick here on the ridge. This allowed some sunlight to penetrate. The immediate warmth of the air—now the Mist was behind them—and the light of the sun dancing on the ground as it shone through the breeze-stirred branches of the trees above, raised Diakrina's spirit. It was suddenly a bright, summer-like day.

It was now close to midday: the morning had been packed with riding and fighting. Strateia, however, seemed to be in no mood to slow their pace. Now the Mist was gone he did, however, relinquish the lead to Captain Kedar. But Diakrina heard Strateia urge him to keep a quick pace.

They soon topped the ridge and began down its other side, remaining always under the canopy of the forest. When they came to the place where the forest ended, the order was given to halt well under the trees to use them to conceal their presence from any Nekros which might be overhead or from any of Anomos' warriors down below. From this spot where the forest cleared out ahead of them, they were still quite high and could see out over the terrain below.

There in the distance was the jagged, immense scar of the great chasm. And on its far side, shrouded somewhat by a haze of golden light, was the Garden. Just the sight of the Garden caused Diakrina's heart to leap into her throat from longing. A powerful sense of what could only be described as an otherworldly intensified homesickness hit Diakrina hard.

In fact, the sensation was so intense, even though it was a very private, psychological event happening in her innermost being, it seemed to fill the very atmosphere—so much so Diakrina had an accompanying sensation of self-consciousness making her feel what was going on inside her had attracted the attention, somehow, of everyone around her. This caused Diakrina to glance around momentarily to see if the others were staring at her.

They were not. In fact, next to Diakrina was Jared. What she saw on his countenance instantly corrected her misconception. If ever a look of longing and homesickness could be written on a face, it was written on his. Diakrina could never be sure—for to have stared at Jared would have seemed like an improper intrusion into his most intimate and secret longings—yet it seemed to her she detected a hint of tears rimming Jared's eyes as he gazed transfixed at the light-shrouded country beyond the chasm.

Then it hit her. Jared had heard of this place all his life. It was the forbidden land from which his great, great, great grandfather, whom he knew and loved, had been exiled. It was the true homeland which he could never see and to which he could never return.

As Diakrina turned her gaze again toward the Garden, it hit her the terrible chasm had never seemed so cruel. In Jared's face she was seeing a pain-saturated longing, which she was sure only someone so close to the fact of the exile could feel with the intensity Jared clearly was experiencing.

In that moment she understood in a new way the terrible ache at the center of all mankind. The sense of loss, the sense of exile, the sense of hearing mere echoes of some music—if only you could truly hear even once—would fill your soul. Such music would quench your deepest thirst and feed your deepest hungers by resolving every soul-twisting question you had ever formed. These questions were constant and passionate desires for … one knows not what … which people of later times would still experience from afar, even though they would be separated from the reality of this Home by an impenetrable mist of time. This, and this truly, was the connectedness of every human soul to something beyond the world's rim: and through this common longing, the connection of every human soul to each other.

Clearly the Spring of Longings flowed with an irresistible current through the whole of human history. It was mankind's common infection—a good infection. And here, so near its source, the current of those longings clearly ran deep and powerful.

A quick, stolen glance around her confirmed every warrior was experiencing the same. This was a shared/private experience: all experienced it; all knew the others experienced it; yet each had such a personal and unique engagement with the moment, it was truly intimate and deeply—almost embarrassingly—personal (though there was really nothing to be embarrassed about). But you could not help—for some reason—but feel your most sacred secret had been suddenly spilled out into full view of the world.

However, a sense of proper decorum was also shared. Each attended to his own soul while being intensely aware everyone around him was properly doing the same.

Diakrina often wondered out loud as to why we are so awkward in such moments. "Could it be," she asked one day, "that our first experiences of these longings, our most transparent engagement of them—though often in false forms—is when we are children? Could it be because they get mingled, like tea in water, with our childish fantasies and dreams? Do we then forever after mistakenly associate them with things we rightly put away when we became adults? Is this why we become so awkward, feeling like an adult male getting caught playing with toy cars? Perhaps this could be one of the reasons He said to us, "Unless you become like little children you cannot enter the Kingdom of the heavens."

She often, as she did on this occasion, left these questions and possibilities hanging in the air without further comment.

It was Strateia who ultimately broke the silence engulfing each of them that day. He pointed to the terrain beyond and said, "There—below us, to the left somewhat, on the top of that cliff in the stand of trees near the chasm—are the ruins of Dorogon."

Strateia then pointed beyond it to where the gaping mouth of the chasm was just disappearing over the horizon. "There is the Tree Bridge. In the forest just beyond the meadow below the cliffs of Dorogon, Anomos has several units stationed to guard the access to the Bridge. We will take up defenses for now in the ruins on the hill.

"Jared," Strateia continued, "as you can see the forest ends beyond us and the descent toward Dorogon is a forestless descent sloping into the small meadow in front of the cliffs of Dorogon. To our left, however, there is a branch of this ridge circling toward the chasm. Down its slopes the forest descends unbroken to the top of Dorogon from behind.

"We need to arc back to our left staying in the trees along this ridge until we have reached the branch of this ridge descending behind Dorogon. This will put Dorogon between us and the meadow beyond it. By descending through the forest of this ridge it will allow us to reach Dorogon without being detected by Anomos' units. Once we have set up defenses in Dorogon, I will go to Captain Moreh and Captain Arioch on top of the mountain to signal the beginning of their quick advance down the backside of the peak."

"Understood," responded Jared. Then turning to Captain Jaros, he said, "Leave one warrior here to wait for the others to guide them into Dorogon by the same route we take. We cannot risk them alerting the enemy units."

"Yes, sir," responded Captain Jaros.

Jared then said to Captain Jaros and Captain Kedar, "Pass the word through all your men we are to ride in silence. Use only hand signals."

"Yes, sir," answered both captains.

Both units of warriors turned left and stayed well behind the tree line and the immediate summit of the ridge in order to be hidden from any watching eyes in the forest below beyond the meadow. They soon came to the place where the ridge branched into two: the main ridge arcing back toward the northeast, while a smaller branch turned slightly and continued due east with a downhill slop.

They followed this eastern branch which was still adequately forested. Though the ridge dropped slightly in elevation along its top as it extended toward the east, the first part of the ridge was still high enough over the meadow below and the ridge out in front of them—which extended southward and then ended at the ruins—they were looking somewhat down on the ruins of Dorogon still out ahead of them and to their right. They traveled this land bridge, picking their way through the trees, until it reached the area behind Dorogon.

There, behind Dorogon, the ridge narrowed into a long land-bridge. It then continued beyond the back of Dorogon going east toward the chasm. However, it was here the ridge on which Dorogon was built reached back to them and intersected this land bridge from the south. Its southern most point ended at the ruins which sat atop a large cliff where the ridge overlooked the meadow below it.

Because the forest thinned out as it approached the backside of Dorogon, the whole of the ruins were quite visible against the sky. Diakrina could make out, from occasional glimpses between the trees, it had the ruins of a large castle at its center, which towered over everything else around it. What was around it seemed to be the remains of a small but once prosperous village. The castle walls were high but breached and tumbled in several places. It clearly showed the signs of having undergone a devastating siege.

They descended until they reached the spine of this ridge which descend into the backside of Dorogon. Here Jared motioned for everyone to come to a halt. He signaled to Captain Kedar who approached him.

"I think it would be wise to send at least four men quietly on foot down into the ruins before we descend. It is not beyond possibility they have stationed a small detachment of warriors as watchmen from the top of Dorogon. Several of the men in your unit are known for their stealth ability. Select your best and send them ahead of us. If the detachment is small enough they can take care of it quietly. However, if it is too large for them to manage, they are to return here to us so that we can, from their report, determine the best method of dealing with them."

"I agree, sir," said Captain Kedar. "But may I suggest an even further precaution. The area behind Dorogon is quite open for several hundred yards. If there is a unit stationed there, they will keep an eye on this natural , descending approach. However, off to the right of this open area, slightly down on the sides of the connecting ridge, there is a boulder field. The boulders are quite large and extend well past the back of the castle and to its south side. If the men use the boulder field, though it will take a little longer, it will allow them to approach the castle ruins without detection and slip into the ruins of the village coming from the west side. This would keep the men out of sight until they have actually been able to get in among the ruins."

"Good plan, Captain," responded Jared. "We will dismount here and give the men time to make the approach by that route."

Four warriors were immediately briefed and sent down the ridge on foot. Everyone else dismounted and gave the horses some time to nibble on the patches of grass lying between the trees.

Diakrina wanted to stretch her legs and asked Strateia if it would be alright if they took a short walk, as she knew he would never allow her to walk alone. He consented and motioned to the east where the ridge they had been following continued to descend amid adequate tree coverage.

Strateia informed Jared where they were going so he would not be concerned. They then began a moderate pace along the ridge. The sun was high in the sky and the slight breeze coming up the south side of the ridge made it a very pleasant, summer-like day.

Diakrina realized this was the first time she had been given any leisure to talk with Strateia since her capture and rescue from Parad. She was full of questions and decided to use these few moments to seek answers.

"Strateia, Parad … the place the Monk took me … it confuses me. I realize it was another out-of-body experience or what those in my time would call a near-death experience, an NDE. But if I was in the realms of Anomos, why was it so beautiful? The whole experience, except for the conflict over the sword, was incredibly wonderful. The explosion of light, color, and beauty. A sense of love seemed to engulf me constantly. The sense of being fully alive and filled with joy, how could it all be evil?"

Strateia, who was slightly ahead of Diakrina, pulled up short and turned toward her. "The very nature of evil is the misuse of the good and beautiful. Experiencing the incredible beauties of the spirit realm, which even in its fallen state can be very overwhelming for your kind, is often mistakenly taken for an experience of Heaven. It is an experience of the heavenly—in the sense this the word is used to describe the spiritual realms. But, as you know, all that is spiritual is not good.

"Diakrina, you must realize by now evil can use the spiritually beautiful to deceive just as it can use the physically beautiful to deceive? The things you experienced were spiritual beauties under the control of evil. They are beauties all the same. Yet they are being utilized to pull a mask over evil's twisted face. While evil can use and misuse the good and beautiful, it cannot create it or sustain it. As I have already taught you, evil is a parasite. It feeds on the good. It uses up the good. But it cannot create or sustain the good."

"But Strateia, the sense of warmth, compassion and empathy coming from the one on that throne—Anomos, I assume—was not anything like I imagined. Is he really a loving and caring being?"

"Far from it!" responded Strateia with a flash of defiance in his eyes. "What you experienced was pure sacrilege. It was the profaning of sensations intended to be engendered by true compassion. They were instead misused in the service of evil. For he intended—in your word, felt—nothing of compassion, love or affection for you. It was pure manipulation. The moment he achieves his desire with a victim, the mask comes off and nothing but evil's distorted face is left. But the mask he weaves himself, by means of these highjacked joys and beauties, is his most dangerous face. It is, therefore, the most evil.

"He deceives and manipulates as he slowly—and often with little to no detection by his victim—attaches his chains of bondage. When it is done, he throws down his disguises and terrifies his victim while laughing at their stunned bewilderment.

"As I told you before, it is the serpent hidden in the gifted bouquet which is the ultimate twist and betrayal. A serpent unhidden and clearly seen can be dealt with more easily."

Diakrina thought for a moment and then said, "There is, then, a great deception going on in my time. Many are claiming such experiences are experiences of God and Heaven. They use them to basically teach all are ultimately cured of evil, and evil does not really exist. They tell people everyone obtains peace and bliss after death."

"It is nothing new, even in your time," interjected Strateia. "This is a very old face of evil. Many of the mystery religions of the pagans were founded on such experiences. And unfortunately, as many in your time who are followers of the true faith are becoming more and more ignorant of what the Living One has said and taught, such deceptions are having a profound impact once again, even among follower of the Living One."

"So," asked Diakrina, "has anyone making the claim to have been near death and seen Heaven and the Living One actually experienced it for real?"

"Yes. Just because there are false experiences does not negate the true ones."

"Then how does one know which are true and which are false?" asked Diakrina.

"By measuring all experienced against the revelation of the Living One given in the Great Book. The Living One is utter truth. Therefore, He never contradicts Himself. This is why He gave you the Great Book.

"Both the spiritual and the physical must be judged by its truth. The Great Book is a standard—a measuring rod, if you please—by which you are made safe from errors and lies if you give heed to it. Not only has He revealed all necessary to protect you, He gives His Spirit to those who truly seek to understand the Great Book. The Spirit provides them discernment and guidance."

"So," interjected Diakrina, "no matter how beautiful and overwhelming such an experience may be, it must conform to the clear teachings of the Living One found in the Great Book? In other words, if He has stated the truth of something in its pages, that truth cannot be invalidated by our experience. Correct?"

"Correct!"

"One more thing, Diakrina. Toward the end of your age the evil ones will use many false, very different, NDEs, attempting to invalidate the power of the Good News. People will have hellish experiences and will claim to have seen many of the Living One's truest servants and leaders, in eternal Hell. It is a subtle claim that faith in the Living One does not rescue eternally and the power of His sacrifice is too weak to keep them from being condemned. It is an attempt to destroy people's faith in the promises of the Living One that those who truly put their trust in Him will never be put to shame.

"Of course, there are false followers and deceitful false teacher and leaders, and yes, many of them in a true near-death-experience might be observed in the dark doom of torment awaiting their eternal sentence and the Lake of Fire. It is the mixing of these false NDE dramas with the true which they will use to obscure the truth and to destroy faith."

While Diakrina would have liked to speak more about this, she had another question eating at her and she did not know how much longer this short pause in their journey would last. So, she changed the subject as they turned to resume their walk.

"Strateia, what of the Atheos? How are we to get it back?"

"Everything concerning the Atheos will be made plain to you soon enough. However, I need to make something clear to you." Here Strateia paused. He seemed to be trying to decide how best to explain what he was about to say, or perhaps he may have been listening for instructions as to what to say. Diakrina could never be sure which it was.

"Diakrina … your quest will soon come to its end. Already it is a success. The Atheos has been secured from the realms of Thanatos. Anomos will not be able to bring eternal damnation to the whole surviving human race by means of it, for it is now locked safe within the crystal container of infinite light.

"If you please, you may think of this infinite light as the boundary where the Living One's sovereignty has now set a limit to the evil that can be done to your race. As long as the Atheos is in the crystal container of infinite light, the graver aspects of its misuse have been forever eliminated.

"As you know, the fragrance from the Atheos can still cause much chaos among men …" and here Strateia paused for a moment, then continued, "… and will."

"What!" interrupted Diakrina. "No, Strateia, you don't mean … surely you can't mean … that we are not going to get it back, do you?"

Strateia did not immediately answer. He simply paused and looked out over the terrain below them. The look on his face made it seem to Diakrina he was not just looking out over the landscape but was gazing down through time. And, as if, coming to her time, he turned slowly toward her.

"Right now, that is not the most important issue, Diakrina."

"Then tell me, what is?" she begged.

"It is you. You are the one weakness in the crystal container."

"But I would never … I couldn't … I would die first!"

"Peace, Little One. I know you mean every word of it. And in a sense it is true. But it is not enough."

"What do you mean?" gasped Diakrina. "You surely know by now I would do anything to finish the quest!"

"That I do," answered Strateia. "But hear me out."

It was hard, but Diakrina held her peace and let Strateia continue.

"You have already seen how they work. They would not give you the option of death. And you have experienced how they have their ways of exerting their will over you. The Living One is not going to let that happen. We must get you beyond their reach."

A question suddenly came to Diakrina, and she blurted it out. "How do they know that I can unlock the crystal container?"

"Such containers are common in the higher realms. They are used to carry one's sacred trust, which is the secret name and identity known only to the Living One and the one to whom it is given. They are normally very small and can fit into the palm of the hand and look like a white stone though they are actually a container.

"Anomos and his minions did not recognize this one as being such a container because the Living One disguised it as a large crystal water bottle—a canteen—as you would call it. These too are common. They are normally not made of infinite light. While they can be locked with a word, and unlocked by repeating that same word backwards, they are not indestructible.

"They have, of course, discovered by now this container is indestructible and know what they are truly up against. And it did not take much insight for them to realize you were the one who put the Atheos in the container—as you were the only one present when it was retrieved in Nekus Canyon. They know you are the key to opening it. This is why they are determined to capture you and why we must be sure they cannot."

"But Strateia, if the Atheos remains among men, even within the crystal container of infinite light, the fragrance, as we have seen, will drive men mad. They will kill and slaughter each other to obtain it. Surely the Living One does not want this to happen."

"Most certainly He does not wish it to happen. However, within the parameters of His higher will, his prime directive of limited, but real freedom for His creatures bearing His image, it may be necessary. But we will see."

"Strateia, I don't understand that! It doesn't make sense to me. The Living One is all-powerful. He could see to it we get the Atheos back. Wouldn't this be His highest will in this case? Isn't that what He wanted me to do?"

"It is what He wished. And He certainly has the power to do as you say. But it is not His highest will. His highest will is to have a creation where genuine, though limited, freedom births the possibility of love and responsibility. If He simply overwhelmed every abuse of freedom by His creatures, then their freedom would be an illusion and so would be any love, meaning or purpose in all their lives.

"He has made us love-capable, purpose-capable and

relationship-capable. This is His highest will—this is His sovereign purpose. It is the prime directive of all moral creation. This means while He has set the boundaries tight enough to ensure the ultimate outcome, He has purposely given enough freedom so the path to the outcome can be, and often is, altered by His creatures.

"This is His will: a world of meaningful relationships which must include risk. Not risk to Him. But there is risk to us when this freedom is abused. In fact, that old word used far too little now in your time, the word, "sin" describes what really is nothing but the abuse of this moral freedom.

"Sin could not exist for a determined being. For if a fully determined being sinned, it would be the determiner who would be sinning through them. But since we have true, though limited, moral freedom, the abuse of that freedom—the sin—is legally and rightly laid to the account of the transgressor.

"So, Diakrina, this means the Living One's creatures really can afflict themselves by the abuse of their freedom. But of course, that is only the necessary corollary to the fact they can also be blessed by the right use of it, which He enables. The power is the same, only the intention and will are different.

"And it is the freedom to choose, within limits, their own intentions and the set of their own will in the exercise of their power—which too is limited—making a meaningful world possible. He will have no other kind of world until the redemption of this world makes a better world possible, Diakrina.

"Regardless of what you and I think—and we can only think because He enables us to think—He considers such a world worth the cost. And He is willing to pay a very high price not only to have it but also to redeem it. Do you understand?"

"Yes … and honestly … to some extent, no," answered Diakrina. "I do see He has sovereignly decreed this limited freedom. I also see no love or purpose or meaningful relationships could be possible without it. And I can also see how our limited freedom, love, purpose, and relational capacities are intended to reflect the deeper, infinite freedom, love, purposes, and perfect relationship always existing in the beauty of His nature, in His Tri-Personal Love. All that I can see with my mind and partially understand its necessity and validity.

"However, I am still deeply troubled evil must be given so much power to inflict pain, destruction and despair. While you have taught me the capacity for good must be equaled by the capacity for evil when this necessary freedom is abused, there is something within me—like emotions deeply troubled and refusing to be satisfied— revolting against all evil beings can inflict on the innocent. I can't calm this stormy sea of militant discontentment within me."

"Diakrina, do not try to bring this troubled sea within you to a calm," interjected Strateia. "It is a proper response to evil.

"Yet, at the same time, do not allow it to eclipse the greater truth. That truth is the ultimate context in which evil exist and in which it will be destroyed and all things set ultimately right—every wrong, every injustice.

"This troubled sea within you does not have the last word on reality. It is stirred up by both your limited perspective and your proper sense of justice crying in hope for all crimes to be avenged.

"And be assured, a Day is set, like no day which has ever been before it, when the cruel spell of evil will be undone. And on that Day all pain will be turned to joy for those who have trusted the Living One; all injustice will meet not only perfect retribution but also perfect healing.

"The rewards given to those who suffered, and yet trusted, will be so great they will consider their past horrors to be as nothing compared to the beauty, joy and ecstasy these sufferings have eternally purchased for them. He offers eternal joy in exchange for a momentary pain ... not a bad trade!

"Diakrina, it is beyond your comprehension now. Yet trust me when I tell you on that Day those who suffered the greatest horrors will dance for joy they suffered them. Not because of the horror— which will always be a horror still, in and of itself—but because of all the good, beauty and joy the Living One has purchased for them by means of it.

"On that Day evil will even be robbed of its cruel satisfactions. Evil now believes even if they are defeated—which they are—at least they will have been able to inflict great lasting harm. It will be no such thing!

"All their cruelest tortures will flower into glory at the touch of the Living One. None who trusted the Living One and were afflicted by them will be a victim then. They will watch their former victims dance in indescribable delight because of the joy the redemption of their sufferings has purchased for them. The Evil One, and all His servants will, on that Day, realize the only lasting horrors they ultimately inflicted was upon themselves."

Diakrina was wide-eyed and silent for several seconds. Then she looked up at Strateia and said, "So, we must humble our troubled thoughts and emotional conclusions in trust to His greater understanding and plan?"

"Yes. It is not possible that His thinking could be wrong and ours right any more than an effect can be greater than its cause. So, it is necessary this present state of creation is going to be worth it whether you and I can understand how or not."

"So, you are saying, Strateia, the road by which the quest will come to completion has been altered as to its course but not terminated, correct?"

"Yes. But the alteration in the road will mean, in this case, Anomos and the fallen men in league with him, have added dangers and pains to its course—this they have the power to do within limits—but they have not derailed the ultimate outcome."

"But what of those along this altered road who will suffer what they otherwise would not have suffered and be tempted with what they otherwise would not have been tempted with, and all through no fault of their own?"

"Diakrina, the Living One does not abandon anyone. And He does not give inadequate grace—desire and ability. Yet, He also does not coerce.

"The reason: forced grace would be a contradiction. He never does the contradictory as it violates His nature. In fact, the very definition of the contradictory from His point of view is, that which His nature will not allow to obtain—to exist. Therefore, the idea of forced grace—irresistible grace—is contrary to His nature and cannot exist. Such "grace" would be contrary to His sovereign will and His deepest nature. No gift is a gift if coerced—forced—upon someone.

"In reality, Diakrina, this altered road of greater trials and pains will cost Him most, not His creatures. He will give them everything they need—no matter how great the need—to overcome and be ultimately healed.

"To use an illustration from your times: the larger the potholes in someone's road of life, the greater the grace He gives to fill them in. Yet, while He gives the grace to fill them in—and even provides the gracious power to accept the grace given, a grace on grace— He will not fill the potholes for them. Each person must accept the empowerment and grace He provides. They must use it as He intends by a grace-empowered act of their will.

"And here is where real beauty often can be seen even in these Severed Lands. His grace is like gold, Diakrina. So, in a sense, those who use it to fill in the potholes of their road of life get gold. And the greater the potholes, the more gold they receive."

"This is really a stretch for me," responded Diakrina thoughtfully. "It makes perfect sense to my head but not to my emotions."

"If you will remember it will cost the Living One the most, as He lovingly embraces every person's pain in order to ultimately cure it, then this fact will give you a healing emotion alongside all your others. It will fill you with a sense of grateful awe.

"The deep secret of the world which evil wants to hide from you is how God bears the true tortures of evil. And, ultimately, it need be only He and He alone."

"How can you say that, Strateia?" interrupted Diakrina. "The history of the world is a long history of cruel suffering and hideous tortures. Millions have suffered."

"Yes. But trust me. At the end, we will see it is He who suffered, not His creatures who trusted Him. By His Spirit He so mingles Himself within each one's being, as they suffer He absorbs it all into Himself. On the Day, of which I spoke, we will witness His undoing every evil suffered by His children. It will be undone so effectively it will be as though they never suffered at all. He will drown its dark terrors into none existence in His infinite Light.

"So, Diakrina, He remedies all suffering eternally for those who let Him. And that remedy will work backwards and turn every tear into joy, every pain into pleasure. It will not be because the tears cease to be tears or pain ceases to be pain, as I said. No, it will be because the context of their indestructible life will be so joy-and-strength-saturated, that tears and pain will be able to be experienced—even at their greatest—as little more than the faintest tingle of which one remains easily unaware.

"Earth as you now know it will be like forgotten labor pains, Diakrina. Those labor pains will have given birth to a love-drenched life. It will be a life in which pain and sorrow can't find a foothold. And that life will so thoroughly saturate all existence with love, so completely remedy every sorrow and pain, it will turn it on its head and make it as great a joy as it was previously a horror.

"Of course, this is also the context of the great, incurable tragedy for those who embrace evil. Evil willingly embraced makes those who embrace it immune to the Living One's grace. And having rejected His grace—His freely provided solution—there is nothing the Living One can do for them.

"They have the freedom to reject Him and His healing. And even their greatest pleasures and joys, resulting from their alienation to Him—who alone can sustain pleasures and joys—will also be turned on their head: every pleasure they experienced in defiance of Him will become a horror.

Their "pleasures" will torture their hearts with the realization of what has been lost. And all their evil and pain will remain unhealed: a forever growing cancer in their being for all eternity. In the end they can retain only the empty, outer darkness of a vacant, suffocating self as they curse their former pleasures as abiding thieves robbing them of all true, enduring pleasure."

"Strateia, you said I have already, in one sense, succeed at the quest. And I now see you mean that to be true in the sense the ultimate calamity has been aborted if I can be kept out of the reach of Anomos. But will the Atheos torment mankind for all of time?"

"No. Even without the Atheos being here, evil will run its terrible, unavoidable course. As you know from the history in the Great Book, this Antediluvian world will become so filled with bloodshed and violence the Living One will have to end this present form of creation with the Great Deluge. Only the one family, with the three sons and their wives, will survive to carry the Seed of the Deliverer forward and replenish the earth.

"And even if the Atheos were allowed to remain among these people, the Great Deluge would remove the Atheos from the realms of men. It would be buried when the great fountains of the deep erupt and turn the earth's crust upside down in thousands of places."

"Strateia, you have just given me hope we will recapture the Atheos. For there is no mention in the Great Book of it being the cause of man's bloody warfare before the Great Flood."

"That is true," admitted Strateia. "And perhaps this may point to our total success, though of course, it could have been the cause and yet was not mentioned."

"True," agreed Diakrina. "Yet it gives me hope it is omitted because we succeed. And," continued Diakrina, "even if we do not get it back, the Great Deluge would finish the quest."

Diakrina would certainly have liked to pursue this line of discussion much further. However, at that very moment, Jared came striding through the trees toward them. When he realized he had their attention, he motioned to them to come, indicating it was time to descend to Dorogon.

Strateia nodded an acknowledgement to Jared, who turned and began walking back to the men. But he took one moment more with Diakrina before they too began the walk back to the horses.

"Diakrina, Dorogon was not an arbitrarily selected site. Though the others do not know it, it is actually our destination. For in the ruins of the Castle of Dorogon there is a door yet in existence—the Door of Dorogon—which we have need of, especially now. It is hidden in the rubble and has been forgotten with time by all but the great father of the Sons of El. It is by means of this door we will be able to get you across the Tree Bridge and back through the Door of the Rose.

"When we get to Dorogon I will make a quick trip to the top of Mist Mountain to start the descent of the warriors. As soon as I return, you and I must find the Door of Dorogon."

Strateia motioned for Diakrina to follow him, and they began walking back to the others. When they arrived, they found one of the warriors who had been sent down to the ruins of the Castle of Dorogon had returned. He reported they had found two of Anomos' warriors using the ruins of Dorogon as a lookout. They had quickly taken them captive before they could signal the units below.

Jared gave the order for everyone to get mounted and begin the descent to Dorogon. He reminded everyone to ride silently and to use only hand signals to communicate.

Within another twenty minutes they were down the ridge and on the outskirts of the ruins. When they got close to the ruins Diakrina could hear the sound of a waterfall. It soon proved to be off to their left where a spring was gushing from the hillside, forming a fall and then flowing toward Dorogon.

To the right of the stream, Diakrina could just make out the remains of a central road leading to the castle and passing through a large, arch-covered gateway. The gateway passed through the ruins of the outer wall. And to the left of the gateway, the stream also passed through the wall by means of a very deep pool having a part of the wall extending down into it, at its center, beyond sight. The pool was filled with debris, yet the water in it was clear, which indicated it was not stagnate but still flowing through the wall.

As they passed inside they were met by one of the other warriors. He came straight to Jared and gave a salute with his head.

"Sir, I don't think we have been detected. However, it has been necessary to gag the two warriors we took prisoner in order to keep them quiet. We have searched the ruins and we are convinced there are no others. Dorogon is secure."

"Good work, Soven," responded Jared. He then instructed Captains Kedar and Jaros to make certain the whole ruins of the castle, indicating, that if needed, it would be the place designated for defense.

Strateia turned to Jared and said, "While you finish with your preparations, I will go to alert Captain Moreh and Captain Arioch and the others to begin their descent. It seems all is ready."

Jared nodded in the affirmative. And with that, Strateia was gone.

Diakrina, who was still on Phos, took hold of Phulasso's rein and led him to where the others were headed to dismount their horses. They made their way through some of the lower ruins to a large gate, which had great doors laying flat on the ground to either side of the entrance. It opened on the inner courtyard of Dorogon Castle. To the left of the road, which passed through this great door, the stream entered through the wall and into the courtyard in the same manner it had passed under the other wall.

The Castle walls rose around fifty feet into the air and encircled a center courtyard of about two acres. There was one large door at the back of the courtyard which entered the castle proper. There were also several smaller doors all around the open area which clearly gave access to different parts of the structure.

Diakrina dismounted at the place where the others were securing their horses and secured both Phos and Phulasso. The place where the horses were secured was by the stream so they could reach the water.

She could now see it flowed through the courtyard by entering through a labyrinth in the wall near the great gate. It then ran along the main castle in an arc. The stream then passed under a small bridge leading to the large door of the main structure. From there it continued through the courtyard, always close to the main castle walls, and then exited on the east side of the castle courtyard through another labyrinth. The stream evidently formed several small waterfalls outside the east walls of the castle. Diakrina could now hear them cascading down the cliffs beyond the castle walls.

Her head was still spinning as she tried to sort out all her and Strateia had talked about concerning the Atheos. She walked toward the bridge leading to the large castle door. She ascended to the top of the bridge, as it was a stone structure built as an arch and sat down to watch the water flowing underneath.

She could sense everything was about to change again. Strateia would be back very quickly. He had said they would begin hunting for this ancient door, the Door of Dorogon he had called it. What would it all mean?

For the first time she found the thought of leaving the Severed Lands gave rise to a kind of reluctance within her. Then she smiled at herself. It was all too clear. She still felt as if she were leaving the quest unfinished: she liked to finish things.

Jared was walking toward her and had just stepped onto the bridge when, suddenly, Strateia was back, standing right beside him.

"The army is on its way," he said. "It will take them about 2-hours to get down to the other side of the meadow and the forest beyond it."

"Is the plan working?" asked Jared with a sense of anxiety in his voice.

"Anomos' warriors are giving chase, if that is what you are asking. So far, this part of our plan is a success. However, you need to know the size of the army is increasing beyond what any of us anticipated. Since the Monk disappeared with the Atheos—and in short order discovered they could not open the container—Anomos sent him to begin recruiting.

"He has gone all through the land of Cain with the Atheos. They are under its spell, and he has promised to make immortal those who distinguish themselves in battle. Not more than twenty miles behind Anomos' first warriors which were attacking your army on Mist Mountain, I detected another larger force—I would guess it to be about 20,000 strong—riding hard to join him."

"Should we try for the Bridge before they can get here?" interjected Jared.

"No. I have scouted the units stationed at the bridge. Anomos put more warriors there than I thought he would. They are far too many for our two units. We will have to wait on the larger force to arrive."

Strateia paused for a moment then continued. "I fear we are going to be fighting a much larger battle than we had planned.

Anomos is in a rage. The Atheos, which the Monk has now delivered to Tubal-Cain, Captain of all the armies of the Sons of Men, will be used to inflame the warriors with a manic passion. Anomos, through Tubal-Cain, will orchestrate that passion into a murderous rage of resentment against us. They will be told we are trying to rob them of their destiny by keeping Diakrina from them. In fact, they are likely being told you actually want the Atheos for yourselves so you can make the Sons of El immortal and wipe them off the face of the earth."

"Nothing could be farther from the truth!" responded Jared with indignation. "And it doesn't make sense. If that had been our motive—as we had both the Atheos and Diakrina in our power—this whole mission would never have taken place: we would never have left our valley."

"True," answered Strateia. "But Anomos does not deal in the truth. He has reduced these men to impoverished motives. And it is easy—because of their desire to justify themselves by jealously accusing those who make them feel inferior—to convince them the motives of others are the same as their own. They will not ask for one shred of evidence because what they are being told is what they want to believe."

Jared seemed stunned into silence by these insights. He looked away but it was clear he was not looking at any physical object: his eyes were filled with thought. Then as if speaking to himself, he said, "It seems the lie is continuing to birth lies."

Then turning again toward Diakrina and Strateia, "And like the Nephilim, each generation of lies seems to be bigger than the last. If this continues down through history, I can see a time when there will be no honor among men."

Strateia and Diakrina looked at each other while Jared searched their faces for a response. Neither of them could bring themselves to comment. But it was clear Jared read their faces with adequate certainty.

"Jared," said Strateia, changing the subject, "we only have a few hours left before your army arrives. And I am not sure they will be far enough ahead of the Sons of Men to engage Anomos' units at the Bridge before Tubal-Cain and his warriors catch up."

Then turning toward Diakrina, "In the meantime, Diakrina and I have an important mission to complete. It could be the key to victory."

Then turning to Diakrina he asked, "Are you ready?"

Diakrina hardly knew how to answer. She had little idea what this search for the Door of Dorogon was about. But if it could somehow give success and defeat Anomos' warriors …

"Yes, Strateia. I'm ready," she answered after taking a deep and determined breath.

Strateia smiled at her and then said, "Come with me."

And with that, Strateia walked past Diakrina and headed toward the large door which was the entrance to the main part of the castle.

Chapter Sixteen

THE DOOR OF DOROGON

As Strateia and Diakrina approached the great door of the castle—which were actually two great doors joined at the center—it became clear the doors were not fully closed. The doors were designed so they opened outward. The left door was open just enough that a man could get his hand behind it.

Because the doors were very large—about twenty feet high and around seven feet wide each—Diakrina was glad Strateia was with her to deal with opening one of the doors farther. There was a lot of debris—branches and leaves—that had built up against the doors. But Strateia took hold of the left-hand door and pulled at it until it began to give way to his effort. The door opened, with a creaking complaint, as the debris was pushed up into a pile behind it.

There was a generous entrance and then, beyond, a large room. Beyond the door it was not totally dark. A very tall window on the far wall, in the large room, which outside shutters had long since fallen from place, allowed light to stream down through the room toward them and land on the floor at the center of the room.

When her eyes adjusted, she was shocked to see someone standing at the room's center, right where the light splashed across the floor. He was very tall and though Diakrina could, at first, only make out a kind of silhouette because of the backlighting, she knew instantly who she was looking at: No other human being could have produced such a silhouette.

There, facing them, as if waiting on them, was Adam. Diakrina's astonishment could not have been more complete. Even though, as her eyes began to adjust, she could see he was smiling warmly at her, she was immediately overwhelmed by his presence.

With her mouth and eyes wide open, she walked slowly toward this god-like mortal. When she came within about six feet of him, she stopped and stood staring as if she were in a trance. He smiled at her and raised a questioning eyebrow.

As he did it triggered a flood of self-consciousness back into Diakrina's eyes and countenance. She immediately sank to one knee and bowed her head in respect.

"Welcome to my home, daughter. Sorry it is in such a state of disrepair. But then, I haven't been here for over three hundred years."

The music of his voice was like the climatic strains of a beautiful and haunting melody. It both surrounded Diakrina and filled her with a lost-world atmosphere: the atmosphere of a greater place and age overwhelming all other senses of space and time.

Adam stepped forward, and bending down, took hold of her shoulders and lifted her to her feet. Then he spoke.

"We have little time for formalities, child. And also, far too little time to do justice to the questions which fill both our hearts concerning each other. Strateia has made it clear to me time is short."

Diakrina wanted to ask how he had come to be here, but nothing would come out of her mouth. Somehow, he seemed to divine her question and began answering it.

Nodding toward Strateia, he said, "After you were taken captive, Strateia came to the valley and told me you might need access to the Door of Dorogon. I immediately mounted my horse and came here by a route through the mountains few know. My being here will save time as I can lead you to the Door of Dorogon instead of you having to search for it. No others know its exact location and only I have the key."

Here, he reached down into the neck of his tunic and pulled out the end of a necklace made of large, beautiful links of golden chain. Hanging from the chain was a key around five inches long. The shank of the key was almost a half inch in diameter. On its end, the key section, there were three square blades radiating out around the end like the points of a triangle. And on the opposite end of the key was a round bow about three inches in diameter.

Adam lifted the necklace over his head and took hold of the chain, just above the key with his index finger and thumb, so the key hung freely below his hand. He reached out toward Diakrina, and with a subtle nod of his head, beckoned her to take it.

Slowly, Diakrina lifted her hand, and Adam lowered the key into her upturned palm. The bow of the key filled Diakrina's hand. As she drew the key toward her she could see the bow was thick and deeply carved with images. The images seemed to almost leap from its surface. In the center of the bow was the face of a great lion which dominated the surface of the bow. From his great mane, in all directions around his head, like the rays of sunshine radiating out from the sun, there were various smaller carved animal images.

In the top righthand corner was a great elephant with his trunk raised in the air as if saluting the lion. In the top left-hand corner was the image of a great blue whale leaping from the surface of the ocean toward the lion. On the bottom left and bottom right, respectively, was a great horse pawing the air with its front feet as it reared and then, a great eagle soaring on its wings toward the lion.

And above the lion's head, right in the center, was the image of a lamb's head. It was not the whole animal as in the other four, but just the head, like that of the lion.

Diakrina could feel by the way the key set in her hand the underside of the bow was also carved. She turned it over. There, in the center of the bow, in the way the lion's head dominated the opposite side, was the head of the lamb she had seen above the lion's head, only now as large as the lion's head on the opposite side. And above the head of the lamb was the face of the great lion, like the face of the lamb had been on the opposite side.

The same four animals that had been radiating out from the head of the lion were, in identical fashion, radiating out around the head of the lamb. Clearly the relationship of the lion and the lamb to the other beasts was being equated.

"It's beautiful," she whispered almost to herself. Then in full voice, as she looked up to Adam, "What does it all mean?"

"It is the key to a life I no longer have the ability to manage or enjoy," answered her great father, looking rather grave. "The Door of Dorogon is a place of merciful imprisonment. It was provided by the Living One after we fell to the great deception of Anomos."

"Imprisonment?" repeated Diakrina.

"If you wish, you may use the word, "vault" in its place. But the vault also imprisons undesired possibilities. That is why it is a merciful imprisonment."

"So," continued Diakrina, "it is a place for safe keeping?"

"Yes."

"Safe keeping for what?"

"For many things," said Adam thoughtfully, as if recalling a host of them. "They are all abilities, innate to our human nature, which I soon discovered were difficult to manage in the weakness of my present condition. I sought the merciful help of the Living One and asked Him to enlighten me as to what should be done. Over time I had come to fear if I passed these abilities on to my offspring, they could pose a great threat to all human history if their weaknesses were like mine or even greater.

"One night I was awakened. And there, at my feet, stood the Living One, Himself. 'I HAVE COME IN ANSWER TO YOUR PRAYER, MY SON,' He said. 'RISE AND WE WILL WALK AND SPEAK OF THESE THINGS.' I rose and He led me out under the stars.

"It had been several years since I had had this privilege. And I was grieved my perception was so dim I could only just discern His unmistakable glory. Before the banishment from the Great Dance, the glory I could only faintly see that night—though to my physical eyes it was overwhelming and blinding, for I was no longer able to endure even the material manifestations of His radiance—I had before been able to fully engage.

"Yet, He accommodated my weak perception by translating His interactions with me into the realm of my physical senses. I can still remember His words as if it were yesterday." Then, as if quoting something set to memory he turned and looked out at the sunlight streaming through the great window.

'THESE LOSSES ARE PART OF THE DEATH OF WHICH I WARNED YOU, MY SON. YOU ARE SLOWLY BEING SEVERED FROM THE POWER TO MANAGE MANY OF THE GIFTS I GAVE YOU.

'YOUR LOWER NATURE IS IN REVOLT AGAINST YOUR HIGHER NATURE, AS YOU NO LONGER HAVE MY CONSTANT RENEWAL TO MAINTAIN THE AGENCIES GIFTED TO YOU. YOU ARE RIGHT TO FEAR THE MISUSE OF THEM BY YOUR PROGENY. THEY WILL BECOME MORE FULLY IMPRISONED IN THE FLESH THAN YOU. AND THE SELF-OBSESSION WITH WHICH ANOMOS HAS INFECTED YOU WILL WORK THROUGH THE INFLAMING OF THIS LOWER NATURE TO MORE FULLY ENSLAVE THESE ABILITIES TO EVIL'S PURPOSES AS THE YEARS DESCEND.

I HAVE COME TO OFFER YOU A MERCIFUL CHOICE.'"

Adam paused here and the last sentence seemed to hang in the air. Then, he seemed to come to himself.

"We haven't time to speak of all transpiring that night. But the short of it is I made a decision to willingly give up certain treasures of our nature lest they prove too destructive to mankind in the misuses of them that would surely follow."

Then turning and looking directly at Diakrina who was still holding the amazing key in her open palm, "That key is to the Door of Dorogon. And behind this door is the vault of my greatest treasures—my greatest abilities. It is the powers I have given into the Living One's safe keeping. He promised me that night only small reflections of these powers would be passed on to my children. He will keep the full manifestation of them in trust behind the door until the time of the great restoration. Then they will once again be restored to those who have accepted the cure when the new creation is materialized."

Then pointing to the bow of the key he said, "So many of these powers which I have willingly entrusted to the Living One's care have to do with my stewardship over this earth. I do not fully understand the meaning of the all the symbols on the key, but He did reveal to me the lion and the lamb are important images of the Promised Seed who will crush Anomos' head. It is he who will restore—and I believe, expand—the full authority of mankind over creation."

Diakrina stared long and hard, first at the key and then at her great Parent. "So, He gave you this key?"

"Yes."

"In my time," said Diakrina, "a time beyond the coming of the Promised Seed, He is symbolized by these two images. They speak eloquently of who He is and what He accomplishes."

"So, you come from the time after the great restoration?" asked Adam with his eyes wide.

"No, not the one you are speaking of, that is yet to come. But the foundation for that restoration has been fully laid and many are awaiting its consummation."

"As I do now," responded Adam. And then looking again out the window, he added, "It is what fills my dreams with hope."

Diakrina started to say more, but Strateia, who had walked around behind Adam as they had been speaking, raised an eyebrow at her in such a way as to command her attention and then subtly shook his head. Though Adam did not see, he seemed to understand from watching Diakrina's eyes what had transpired.

"Come, daughter, I have a gift for you from beyond the Door of Dorogon. I believe it will give us what we need to get you over the chasm and safely back to the Garden."

With that he turned and began walking to a door at the far-right side of the room. He opened it and Diakrina could see that some stone stairs descended beyond the threshold. She was momentarily taken back a little when his walking through the door caused light to flood the stairwell. It was hard to remember the technological sophistication of these ancient times.

Once again, the light seemed to come from every surface: walls, ceiling, floor—in this case, steps and landing—handrails, etc. When

Diakrina peered past Adam down the stairway, she was surprised to see the stairs did not come to a landing after a few steps. Instead, they extended forty feet downward in a gentle slope without turning or being interrupted.

When they arrived at the bottom of the steps there was a landing which had a doorway to the left. As they passed through the door, light flooded a large room in which were all kinds of strange objects. They were machine-like objects. But for most of them she could make out nothing looking familiar.

"This was my place of creativity. My first two sons and I spent many happy hours here creating and building."

Diakrina immediately made the connection this was something like an inventor's laboratory for experimentation. And as this realization came to her, she found herself pointing out the obvious to herself, "Of course, all the technology began with Adam. What is it Plato said of Adam? Something to the effect, 'Our first parent was the greatest philosopher who has ever lived.' And of course for Plato, a philosopher was a man of science in all senses of the word and would include even the physical sciences."

The room was large and the ceiling as high as the stairs they had descended. Adam turned again to the right and led them through a winding path of dormant machines. On the far wall was a large arrangement of shelves in five sections covering the whole wall, up to about fifteen feet, with something like bookshelves lacking any books. Instead, there were smaller devices all properly arranged in an orderly manner up and down the shelves.

Adam walked up to the center section. He reached into one of the shelves and took hold of a handle cut into one of the upright sidepieces. He pulled and the shelves began moving outward as if on hinges. He continued pulling until the set of shelves was ninety-degrees to the wall.

Behind the shelves was a tall, inset doorway with an arched top. There was no door visible at first, but then Diakrina realized it was set back from the wall about five feet. This door proved to be made of some kind of wood looking like very dark oak. The door looked quite massive. At first Diakrina was sure this must be the door which was their destination. But that proved to be untrue.

Adam reached up on one of the shelves still against the wall and took down a three feet long piece of wood which top end was wrapped with some kind of cloth which had been soaked in a black pitch. The pitch was dry but would still clearly burn if lit.

"There is no provision for illumination beyond this door and we have some distance yet to go," he explained.

Adam was about to reach for something else on the shelves, presumably something with which to make a flame and light the torch. But Strateia who had already anticipated the need stepped forward with his sword drawn and touched the torch on the side of the pitch. It instantly burst into flames.

Adam nodded an obvious, thanks, and walked into the arched inset. The door had a thick iron latch sliding into the doorframe and indeed looked as if it had not been moved in centuries. It had a large handle on it and Adam took hold of it and began pulling. Ever so slowly the rust and dirt gave way, and the latch began to slide back. When it pulled free of the frame, Adam pulled out on a handle below the latch. After several very powerful pulls the door began moving. When finally it was fully opened, Adam led the way with the torch into the darkness beyond.

Immediately they were in a long earthen tunnel slopping downward at a very steep angle for about a hundred yards. It proved to empty out into a large cave.

The first part of the cave was an immense cavern with a high vaulted top. There were some massive formations towering into the air all around the gigantic cavern yet failing to reach all the way to the ceiling.

As they walked out into the cavern, Diakrina immediately became conscious of the sound of rushing water, like that of a river, echoing all through the large space. Adam turned right again and began leading them through the underground cathedral. They had to climb and descend several times as they made their way toward a place where the cavern ceiling seemed to be narrowing, but not descending.

The large room soon dovetailed into a much narrower branch of the cave, which was only about forty, to fifty feet wide in most places. Because the top of the cavern did not become lower, it was like walking into a very narrow, underground canyon with sheer walls on either side.

Adam led the way down this branch, which was descending all the time, and almost immediately the sound of the river began to subside. They had not gone far until it branched into two. Once again, he stayed to the right. This branch of the cavern kept descending. Somewhat farther they came to a place where it branched off in three different directions, and again, Adam took the branch farthest to the right.

This branch also kept descending. After about five minutes of walking Diakrina began hearing water again. Only this time it was the sound of falling water. They continued for about another ten minutes when, suddenly, this branch of the cave emptied into a large cavern which seemed to have no floor. It was round like a great shaft and seemed to descend deep into the earth. It was about fifty yards across, and you could just see by the flickering of the torch the cave continued on its far side.

Diakrina looked up but the light of the torch did not reach far enough to see any top to this enormous hole. But what was most impressive was that a large waterfall was pouring out of the wall of the cavern about twenty feet up to their left. Adam turned left and Diakrina realized a spiraling ledge circled downward around the circumference of the shaft. It was not so narrow as to be difficult or fearful to navigate—about three to four feet wide in most places—but the great sense of height created by a shaft which descended into darkness, without any indication of having a bottom, was very sobering. The ledge passed behind the falling water under an overhang which was the edge of the waterfall above them.

The descent was steep, and they traveled around the shaft until they had encircled it a full three times; each time passing behind the falling water. When they were almost exactly under the opening where they had entered—by now about a hundred and fifty feet above them—Adam turned to the left into another long cavern. This branch soon began to get narrower until it was only about five feet wide. It continued for about another sixty yards at this width and then it widened out again—to about twenty-feet—ending abruptly.

There in the very center of the cavern wall was a door about twenty feet high, and ten feet wide. It was a massive wood door with carvings all over it. About six feet up the door was a large and impressive carved head of a lion with his mouth open in the act of giving a terrible roar. But as Adam approached closer to the door, Diakrina was shocked to see the head of a lamb looking serenely out from the center of the lion's mouth.

And there, below the face of the lamb, in the lion's curled tongue, was a triangle shaped keyway. Outside the head of the great lion, radiating from his mane in all directions, were carvings of thousands of different animals. All of them seemed to be somehow looking toward the lion and the lamb.

As Adam came up to the very door itself and held the torch high, Diakrina could see at the top part of the door were carvings of suns … and stars … and planets … and galaxies! Whoever carved this door knew the structure of the universe!

Adam stood looking at the door for a moment. Then he turned to Diakrina and Strateia. To Diakrina he said, "You are the only other human on the face of the earth besides me who has ever seen this door. Not even your great Mother has been here."

Then looking very serious indeed, Adam knelt on one knee so as to be on Diakrina's level (for you must remember he was over eight feet tall). He looked deep into her eyes as if searching her soul.

"Daughter, I have never opened this door. And I would not open it now if it were not clear to me from the Living One it is necessary for it to be opened."

Then taking a deep breath, he continued.

"I want you to place the key into the mouth of the lion, and I will then tell you how to turn it. When the door opens—for it will open of its own accord—you are to hold the key in front of your face with your right hand, with the three blades of the key on top. Then walk into the light.

"Once you are within, you will see six shelves in front of you, one on top of the other. On each shelf will be a single golden box. Place your hand on the box which is on the third shelf from the bottom—do not touch any of the other boxes. Remove your hand and wait for it to open. When it opens, lift it to your face until it is touching. Look deeply within it and take several deep breaths. Then place the box back on the shelf and wait for it to close. Then return to us."

"Is that all I have to do?"

"Yes. And I warn you, very sternly, do nothing else besides."

"I will only do as you have said," answered Diakrina in her most reassuring voice.

"Then the time has come," said Adam as he rose from his bent knee back to his considerable height.

Diakrina moved toward the door as Adam held the torch over the lion's mouth so she could see the keyway. It was six feet high on the door. And even though Diakrina was five feet, seven inches tall, she had to reach with all her capacity in order to keep far enough away from the door to see into the lion's mouth and reach the keyway at the same time.

She did reach it, however, and she pushed the key firmly into the triangle until most of the shaft of the key was within the keyway.

Then Adam said to her, "Turn the key to the right a half a turn, seven times."

It seemed like an odd way to say, "Turn the key to the right for three and one-half complete circles." But in reality, it amounted to the same thing in slightly fewer words.

Diakrina turned the key one half turn, then another, and another, and another. That was two full turns. She then turned it another half turn, then one more and then, finally, the last one. As the key clicked into place on the last half-turn, it was immediately pushed out of the keyway back into Diakrina's hand.

At that very moment the door began glowing. Diakrina was so startled she jumped backwards and almost drop the key. She managed to hang on to it, however, and took several steps backwards to watch from a safe distance what was happening.

Adam placed his hand on her shoulder and said, "There is nothing to fear. The opening door will do you no harm."

The door continued to glow ever brighter, until it turned from its wood color to a golden color. The intensity of the light continued growing until this golden color began to give way to an ever-whiter glow as the intensity of the light seemed to be translucing the features of the door.

Then without warning, the door began becoming totally transparent from the center outward. That is when it hit Diakrina this door was opening in the same manner as the Door of the Rose which had brought her to this side of reality, to the Garden and to the time of the Antediluvians. In about ten seconds it was completely opened.

The light from the door, as it was opening, was very intense. Beyond it was a narrow room which seemed to be made of the same material as the door only it was still fully opaque and bathed in a soft gold-white light. It was about ten feet deep and ten feet wide, like the door.

"Lift your key to your face and enter now, daughter," instructed Adam.

Diakrina lifted the key with the three blades on top and began walking toward the door. She was almost to the surface of the translucent door when a face of a lion, bigger than any she had ever seen in real life, appeared in the substance of the door.

Diakrina froze.

The lion looked intently at the key and then deeply into her eyes, holding her gaze for several seconds. Then, as if losing interest, he blinked, lowered his head, and turning away, disappeared.

"You have been approved, daughter. Continue," said Adam.

Diakrina stepped into the surface of the door, and it was like walking into very viscous water. The door was about three-feet thick, so it took a couple of small steps to put her through the substance of the door and on its other side.

When she exited the door, she was completely dry and without any sign of having passed through anything. There on the far backwall were the six shelves, one over the other. Each shelf had a single, glowing golden box sitting at its center. Each box was about fourteen inches wide, about ten inches tall and proved to be, once she was close enough to see, about ten inches deep.

Diakrina noticed the box on the bottom shelf seemed to have rocks and crystals, perhaps, diamonds, protruding from its top. The box on the second shelf had the branch of a tree growing out of it with fruit on it.

The box on the third shelf, the one she was to open, had what appeared to be miniatures of animals on a savanna-like plain. She peeked briefly at the fourth and fifth shelf—for the sixth one was too high for her to see the top of the box—and on the top of the fourth was what appeared to be human made structures. On the fifth was something like a replica of the solar system with all the planets in motion. She was tempted to reach up to the sixth shelf and pull its box down just so she could look at its lid. But she remembered she had been told not to touch any box but the third one from the bottom.

She reached out and placed her hand on the top of the lid of the box on the third shelf. When she lifted it off, instantly she heard, as if at a great distance, the sound of the cries and calls of every kind of animal she had ever heard and many she was sure she had never heard before. The box began to glow, and the lid slowly opened until it was standing fully upright.

Diakrina very cautiously lifted the box toward her face. The closer it came to her face the more the inside of the box seemed to expand outward until it was a scene which engulfed her. Suddenly she was standing in a vast bowl-shaped landscape. And all around her were animals of every possible description. They began with a tight circle of about ten feet in diameter and filled a massive landscape from there as the bowl spread up and away from her on all sides.

Amazingly, all the animals were giving their full attention to her. And as she looked into the face of any one animal, she seemed to know something of its desires and could even understand something like very simple thoughts.

Some of the animals had thoughts closer to human-like thought than others. The others had thoughts which were much less structured. However, while none of them approached anything like reason or conversational intelligence, somehow, she could adequately read them.

What is more, she also knew in this place, she had an ability to cause them to understand her intentions, desires and directions. And most importantly, they all seemed eager to please her and fulfill her wishes.

She remembered she was instructed to take several deep breaths. This she did. And as she did so, it seemed every animal all around her stirred to even greater attention—more so than before. And instantly she was filled with a new knowledge and appreciation of the animals she could not have conceived of in the previous moments. It was like being introduced into a whole different realm of existence where she was some kind of queen who had a huge variety of subjects, all of which she cared for very deeply and delighted in each in very particular ways.

She was filled with delight and began to breath very deeply indeed in order to insure she would not miss obtaining any of this wonderful new ability. After she had taken four deep breaths the scene vanished, suddenly. She pulled the box from her face and placed it back on the shelf exactly as she had found it.

Diakrina knew she was different. Something incredible had been given to her and already she began to understand how it would help her make a successful run for the Bridge.

She turned and walked straight for the door and pushed through it. When she got to the other side, Adam was standing there holding out his hand to receive the key.

"Well done, daughter. Now give me the key and turn looking away from the door."

Diakrina did not understand, but she obeyed and walked over to where Strateia was standing.

"He is locking the door again. And the number of turns he

uses to lock it will become a new combination for unlocking it," said Strateia.

"You mean, it will not be the same as before, seven half turns to the right?"

"Correct. Once again, no other living human will know how to open this door even, if somehow, they could obtain the key. For the combination must be right the very first time or the door will not open—no second chances."

After a few moments it was clear the door had closed because the light flooding the area ceased.

"You may turn around now, daughter," said Adam.

When Diakrina turned around, the door looked as she had first seen it.

Adam placed the key back around his neck and dropped it inside his tunic. Then taking the torch in his hand and looking at Strateia he asked, "Shall we go?"

Strateia nodded in the affirmative and they all began the long trek back out of the cavern.

Chapter Seventeen

AN ARMY WITH TEETH AND CLAWS

They were about to ascend the final stairs when Adam paused before mounting them. He turned to Strateia and Diakrina.

"I left my horse, Equus, in a small courtyard on the backside of the castle. I believe it would be faster if I led Diakrina to the prides."

"I agree," said Strateia. "However, you need to explain to me your intended route so I can check to see if it is safe before you leave."

Adam nodded in the affirmative.

"The prides you referred to, I assume," interjected Diakrina, "are lions?"

"Yes," answered Adam. "I am taking you to meet an alpha male who can command the respect of more than one pride. He is the grandson of the first lion, which I named, Lavi. Lavi was with me in the Garden." And here, almost as if speaking of the passing of a friend, Adam added, "Lavi died at four hundred years of age."

Then, as if coming back to the purpose, he continued, "One of Lavi's sons still lives, which I named, Leōn (he pronounced it with a long O). He is the father of Lāvōn (which he pronounced with a long A and a long O), who now rules the prides. It is Lāvōn I am taking you to meet."

Now at this point I must explain to you what Adam, Diakrina, and of course Strateia, all understood without having to say it.

Diakrina had been given, in undiminished potency, Adam's original gift of ruling the animal kingdom. No son or daughter of Adam had ever received this gift except in a very diluted form (we have all met those who have a special knack with animals), but at it greatest this diluted gift is not even one-thousandths of the original.

Though Adam had given up the power to transmit this gift to his children, he still possessed it himself, though he informed Diakrina that since he had been severed from the Great Dance it was beginning to diminish to some extent. But Diakrina had been given the gift in undiminished power. Along with this power an innate knowledge of how it was to be used had accompanied it. What she had experienced in those few moments when she lifted the golden box to her face made it perfectly clear to her, she could now—in some fashion hard to explain—communicate meaningfully and very specifically with all animals.

This communication was not particularly verbal, though words could be used and an animal made to quickly attach (without long training as today) the desired meaning to it. And, of course, the animals had no words; they could not talk. But they didn't need to talk. Diakrina could read their eyes, their faces, their bodily gestures and movements. And what is more, she could intuit very accurately their thoughts, and in some manner, they too understood—could you say, intuited—her thoughts, or at least her intentions and commands.

It was, in many respects, like learning a new language with all the novel human expressions, connotations and culture it opens to you. But in another way, it was nothing like it. This was not another aspect of the world of men she had been given access to. It was the world, the culture, if you please, of beasts. It was lower and more instinctive; and in a way it was very alien. It was devoid of rational reasonings and justifications. Yet, it was also intriguing in its simplicity. Its very adequacy through simplicity testified of something designed and given to the beast. Diakrina could clearly understand the great gulf between the beast who utilized it and the design of the ability they utilized: they could never have evolved it on their own.

And, yes, Diakrina had also come to realize in those few moments, when the golden box was at her face, that within this larger system of communication each species had its own dialect or tongue. She had been given the knowledge of all their various tongues—you could say she was given the ability to speak lion, or zebra or horse, etc.—while each of the beasts had only been given the knowledge of that tongue specific to its kind.

Entering this new world and finding she had been given a designed place and function within it, gave Diakrina new insights about the beasts and their intended relation to people. It slowly dawned on Diakrina this animal kingdom, which was divided from each other by these different tongues or dialects, found unity only in someone like Adam—or now, her—who transcended them all and understood them all. They could only be an animal kingdom, in the truest sense of that word, by means of someone who was more than an animal. Outside of a relationship with someone who transcended them they could not properly relate to each other.

In this she began to see the deeper reason for the realm of the animals becoming red in tooth and claw. Without mankind as its benevolent ruler and source of unity, it was a shattered kingdom, where not only every species was in some sense—large or small—in competition with all the other species for survival, and often each member of each species was in competition with its own members for survival.

For in this domain of animals, no longer united to mankind, and by mankind, the instinct to survive had become undirected—therefore, misdirected—and desperate. Just as men without the One above them are misdirected and desperate about love, meaning and purpose, so were the beasts about existence and survival.

Humans die without love, meaning and purpose—first on the inside, and then throughout. Animals die without the survival instincts that enable their continued existence. But when they are severed from their rightful sovereign, who is both above them and one of them, those instincts become corrupt and savage. All their days are consumed with existing, and finding a way to keep existing, by any means. And without mankind they can rise no higher.

Certainly, the most corrupt humans seem to descend into their baser nature until they become animal-like in this way. And when they do, they renounce their true humanity, which is created for higher things. For is it not the absence of acknowledging the One who transcends them that results in people being doomed to such reductionism and inevitable competition?

Diakrina also sensed, and was now about to discover by experience, this new ability came with some kind of absolute authority over beasts which they recognized and willingly obeyed. And it was this causing Diakrina to understand best why Adam had not wished to pass this power on to his fallen progeny. Such absolute power over beasts would have made them slaves and servants of war in ways far more tragic than any which history has recorded.

The machines with which later generations would learn to kill each other would have been upstaged for many thousands of years by natural and intelligent machines of beasts mastered by men. The whole planet would have been stained with the blood of men and animals too deeply to contemplate.

After they had climbed the stairs back to the main level of the castle and reentered the sunlit central room, Adam put out the torch and then closed the door and latched it again.

"Diakrina," said Strateia, "I will go out the front and bring Phos around behind the castle. You go with your great parent to the small courtyard where he left Equus. You will begin your mission from there to prevent the others asking too many questions. I will inform Jared of what is happening for he must know. But that will be enough for now."

Then turning to Adam he said, "After I bring Phos to you, explain to me the route which lies before you and I will make a quick survey of it to ensure you will not encounter any of Anomos' minions, nekros, Nephilim or men. And while you journey, I will check on you repeatedly from time to time. For I must stay here to help Jared and the others engage the battle in the most hopeful manner. Yet, I cannot risk you two being taken captive."

Then looking again at Diakrina, "Jared and the army must hold out until you return."

Diakrina nodded, slowly.

Strateia left through the front door and pushed it closed behind him. Adam turned and motioned for Diakrina to follow him to the other end of the room. In the far back corner was a doorway with no door and it led to a long hallway that was quite wide. They soon came to another larger room, something like a great ballroom, and Adam began to transverse it to the left toward its far back corner. In this corner there was a door in the sidewall. Clearly it had been opened earlier as the dust around it had been pushed back where the door had swung open. Obviously, it was Adam who had entered by this door when he arrived.

Adam opened the door and Diakrina followed him outside onto a large, covered, stone porch about twenty-feet deep and fifty-feet wide. To the right, down several steps, was a small courtyard with high, stonewalls all around it and an arched gate in the center of the back wall.

There, eating grass from an area in the center not covered with paving stones, was the greatest stallion Diakrina had ever laid eyes on. He was coal black with not a hint of any other color. His coat shone with a luster which dazzled the eyes. His conformation was much like that of the other horses but more defined and rippling. He stood a full twenty-four hands tall. His long flowing mane and tail were textured and regal.

When Adam walked onto the porch, Equus quickly lifted his head and threw it lightly into the air in greeting. Then totting over to Adam he put his great nose in his master's hand.

Only then did Equus look at Diakrina. And with that one look Diakrina knew instantly how greatly this gift had changed her. The first thing she noticed was her delight at realizing the horse had communicated to Adam when he looked at her. And his openness to her, his fearless inquisitiveness, was instantly real to her in some very objective way.

Equus investigated the face of his master. Adam smiled. Diakrina discerned what had passed between them as surely as if she had overheard a conversation. Equus had clearly asked if it were alright to interact with Diakrina. Adam's smile had communicated all. The stallion lifted its head from Adam's hand and came over to Diakrina who was reaching toward him. He placed his nose in her hand and instantly they had their first conversation.

Diakrina could never quite explain how this conversation actually transpired. But by the touch of her hand on this horse's willing nose she knew him—his every like and dislike, his fiery nature and thunderously strong determination to fulfilling Adam's every wish. And somehow, he knew her too, in some manner adequate to a horse. She was instantly one of those he wished to please, though he still knew who was his true master.

"Seeing your eyes shine as they do," said Adam, looking intently at Diakrina, "makes me hate evil even more for making it necessary for me to deprive my children of this gift … this whole other world of experience and joy intended for us."

What stunned Diakrina at that moment was Equus seemed to interact with this emotion of his master, and he tossed his head up and down as if trying to agree or enter into the sense of loss. She could intuit his discernment of their shared emotions.

When Strateia came riding Phos through the gate, Diakrina relinquished Equus' head. Strateia rode Phos up beside Equus. It was the first time Phos had looked small to Diakrina. That was the effect of the great stallion as he towered over Phos.

When Strateia handed Diakrina the rein, after stepping down, and she took hold of Phos' head to pat him, it all happened again. She suddenly knew this horse she had been riding for two days. It was quite a stunning moment for both Diakrina and Phos.

Adam walked up beside Diakrina and patted Phos' head. He pulled the bridle and rein from Phos' head and, coiling it up, put it in one of the compartments of the saddle.

"You will no longer need this," he said smiling at her.

That is when it hit Diakrina that Equus didn't even have a bridle. Instantly she understood why.

"This is going to be riding, indeed," she said with a sparkle in her eyes.

Phos tossed his head as if in agreement and all three—Adam, Diakrina and Strateia—laughed with delight.

"You weren't saying I gave bad directions with that reign, are you?" said Diakrina to Phos in a tone of mock offense. And in any other time and place the horse would have been oblivious to the play acting going on: he would have been an unaware participant with the joke being understood only by the humans. Of course, Phos didn't get the joke, but he did sense the continuing delight and continued to shake his head up and down. This had all three of them roaring with laughter.

Even Equus seemed to enter into the mood and he too was shaking his head and pawing the ground with excitement. And it was this pawing which reminded them all they needed to be underway.

Adam turned to Strateia and began explaining the route to him. It took about thirty seconds to convey a full description.

Strateia then turned to Diakrina and helped her up onto Phos' back.

"The quest comes to a point, Little One," he said looking up into her eyes (it was one of the few times she was higher than Strateia and didn't have to look up herself). "The beasts you bring must come in fast and hard from the north when you attack. Come down the open area of the ridge we avoided for fear of being seen. For the battle will likely be waged in the large meadow below Dorogon Castle.

"I am now sure we will not be able to take out the units at the Bridge because Anomos' army will come too quickly behind our army. In reality, our army is going to be caught between Anomos' army and the units at the Bridge.

"Our one advantage is that we will have the two units here, which they are unaware of, using their bows from the top of the cliffs. This will greatly increase our power and will enable us to hold them for a while.

"You must get here before the larger force of Anomos' arrives—some twenty-thousand strong. It will be close. Our goal will be to control the eastern side of the meadow forming a defensive line from the cliffs of Dorogon to the Bridge.

"If we have been able to hold them back, there will be space behind us. You should bring the beasts in as close to the cliffs as possible and fight your way to us and then behind us. Then using the beasts as your guard, make for the Bridge.

"If we have not been able to hold them back and give you this protected path to the Bridge, when you get to the top of the ridge, look to see where the armies of the sons of Cain are concentrated. The sons of Cain will not be able to withstand the beasts. Direct the beasts to attack there and avoid Anomos' warriors.

"Have the beasts roar at the top of the ridge as you start descending. When we see you coming, we will make an all-out, single-point attack toward you to cut a path to join up with you. Have the beasts keep you well among them—surrounded so no one can get close to you. You will be in no danger from arrows, yourself, for they want you alive. So, if the beasts stay tightly around you during the charge, none of the sons of Cain will be able to reach you.

"Our goal will be to join up with you and then turn and make for the Bridge while then using most of the beasts as a fighting shield between us and the army.

"Do you understand, Diakrina?"

"I think so."

"You must not be slow, so ride both ways like the wind."

And with that Strateia was gone to scout the route. Within three minutes he was back high above the gate.

"Ride! The way is clear."

Equus and Phos, in full awareness, jumped into action and they thundered through the gate with Adam and Equus in the lead. Even though Diakrina felt the gravity of the moment she couldn't help finding instant delight in her newfound cooperation with Phos. The willingness of the horse to make itself available to her seemed to be without reservation. And her ability to discern his impulses which preceded his actions, and his ability to discern her intentions and commands, made her and Phos become one physical organism as to unity of action.

Diakrina felt as if she actually had four legs thundering under her which she was controlling with Phos' help: like power steering on a car. But she soon rejected this image for a better one.

Diakrina began to imagine this is what it would have been like to be a centaur—if such a mythological creature had actually existed. And then it hit her this kind of experience could give rise to such an image in the mind of anyone who had experienced it.

Could Adam have been the source of this image? He certainly had experienced this sensation in riding all his life. Had he handed down this image as a means of conveying to his sons and daughters what it was like to ride, or better yet, to charge into battle with the rider and horse so completely welded together in common action they were as one entity?

As she looked ahead to the amazing man and horse acrobatically thundering through the forest ahead of her, she realized how many questions she longed to ask him which she would never have the leisure to ask. It didn't seem fair. Who in all the later history of the world had this access, which she now had, to the one man who knew the beginning of things? It seemed like such a terrible injustice to have no time to inquire of him with the thousands of questions she knew would spill out of her if such an opportunity were given.

It was in the midst of these thoughts and this sense of loss that Diakrina seemed to hear His voice on the wind rushing past her ears. "PEACE, CHILD, THE TIME FOR SUCH QUESTIONS WILL BE GIVEN LATER."

The word, "LATER" somehow carried with it the meaning of, later in another time and place, not later in the present time. And with His voice a sense of peace and the awareness of the continual presence of One greater than Adam, who could answer all questions, came flooding over Diakrina.

They thundered up the forested ridge with speed and agility which cannot be conveyed with words. And yes, Diakrina's serious delight at being given such ability, when it was so greatly needed, caused her to bubble over with the thought—almost out loud—"Now this is riding, indeed!"

She now recognized what had happened before as the units had descended through the gorge—where they and their horses had become like a synchronized, flowing wave, rushing down the gorge—had been a small reflection of what she was now experiencing riding with Adam, Equus and Phos. What had slowly, and dimly, emerged over hours of riding was now instant and ever-present.

When they reached the top of the ridge they kept going straight north over to its other side. The forest was still quite predominating here. But as they continued down the ridge it began to thin out so there were larger open areas between the great trees.

Here it became possible for Diakrina to see some of the terrain which lay below them. This ridge they were galloping down ran in a nearly true east-west orientation to their right and left. To their left, out in front of them, she could see the greater ridge—which this ridge had divided from up to the west—continuing toward the north-northeast. And below them, in a V-shaped area between this north-northeastern ridge and the ridge they were descending, was a large open savanna-like area extending and expanding outward toward the north and east. Diakrina could not but believe this would be the area where the lion prides would be found.

Before long the side of the ridge they were descending began to level out. Almost immediately they came to a place where she could see a treeless savanna up ahead, beyond a place where the forest ended.

They galloped onto the savanna and Adam turned Equus northeast to travel down the very center of the expanding V-shaped area between the two ridges. Here the horses had no impediments. They stretched their necks forward slightly and began to run, not gallop. Their pounding hooves, their amazing speed … it all made Diakrina's heart race with excitement as the wind in her face began to make her eyes water from its sheer velocity.

No Kentucky Derby ever saw two horses race this fast. Diakrina sensed Equus had stretched Phos to his maximum, which Phos was doing with ease. But it was clear from the greater ease with which Equus was running he was holding back.

The epic of this moment came over Diakrina: she was racing on horseback across a savanna on a horse of near other-worldly strength and speed, with no need to use reins or give guidance with leg pressure. And she was riding beside the proto human, the father of the human race. Who would ever believe it!

They pounded the savanna and rode over its rolling gentle hills and hollows for about twenty minutes. The savanna was filled with wildlife. And even racing past the various creatures with such speed was, for Diakrina, an amazing introduction to the world of animals. If a deer looked up at her and she caught its eye, she entered the world of the deer temporarily. She instantly identified with them and understood them.

She caught the eye of a reem as they raced through a low place. It was grazing and looked up as it heard their approach. She felt the reem's immediate concern, not alarm, and then felt that concern subside as it realized they were no predator. At the same time, she sensed something in the reem which, if it had been sensed in a human, you would have called, sturdy confidence. It was a fearless warrior among beasts and would not hesitate to defend itself against even a meat-eating dinosaur. And its great size and strength, along with its massive, razor-sharp horns, would likely give it every chance of winning such a contest.

They topped one hill and down below them in the next hollow was an area dotted with large broom trees. And under the trees were lions taking their rest in the shade.

Adam turned slightly right—more east—toward one of the largest broom trees under which about twenty lions were lying. Diakrina could tell immediately these were lions the size of the Smilodon she had encountered in the Great Meadow: the one on which she had been given her first sword lesson! They were the size of small modern-day elephants in height and several feet longer as the body of a cat is not boxy like that of an elephant.

As they approached to within fifty yards, a male lion much larger than the others stood up and came to the edge of the shade to survey them. Diakrina knew immediately there was zero fear in him! He was merely curious.

Adam pointed Equus in the large lion's direction. He showed not the lightest fear for himself or Equus, nor for Diakrina and Phos.

Normally Diakrina would have been full of questions about what was safe and what was not. But she had no need. She could read the lion's eyes, and she knew his intentions. She also knew that Equus and Phos were safe because they were secure in Adam and Diakrina's care. The lion and his pride would do nothing against their wishes.

As Diakrina had guessed by the time they reached him, this large male proved to be the alpha male, Lāvōn. When they got within ten yards the lion, according to his nature, gave a subtle, quick growl to confirm his status as the one in authority over the pride. Adam smiled and brought Equus to a stop and dismounted. Diakrina did the same.

Several of the other lions, out of curiosity, came up close behind on either side of Lāvōn. But it was clear that none of them would dare step closer to the approaching humans than their king.

"It is good to see you, my old friend," said Adam as he walked up to Lāvōn and placed his hand on his forehead. The great head of the lion dipped slightly for a second as his eyes closed momentarily in acceptance of Adam's touch. Then he sat down and looked attentively into Adam's face.

"I have brought one of my daughters to you, Lāvōn. We are in need of your help."

The lion's head turned slightly sideways and upward and he gave a small snarl. It was a lion's expression of excitement and anticipation.

Adam motioned for Diakrina to come. As she walked up to Lāvōn and reached out and touched him, his whole world opened to her. It was shocking and savage by human standards, but Diakrina had been given an innate knowledge of animals allowing her to contextualize what she received. The savage strength and ways of this beast was right and proper to him.

In that touch Lāvōn also came to know Diakrina—in the way lions know things. And it was clear some kind of rudimentary understanding of needing them to fight and conquer some foe—though it was linked to the idea of hunting in his understanding—was immediately understood by Lāvōn.

Diakrina quickly learned one characteristic of lions: any suggestion that might lead to a hunt was relished. And the desire to serve Adam, and now her, was so complete, even in these most fierce of beasts, their intuition of a coming conquest allowing them to do both—hunt (fight) and serve—immediately gave them a raw, vibrating passion of anticipation. Lions give themselves without inhibitions to their instincts to fight and conquer; it is a wild and over the edge surge of exhilaration which has no rein of reason to check it.

Lāvōn immediately turned toward the pride and gave a roar making the ground shake under their feet. Instantly, as if a bolt of electricity had hit them all, every lion and lioness leapt to all fours. This started something like a pregame hype as lions pawed wildly at the air or each other without causing any harm as they were snarling their readiness.

Adam walked up beside Lāvōn and said, "The fight will be very big, Lāvōn, with very strong and deadly men. I need you to call every pride within hearing to the hunt."

Lāvōn, without delay walked to the other side of the large broom tree and lifted his head toward the horizon of the savanna. What came out of him next shook not only the ground but made it necessary for Adam and Diakrina to cover their ears to protect them. Diakrina was sure no modern-day lion, which would be a quarter of Lāvōn's size, could produce anything remotely like it. She felt her insides vibrate from the rumbling, ground-shaking tones filling the air.

Within five seconds there were answers in kind coming back at them from every part of the horizon. It sounded as if twelve to fifteen different responses came rolling at them.

Adam turned to Diakrina and said, "I will take the horses with me and ride back to Dorogon by the same route we just transversed. Perhaps I can be of some use."

For a moment Diakrina was a little confused at his indication he was taking both horses. Adam noted her expression and immediately explained.

"You are going to lead this army. And Lāvōn will be your mount. Trust me, it will be quite a ride. But large, thick manes make it easy to stay in place. By your constant touch and communication with Lāvōn, you will be able to give direction to all the lions through him.

Adam then said to Lāvōn, "My daughter is to be your master in this battle. You are to protect her at all cost. Keep her well within your midst so none of the dangerous ones can get near her. The goal is to get her to the Tree Bridge without harm and without being captured: you know the place."

Lāvōn's eyes brightened, and he growled an affirmation. And in that moment Diakrina learned when the objective of a hunt or battle is given to a lion, he locks in on that objective and brings all his instincts into the service of realizing the objective. He thinks of nothing else without it being somehow related to the prime directive until it is accomplished, or it is clear it cannot be done. From that moment she had Lāvōn's full attention, and he kept his eyes on her awaiting her command to begin.

The roaring and striding continued for several minutes all around Lāvōn, Adam, Diakrina and the two horses. The whole pride was ready to begin. But of course, they had to wait for the others.

It wasn't too long before Diakrina saw hundreds of fast-moving grass streams and rivulets coming at them on the horizon. Lions in fast, loping gates were covering the ground between them quickly. Lion battle cries were filling the air. Lāvōn gave a roar calling them all to come to him and follow.

Then Lāvōn turned to Diakrina and lay down for her to climb on his back. Even lying down, she could not possibly get on him without climbing by grabbing handfuls of mane and pulling herself up like a rock climber. At first, she was afraid Lāvōn might not like his mane pulled on so hard and used to climb with. But she soon realized it gave him not the least discomfort, as she was too light to cause it.

It took some creative mountaineering, but after about ten-seconds of scramble, she was finally on Lāvōn's massive back, right behind his mane. She grabbed two large handfuls and looked down at Adam. He was smiling up at her and had evidently found her means of getting in the saddle amusing.

But then his smile took on a proud and reassuring look of

determination. "The blessing of the Living One be on you, my daughter. We will meet again. If not in this time, beyond it."

He gave Diakrina such a look of approval and confidence she felt as if her heart would burst from the joy of it. Then without another word, he turned and mounted Equus with a single, fluid motion. And calling to Phos to follow, gave Diakrina one last nod of grace and then shouted, "To the battle."

Equus pawed the air and leapt to action with Phos right beside him. Lāvōn gave a roar that was deafening and which made Diakrina's whole body vibrate so intensely she took hold of his mane with all her might for fear of being vibrated right off his back.

It was a good thing she had. For the next moment Lāvōn sprang forward like he was ambushing prey. There were roars and snarls rolling over the grassland as an army with teeth and claws burst to life and poured over the savanna in pursuit of the steeds.

Chapter Eighteen

THE BATTLE OF DOROGON

"Oh! OOOOOOOH!" is all that was coming out of Diakrina's mouth for the first few seconds. THIS was riding indeed! Diakrina claims if you have never ridden a large, elephant sized lion at full charging speed—and of course, who has!—you have never yet lived.

"It is hard to put into words," she explained. "It is the difference between the thundering, hoof-pounding ride of an antediluvian steed and the raw, muscles-rippling charge of an antediluvian lion whose great feet are padded and soft but whose power is hard, forceful and frighteningly dynamic. It might be something like having a cushioned, coil-spring ride which levels out everything even while you are on the back of a bucking Brahma bull. Something savage and unrestrained is going on under you. But somehow, you are flowing with the lion's ability to interject stealth and seamless coordination into its every movement.

"All I could do was grasp more firmly to the hands-full of mane I had and hold on with everything in me." Then Diakrina's nearly clear, blue eyes took on that faraway look which always filled them whenever she was remembering something so intensely, she was reliving it.

"In less than a minute Lāvōn and I were in clear and constant communication. I had entered his world without leaving mine. And by means of that foothold in my own world, I—somehow the stronger in this sense—could pull Lāvōn up with me into my world. As we charged across the savanna, I filled him with the knowledge of my quest and with an understanding of what was at stake.

"By means of this interaction Lāvōn's knowledge clearly rose, by my gift to him, beyond that of a lion. However, his response to it was still that of a lion. When he understood Anomos' deadly plan and its ability to extinguish all hope for the whole present creation, I felt a deep rumble of anger and raw rage within Lāvōn's body. It seemed to cause him to lunge forward with even greater speed and determination to reach the battle."

Diakrina's passions and motives were communicated to Lāvōn in a way a lion could understand. But more than this, Lāvōn was raised above a lion's understanding by being united to Diakrina. It must have been for Lāvōn almost like it is for a human when an angel visits and reveals things which were before unimaginable. In a phrase, Lāvōn was having an other-worldly-experience.

And of course, so was Diakrina. If she had been delighted at feeling as if Phos' four powerful legs were under her control, imagine what was going on in her as she and Lāvōn increasingly merged into a single motive force in regard to action.

Lāvōn was one of the most powerful and agile creatures to ever come from the hand of the Creator. To have such raw power, instincts, agility and fierce intentionality under the control of her every thought was intoxicating to say the least. In these moments she knew what it was like to be a lion without ceasing to be human. And in some sense Lāvōn was experiencing something of her humanity. And by doing so he was more fully a lion than he had ever been and Diakrina by doing so was more fully human than she had ever been.

As Diakrina came to understand, lions were created to know humans and humans to know lions: at least that is how it had been in a better world. And both find some aspect of their true lion-ness or humanness by means of the other. "And perhaps," added Diakrina, "it is so with all the other animals and a human when this communication is undiminished."

Diakrina said it is hard to explain the mixture of wonder and delight, which at the same time was mingled with serious resolve and deadly intentions. Both she and Lāvōn were experiencing an expanded capacity to accomplish their objective. He was filled with her understanding and intentions, she with his mono-focused, beastly resolve.

This army, fierce beyond modern mind's ability to conceive, covered the savanna in a blaze of speed. And you must remember in these ancient times the thicker atmosphere, the higher oxygen content and the greater vitality of living things, made it possible for all creatures to run or work without tiring for long periods of time in a way which would be impossible today.

When they reached the point of the savanna where the two ridges came together, this army of teeth and claws began flowing up the ridge, in and around the trees of the forest, so there was not a single space between the trees in which a charging lion or lioness was not bounding uphill. Lāvōn began to give low, guttural, almost subsonic groans from his body which all the lions, for hundreds of yards in every direction, could hear and understand. He was communicating in lion the importance of the battle, the importance of protecting Diakrina, and the absolute necessity of being willing to die, if necessary, to see this objective accomplished.

In response there were deep, guttural subsonic groans which erupted all around Diakrina and Lāvōn. She felt them more than heard them. And before Diakrina knew what she was doing she was talking to all the lions through Lāvōn. Her thoughts and intentions and commands were given to Lāvōn and he translated them to all the others by this subsonic communication.

The result was Diakrina was not just controlling the body of the lion on which she was riding, but now, also, through an inexplicable connection, controlling a flowing wave of savage, fierce lion-power, filled with vicious intentions. Through her all the lions, which she now, somehow, knew were 294 lions and lionesses, became like a mythical, single beast covering the landscape. They were coordinated with the intelligence of a human at their head and the power, agility and killing instincts of lions at the point of execution in 294 places.

This army of 294 had the killing power of 294,000 humans. Diakrina could feel the anticipation of the lions as they began to use her gift of imagination, which was available to them through their connection with her, to visualize attacking the human warriors of Anomos. Their instinct for fighting factually conveyed what would be the results.

And Diakrina needed all her contextualizing powers to handle the bloody-red surge of passion filling the lions as the scenes of massive slaughter unfolded before her mind. Indeed, these lions would cut a swath of corpses through the Sons of Cain, carpeting the earth with lifeless men faster than she could count them. Diakrina began to see an average of one man would die every six seconds for each and every lion: which would be 2940 men a minute. This could translate into 29,400 men in just ten minutes if allowed to continue unchecked.

It was this insight which caused Diakrina to realize she must convey some limits to the lions' passions to kill. They must kill for the objective, not merely for killing's sake. Fortunately for Diakrina, lions are wired by their hunting instincts to understand conservation of energy toward a purpose. And she immediately sensed their conformity to her redirection of their savage impulses.

Yet, while it was redirected, it was not lessened. And Diakrina knew it. She couldn't help beginning to form a kind of prayer of compassion for the enemy and the bloodshed they had made necessary, "God help any man who gets in the way of the objective!"

Equus and Phos, under Adam's command, continued to lead the way toward the top of the ridge. As the trees became more closely set you would have thought it would necessitate slowing down. Not so. Both the horses and the lions were the very incarnation of agility.

It soon became clear to Diakrina Lāvōn was even aware of the need to avoid going through places too narrow or too low which might endanger Diakrina's ability to stay mounted by dragging her off. His natural ability to determine if a space was large enough for him to pass through now included Diakrina. And his eye was never wrong: even though a few times Diakrina found herself wondering if he had miscalculated. Yet in every case, even though she ducked out of reflex the first few times, his judgment proved to be correct and the space was always adequate by inches.

As she could also perceive his forward-looking decision-making, in a sense Lāvōn was training her in how to read his spatial perception as he picked their path forward. The result was her growing trust in the lion's abilities caused all her fears to be vanquished. She and Lāvōn became united in coordinated responses to every leap, every sideways dart, and, yes, even every bounce off the sides of tree trunks, which gave them another dimension—up—in which to find adequate spaces to continue forward without hesitation. For unlike horses, lions are at home, like any cat, using vertical surfaces; they are a natural part of their considered options in transversing any space.

Because Diakrina could anticipate each turn, leap and ricochet off tree trunks along with Lāvōn, it made it possible for her to ride him as if she were part of his body. Without this ability no human could have managed to remain on Lāvōn's back. But because of this ability she and Lāvōn performed a kind of high-speed ballet through the forest.

Adam had not led them back up the way he and Diakrina had come down the ridge. He constantly veered right—west—in order to bring them up the ridge at the point where it joined the larger ridge. They were not going down to Dorogon. Strateia had made it clear they were to come down the open slope into the meadow to the west and below the cliffs of Dorogon.

Diakrina knew she would need a few seconds once they reached the top and could see down into the meadow to determine the state of the battle and which army occupied which part of the valley. Presumably the Sons of El would be close to the cliffs and fighting a two front battle: the larger army of the Sons of Cain coming down the mountain behind them, and the other units in front, between them and the Bridge. Of course, the goal was to quickly eliminate the units at the Bridge so a clear path to the Bridge could be secured behind their lines.

When they actually topped the ridge the roar of battle came up to meet them from the meadow below. Diakrina gave a command for her army with teeth and claws to come to a pause well back, out of sight, so none below would see them. To the lions this was a stalking moment and they knew well how to comply.

Diakrina had Lāvōn creep forward so she could just see over the top of the ridge. In this way she could determine what they should do next. Adam, who had reached the top slightly ahead of them, had also stayed well back. He came riding along the ridge toward Diakrina.

"Beware the nekros, daughter. I have counted three in the skies over the battle and they are large and formidable. Instruct Lāvōn to have six lions to surround him and you with their primary concern being to keep any attacking nekros from you. If the nekros come low enough to get at you, the lions can reach them and bring them down with a coordinated effort."

"What are you going to do?" asked Diakrina.

"I will go to the top of Dorogon and help indirectly," answered Adam.

Then seeing a questioning look on Diakrina's face, Adam added, "I will not kill any of the sons of my firstborn, Cain, with my own hand. It is not for a father to kill his own with his own hand no matter how wrong they have become." Then pausing for a breath, he added, "At least … I hope it will never come to that."

In that moment, Diakrina saw the whole terrible conflict below them through different eyes—Adam's eyes. The pain she discerned in his words nearly broke her heart. There in the valley, locked in blood-soaked battle, were his sons; they were all his sons. And though he understood the necessity of the battle and sided with what he knew to be right, he was still the father, grandfather and great grandfather, etc. of every man killing and dying below them.

For a fleeting moment Diakrina saw behind his courageous eyes and beheld the dreadful sense of responsibility he bore for it all. How many times had he spent a sleepless night wishing he could undo one fatal decision which had given it all birth?

Then regaining himself, Adam said, "Courage daughter. We will gain the Bridge. I'm sure of it."

Then he pulled Equus alongside Lāvōn, and reaching out his hand onto the top of her head, he looked to the sky.

"Living One," he pled, "shield her with Your Light on all sides, as well as above and beneath." And with that, he and Equus and Phos turned and galloped down the top of the smaller ridge toward the place where they could pass down into Dorogon.

It took only a moment for Diakrina to see the state of the battle and it was not good. The battlefront was easy to see because the Son of El were all dressed in their bright blue with their swords made of the shiny, bright, bluish metal. The Son of Cain were dressed all in black with black metal swords. They looked like a wave of darkness trying to overrun the courageous wave of bright blue warriors withstanding them.

Diakrina could see that near the Bridge, on the far side of the trees lining the meadow to the south and west, there was still a small force of the Sons of Cain holding a position which gave them control of the Bridge access. The Sons of El were trying to fight their way through. But some of Anomos' warriors from the first force which pursued them down the mountain had fought their way to the area and were holding out against the Sons of El. They were keeping them from being able to make any progress.

The army of the Sons of El filled the area between the cliffs and the tree line, which was about 200 yards from the point of the base of the cliffs. But out in front of the cliffs and to the west of them, up to where she and her army stood, they were pressed back nearly to the very cliffs themselves. They held only a small alley along the eastern side of the meadow, and they were clinging to it only by fierce fighting. It was primarily the help of the archers at the top of Dorogon keeping them from being overrun.

The rest of the valley was filled with Anomos' forces. They were organized so as one unit fell along the front, another would take its place. Their manner of execution of this kind of death-march tactic looked as if they were in some kind of hypnotic spell.

The Sons of El were clearly the better warriors and were taking down Anomos' frontlines of warriors ten to one. But they were gravely outnumbered and could not keep up such a fierce blood brawl much longer.

Every unit they eliminated was replaced by another coming behind it. Anomos even had units of warriors which were not fighting but whose job it was to pull the dead away from the front so their bodies would not hinder the advance of the next wave of warriors they were sending against the Sons of El.

Diakrina knew she had to think and act quickly. She determined the best course of action was to bring her army down the slope into the side of Anomos' forces, right where the battlefront was formed near the cliffs. In this way, her lions could blindside them and the Sons of El could surge forward to move the front out away from the cliffs toward the west, deeper into the meadow. She made it clear to Lāvōn he and the six other lions that would be with her were to keep to the left of the charge so they would be closest to the front and nearest to the warriors of the Sons of El.

She remembered to tell the lions they were to give a thundering roar as they descended the ridge. All seemed ready. Yet, she was still hesitant to give the command for the lions to charge. She was second-guessing herself. Had she made the right decision about where to attack? Clearly, she had no time left for more consideration. Yet, she must be sure she was doing the right thing.

Suddenly, Strateia came to a stop in midair out in front of her and Lāvōn. Diakrina was so relived to see him. Somehow he knew her decision. (It is likely he had been told.)

"You have decided correctly, give the command now! The larger force of Anomos is about to come over the ridge to your right. You must be well ahead of them. When you get near the Bridge I will come to you. Anomos has his demon warlords helping the units there and you will need the help of my brothers and I to deal with them."

By demon warlords, Diakrina knew he meant the wicked demon warriors like Sarx and Desmos and the contemptible Monk. She certainly had no desire to content with them again. Yet it seemed it was going to be unavoidable. Still, she could take courage Strateia was aware of them and had mentioned his brothers—likely the ones who had come with him at her rescue. She would not be alone.

Strateia was instantly gone and Diakrina wasted not another second. She drew her sword, pushed her shield a little farther up her left arm so she could get a firmer hold on to Lāvōn's mane with her left hand, and then gave the order.

Thunder filled the air as every lion sprang forward and let loose a roar shaking the earth. Lāvōn's roar was so loud its affect on Diakrina was like being in Nekus Canyon near the falls. Even the sound of the battle below which had been so loud only moments before was vanquished by this terrible blast.

The wall of lions surging down the ridge was over a hundred yards wide and two to three lions deep in all places. Diakrina took note every warrior in the valley looked either to his right—Sons of El—or to his left—Sons of Cain. Evidently Jared had informed his men in Dorogon and sent word down to the army below about the coming of the lions, for there was a shout of triumph that rose from the Sons of El. But the look on the faces of Anomos' army was one of pure shock and then unadulterated terror.

There was a desperate attempt by a few of the captains among the Sons of Cain to turn the warriors toward the coming wave of teeth and claws. But they had little success. Their warriors were dumb struck at what they were seeing.

As the lions came closer to their ranks, another earth-shaking roar rolled out of them. More than half the warriors turned and fled. The others which tried to hold their ground were mostly paralyzed with fear. They didn't have a chance.

The lions hit the warriors at full speed and body parts began to fly in every direction. It seemed every lion was swatting with both front claws as he ran. Every swat shredded some warrior into pieces. Several lions also caught up warriors in their jaws as they continued through the ranks slashing and mauling. These were usually bitten nearly in half and the mangled body sent spiraling through the air by a quick shake of the lion's head in one direction or the other.

It would not be proper to give detailed, blood-drenched descriptions that could add pages to this book concerning the carnage the lions exacted on the Sons of Cain who served Anomos' army. It was devastating to say the least. Everywhere there was blood splattered on pieces of black uniforms—few were in one piece and connected to a whole body.

As the lions passed through the ranks of the army all along the front, behind the lions as they passed, the Sons of El pushed forward and moved the battle line out into the meadow. Diakrina really had no opportunity or need to use her sword on anyone as there were no live warriors who even came near her: though not a few parts of dying ones flew past.

However, she needed her sword when the nekros descended. Two nekros came diving out of the sky. Clearly, they had the intent of snatching up Diakrina from off Lāvōn's back. As the first swooped down and was almost on her with both its talons extended toward her, two of the six lions surrounding Diakrina and Lāvōn leapt high into the air. Each lion's mouth clamped down on one of the legs of the nekros. It tried to reverse itself in midair. But while the nekros was much larger than the lions it still could not lift two of them into the air. It struck downward with its fang-filled mouth at one of the lions. That was its fatal mistake.

A third lion, which was waiting just for that kind of move by the nekros leapt into the air and wrapped its claws and teeth around the neck of the beast and bit down with savage force. The three lions now pulled the nekros from the sky as several more lions then climbed on. Within two seconds of the beast hitting the ground they had severed its head from its long neck.

However, a second nekros came falling out of the sky to Diakrina's left. She just caught a glimpse of it before it was on her. She turned and swung hard in the direction of its outstretched talons. At the same moment she began to make her swing she sensed Lāvōn had determined to act as well. She instinctively knew as she swung her sword she must hold onto his mane with all her strength.

Lāvōn leaped into the air and turned left toward the nekros as Diakrina swung. Diakrina and Lāvōn were so synchronized his powerful turn added force to her sword swing. Her sword hit its mark and the left appendage of the nekros came off.

Lāvōn also fastened on his mark. His jaws clamped down on the nekros' right leg and he pulled down hard on it with a powerful surge of his whole body. The beast was slung past them down to the ground with a crash. It had no chance from there. Three other lions were on it by the time it hit and the rest you can imagine for yourself.

However, as clearly as Lāvōn and the lions were giving the Sons of El the edge in regard to the part of Anomos' army which was composed of the Sons of Cain, this was not the whole of Anomos' forces. The closer they came to the point of the cliffs and the tree line of the forest beyond it, which was about 200-yards away, the clearer it became to Diakrina there was another force gathered there which was holding back the Sons of El.

In a strip of forest, which was about 250-yards deep, and lay between the Meadow of Dorogon and the small clearing leading to the Tree Bridge, where the other units of the Sons of Cain were guarding the access to the Bridge, Anomos himself and several of his demonic warlords—among them were Desmos and Sarx and about 11 others like them—had formed a line.

It was clear they intended to block access to the Bridge and the Sons of El were falling back away from them. The warriors could not engage them because these demon warlords were standing in a row along the front of the forest creating a greenish, pale line of glowing flames between them and also out in front of them. These flames blazed out from them with fierce heat which drove the warriors backward.

The question beginning to rise in Diakrina's mind was if the lions could actually take on these warlords and their greenish blaze. They were not material beings. They were spirits—depraved, fallen elohim. Their powers clearly far exceeded that of material nature in any of its forms. Did Strateia have a plan to deal with them? He seemed to indicate he had been given reinforcement to fight them. Diakrina could only assume these meant warriors of the Living One, much like the ones with him at her rescue from Parad?

Yet, there was more than these demon warlords to worry about. Diakrina knew a large force of the Sons of Men, which had been recruited some 20,000 strong, were marching on the valley. Diakrina turned her head to look back to the northwest where Strateia said this force would come from.

Her heart sank. There, at the top of the ridge, the front lines of this force were just appearing. Their captains were overlooking the

Valley of Dorogon to determine where to best deploy their warriors. If she and the Sons of El did not move fast they would be sandwiched between these converging forces.

The whole of the warriors of the Sons of El were falling in behind Diakrina and Lāvōn and the other lions and starting to fight a retreating rear guard action against anyone trying to catch up to Diakrina and her army of lions. This meant there was no place to go but toward the Bridge and toward Anomos and his demon warlords. But was this what they were to do?

Clearly, dealing with the demon warlords was still the big issue. And Strateia and his fellow warriors were the only ones who could engage them.

While these thoughts were going through her mind, Diakrina suddenly heard that silver voice of Strateia, which he said only she could hear.

"Diakrina, turn to your left and come toward the base of the cliffs of Dorogon, right at its point which reaches farthest out into the meadow toward the forest. DO NOT ATTEMPT TO ENGAGE ANOMOS AND HIS WARLORDS WITH LĀVŌN AND THE LIONS!" He said emphatically. "Rather, bring all the prides to the base of the cliffs to form a defensive barrier back toward the army that will advance down the ridge. Have Lāvōn direct all the lions to form a defensive barrier in a half circle all around the point of Dorogon. Jared and his warrior are to form a line behind them. You and Lāvōn, with the six-lion unit which are guarding you, are to take your place near the cliffs behind these two line."

Then there was a pause, and she heard Strateia say, "A very different kind of battle is about to begin. Your part is to be ready to follow my orders from behind the lines being formed. And whatever I tell you to do, do without hesitation! Act immediately. Understood?"

"Yes!" shouted Diakrina knowing somehow Strateia could hear her.

Diakrina communicated to Lāvōn Strateia's orders and all the lions began clearing a path to the base of Dorogon. From this point, where Strateia had instructed her to go, it was only about 500-yards to the Bridge. As mentioned before, there was about 200-yards of open meadow and then about 250-yards of forest. Beyond the forest, 50-yards from the Bridge, there was a final clearing which would have to be crossed. It was in this clearing where the units guarding the access to the Bridge had formed a final line of defense.

Certainly, with Anomos and his demon warlords only 200-hundred yards away at the edge of the forest, this part of the battle seem to be ready to erupt into something very otherworldly.

When Lāvōn and Diakrina and the other six lions reached the point of the cliffs of Dorogon, the warriors who were already forming lines there, opened their ranks and allowed them to pass inside. The other lions, however, turned and began forming a new line in front of the one the warriors were defending.

The lions did this by decimating the units of the Sons of Cain fighting there and then forming an arc which they kept expanding out around the point in both directions: toward the northwest, where the large force was organizing to charge down the ridge, and toward the south in the direction of the Bridge and Anomos' warlords.

This new line brought the battle somewhat to a standstill as the Sons of Cain began to draw back from the lions and would not engage them. The lions stood facing them, each about four feet from another lion, roaring and pacing back and forth and daring any warriors to advance.

They didn't.

This momentary still in the storm, which had begun to descend over the valley of Dorogon, was only like the eye of a hurricane. For the battle erupting next made both men and lions seem secondary members of the conflict.

Chapter Nineteen

THE BATTLE FOR THE TREE BRIDGE

As Diakrina and Lāvōn looked toward the warlords of Anomos, in this momentary quiet, Diakrina had no sense of what might happen next. She took advantage of the moment to make sure she had everything in place: her sword and its sheath, her shield, the glowing page from the book, which she kept folded inside her dress just above the belt which held her sword and scabbard. Instinctively she started to check for the crystal container but then remember she didn't have it.

It seemed so strange to her not to have the crystal container with the Atheos. Strateia seemed to indicate it likely would not be recovered from Anomos. However, it was secured inside the crystal container of infinite light which not even Anomos could penetrate. In that sense, at least, her quest was a success. Yet, somehow, she hoped it would be recovered.

Diakrina began to imagine what would happen if Anomos indeed did succeed in keeping the Atheos in the Severed Lands. Even though he could not carry out his plan to create a race of immortal humans who were forever doomed to serve him, he could, nonetheless, use the overpowering fragrance of the Atheos, which came through the crystal container, to manipulate men. Men seemed helpless against the desires to obtain it which the Atheos kindled.

The Atheos would be something always out of men's reach; something they could never actually obtain. Yet, in the madness and obsession it would create mankind would kill and slaughter one another just to possess the crystal container and to have the kindled desire of the Fruit in their possession: "Better to itch than not, even if you can't scratch, is the philosophy of the madness it kindles in men," thought Diakrina.

The passion for paradise which the Immortal Fruit kindles, but which evil puts out of reach as long as it infects you, torments men's souls. And this manic torment would actually destroy all possibilities of any degree of paradise in the Severed Lands. Bloodshed, war, greed and destruction would reign where men and tribes fought to obtain the Immortal Fruit.

Something so beautiful and good in its essence, when placed out of its proper context and, by a severe mercy, placed out of people's reach—but not their sight and senses—would be one of evil's most terrible weapons: insane longings severed from the hope of fulfillment. Diakrina realized the history of the world she knew, which in this time and place still lay before her in unfolded ages, revealed this to be the trademark of evil.

Evil stirs up a sense of loss which enslaves the soul. It kindles a fierce, uncontrollable obsession and pursuit—an irrational pursuit—of what you ultimately will come to realize is forever beyond your grasp. Thirst with ever-retreating water in sight. Hunger with food always just beyond your reach.

Perhaps it would be this trait of evil magnified by the presence of the Atheos that would doom the Antediluvians to such bloodshed and wickedness the Living One would determine to wipe all the earth clean and make a new start. This world, as she was now experiencing it, would be obliterated by a great judgment with only a remnant of mankind and beasts being preserved.

Diakrina was startled out of these thoughts by a stinging acrid ray of greenish light radiating from over the horizon. It was coming from behind the place where the demon warlords had taken their positions. Coming from the area where she had first encountered the Mist outside the cave, was an all too recognizable and overwhelming presence.

Anomos had summoned Bellicose. He was not yet in sight, but

his acrid, stinging stench was broadcasting his approach. And the fear which this realization cast over every warrior's soul created a visible change in each man's countenance.

Then he rose. Anomos, himself, rose like a bright star from the forest over the whole Dorogon Valley, filling the sky like a second sun. Diakrina had to shade her eyes from the brilliance of his illumination.

Higher and higher he rose until he was several hundred feet in the air. Then he came to a standstill in the sky.

Between the acrid stinging stench of Bellicose, radiating in the air from over the horizon, and the blaze of light coming from Anomos, it was hard to see anything without squinting and constantly wiping one's watering, stinging eyes.

"I am the prince and power of the air," came a voice which thundered and rolled over the valley. "These Severed Lands are my right to rule."

Then from somewhere behind Diakrina, high up, came a voice like a trumpet. It was a voice which Diakrina recognized. But she had never heard it used with this kind of intensity and power.

"True, Anomos Poneros—yet not the whole truth. You rule in these Severed Lands by having usurped Adam's authority through deceit. And you are, yourself, ruled by the Living One, the true King who has no equal and bows to none. You rule at His pleasure until your appeal is answered. Then your rule will end. For you have been condemned."

"Who dares to speak to me in this manner?" roared Anomos with a flash of lightening filling the sky.

"I, Strateia, servant and warrior of the Living One, have spoken to you. And the words I speak to you are not my own. They come from the Throne which rules you and all that exists. Otherwise, I would not speak."

"Strateia! I know your name. You are called warrior. Well, we shall see how well you and your warriors can fight!"

Then Anomos turned and looked in the direction from which the acrid stench of Bellicose was radiating. "Come!" He bellowed in a voice shaking the whole valley.

Diakrina knew what the outcome could be if Bellicose came among them. All the men, Sons of El and Sons of Cain alike would perish. And obviously Anomos cared little He might be slaughtering his own human troops as well as those which opposed him.

But Diakrina knew Anomos would not allow the radiating flames of Bellicose to consume her. For that would defeat his purpose. What was his plan? How did he intend to shield her while unleashing Bellicose on all the others?

One thing she was certain of: she could not let it happen. Somehow, she had to find a way to expose herself to the danger of Bellicose in such a way it would protect the others. No matter what protection Anomos might attempt to put over or around her, she must find a way to put herself beyond it—positioning herself so he could not expose the others to Bellicose without exposing her as well. It was the only way to save the others.

Yet, on the other hand, if she exposed herself, and Anomos captured her, all would be undone and his scheme would succeed. For she now understood well the powers he had to bring her into subjection to his will and make her retrieve the Atheos. She couldn't risk letting that happen.

Lāvōn could sense Diakrina's desire to do something. But he equally understood her hesitance. But more importantly, Strateia understood her thoughts. And this soon became apparent.

In that silver voice, which only she could hear, she heard Strateia interrupt her thoughts.

"Diakrina, there is some warrant to your strategy. However, it is very precarious. Anomos has already dispatched Desmos and Sarx along with four other dark warriors. They will attack the defensive line the lions have established with only one goal in mind: to break through to you and take you captive."

Just the thought of those two demon warriors, and the others with them, made Diakrina shiver with disgust and fear. She had no desire to become their captive. And she knew if she did, the vile Monk would not be far behind.

Strateia interrupted her thoughts again.

"Diakrina, a battle of Titians is about to explode over this area. You will understand what I mean in just a moment. If we time everything exactly right, Lāvōn and the six lions with you can take advantage of the explosive eruption in the battle to make your move for the Bridge. This will force Desmos and Sarx to back track their charge and try to overtake you at the Bridge. And it is likely the Monk will make his appearance once you are at the bridge.

"But don't fear, we have a little surprise in store for him and Anomos."

Diakrina could not help but interrupt Strateia. "What of Jared and his men. How will they survive? Bellicose's radiating acrid flames will consume them. We can't let that happen, Strateia!"

"Leave that to me, Little One. I have a small army of the Living One's warriors hidden here near me. They are prepared to create a shield over the Sons of El to protect them from more than Bellicose."

"More than Bellicose?

"Yes, I told you this battle is going titanic."

"But what of the Sons of Cain. I am sure Anomos has no intentions of having mercy even on his own human troops. They will be burned to ashes."

"Most will flee. Many will perish. I cannot protect them from the consequences of their unfortunate alliance with Anomos. They have embraced darkness. Many will now discover what darkness really means. For Anomos always rules by betrayal."

Diakrina could not help but feel deep sorrow for these wayward sons of Adam. "What must Adam be feeling now," she thought, "as he watches from the hill of Dorogon?"

"Diakrina, the moment is here," said Strateia. "I can see the dark warriors of Anomos making their way toward the line of lions on the south. Just as they attack, you and Lāvōn and the other six lions are to make your move and head straight southeast for the Bridge. At the same moment I will engage Anomos and will unleash our remedy for Bellicose. He—this remedy—will become the shield between you and

Bellicose's acrid beams. Be ready to move at my command."

Diakrina had no idea who, or what this "remedy for Bellicose" could be, but Strateia's confident mention of such a remedy was very reassuring.

Suddenly there was an eruption of roars and battle cries from the defensive line to Diakrina's right. Clearly the dark warriors were making their move. At the same moment a flash of pale green, acrid beams came blazing over the horizon as the head of Bellicose rose high in the sky. Anomos, who was still suspended high in the sky, placed himself between Bellicose and the location of Diakrina and Lāvōn. He purposely cast a long shadow out toward them that was clearly keeping the greenish flames from hitting her.

However, the flames hit with force everywhere else. The warriors of the Sons of El, gathering in protective formations, joined their shield in such a way as to form a combined covering. All around them the terrible heat began to burn the grass and earth.

At the same moment three other things happened. Strateia came shooting into the sky in the direction of Anomos. As he did, a large unit of golden warriors like Strateia filled the sky between Bellicose and the Sons of El gathered near the cliffs of Dorogon, and on its top in the ruins.

Like Strateia had done in the cave—which Diakrina had only learned about later—they spread their robes of light over the sky to form a golden protective canopy above the army and Diakrina. This canopy was formed from the cliffs out over the army and in the direction of the Tree Bridge, which gave Diakrina and Lāvōn a corridor toward the Bridge protected from Bellicose's flames.

However, there were still several of the Sons of Cain between them and the Bridge and she and Lāvōn and the other six lions would have to fight their way through them.

The third thing which happened—at the same moment all the other was happening—was a massive golden, blue, and white light flooding the horizon from beyond the Tree Bridge. It came from the direction of the Garden. It was like the rising of a hundred suns. And suddenly, in swift flight, Diakrina saw a sight which took her breath away.

The great Guardian of the Tree, which stood over 450-feet high and burned like a white-hot furnace—the one who had been standing at the gates of the Garden; the one giving Strateia permission for Diakrina to be in the Garden—came flying through the sky on wings of terrifying flames. He flew behind Strateia who had flown directly at Anomos.

Strateia's voice suddenly echoed all around them. It sounded like a silver trumpet of immense size. His words shook the whole valley.

"IN THE NAME OF THE LIVING ONE, ANOMOS, YOU WILL ANSWER TO THE GUARDIAN OF THE TREE WHOSE TRUST YOU VIOLATED. JUSTICE IS IN HIS SWORD AND THE COURTS OF THE LIVING ONE WILL UPHOLD HIS GRIEVANCE AGAINST YOU. HE HAS BEEN GIVEN PERMISSION TO UNLEASH HIS WRATH WITHOUT RESTRAINT."

Anomos roared a defiant curse and turned toward Bellicose. "Stop him, Bellicose! Stop him! Now!"

Bellicose lifted one arm and threw his hand toward the flaming Guardian of the Tree. Greenish balls of fire looking like flaming brimstone came streaking from his hand. They were bolder-sized missiles. But the Guardian's flames, which surrounded him for hundreds of feet in every direction, only disintegrated each flaming fireball before it could touch him.

And while all this was commencing in the sky above Dorogon valley, Diakrina, Lāvōn and the six lions made a break for it. Diakrina pulling her sword gave the command. Lāvōn and the lions leaped into action as a single unit.

When they reached the defensive line between the two armies, the Sons of El's lines opened. Diakrina found the soldiers of the Sons of Cain on the other side distracted and overwhelmed with all happening above them. This is what Diakrina had counted on.

When the warriors saw the seven lions charging toward them, they gave no contest. Instead, they leaped to the right and to the left trying to avoid their teeth and claws. Some of the quicker ones were successful, but several were shredded where they stood.

Instantly, Diakrina and the lions were in among the warriors of the Son of Men. The soldiers were so tightly ranked the lions were treading more on the bodies of men than they were on earth. Diakrina heard a captain up ahead of them scream an order for the warriors to form a defensive line and stop Diakrina and the lions. There was enough threat in the captain's voice his men took a battle stance with their swords and lances positioned to meet the lions' advance.

Diakrina realized immediately the lions would be impaled on the lances if they tried to charge straight at the line. However, she instantly knew what they needed to do, and she communicated it quickly to Lāvōn, who almost simultaneously conveyed it to the other six.

Diakrina directed the lions to turn to the left and hit the line at an angle using their great claws to strike the side of the lance points and slap them down toward the ground. Then continuing in this angular manner, they advanced into the midst of the troops until they surpassed the frontline lance defenses.

Diakrina had her sword in her hand and the blade was blazing with intense crimson light. When the six lions in front of her and Lāvōn hit the defensive line of lances Diakrina could not have believed the strategy would work so well. Lances and men were actually upended by the powerful swats of the lions' front paws. Immediately men and lances were flying in all directions. The lions also kept their teeth busy snatching up warrior after warrior and slinging them into the warriors ahead as they severed their bodies into pieces. This created total chaos among the ranks in front of them.

Only a few warriors managed to weave through the six lions and get close to Diakrina. However, that was their last accomplishment as Lāvōn made short work of most of them and Diakrina managed to strike down about four or five with her sword.

Unknown to Diakrina, Strateia had directed Jared and several of his best units to fall in behind Diakrina and the lions. Their purpose was to fight a rearguard action to keep the warriors of the Sons of Men from trying to overtake Diakrina from behind.

Strateia had also sent seven of his fellow warriors with Jared. He knew the moment Diakrina and the lions started moving, and Desmos and Sarx, and the other four demon warriors with them realized it, they would turn and begin to give chase. Jared and his men would be no match for these dark gods. And Strateia was not about to allow them to be slaughtered as a sacrifice.

The warriors of the Living One did not strike down the human warriors of Anomos, but turned their backs to Diakrina and Lāvōn and formed a line in the air just above the heads of Jared and his men. They had their eyes fixed on Desmos and Sarx and the other four warriors with them.

Suddenly, the whole earth shook like a number 10 magnitude earthquake had just hit. What had actually happened was the Guardian of the Gate had flown swiftly toward Anomos. The Living One had given the Guardian authority to right the wrong committed against his trust. This gave the 450-foot flaming titian inconceivable power.

Anomos, sensing he could not withstand the great Guardian's charge, had retreated behind Bellicose, whom he had ordered to stop the Guardian. When the valley had shaken with a massive earthquake-like tremor, it was the result of the very moment Bellicose and the Guardian collided in combat. What is more, intense waves of white, gold and blue flames intermingled with greenish, stinging, acrid flames. Together they exploded outward from the two titians like the rings from an atomic explosion.

In the same manner in which the explosive force of Mount Saint Helen's eruption had leveled 230-square miles of timber, these waves leveled almost everything in the Dorogon valley. It was only Diakrina and the six lions, along with the other lions and warriors of the Sons of El, that were kept from experiencing the direct blast. They were covered by the shield of the Living One's warriors.

Many of the warriors of the Sons of Cain, the ones closest to the Tree Bridge, were instantly vaporized. However, the shield keeping the Sons of El protected also deflected much of the force upward and away from the other warriors of the Sons of Cain who were further into the valley. However, even with this benefit, it resulted in them being temporarily knocked either unconscious or dazed so badly they were staggering helpless trying to recover their wits.

With all this protection being provided to Diakrina and the Sons of El, the impact of the shaking of the earth was still so intense almost everyone lost their footing. Even the lions, as nimble as they were, were fighting to keep their balance.

Diakrina had to grasp Lāvōn's mane with both hands, even though she also had to keep hold of the handle of her sword. To do this, she simply grasped some of his mane with her hand opened around the handle. Then clamping down on Lāvōn's strong locks against the handle of the sword she was able to get a second firm grip.

It was good she did. The earthquake-like trembling of the earth had dislodged a large tree, and it came crashing down toward Diakrina and Lāvōn. Realizing he could not get beyond the place where the tree was going to land, because it was so large, Lāvōn and Diakrina—for you must remember they were in constant instant communication through Diakrina's Adamic gift—made the decision to stop abruptly. Then Lāvōn spun instantly 180-degrees and gave a mighty leap which landed them some 35-feet back in the direction from which they had come. As the tree was descending to the ground Lāvōn spun around again and sprang high into the air toward the topside of the falling tree. As they soared into the air Diakrina found they were, for a moment, almost even with the falling tree trunk, then, in the next split second, they were above it. As it hit the ground, Lāvōn and Diakrina, only milliseconds behind its thud on the ground, landed on top of the tree.

It was quite a ride!

The other lions had been far enough ahead they were able to surge forward beyond the place where the tree fell. And Jared and his men were far enough back they were not in danger of being hit by the tree's great trunk, although a few warriors did sustain injuries from large, falling limbs.

The result of the great tree falling was Diakrina and Lāvōn had to leap down and forward off its massive trunk in order to rejoin the other six lions which were their fore-guard. However, this also meant they would be cut off temporarily from their rearguard as Jared and his men could not get over the large trunk and would have to find a way around it by going several hundred feet in one direction or the other.

Diakrina was about to tell Lāvōn to make the leap down from the trunk when, suddenly, three demonic warriors landed to their right and three to their left on top of the trunk. The two closest on each side was Sarx on the left and Desmos on the right. They were in the act of reaching for Diakrina when Diakrina screamed for Lāvōn to jump.

Jump he did. But Sarx and Desmos both leapt at the same time and were reaching to take hold of Diakrina and lift her from Lāvōn's back. But it was then two amazing things happen almost simultaneously. Diakrina somehow knew in an instant what Lāvōn was doing, but it wasn't exactly like she had warning.

Lāvōn, with catlike reflexes, twisted in the air so Diakrina was spun to the bottom and His four clawed feet were spun to the top. He made good use of his two back feet and thrust them deep into the chest of both warriors: one for each. This sent the two demons tumbling backwards. But not before one of them slashed at Lāvōn's underside with his greenish glowing blade and landed a savage blow into his rib cage.

Diakrina, who was holding on with all her might, felt the blades strike: but not as you might imagine. She was so attuned to Lāvōn, she felt the pain he felt. She did not feel it in her own body but felt it in his body as if his body were an extension of her own. And she knew immediately it was a near fatal blow.

Yet, somehow, Lāvōn continued his twisting leap by thrusting off of the two warriors with his powerful back legs and like cats can do, kept turning in the air so he landed on the ground on all fours in a crouched position.

At that very moment, Diakrina heard a terrible clash above her head and looked up. The seven warriors Strateia had sent came blasting through the air and collided with the six demon warriors. Two took hold of Desmos and each of the others took hold of one. They were moving at such a high velocity their collision with the demon warriors made a shattering sound. But their speed never diminished in the least.

Both the warriors of the Living One and the demon warriors disappeared. The Living One's warriors had taken them with them high into the sky not far from where the battle between the Guardian of the Gate and Bellicose was still raging.

Diakrina turned her attention immediately back to Lāvōn. She could feel the strength slowly bleeding out of him. She was sick inside at the sacrifice he had made. It would likely cost him his life in a matter of minutes.

"Oh, Lāvōn!" she heard herself cry. "What are we to do?"

But the answer of the lion was to teach Diakrina something about a lion she as yet had not learned. The only response of Lāvōn was a fierce surge of adrenaline. Diakrina felt a brutal and violent resolve rise up inside the great lion. Instantly, before she could hardly collect her wits about her, the lion went into a rage of action. And immediately she knew he was determined to cross the last 100-yards between them and the Tree Bridge.

Diakrina was overwhelmed with both wonder and grief at one and the same moment. She could hardly conceive of the power and agility surging through Lāvōn. And she knew he was purposely pouring the very last of his reserves of strength into the final few seconds of his life in a stern intensity of determined actions.

The other six lions instantly discerned their leader's intentions and they too flew into a rage of action that would have melted the hearts of the bravest of warriors. And while the earth continued to shake, and the titians battled overhead, and the warriors of the Living One subdued the demon warriors of Anomos, Lāvōn and the six lions shredded any human warriors who dared to stand between them and the Bridge.

All of a suddenly the Bridge loomed straight ahead. When they were within 30-yards of it, Diakrina realized some of the warriors of the Living One Strateia ordered to provide the overhead shield from the acrid rays from Bellicose and the powerful laser-like light coming from the Guardian, had moved low overhead, right up to the Bridge. The wings of their robes of light joined seamlessly together to form a dome over an area about 50-yards round, right down to the ground. Diakrina and the lions were inside a tightly sealed shield.

She soon realized why. The warriors of the Living One seem to be able to be in constant, instant communication at the speed of thought with each other. The Guardian had found a hole in Bellicose's defense. All the other warriors instantly knew he was moving in for the kill, so to speak—even though such beings as Bellicose cannot actually be killed. But they can be mortally disabled or chained in confinement.

Out of the sky came an explosion of blue, gold and white flames. Diakrina looked up to see two titians towering over them all. And what she saw was the Guardian had his sword thrust deep into Bellicose's forehead. The massive crimson blade began to cause crimson light to pour down through Bellicose's whole mammoth form. The towering demon gave a sickening roar lasting for nearly 30-seconds. And all the while it lasted it was descending in both volume and pitch.

The Guardian drove forward with his sword and turned its point, which was coming out of the back of Bellicose's head, downward. He drove the acrid, greenish lava-like creature down to the ground.

But he didn't stop there. The Guardian's sword continued into the ground and began ripping a great fissure in the earth. This fissure continued to open wider and wider. The ground around everyone began to shake violently, as the fissure began opening toward the Great Chasm on the far south side of the Tree Bridge: about 100-yard beyond the Bridge.

The Guardian, with his sword still in Bellicose's forehead, drove him into the depths of the fissure and pushed him deeper and deeper into it and then along its length until he had taken Bellicose to the very rim of the Chasm. Then with a great surge of power, he thrust downward and forward on the sword and drove Bellicose out over the Chasm.

There, in midair over the Great Chasm, the Guardian came to a standing position. Bellicose, still helplessly lying horizontal with the crimson sword embedded in his head, lay in midair at his feet. The Guardian lifted one foot and placed it on Bellicose's great face. And then with a force hard to conceive of, he shoved down violently with his foot so Bellicose was pushed off his sword and at the same moment sent hurling downward into the bottomless abyss of the Great Chasm. Down, down the screaming, greenish, lava-like creature fell until he was finally so deep the darkness swallowed him completely out of sight and his roars of rage were drowned in the depths of the Chasm.

The Guardian then turned his attention toward Anomos. He flew to a position where he was between the dark lord and the Tree Bridge. Anomos dare not make a move. For the power of the Living One was in the Guardian and he could do to Anomos what he had just done to Bellicose.

The Guardian lifted his blazing, crimson sword and pointed it straight at Anomos' face. It was clear Anomos now stood in dread of the Guardian and feared to move.

Meanwhile, Lāvōn had not stopped his ferocious charge toward the Bridge. There were a few warriors standing about 20-feet from its end. That was as close as anyone could go without being challenged by Nemesis. And none dared her challenge.

From what had just been witnessed in the skies above, these warriors realized there was no point in trying to resist the lions; nor could they have done so. They scattered toward the southwest as the lions covered the final few yards.

Lāvōn, still about 10-yards away, suddenly stumbled and fell. Diakrina kept her hold on his mane, but she could feel the life draining from him.

"No, Lāvōn! No, Lāvōn, don't die!" she was saying softly in his ear as she leaned forward.

And once again, this great lion had something to teach Diakrina about a lion's heart. She felt a surge of strange, almost spirit-like determination rise within Lāvōn. Before she could tell him to lie still— tell him she would walk the last few yards—he suddenly lifted himself, stiffened himself straight, and then made three stately large strides forward. After the third stride, he stumbled and fell forward and his head landed touching the end of the Great Tree Bridge.

Diakrina heard Lāvōn take a deep breath. Then slowly he began to exhale. Diakrina jumped down and ran to his face. The great lion's eyes were closed, but as she touched his face, he opened them and looked into her face as if studying her every feature. Then his eyes closed again. And as the last of his final breath came slowly out, his eyes opened slightly, and Diakrina could see the light of life had left them.

And though she had only known this great lion for a few hours, it now seemed like a lifetime because she had known him so deeply. Diakrina buried her head in his great mane and could not help but weep.

Chapter Twenty

THE LION AND THE LAMB

Strateia was the one who ultimately placed his hand on Diakrina's head to bring her back to the moment. She lifted her head out of Lāvōn's mane and saw Strateia and several bright and fearsome warriors stood all around her and Lāvōn and the other six lions.

Out beyond them, the Sons of El were starting to gather in a circle as the warriors of the Living One overhead, who were spreading their shield like a dome, lifted it about 15-feet from the ground to allow them to enter.

And in the sky above, towering 450-feet above the whole scene, was the Guardian of the Gate with his sword pointed straight at Anomos' face. And strangest of all, the sounds of battle, both titian and human, had ceased.

Diakrina was shocked to hear the sound of a lone bird singing from across the Great Chasm. It was indeed the song of the Garden.

Now if you remember, the Tree Bridge was made of a tree that was very tall—over 500-feet tall—and with a very great diameter. It had fallen across the 300-foot Chasm and Strateia had cut away all its limbs but two, one on either side opposite each other. They were attached to the trunk about 30 feet after the tree came aground and then the trunk continued onto the Severed lands about 120 feet beyond the two limbs.

And yes, from the air the Tree Bridge looked very much like a cross in shape. It was at the tip of this great tree Lāvōn had fallen, with his face touching the end of the tree trunk—or symbolically, the top of the cross.

Without warning, the quiet began to be filled with whispers as the men in the gathered groups began to pull back. The cause of this was the slow appearing of a large golden glow of light at the top of the Tree Bridge at its very end.

The glow was soon so bright it began to cast a shadow of golden light over everything. It was this glow which caused Diakrina to slowly rise to her feet and look up toward the top of the Bridge.

There at the top of the Bridge, looking down on them all, was a lion composed entirely of golden flames. He was larger even than Lāvōn. And as the moving flames of Revelation had obeyed some very precise design so as to give his features very clear distinction even though they were composed of flames in constant motion—in his case white, gold and blue flames—in like manner, this lion's every features was clear and distinct. Yet his whole being was composed of golden flames of differing shades and hues that poured golden light everywhere around him.

Strateia placed his arms around Diakrina's shoulder and looked down at her.

"You have done well, Little One. The Tree Bridge has been gained. And now it is time for you to get ready to utilize everything you have been given, in order to be allowed to cross back over the Tree Bridge and back into the Garden."

"Is there no chance, Strateia," asked Diakrina with a deep sense of hope, "that the Atheos can be recovered."

Strateia smiled at her and then said, "I thought you would never ask. My warriors have a present for you."

He motioned toward some of his warriors. Hidden in among their ranks they brought out the Monk. He was bound by some kind of large scarlet ropes tied around his hands and his feet. One of the warriors picked him up by his shoulder and brought him out of the warriors' midst and deposited him on the ground in front of Strateia and Diakrina.

Immediately, the golden lion gave a great roar. The whole of the Dorogon valley shook. Diakrina then heard the thunderous voice of the Guardian of the Gate.

"THE LIVING ONE COMMANDS YOU TO ORDER YOUR MINION TO GIVE BACK THE CRYSTAL CONTAINER OF LIGHT TO DIAKRINA WITH THE ATHEOS WITHIN IT. AND IF YOU DO NOT, I HAVE PERMISSION TO DO TO YOU AS I DID TO BELLICOSE."

With that said, the Guardian moved the blazing, crimson blade slightly closer to Anomos' face. Anomos was quiet for a few seconds and then said in a commanding voice, "Hairesis, hand over the crystal container with the Immortal Fruit within."

The Monk snarled. But he managed to get himself upright. And though his wrists were bound together with scarlet rope, he managed to get the palms of his hands separated out from each other. Then he blew over the space between them and the crystal container, with the Immortal fruit within it, materialized between his hands.

Strateia reached out and took it from him. Then motioning for Diakrina to lift her shield, he placed the strap over her head and left arm and allowed the crystal container to come to rest at her left side.

She dropped the shield over it immediately. For even in the short time Strateia was lifting the strap over her head to secure the container in place, already she was immersed in its delicious fragrance, and she could feel the effects of its hypnotic influence.

Strateia then looked down at her and smiled. "Now, Little One, you have everything, don't you?"

Then to remind her he added, "You have your sword, your shield, the Atheos in the crystal container. Do you still have the shining page from the book you were given as you exited Nekus?"

"Yes. It is right here," answered Diakrina reaching inside her dress and pulling it out.

"Keep it at hand, Little One," said Strateia, "you will be asked for it soon."

"Strateia," said Diakrina, "I guess this means the Atheos within the crystal container will not be here to torment mankind."

"Yes and no, Little One." And with this he looked straight at the Monk but turned and lowered his voice so only Diakrina could hear him. "The Monk has made a counterfeit of the crystal container and the Atheos. He has captured the fragrance seeping through the real crystal container from the real Atheos and used it to saturate his counterfeit. The fragrance of the counterfeit is real and will be used by Anomos to create war and blood shed as men seek the possession of it. However, everyone who battles to secure it will only win a lie. For there will be no true Immortal Fruit within. Yet the illusion will achieve its purpose: the near total corruption of mankind. This, along with the impure Nephilim bloodlines corrupting humanity, will make the judgment of this present world unavoidable."

Diakrina was stunned at this revelation and wanted to ask Strateia if anything could be done to get the counterfeit from the Monk. But Strateia, knowing her thoughts, looked deep within her eyes and shook his head to abort her question.

"We will speak later, Little One."

Then stepping back and looking up at the glorious, golden flaming lion he said, "It is time."

"Will you be going across with me, Strateia?" asked Diakrina hopefully.

"No, Little One. There would be no point."

Then looking up at the great lion, "He alone can take you to Nemesis and satisfy her trust. You must go with him."

It was then Diakrina really took a long deep look up at the lion. And as she looked into his flaming eyes, she realized she wanted to go with him more than anything else in the world.

Diakrina noticed Jared and most of his men had gather around opposite the warriors that accompaning Strateia. She walked over to Jared and clasped both his hands.

"Thank you for all you and your people have done. We would not be standing here right now without your help."

"It was both our duty and our great honor," answered Jared.

Then he reached inside his tunic and pulled something out. It was a key. It was the Key! The key to the Door of Dorogon.

"Our great father asked me to give this to you. He mentioned it will be safer with you where you are going. He said you would understand."

Diakrina took the key and looked again at its beautiful lion and lamb design. She could not believe she was holding it in her hand again.

"Tell, our great father, for me," said Diakrina, "I will treasure it beyond all other possessions. And the key will indeed be safe, and mankind safe from it, where I am going."

"I will tell him," answered Jared.

"And," added Diakrina, "tell our great father this gift, and the gift it gave, pleases me greatly. Tell him I will always remember him when I hold it in my hand. And often when I think of him, it will help to be able to hold it again."

"He will smile when he hears these words," said Jared.

Then Jared placed his hand on the top of Diakrina's head and said, "On behalf of the Sons of El, I give you our thanks and the blessing of the Promise of the Living One. We will meet again in the Day of ultimate fulfillment."

And all the Sons of El behind him responded with a loud, "May it be so!"

Diakrina smiled at Jared and the others and responding back to them said, "Indeed, it will be so!"

Then Strateia motioned to her with a lift of his eyebrow and said, "We can wait no longer, Little One. The time is now."

Diakrina walked over to Strateia who was still standing by the fallen body of Lāvōn.

'Strateia, I have a request."

"What is it?"

Then looking at Lāvōn she asked, "Can anything be done? Can he be restored?"

"That is beyond my area of ability or responsibility," responded

Strateia. "But you might ask Him," he said pointing up to the top of the Tree Bridge where the flaming lion stood looking down on them. And the way Strateia said, "Him" made it clear that somehow this flaming Lion was more than an awesome, flaming creature. He was, The Lion: He was a manifestation of the Living One Himself.

Diakrina looked up and her eyes met the Lion's eyes of fire. They were full of knowledge and understanding and instantly she knew she did not need to repeat her request for He had heard it and already knew it was in her heart before she had uttered it.

The eyes of the great flaming Lion squinted slightly. When they opened again a mist of golden glory came radiating out of them. Diakrina could not be sure, for this mist of golden light swirled slowly downward and was in constant motion. Yet, it seemed to her she was also seeing the form of a lion taking shape: a great lion looking very like Lāvōn.

When the swirling light reached Lāvōn's lifeless body, it began entering his body through the wound in his side using a corkscrew-like motion. When finally all the golden light had vanished within Lāvōn's body, Diakrina was startled to see the wound in Lāvōn's side begin to close and heal over until not even a scar was left.

All was still for several moments as neither human nor spirit dared to move. Then suddenly Lāvōn's great sides heaved outward and the sound of a great intake of breath could be heard. Immediately, he began breathing normally. And after only three of four breaths, his eyes slowly opened and he raised his great head and mane and turned up onto his stomach. Then he gave his head and mane a great shake.

Diakrina could see the light of life had returned to his eyes and she buried herself in his great mane in an attempt to hug as much of his great bulk as she could encompass. When finally she pulled back to look into his face, Lāvōn blinked and then softly touched the tip of his tongue to her cheek which was wet with tears of joy.

Diakrina didn't know which lion to speak to first. But she soon resolved it and turned her face up to the flaming Lion and said, "Thank you." The flaming eyes of the great King shut slowly and opened again in a kind of nodding acknowledgment of her gratitude.

Then turning to Lāvōn who was now sitting upright, she looked up into his eyes and said, "Thank you for what you did for me. I will never forget you as long as I live."

Lāvōn lowered his head and Diakrina touched his great face. And in those few seconds great expressions and conversations passed between Lāvōn and Diakrina. Lāvōn gave a low, almost subsonic deep growl and the other six lions gave a slight roar and came crowding around him and Diakrina. She touched the face of each one in turn and then said out loud to Lāvōn, even though it was not necessary to do so, "Please give all the lions my gratitude."

Strateia came up behind her and turned her around toward him. "I am sorry, but it must be now."

Diakrina nodded her acknowledgement there could be no more delays. And then turning to give a last wave to Jared and his men, turned back again and looked up into the great warrior and friend's face and said, "I'm ready."

Strateia then reached out and took her by the shoulders. Suddenly they both began to rise together toward the top of the Tree Bridge. As they rose, Strateia turned in the air so they exchanged places and Diakrina was closest to the Bridge.

When they reached the top, without setting a foot on the Bridge himself, Strateia set her down lightly upon its surface next to the great golden, flaming Lion.

"I will meet you on the other side, Diakrina," said Strateia. He bowed his head in a salute to the flaming King, and with that he was gone.

Diakrina turned toward the golden Lion and looked up into His face. (She had to look up for He was very large.) Indeed, He was not just a lion! And everything in her knew it, instantly.

She took out her sword and standing the point of it on the Tree Bridge, she took hold of its handle and knelt on one knee and bowed her head in a salute of honor. In her heart a fountain of joy began bubbling up as tears of joy streamed down her face. In His presence her heart felt at home!

Then she heard his golden voice in her head say so softly and gently, "Daughter, follow me."

The flaming King then turned and began walking toward the Great Chasm and the middle of the Tree Bridge. Diakrina fell in behind Him and immediately a great golden mist of light enveloped them. It was like walking in a fog composed of very dense light. Yet, in another sense, fog is the wrong expression. Opaque radiance would be more fitting. And it seemed to be coming from the flaming Lion.

The golden light became thicker and thicker until Diakrina could see almost nothing but the Lion ahead of her. And she could make out His form only slightly. She was glad she could not see the Great Chasm for she remembered how terrifying it was to be out on the bridge over the massive, bottomless canyon.

They walked slowly for several yards. Then up ahead in the golden mist of light, Diakrina began to see a white light. They had not walked much further when there was a flash of brilliant beams of light in all directions. And when the flash was over, there in front of the Lion, suspended in the air, was a lady of great size. She was very beautiful, yet she looked fierce at the same time. She was shrouded in a flowing robe covering her from a tight collar around her neck down to her bare feet. She had a wide golden belt with a sword sheath attached to her left side.

The robe was flowing out behind her as if she were in a strong breeze. In her right hand she held a very large double-edged sword which blade was tortured with waves along its edges from the hilt to its very sharp tip. It glowed a very deep crimson and Diakrina immediately felt afraid of the great weapon.

Diakrina knew this must be Nemesis. Strateia had said she guarded the reentry into the Garden at the Tree Bridge and was greatly to be feared. For she had been given power to enforce her charge of not allowing any from the Severed lands to crossover again to the Garden until justice was fully satisfied. She and the Guardian of the Gate had a common trust in this regard.

The flaming Lion stopped in front of her. Nemesis looked down at Him from her great height in the air and bowed her head in a salute of honor. Then she spoke.

"I give way to my Master. There is no injustice in You. You are eternally perfect. No realm can be closed to You who is the Creator of all realms."

Then she paused and looked beyond the golden, flaming Lion and asked, "But what of her, why do you bring her here with You? You know I cannot betray the trust You have given me, and I also know You would not ask it of me. I cannot let her pass if I am to be faithful to Your commands."

Then Diakrina heard a voice that seemed to be coming from everywhere. And instantly she knew it was the voice of the Living One.

"DIAKRINA, TAKE OUT THE SHINING PAGE YOU WERE GIVEN AS YOU CAME OUT OF NEKUS AND GIVE IT TO NEMESIS."

Diakrina reached inside her dress and pulled out the shining page and unfolded it. On its surface there was a constant motion of images like a movie being shown at hyper speed. She walked up beside the great flaming King, and when she was standing just under His head, she lifted the page up toward Nemesis.

The goddess-like being reached out her hand toward Diakrina and the page was slipped out from between her fingers and began rising in the air toward her. It rose until it was in front of Nemesis, about 4-feet away from her face. She reached out and touched the page and it suddenly expanded—silently—though the speed was almost that of an explosion, until it was the size of an IMAX movie screen.

The images could be seen on both the front and the backside of the now, very large, page. But still the scenes were moving at such a speed Diakrina could not follow anything with much detail. However, she did catch images here and there. And she soon was able to discern this was a record of her life from birth until now, and to her amazement, beyond.

For when she began to see images having to do with her quest here on the other side of reality, as she called it—such as the Door of the Rose, the Great Dance, the scene of the ripping of the Great Chasm, a passing view of the massive Nekus Falls in Nekus

Canyon, her encounter with the great Smilodon (the Chisel-tooth cat), a passing glance of the great columns of the Greater and Lesser Porticos of Sapient Castle, and a glimpse of Bellicose passing by her and Strateia on top of the plateau, a quick view of the great pyramid which housed the Great Hall of the Sons of El, the face of Adam, her journey into Parad, her rescue by Strateia and Jared's men, the flight through the Mist Forest, the ruins of Dorogon, her riding into battle on the back of Lāvōn, etc.—it did not stop at the point of time where she now stood. The scenes continued onward. Yet, Diakrina could not recognize much of any of it as nothing she saw could be fitted into a memory, as it was clearly future events she was viewing.

When finally the images stopped, Nemesis reached out and touched the shining page and it returned to its original size and fluttered back down to Diakrina, who reach out and snatched it out of the air. She then folded it and returned it to its place.

Then Nemesis spoke to Diakrina.

"I see you have come through the Door of the Rose. You have temporarily been dislocated in time. Yet, I see it is decreed that you are to go back through the Door of the Rose to your own place in the stream of existence."

Then she paused and said, "You come from a time beyond the fulfillment of the Great Promise. And it is clear you are one who trusts in the Living One and what He has done for you. I see your shield and I ask you now to show me your sword."

Diakrina pulled her sword, and the blade began to glow bright crimson.

"You still have the sword of the Living One in your possession and I saw, on the shining page, how it has penetrated your soul in the dark cave. Therefore, all is satisfied in regard to justice except for one issue."

When Nemesis mentioned the one issue, as Diakrina was re-sheathing her sword, her heart sank into dread. "What could be missing? What issue?"

"Since you have been brought through the Door of the Rose, you have fallen in the Great Dance, you have often forgotten to trust the Living One, and only returned to trusting the Living One, once you ran out of options.

"Justice demands perfection; it is necessary. And your actions while here are not yet covered by the fulfillment of the Great Promise. There must be some means of its future merits being credited to you now. Justice demands it. I am ordered to obey all the dictates of justice.

"Unless this connection to the merit available from your past, future life, and your future, future life can be made, so that the merits of the Great Promise fulfilled flow over you and pay for your imperfections in this moment, I cannot relent and let you pass."

Diakrina was dumbfounded. Her thoughts began to race. "Had she come so far, and survived so much to now be turned back into Anomos' hands. Surely Strateia had not left her without the means of being able to return to the Garden.

"And I also knew that beside me, in the image of the golden, flaming Lion, was the presence of the Living One, Himself," said Diakrina. "Hadn't He brought me to this point? Surely, He would not have done so knowing I would now be rejected and not allowed to pass!"

Then that voice seeming to come from everywhere spoke again.

"DIAKRINA, PLACE YOUR HAND ON MY SON."

She instantly knew, "My Son," meant the flaming Lion.

Diakrina reached up and placed her hand on the side of the front leg of the great Lion.

"DIAKRINA," came the Voice again, "KNEEL WHILE KEEPING YOUR HAND ON MY SON."

Diakrina knelt, which meant she was now touching the great Lion near His feet.

Then the Voice, which came from everywhere, spoke to Nemesis.

"MAKE READY YOUR SWORD."

Nemesis moved down to the surface of the Tree Bridge. She was now standing right in front of the great Lion and Diakrina. She had her sword stretched forward in her right hand.

Then everything began to change. The great Lion began to change. The golden flames of His body began to transform in shape, and He began to grow smaller. As He did, His appearance altered increasingly as His form descended into a smaller and smaller size.

When finally the transformation was complete, Diakrina was shocked to see she had her hand on the shoulders of a perfectly, white lamb, who too was composed of moving flames.

Then the Voice spoke again.

"RISE DIAKRINA AND PLACE BOTH YOUR HANDS ON THE SHOULDERS OF THE LAMB. PUT ALL YOUR WEIGHT ON ITS SHOULDERS. THEN CONFESS YOUR SINS AND SHORTCOMINGS, PLACING THEM INTO THE LAMB."

Diakrina stood and what she was about to do so overwhelmed her she began to weep. Yet, somehow, she managed to stand and place both her hands on the shoulders of the small lamb. She leaned down upon his shoulders and she felt him sink slightly under her weight as if something more than her body weight were bearing down on Him.

"NOW CONFESS, DIAKRINA, YOUR SINS AND YOUR SHORTCOMINGS. THEN RENEW YOUR OATH OF ALLEGIANCE TO THE LAMB," came the instructions again.

Diakrina opened her mouth and out of her broken heart she began to confess all her selfishness, her attempted self-sufficiency, her self-absorption, and her many acts of willfulness in attitudes and actions, in desires and motives. She says she cannot remember how long it took for it seemed to pour out of her. And the more she confessed the more the lamb seemed to sink under some unseen burden that was continually growing.

Then her confessions came to an end. And she found herself then repeating the covenant she had taken to always maintain the possession of the Living One's sword given to her:

"I HAVE SWORN ETERNAL ALLEGIANCE TO HIM WHO ETERNALLY WAS, WHO ETERNALLY IS, WHO ETERNALLY IS TO COME. I BREATHE HIS LIFE, I AM EMBRACED BY HIS LOVE, I AM SURRENDERED TO HIS TRUTH, I SEE ALL THINGS BY HIS LIGHT."

When she finished, the Voice from everywhere spoke again.

"NOW, DIAKRINA, STEP BACK. YOU CAN GO NO FURTHER."

Then the Voice addressed Nemesis.

"ANGEL OF JUSTICE AND RETRIBUTION, TAKE YOUR SWORD OF JUSTICE AND CUT THE LAMBS THROAT."

Nemesis looked up into the golden glory all around them and said, "How can I do such a thing to your Son whom I love and serve? Why do you call for justice to seek such overpayment?"

"PEACE, MY SERVANT. TRUST AND DO AS YOU ARE TOLD."

And with that Nemesis stepped forward and placed the crimson, undulating edge of the sword blade under the Lamb's neck. And with a quick, short stroke she slit one of the main veins in the Lamb's throat.

Blood poured out onto the Tree Bridge. And as it did Diakrina fell to her knees weeping with her head in her hands. Her sins had caused this. She was undone.

As she covered her face in her hands and wept, she heard His Voice speak to her.

"LIFT YOUR HEAD, DIAKRINA."

Slowly, Diakrina wiped the tears from her eyes, so she could see, and then lifted her head. What she saw next stunned her.

There on the Tree Bridge, lay the lamb in a resting position with blood pouring from His neck down onto the wood of the Tree. And the blood was like flowing and pooling as red flames which were alive with motion like the flames of the great Lion and the Lamb. And out of the golden glory all around her a Hand, which could only be seen up to the forearm, which was protruding out of the dazzling sleeve of a perfectly white robe, reached down and dipped its index finger into the pooled flaming blood. Then the Hand moved toward Diakrina.

As the Hand came near to her face, she could see it had deep scars at the base of the palm, right where the Hand joined the wrist. And somehow, she knew this was the same Hand she had seen as she drank from the cup on the stairs of Sapient Castle.

The Hand touched her forehead and made an upright streak of flaming blood down the center. Then it crossed it with a horizontal streak of flaming blood, forming the symbol of a cross.

And as the Hand formed the symbol on her forehead the Voice from everywhere said, "YOUR SINS ARE PAID IN FULL. YOUR TENDENCY TO TURN FROM ME IN SUSPICION AND GO YOUR OWN WAY HAS BEEN TAKEN AWAY."

And immediately, the Hand was gone. Then, the lamb, who had looked lifeless for the few minutes since the wound had been given to it, stirred and rose completely whole. It was then the flames of its body began to transform again. Up and up the golden flames rose until the flaming Lion stood before Diakrina in all His glory and strength.

Nemesis bowed down with her face to the ground and laid her sword at the great Lion's feet.

"Justice is more than satisfied, my great King," she whispered in a voice of sacred awe.

The Lion turned to Diakrina and looked straight at her. And in His eyes she saw dancing love and joy that made her want to jump up and clap her hands with glee.

Then for the second time the great Lion spoke to her mind.

"Daughter, follow Me," He said.

He led Diakrina past the prostrate Nemesis and down the center of the Tree Bridge. And after a minute of walking, in which the golden glory around them seemed to be getting thicker and thicker, and her ability to see the Lion up ahead was becoming more and more difficult, suddenly the great Lion disappeared completely, and she walked immediately out into a glorious scene as the Garden emerged in front of her.

She was back!

Chapter Twenty One

THE JOURNEY
AT THE END OF THE QUEST

The emotional relief and the physical exhaustion flooding over Diakrina as she relaxed after her long, attentive vigil left her filled with a mixture of weariness and joy. She was shocked at the fatigue descending over her body as her muscles, the very beating of her heart, and her mental frame of consciousness turned loose of what had been a long quest. It had been so long her whole being had been continually standing alert for danger or involved in fighting some assault.

Yet, with all the weariness descending over her she was still filled with a relief-enhanced joy. Just standing at this end of the great Tree Bridge and feeling the very atmosphere of perfect safety and wellbeing surrounding her, which was taking her in again, filled her with a sense of quiet triumph.

She felt she should be jumping and celebrating. But somewhere, deep inside, there was a sacred awe filling her. What she had just experienced on the Tree Bridge transmuted the celebration into an intense gratitude. It could only be properly expressed with an act of worship.

What is more, she now knew the utter sacredness of this place. She had viewed it from the Bridge of Trust through the roof of the Smaller Portico, which connected Sapient Castle to the Great Portico of communion with the Living One. She had just personally witnessed how the Living one used this Tree Bridge—this Cross—to make a way back Home for all who are willing.

Diakrina looked around. Yes, it was massive and would have been a spectacle in her world simply by its size. But here, not so much. Such massive trees were everywhere.

If one did not know what she knew, it was a rather common looking sight … just a fallen tree lying across a gorge. And in that moment the irony of how the Living One could accomplish such great things with such seemingly mundane, commonplace things, invaded Diakrina with wonder.

But on this side of reality, where the deeper truths were engaged, Diakrina could take no common view of it. It was a place of worship; sacred space; holy ground. It was a place for giving voice to her great gratitude and thanks to the Living One for His amazing Love.

And it was more for this reason, than for her weariness, Diakrina pulled her sword and fell to one knee. She placed the point of the sword down onto the Tree Bridge. Putting one hand over the other she rested them both on top of the sword handle. Then bowing her head onto her hands she whispered a short prayer:

"Living One, please receive my gratitude and praise. It is because of You, and You alone, I stand here now as a victor in the quest You entrusted to me. Trusting and following Your footprints have led me through death and back to life again. You gave me constant assistance by means of Your servants, both spiritual and soulical, enabling me to prevail. You, and You alone, are the Great Warrior, the Great Lion, which none can face in battle. Yet, also, in Your infinite Love you reach toward us. And in that reaching You take on our weaknesses as the Lamb and become the great sacrifice, which Anomos cannot discredit. You embrace our weaknesses so You can lift us into Your strength. You take into Yourself our sicknesses and drown them in Your infinite health. You invade our darkness, which holds us in blindness, and banish it with Your infinite Light. I am honored to be the least of Your servants. For to serve You is Life and Joy, itself."

Then raising her head and looking up toward the high eastern mountains of the Garden, which tops could not be discerned, she added:

"Please grant that I may come to You soon. For I long to drink from the fountain of Your Joy at its undiluted source. I desire to gaze upon Your beauty forever. For this, I know, will be the great, unending adventure of all eternity. As You have promised us: in Your right hand are pleasures forever and ever."

Then with a passion to declare her love and allegiance to Him, she broke out again into her covenant pledge:

"I HAVE SWORN ETERNAL ALLEGIANCE TO HIM WHO ETERNALLY WAS, WHO ETERNALLY IS, WHO ETERNALLY IS TO COME. I BREATHE HIS LIFE, I AM EMBRACED BY HIS LOVE, I AM SURRENDERED TO HIS TRUTH, I SEE ALL THINGS BY HIS LIGHT."

It was then she heard His voice surrounding her again:

"DIAKRINA! THAT IS YOUR NAME. AND WHEN YOU FIRST CAME THROUGH THE DOOR OF THE ROSE, IT MEANT, DOUBT, INDECISION AND CONFUSION, AS THESE ARE THE NEGATIVE MEANINGS OF YOUR NAME. NOW, YOUR NAME IS DIAKRINA STILL. BUT THROUGH YOUR TRUST-GENERATED COURAGE, YOUR NAME HAS TRANSFORMED TO IT POSITIVE DEFINITIONS AND NOW MEANS, DISCERNMENT, JUDICIOUS DECISIVENESS AND PRUDENT JUDGMENT.

"I WILL SOON SEND YOU BACK THROUGH THE DOOR OF THE ROSE. YOU WILL RETURN TO YOUR OWN TIME AND YOUR OWN PEOPLE. AND THE LIFE THAT LYING BEFORE YOU IS YOUR NEW QUEST. PROSECUTE IT BY MEANS OF THE NAME YOU NOW BEAR, FOR THERE MAY YET BE MANY REASONS TO TAKE COURAGE. AND I WILL BE WITH YOU EVERY SINGLE DAY UNTIL YOUR PATH LEADS YOU HOME TO MY DOOR."

Then He added: "YOU WILL FIND THE DOOR STANDING OPEN!"

Diakrina confessed no expression could convey the joy these

words produced in her. For these words were also His very presence: for He was in His words. And she was inundated and saturated in His Love for several moments. It was almost as if she were getting a Father's embrace and blessings.

Then the glorious solitude lifted, and she was instantly aware of her surroundings as the songs of the birds and the sounds of the Garden came tumbling in on her. She stood and turned around to look back over the Great Chasm to the west. The sun was setting, and it would be night soon.

Diakrina turned back toward the Garden and sheathed her sword. She then began searching for a way to climb down from the great trunk of the Tree Bridge. When finally she had managed to reach the ground, she turned toward the Garden and was delighted to see several squirrels out of curiosity had come out of the trees and were standing only a few feet away on their hind legs watching her.

She walked a few steps toward them and then, kneeling down, beckoned to them. Without the slightest sense of fear, they scampered over the few feet between and began pressing against her knees for petting and attention. Their total lack of fear and absolute sense of trust was like a splash of delight to Diakrina. How different from the Severed Lands!

And of course, Diakrina still carried in her the gift from the Door of Doragon. This made her interaction quite different than it would have been before.

Diakrina petted their little heads and said to them softly, "Our last meeting was rather rudely interrupted, wasn't it."

"I see you have found your welcoming party," said a familiar voice.

It was Strateia.

As weary as she was, Diakrina jumped to her feet and ran to him. He clasped both her hands and with a smile only an angelic being can convey, he beamed down on her and shook his head with delight.

"There is nothing like the peace following a righteous victory," the great warrior said as he looked into Diakrina's eyes. Then he added, "On the Great Day, all in the New Creation will know this peace."

All Diakrina could do was smile and lift her eyebrows in acknowledgement as she nodded her head in agreement.

"I know you are weary, Little One," said Strateia, "but we have one more important thing to complete before you rest for the night."

"You are referring to the return of the Atheos, aren't you?" asked Diakrina.

"Yes. But here, in the Garden, it is no longer the Atheos. It is again, Immortal Fruit. And the Guardian of the Gate is back at his station and awaits us. When you have personally handed the Immortal Fruit to him, this quest will be coming to its end."

Then he looked at Diakrina and said, "I know you are very weary and tired, and it is quite a hike around Perath, the large lake at the center of the Garden."

"I have wondered about this large lake," interjected Diakrina. "It seems to be the headwaters for all the rivers coming from the Garden. And though its waters are not hot, but rather cool and clear, it seems to boil from some deep underground source like a gigantic geyser."

"You are correct about this, Little One," answered Strateia. "The word, Perath, means, 'to break forth.' And indeed, Perath breaks forth from the deepest depths of the earth. It gives its name to the first river coming from it which we also call, Perath, which in your tongue is, Euphrates. From this river the other three divide off to make the four which exits the Garden through the deep reservoirs in the walls.

"As I was about to suggest, since it is quite a distance, to save us the hike I have permission to transport you to the other side of the Garden to meet the Guardian."

Diakrina's eyes widened.

"By all means!" she said excitedly.

Strateia turned Diakrina around so that her back was to him. Then he placed his large hands around her waist. Suddenly the earth beneath them began to fall away and Strateia turned toward the east and headed across the Garden.

As they crossed the great lake of Perath, Diakrina was entranced at the enormous volume of water rolling up out of the earth's crust. It looked like the volume of three or four Mississippi rivers combined. She could see the largest of the four rivers, the Euphrates coming from the rolling lake. And not far from the lake it began branching and feeding three other rivers finding their way through the Garden and ultimately to one of the four deep exits in the Garden walls.

Soon Diakrina saw the large black gates of the Garden coming into sight. And she also, out of the right corner of her eye, just spotted the small hillside covered with roses and the Door of the Rose in its face, as they were passing over.

But of course, it was the 450-foot-tall Guardian which was most visible. He stood on the other side of the gate. But instead of facing away from the gate, he was turned toward the gate and looking in Strateia and Diakrina's direction.

He was obviously prepared to receive them.

When they were within a hundred yards of the gate, and the great Guardian was towering over them, Strateia took Diakrina to the ground.

"We will walk up to the gates from here, Little One," said Strateia.

"I remember the terrible temperature of approaching the Guardian last time, and already I can feel the waves of heat," said Diakrina.

"I will take care of that," said Strateia.

And with that he extended, like a large wing, a fold in his tunic of light and it covered Diakrina like a large dome which went nearly to the ground. The dome was absolutely clear so Diakrina could hardly tell it was there except for the obvious reduction in heat she immediately detected.

They walked together toward the great gates of the Garden. When they were about 50-feet away, they stopped. This time it was the Guardian which spoke first.

"GREETINGS, MY BROTHER STRATEIA! IN THE NAME OF HIM

WHO WAS AND IS AND IS TO COME, I WELCOME YOU."

Again, Diakrina was overawed by the melodious thunder of the Guardian's voice. Words carried on such a medium seemed to penetrate your very soul as they made the ground beneath her feet tremble in harmonic resonance.

"I ALSO GREET DIAKRINA, WHO'S FAITH IN THE LIVING ONE HAS BROUGHT US TO THIS HAPPY MOMENT. THE LIVING ONE HAS MADE YOUR NAME REVERED AMONG YOUR KIND. IN THE WORLD TO COME, YOUR STORY WILL BE REMEMBERED WITH HONOR AND JOY."

Diakrina didn't know how to respond to being honored by such a being. She simply bowed her head in acknowledgement of his praise.

"Guardian, we are indeed happy to come to this moment," said Strateia. "The Immortal Fruit which was stolen from your trust will now be returned.

"It was first made secured against its ultimate misuse by means of Diakrina obtaining it in the realms of Thanatos and placing it within the crystal container of infinite light. And though lost to our possession temporarily in the battle to remove it from the Severed Lands, the fact of its security within the crystal container being impenetrable, led to our being able to retrieve it. Thanks to you and our brothers and the Son's of El, the Living One has given us success."

"HIS NAME IS GLORIOUS AND IS NOT DIMINISHED EVEN WHEN HE STOOPS TO WORK THROUGH US, HIS CREATURES. INSTEAD, WE ARE EXALTED TO BE HIS SERVANTS."

"Amen!" answered both Strateia and Diakrina.

Diakrina realized the moment had come. So, she lifted the shield up for the last time to remove the crystal container with the Fruit of Immortality within. As she lifted the strap of the crystal container over her head, the incredible fragrance enveloped her instantly. Her eyes widened and it seemed her spirit would leap out of her body because of her instant longing for it. Strateia had anticipated this effect and placed his hand firmly and reassuringly on Diakrina's right shoulder. She steadied herself and elevated the Immortal Fruit into view and took one last, long look at its beautiful, swirling, golden radiance.

"INDEED, MY EYES SEE WHAT THEY HAVE LONG LONGED TO SEE!" said the Guardian.

Strateia looked at Diakrina and smiled. "Go ahead Little One, the honor of handing off the prize is yours." And seeing the hesitation in her face Strateia added, "Don't worry, I have you covered, and the Guardian also will withdraw his flames away from you. Simply lift it to the outer edge of my protection."

Diakrina took a couple of steps out in front of Strateia and lifted the crystal container high with both her hands. But she was careful to hold it by a generous length of strap so the Guardian could take hold of the crystal container without having to touch her.

"Guardian of the Tree, I, Diakrina, return into your keeping the Immortal Fruit stolen by Anomos, whom we have defeated by the grace of the Living One. By His constant presence and power, I have overcome the lies of Anomos and the temptations to partake myself. Please receive this treasure from my hands as I release it back into your trust."

The Guardian bent down and reached out his hand toward the container. The effect of someone so tall, composed of billowing flames, descending toward her caused Diakrina to have to steady herself to keep from fleeing. It was, of course, the knowledge she was in no danger from the Guardian—he had no desire to harm her—which helped hold her steady. But even with this, his immense presence was overwhelming and took all the self-control Diakrina could manage.

When the moment came that his hand reached the container, he took hold of it between his thumb and index finger. It looked no larger than a small seed between his fingers. As Diakrina turned loose the strap, the Guardian lifted the container, as he stood back upright. The leather strap instantly disintegrated from the flames. However, it was clear the crystal container of infinite light was not damaged in any way.

"YOU HAVE RESTORED THE WHOLENESS OF MY TRUST, DIAKRINA. NOW THE LIVING ONE HAS GIVEN ME A QUESTION

FOR YOU. ARE YOU WILLING FOR THE LIVING ONE TO SEAL THIS
CONTAINER AGAINST YOU SO YOU CANNOT NOW OPEN IT?

The great Guardian then waited for Diakrina's answer. At first,
Diakrina was confused. Why would this be needed. The Immortal Fruit
was now out of her control. Yet, deep inside she knew with certainty
the Living One does not ask questions without a purpose. And of
course, she trusted any measures He considered necessary.

"Yes, of course," answered Diakrina when she found her voice.

"VERY WELL, THEN. IT WILL BE DONE."

With that the Guardian lifted the crystal container high over his
head. Diakrina watched in wonder as it was lifted so high, she could
not have seen it at all if it had not been for the radiance of the Fruit
within, and the additional fact the sunlight reflected so brightly from
the surface of the crystal.

As the Guardian held it there in the sky, a beautiful hand came
reaching out of the sky toward the container. The hand took the
container from the Guardian. It then closed with the container inside
and held it fast for several seconds. Then opening, the container could
be seen shining as it lay in the upturned palm.

The hand lowed slightly, and the Guardian took the container
once more. Then the hand retreated into the blue of the sky again.

The Guardian then bent down and reached toward Diakrina
and clearly indicated she should take the container from him.

"THIS IS YOUR TRUST, NOW. I BEQUEATH IT INTO YOUR CARE."

Diakrina hesitantly reached for the container. She was surprised
to see there was a new strap on the container, but not one like the
first one, made of leather. It was rather one looking, for all the world,
like it was made of the same material as the container itself, yet
somehow, it was flexible like the leather strap had been.

The Guardian spoke again. "QUICKLY PLACE THE IMMORTAL
FRUIT AND ITS CONTAINER UNDER YOUR SHIELD. STRATEIA WILL
GIVE YOU FURTHER INSTRUCTIONS. BLESSINGS MY LADY. MAY THE
PRESENCE OF THE LIVING ONE BE WITH YOU ON YOUR CONTINUED
QUEST."

And with that the Guardian stood up and returned to his station at the gate with his back to them.

It was then the fragrance from the Immortal Fruit reached Diakrina. It was a severe delight which called for immediate action. She quickly pulled the crystal-clear strap over her head and swung the shield over the crystal container as it came to rest on her left hip.

She then turned to Strateia, with confusion on her face and questions in her eyes.

"Come, Little One, we will talk once we have you safely out of the reach of the Guardian's flames."

With that Strateia turned and motioned for Diakrina to follow.

They turned and began walking down the slight hill leading toward the flowering trees to the northwest. Once again, they passed through the red-, purple- and ivory-colored flowers on the tree branches that were within reach and had so delighted her when she touched them the first day in the Garden. However, Diakrina was too deeply in stunned thought to take much notice of them.

They turned left near the rolling lake of Perath and made their way back southwest not far from its shores. Within 15-minutes they were climbing the slight rise which led to the rose-covered hill in which was set the Door of the Rose.

When they reached it, Strateia pointed to a place off to the right of the hill where there was a large spreading tree and some deep grass.

"We will make camp—as your people say—here tonight. In a minute I will go and retrieve something for the evening meal. But I am sure you have questions first."

Diakrina walked over to the tree and sat down on the soft grass. She looked up at Strateia and all she could manage to say was, "Why?"

Strateia smiled at her and responded, "That will be answered very adequately this evening. In the meantime, let me point out you are made perfectly safe against consuming the Immortal Fruit; you have no access now: it is sealed against you. Only the Living One can now open the crystal container. However, you are not safe from being driven mad by desire for it if you were to carelessly expose yourself to it. I urge you to keep it under the shield. For if you begin breathing its fragrance and staring into its swirling beauty, you will soon be able to do nothing more. You will turn it into the Atheos again and you will be its slave by being driven mad for want of it."

"But why must I carry this beautiful danger?" asked Diakrina with a sigh of weariness.

"It will not be for much longer. That burden will be lifted this evening. What you are about to accomplish will complete your quest in a very satisfying way. Until then, take the container off your shoulder and place it on the ground under your shield. Once I return with food, we will set up camp and talk. You can take your rest here in the soft grass until I return." And with that Strateia disappeared.

Diakrina was not sure what he meant by, set up camp, but she was certainly ready for a rest. She took off her belt with its sword and sheath and, wrapping the belt around them, laid them on the ground close to the great tree. But the glowing page she kept inside her tunic above where the belt with the carved roses was tied around her waist. She took off her shield and put it next to them and then quickly removed the crystal container from her shoulder. Yet, before she could place it under the shield the glorious fragrance seemed to drench her in passion.

She knew what she should do, but somehow, she didn't do it. She glanced down at the container and time seemed to come to a standstill. Instantly she was pulled in, mesmerized. While telling herself not to do it, she nonetheless lifted the golden beauty up toward her face.

In an instant two contrary things happened. First, she felt like she was being pulled nearly inside out with desire for the Fruit. At the same time there flashed a terrible picture of a boiling lake of fire and also another mental image of the rolling black rings of Serpents of Paranoia. She could feel the fear roll at her.

These were of course the two images Diakrina had been training herself to attach to the fragrance of the Fruit—the Atheos as it was then, and in a sense, still was to her now. She was shocked out of her trance-like state and with wide-eyed alarm at how close she had come to being reeled in like a fish on a hook, she quickly thrust the crystal container under her shield. The relief was immediate.

However, the fragrance had so energized her she found she no longer wished to rest. She was too filled with energy. She looked around her and immediately spotted the Door of the Rose about 20-yards away. Her interest was immediately peaked.

Diakrina couldn't help but wander over in the direction of the great crimson door. When finally she stood in front of it, the carving of the massive crimson rose, which covered the whole of its surface in its impressive relievo style, was so striking and perfect in its shape and lifelikeness, she couldn't help thinking it was an actual living rose of immense size. And it was so perfect she couldn't help but think that, somehow, she was looking at the archetype after which all roses are patterned.

And the depth of its surface, which seemed, as Diakrina had first called it, "a bottomless, horizontal ocean," captured her in its extra spatial dimensions. Diakrina stood there looking into its depth and began to think how she had traveled through both time and between the realms of the material and the spiritual by means of it. She knew deep inside its extra dimensional characteristics were a testimony to its function.

It was while she was looking deep into its surface her eyes traveled toward the center of the rose, which was the door. She noticed something that seemed unusual. She stepped closer to get a better look and was instantly surprised to see her foot-warmers, which had ended up embedded in the door when she almost failed to get through it, were still there. However, the reason she had not noticed them before now was they had changed.

The original color of the foot-warmers had been white. But now they were a deep crimson red like the door itself. They blended in as if they were rose petals, except they were not quite the right shape nor lay quite right as they hung vertically down from the toes.

Diakrina noticed they were held by only the very smallest part of their tips. And she could not help but wonder if she could free them from the surface. She stepped forward and reached up and took hold of one of them in her hand and was about to give a slight pull.

However, the foot-warmer released before she pulled. The sensation was like the door had turned lose its grip on the foot-warmer the instant she touched it so it merely dropped into her hand.

Diakrina smiled and then reached for the second one, which dropped in the same manner when she touched it. What Diakrina immediately noticed was the foot-warmers were not only changed in color, but they were also changed in texture. They felt very different. They were smooth to the touch and felt like the live petals of a rose.

She folded them together and placed them inside her tunic along with the glowing page. She was so close to the Door of the Rose, only an arm's reach away, when she looked up again, the sense of depth coming at her from the surface made her feel, for a moment, as if she were falling into a great crimson void. Instinctually, she stepped back to regain her equilibrium.

She stood there for a moment and then began to wonder what the surface of the door would feel like if she touched it. She eased forward a step and reached out her hand and placed it lightly on the door's surface. Two amazing sensations greeted her fingers.

The first was the door did indeed feel like touching the petals of a very soft, immense, perfect rose in its prime of life. The second sensation, which accompanied the first, and was just as pronounced, was the door seemed to be like a very impenetrable substance one could not push against or move even a millimeter. She said it was hard to imagine the two very different sensations being simultaneous. And in fact, if she lifted her hand off, she could not imagine it or remember exactly what it felt like until she placed her hand on it again. Clearly there were extra dimensions in operation in the substance of this amazing door.

"Beautiful, isn't it," came Strateia's voice from behind her.

Diakrina turned around to see him standing there with an armload of various fruits. They were all beautiful and the fragrance coming from them was delightful.

Strateia walked over to the large tree and sat down. He then spread the fruit out onto the grass in front of him and motioned for Diakrina to come sit next to him.

The meal following was incredible. And to her utter surprise Strateia joined her in the meal. Indeed, he could consume material food. Yet, she sensed he was doing it as an act of fellowship more than out of any need to eat.

The meal left Diakrina fully satisfied. But even more than satisfaction it filled her with a new sense of wellbeing running through her every limb. Once again, her body was being healed and renewed from the toll the battles of the last few days had imposed.

While Diakrina leaned back against the large tree trunk to watch the last of the sunset in the west, which was to her left, Strateia rose and indicated he would be back in a moment. And with that he was gone.

When he reappeared a few moments later he was carrying an armload of basketball-size rocks—seven in all—piled into a kind of pyramid shape in his arms for carrying. The stones were rough but mostly round and they looked to be something like granite.

Certainly, no mere human could have lifted such a mass of stones. But for Strateia it was like a load of beach balls. Everything material seemed so non-dense to him as a pure spirit being.

Diakrina watched Strateia kneeling to make a pile of them on the ground about 10-feet away. She began to wonder if the fruit he had shared with her had any sense of real substance for him or was it merely like the consistency of eating something like air-puffed Cheetos? However, these thoughts would go no further as she became engrossed in what Strateia was doing.

He didn't just pile the stone together in a heap. Rather he laid three stones side by side. Then he put two stones on the ground alongside them so that each one nested in one of the spaces between the middle stone and the two outside stones. He then placed a sixth on the ground, so it nested in the space between the two stones he had just placed. This formed a triangle on the ground if you were looking at it from above. He then placed the last stone—the seventh—at the center point on top of the stones, where the first row of three stones and the second row of two stones met.

Strateia then took out his sword and began walking around the pile touching each stone in turn. As he did, each stone would begin to heat and turn cheery red, with patches of orange and whitish-yellow, as they began to glow. The heat and light seemed to move inside the stones, and it made them as interesting to look at as the dancing flames of a fire.

There was no need of the stones for warmth as the temperature of the Garden was perfectly delightful already. But as the sun passed below the horizon and the stars began to appear, the light from this unusual campfire cast a welcome glow over the whole area under the great tree.

Having finished this task, Strateia walked back over to where Diakrina was still leaning against the tree and took a seat on a nearby boulder just beyond her. Neither of them said anything for several minutes as Diakrina studied the swirling radiance that seemed to move inside the stones. And even though there was no chill in the night—only a slightly cool breeze detectible now and then—the small amount of heat radiating just enough for Diakrina to feel it on her face from 10-feet away was welcoming.

Somewhere in the distance a nightingale began to sing. It was the perfect touch as a large moon, rising in the east to their right, began to splash its golden light across the landscape and the rolling lake below them.

Before long the little nighttime chorus of tree frogs and crickets began providing an almost hypnotic background softly surrounding them. How long they sat there and drank it all in Diakrina was not sure. Presently, though, Strateia spoke.

"In the morning you will go back through the Door of the Rose to your own time and place. However, before the morning comes you and I have a journey to take together."

Diakrina roused out of her restful trance and looked at Strateia. "A journey before morning?" she questioned.

"Yes. And it is time for us to begin."

Strateia stood and looked down at Diakrina and then walked over to the glowing stones. Once again, he took out his sword and this time touched only the top stone. Slowly a glowing, radiant spot began to form above the stone. It continued growing until it was nearly ten feet round. At first the light within the radiant circle only moved back and forth like the surface of water.

With this done, Strateia walked back to where Diakrina was seated and sat down beside her. He then began by asking Diakrina some questions.

"Do you remember the Spring of Longings?"

"Yes, of course. I shall never forget it."

Diakrina was shocked, then delighted, when suddenly the waterfall of the Spring of Longings appeared in the radiant circle with vivid realism. The glowing spot was now like a 3-D IMAX screen complete with sound.

Strateia motioned toward the image and asked, "Do you remember it primary purpose?"

Diakrina thought for a moment and then responded, "To infuse the waters of the Severed Lands with a hint of longing for the Kingdom beyond, the Kingdom which mankind has lost access to but was created to live within."

"Correct," answered Strateia. "And that hint of longing, though diluted in the rain and the streams and rivers, and even within the plants drinking up its waters, is a way to graciously haunt mankind—a proper kind of haunting—with a sense of their loss of the Kingdom beyond the world's rim. It is a way to keep them from being made hopelessly dull and below desiring the things for which they were created. It is constantly rekindling a longing for something beyond. It is a way of reminding them of their true Home, which almost all of them have never seen.

"It draws out the secret signature of each soul which is seeking to know and be known. Yet it is so personal they hide it from one another and suffer in private these moments of discontentment.

They will even sometimes disguise it from each other by calling it anything but what it is. They'll label it a fit of nostalgia, or childish enchantment, or the magic spell of a haunting melody. They will often tell themselves, and each other, it is only a desire for safety, or romance or pleasure or recognition and fame. And they will pursue these things hoping to find what it is that calls to them. But they always come up empty.

"In the end the disguises they have used are all ripped from its face, and all the things communicating it to them go dumb. It is maddening, but it is intended to make them look beyond their world and to realize they have longings nothing in their world can satisfy. It may come through a distance landscape, but it is not the landscape they want. It is something reaching them by means of it; something from beyond they hunger and thirst for.

"And we hope to cause them to reason that if one desires bread, so to speak, well, is it not likely bread exist? If one is thirsty, is it not likely water exist? We want them to ask if perhaps they were made to inhabit a world where such bread is eaten, and such water is available to drink.

"While it may be painful and sometimes confusing, it is a common grace—even a prevenient grace—give to all mankind as a severe mercy. It calls them to the Living One's heart and His solution for their return. It is part of what is their only hope."

"Yes," responded Diakrina. "It is both a painful and pleasurable experience. I have had it many times as a child growing up. And the longings can be so intense, that even though it is a deep pain— because the satisfaction is not near at hand—one would rather have that longing with its pain than all the pleasures the world around you can offer. Just the desire for Heavenly things is more wonderful than the fulfillments offered by earthly things."

"Then," interrupted Strateia, "you will understand what you are going to be asked to do with the Immortal Fruit. For does it not also create this longing, but to such an extent it is far too intense for sanity to be retained?"

"Yes," said Diakrina thoughtfully, "the fragrance is like the longing only a 1000-times stronger. And of course," she added, "it comes with the horror of possibly succeeding in attaining it when it is available to you, which I take, would not be the same as what we are discussing."

"True," admitted Strateia. "But that was your burden. No others have faced it. And it is no longer an issue. The Fruit is forever beyond being obtained in a destructive way—as an Atheos. It will be consumed one day in the Kingdom, but then it will only be the highest pleasure and joy leading to abundant life."

"So, what am I to do with it, now?"

Strateia rose and motioned for Diakrina to do the same. "Get all your things. We are taking a short trip."

Diakrina began putting on her shield, sword and placing the crystal container over her head and under the shield—which once again shocked her with the Fruit's incredible fragrance—while she questioned Strateia, "Can I ask to where we are going?"

Strateia pointed to the Spring of Longings in the radiant spot above the stones. "We are going there."

Strateia led Diakrina to the stones, and the radiant spot with what Diakrina thought was a representation of the Spring of Longings within it. But as they came near, she felt the mist from the waterfall and could even smell the atmosphere of a cave and the dampness common to such places.

"Is that the real …"

"Follow me, Diakrina." And with that Strateia step into the circle of radiance and then turning around, standing with the waterfall of the Spring at his back, looked toward Diakrina.

He smiled again and said, "Come."

Chapter Twenty Two

JUST REVENGE

As Diakrina stepped into the radiant circle the Garden disappeared, and she was immediately standing in the cave at the waterfall of the Spring of Longings. She could hardly believe it.

"I assumed from the start this was only a projection of some kind. How did we ... never mind," she said thinking better of her question. "I am sure I can't understand how we were able to move from one place to another instantaneously." However, she got more of an answer than she thought possible.

Strateia smiled at her and simply said, "It has to do with accessing dimensions beyond the four of space and time you normally interact with. You might realize we also passed through many solid material things as we came here. So, it is not just a movement from one place to another, but a totally different interaction with material reality.

"You might recall after His conquest of death, the Living One appeared and disappeared in places and ways much as we just did. In His glorified form His physical body was able to access more than the four dimensions of space and time. And when your race is totally restored, so will you."

"You mean to say, this will be normal in our future existence?" asked Diakrina with a sense of amazement, and even a little hint of incredulity.

"It is normal. You must remember in your present state you are subnormal," responded Strateia in a very matter of fact way. "In fact, it might occur to you this is exactly how the waterfall of the Spring of Longings comes to this place." And Diakrina could see as far as Strateia was concerned, the subject was closed.

"Come, Diakrina," said Strateia while turning toward the waterfall falling from what looked like an opening in the roof of the cavern. Diakrina at that moment recalled being told the roof where the Living Water of the waterfall was coming through was materially solid. And while this was true—evidently, if you were accessing only the normal four dimensions—it would not be true if you could access more than four dimensions.

"We are back in the Severed Lands, then," stated Diakrina.

Strateia stopped and turned around to her once more. "Yes … and no." As he often did, he allowed the seeming contradiction to hang in the air between them.

"We have not only relocated in space we have relocated in time. We are on your side of the Great Flood; in fact, only days after Noah and his family have come out of the Ark."

Diakrina did not know how to contextualize any of this and the only response she made was with her expressions of astonishment. So, Strateia continued.

"The mouth of this cavern, where we entered the first time, no longer opens above ground. The cavern has been altered so it descends as you travel toward what was the opening to the outside.

"If you and I were to walk down that way it would soon be clear we had descended several hundred feet. And we would eventually come to a place where the water of the Spring flows into a deep pool. The surface of this pool is the same as the surface of an ocean several hundred feet beyond. But the water will reach the ocean by descending deep into the pool, where the cavern forming the pool will make a horseshoe like turn toward the ocean and then re-ascends through another cavern to the surface.

"Where it comes out and mixes with the ocean is still under a ledge of rocks reaching some several hundred feet outward as part of a mountain lying overhead. In this way the Spring of Longings is hidden but can influence the whole planet as it flows out to mingle and ultimately infuse all the water both in the oceans, but also on the land—as it is caught up by evaporation and rained down all over the earth.

"This Spring will stay hidden until the renewal of all things for the present earth, which will last a thousand years. At that time, it will be given a different channel to the surface and will come above the ground in the renewed Temple in the restored capital of the Holy Lands. For we are presently under the location where the city and the Temple will be in the future."

Then Strateia began to quote a passage from one of the ancient prophets from the Great Book:

> On that day Living Water will flow out from Jerusalem, half to the eastern sea and half to the western sea, in summer and in winter.

Diakrina's head was spinning a little trying to keep up with it all. It was then Strateia turned again and began to walk toward the edge of the pool where the waterfall fell at its center. Diakrina followed.

When they were at its shore, Strateia stopped and pointed to the roof high up where the water entered. "Up there, in the middle of the Hole in the World, the Living One has prepared a very sturdy hook made of infinite light. It is in the very center of the mass of water pouring from the roof, which as you can see, is around 40 feet in diameter. Here is what you are being asked to do.

"You have taken note, I know, that a very different strap has been attached to the crystal container. It too is composed of infinite light and will never age nor become weak. You are to hang the crystal container on this light-hook and leave it there to infuse its fragrance into the Living Water of the Spring of Longings."

"Two questions, Strateia," interrupted Diakrina. "First, how can I possibly do such a thing as it is 70 feet to the roof and the mass of pouring water coming down will not allow me to get to the light-hook at the middle of the waterfall? And second, (Strateia allowed her to continue) what is the purpose? Isn't the Living Water of the Spring already able to create the longings for the lost Kingdom? Why is this added enticement needed?"

"I will answer the second questions first," responded Strateia. "The humans of your time are becoming increasingly insensitive to the realms of the spiritual. As I said before, a physical word picture would be like someone being born without any ability to see, hear, taste or touch; only the ability to detect odors is left to them—the sense of smell. Such a person would know almost nothing of the material world around them, even though they lived in it. However, they would still have occasional experiences of scents telling them there was indeed a nature around them they could not otherwise detect.

"Your race, in your times, have not only been robbed of most of their spiritual perception, what they do have left is very limited—as if the sense of smell in our illustration was only partially working. For any fragrance to awaken any such person to awareness, it would need to be very much strengthened to be detected. And Anomos has slander even this partial awareness and educated the younger generations to believe there is nothing but the material realm. Experiences of longings and spiritual thirst are to be discarded as a disguised longing for something in their physical world.

"So, our purpose is to increase the catalysis effect of this Spiring that stirs such longing by the hanging of the Immortal Fruit within the waterfall at the Hole in the World. This will infuse a much stronger scent, so to speak, into the Living Water. This will make it impossible for even the most hostile to not have some moments when the spiritual longings break in on them. They may ignore them or try to explain them away, but the experiential testimony will be there all the same. And they will have to answer for how they responded to this grace-kindled awareness."

"It will not be too strong?" asked Diakrina.

"No, the great volume of water will dilute it to a useful, but not dangerous level. What is more, it will be coming from everywhere—in the rain, in the fragrance of a flower nourished by water; from a bubbling brook, from the light passing through the vapors of ascending clouds as the sun rises or sets—thus it will not cause the pursuit of any one object. In fact, most will go from object to object to object trying to find the material source before they come to realize it is not the material objects they desire, rather it is something calling to them from beyond the objects and through them."

"I understand, Strateia. And, yes, I realize now—though I did not until I was brought through the Door of the Rose—just how severed we are from the true source of all reality. I am thankful for this common grace."

Then with a light of joy in his eyes, Strateia said, "Is it not a just revenge that what Anomos wished to use to destroy all hope, will be used to draw people toward the true hope by awakening the latent longings of their soul?"

Diakrina could not help but smile with delight at this thought. She looked up at the waterfall coming from the roof and then responded, "However, it remains … how can I possibly reach the light-hook you mentioned?"

"By means of our teamwork and by following my instructions," answered Strateia. "Are you willing?"

"Of course."

"It will not be as easy as you might imagine," added Strateia. "You will need to ask the Living One for much strength to do what you must do. And here is why: You will need to take the crystal container off your shoulder and hold it by the light-strap in your left hand. Then you will need to take your sword in your right hand to use to part the waters of the waterfall. Your sword will do this and make an opening for us to pass into. I will raise you to the necessary height.

"However, here is the part you will find most difficult. You will be exposed to the fragrance of the Immoral Fruit for the whole time we are rising and while we are performing the procedure. You must keep your head clear and your resolve strong. Only in this way will you be able to turn the container loose and hang it on the light-hook. It will not be easy."

Diakrina realized instantly how hard this would be. In fact, she found herself wondering how it would be possible. The power and impact of the Fruit was not something she could control; and it certainly would tend to control her. This she had repeatedly experienced.

"Is there no way for me to be protected from the impact of the fragrance of the Fruit?" asked Diakrina hopefully.

"Not from the outside," said Strateia, "only from within you, by seeking the Living One's strength to empower you beyond your natural ability. The victory will come from within you by His Spirit empowering your will. For His way is not to work around your will, but through it. Thus, you become a co-laborer with Him by means of His Spirit in you."

Diakrina had too often felt the mesmerizing power of the Fruit to think for even a moment she could, on her own, be anywhere strong enough to master it. And she realized she could not complete her quest unless she could do this. It was very unsettling. But ... she was determined.

Yet, she knew this alone would not be enough.

She looked at Strateia and asked, "May I have a few moments to prepare?"

"Most certainly, Little One. I think you must."

With that said, Diakrina walked a few steps away and knelt on her left knee. Then placing her right elbow on her right knee and her face in her right palm she began to address the Living One.

"Please, Living One, strengthen me. I need Your help, or I will fail."

She then looked up at the opening, which Strateia called the Hole in the World, and looking into the light and the Living Water coming from it, said, "I trust You to strengthen me. I know You will not let me fail."

From behind her Strateia walked up and place his large hand on her head and said, "The strength of the Living One is yours."

Peace descended over Diakrina. She rose with trusting resolve.

"I am ready, Strateia."

"Wait until I am ready to lift you. Then pull your sword with your right hand. Then lift your shield and remove the crystal container by its light-strap with your left hand. As soon as you have done this we will ascend."

"Understood," said Diakrina.

Strateia took his place behind her and placed his hands on her waist. Diakrina took a deep breath, pulled her sword, which immediately began to glow crimson, and then, lifting the shield, as she lifted her left hand to reach over her head and remove the light-strap from off her right shoulder.

The strap was long enough as she lifted it over her head and then extended her arm, the shield passed easily through the strap which allowed Diakrina to extend her left hand fully out to the left as far as possible with the strap in her hand.

Midway through this motion, the fragrance from the Fruit of Immortality hit her full force. The impact made it necessary for Diakrina to focus with all her resolve just to keep her left hand moving in order to keep the Fruit as far from her as possible.

Immediately Strateia began to lift her toward the roof of the cavern near the very sides of the waterfall which poured straight down in a column from the roof.

Already Strateia could feel Diakrina's body go tense as she was now in full combat to control her every movement against the inclinations the Fruit was inducing. For Diakrina it was necessary she focus her eyes upward toward their destination and not look directly at the radiance of the Fruit.

By the time they reached the roof, Diakrina was shaking all over with the effort to keep the container away from her. She was consciously picturing the rolling, black rings of the Serpents of Paranoia and the awful moment of realized hopelessness she had experienced in the vision of the doom of the Atheon as she was about to be cast into the lake of fire.

Even with all this effort at negative associations, she was groaning with intense pain as she fought to keep control.

"Help me, Living One," she quietly pleaded. And even though

she knew He was doing just that, she had moments when she was sure the pain and force would be too much for her to bear or overcome.

Yet, just when she was sure she would collapse under the pressure, a renewal of strength would flow into her enabling her to continue to fight the pain and hold out.

"Put out your sword in front of us," came the command of Strateia. Diakrina, with all the strength and resolve she could bring to focus on this small task of lifting the sword, slowly, yet surely, lifted her right hand straight out in front of her.

As Strateia began to move forward so the blade of the sword would intersect the falling water, Diakrina could not help but wonder if she would be able to hold the sword against the massive current of the waterfall.

Yet, when the blade entered the fall, she felt no pressure from the water. Crimson rays from the sword parted the falling water to a wide opening extending both upward above them and downward below them. It was about 7-feet wide, and it was, therefore, possible for Strateia to move them forward into the dynamic tunnel being formed.

Inch by inch, foot by foot, they pushed forward until they had gone about 20 feet into the cataract. And then, there it was. The light-hook, shining with a subtle white radiance, was fastened to the roof of the cavern in such a way it formed an almost total circle with only a small opening near the ceiling for the strap to pass over and through into the saddle of the hook.

"Now! Diakrina. Reach out and place the strap on the light-hook, now!" shouted Strateia.

Diakrina reached out with her left hand toward the light-hook. Unfortunately, this brought the Fruit not only closer to her, but it made it impossible for her not to see it.

Immediately, the fragrance of the Fruit saturated her. And as it did so, everything seemed to go into slow motion. She realized she was staring at the Fruit with a look of absolute horror as she could see her left arm bringing it toward her. At the same time, the delight and pleasure it generated in her cried out for the container to be pulled completely to her face.

"NO! I ... must ... put ... it on ... the ... hook!" Diakrina was saying with clenched teeth. But she was not sure she was succeeding.

It soon became clear this was a total standoff. The container was not moving toward her nor away from her. Yet she was shaking all over. Every muscle in her was trying hard to put the light strap on the hook, yet it was a momentary deadlock.

Again, she cried between clenched teeth, "Please ... help me, ... Living One! ... Please!"

At that instant, blue, white, and golden rays of light exploded from her shield still on her left forearm. The explosion cleared the air of the Fruit's powerful fragrance. Immediately, Diakrina found she had less pressure pushing her left arm toward her. With all the strength she could summon, she pushed the light-strap toward the light-hook.

The effort caused a long, agonizing groan to escape her as the strap was lifted toward the hook. But she seemed to be succeeding. However, when she reached it, her strength failed somewhat, and she fell short of getting the light-strap over the end of the hook and into the hook's saddle.

Her arm fell a little. But she gathered herself and made another attempt. It felt like it was going to make her whole body explode. But just when she thought she could not do it, her hand hit the light-hook and the strap slid through the slot and down into the saddle.

Diakrina's whole body went limp as she collapsed in Strateia's hands like a rag doll. Strateia quickly flew backward, and the channel created by Diakrina's sword quickly vanished.

When he was well clear of the waterfall, Strateia pulled Diakrina close and wrapped his arms around her to make her more secure. When they reached the cavern floor, he set her gently down, which resulted in her going down into a sitting position with her legs somewhat out to her right side.

Strateia then placed his right hand on her head and said, "Be made strong again, Little One." Lifegiving energy rushed down through Diakrina's body and she came fully alive in an instant. She leaped to her feet and began to jump up and down like a young girl as she clapped her hands and cried, "We did it! We really did it, Strateia!"

Strateia was all smiles and gave Diakrina a noble hug as she forgot herself and threw her arms around him as high up as she could reach, which was only a little above the great warrior's waist.

Then coming to herself, she quickly backed off. For a moment she was a little embarrassed at herself. But Strateia only laughed with delight at her, which broke the ice off Diakrina, and she too joined in his laughter.

Chapter Twenty Three

THROUGH THE DOOR AGAIN

Diakrina was full of unquenchable joy with the realization of the success of her quest. She and Strateia passed back through the portal, as Diakrina was now thinking of it, and stepped out onto the grass in front of the glowing stones.

She and Strateia walked over to the large tree, and both found a place to sit and lean back against its massive trunk.

Strateia and Diakrina talked on into the night and Diakrina realized how at home she had come to feel in the presence of this noble warrior. She would miss him. Yet, somehow, she knew time would not separate them for long.

Strateia spoke to her of a quest still laying ahead of her in her own time. He said it would have some connection to what she had experienced here in the time of the Antediluvians. They spoke about it, but Strateia seemed to have little information to share.

When finally the sun began to rise in the east and cast shadows toward them, Diakrina knew the time had come for her return. But before she stirred, she turned to Strateia and asked a question.

"Do you know any more you could share with me about this quest lying before me in my own time?"

"Yes, but not much more," answered Strateia. "However, I can tell you the counterfeit Ātheos will be used this side of the Deluge to create much bloodshed and war.

"As you know, the Antediluvians still retain much more spiritual perception than the people of your time. This could have been a strength to draw them back closer to the Living One. However, for most, it will be turned into a weakness as they seek to obtain what they can never have by their own power. Much bloodshed will be the result. You know the outcome that will become necessary as it is written in the Great Book your time possesses.

"The Living One will see to it that the breaking up of the earth and its crust, by the eruption of the fountains of the deep, will bury the false Ātheos with this world. This world will disappear for the most part. Its vast vegetation and wildlife will be buried deep within the crust of the earth to create the oil and coal of your time. And as you know this will also result in billions of fossils found in the rock layers deposited by the Deluge."

"Is it possible," interjected Diakrina, "the Evil One—Anomos—will seek to uncover this false Ātheos and use it in my time."

"Yes, it is possible."

"Then could that be part of my quest?" asked Diakrina. "To hinder him?" she added.

"Up to this moment I have not been told, Little One. But I do know I will be sent to you again when it is time for your quest to begin. Only this time I will come to your side of the door. By that time, I will have been informed as to how I am to direct you and help you."

"Then," said Diakrina, "sometime after I arrive home you will come to me?"

"Yes. I don't know how long after you arrive home. It could be days or years. I have not been told."

Then with a slight twinkle in his eye he added, "But remember, Diakrina, however long you wait for me, I will have waited much longer. I will not be using the Door of the Rose to come to you from this age. I will live and work all through the ages between now and then. I will have grown and changed much in my experience by the time we meet again."

Just the thought that while she returned almost instantly back to her own time and family, she would be bypassing ages of time through which Strateia would live and serve the Living One, was a rather overwhelming thought to Diakrina. Then with a twinkle in her own eye she said, "You will not have forgotten me by then, will you?"

Strateia smiled and answered, "Those of my kind never forget. And you never forget that!"

Diakrina smiled back.

Both knew the moment had come to get her ready to return. The orb of the sun was fully above the eastern horizon and the birds were in full voice singing an incredible symphony of joy as the squirrels chased each other from tree to tree and the rabbits came out of their burrows to greet the day. And in the distance by the lake Diakrina saw a doe with her young fawn dipping her head for a morning drink.

Diakrina tried hard to drink in all the magic and glory of the atmosphere around her. She breathed deeply as if trying to imprint the very freshness of this morning on her soul and store it deep inside.

She stood and made sure she had the glowing page safely tucked inside her tunic. She walked over to her sword and shield and picked them up. For the first time she found herself asking if she was indeed going to be allowed to take them with her through the Door of the Rose.

She knew she could not relinquish them—that was her sacred vow. But where she was going people did not walk around in public with a sword and shield.

Strateia had noticed her hesitation as she picked them up. He walked to where she was standing. Taking hold of her shoulders, he turned her round so she was facing him.

"Diakrina, of course you will take both your sword and your shield with you. However, they are dense spiritual reality and will not be discerned by those around you who only perceive the physical world through their five bodily senses and very little, if any, of the spiritual world.

"What is more, you will carry them very differently for a short time while back home."

Then reaching out his hand toward her sword he said, "May I?"

Diakrina surrendered the sword to Strateia when he instantly gave the necessary oath to the Living One. He then took the sheath off the belt and began wrapping the belt around both it and the sword in a very intricate pattern which secured the belt to the sheath. Then turning the sword and sheath so the handle was pointing down, he handed the sword back to Diakrina.

"Now hand me your shield," said Strateia. "I will hold it while you follow my instructions."

Diakrina took her left arm out of the straps on the back of the glowing shield and handed it to Strateia.

"Now," said Strateia, "take the sword and sheath and belt—keep them pointed up as I have handed it to you—and embrace them to your breast."

Diakrina wrapped her arms around the sword, sheath and belt and pressed them close to her breast. Slowly the sword's crimson light began to glow through the sheath and the belt. Then, ever so slowly, the sword and sheath with the belt began to slowly sink into Diakrina's body just like the swirling rainbow of light from the Altar of Sapient Castle had dissolved deep within her.

"Now the sword is in your inner being. It is also in your mouth, Little One. You will wield it by speaking His word."

Then Strateia held out the glowing shield.

"Take it and do the same with the front of the shield facing outward as usual."

Diakrina took the shield and embraced it. Rays of blue, white and gold light began to pour from its face as the sword had done. The shield too sank deep within her.

"When you courageously trust the Living One and go where He sends you, your faith will still be with you as an impenetrable shield," said Strateia.

Diakrina felt a little naked at first not having the sword and shield to wear. But then, somehow, she sensed their presence. They were with her in a new and satisfying way. Because of the intuition of their true presence, she felt naked no longer.

Strateia smiled at her and reached out his hands and took her by the shoulders. Diakrina looked up into his noble face and tears— both for the parting she knew was coming, and for the joy which she still possessed in this noble friend—filled her eyes.

Warrior angels can't cry but Strateia did the equivalent. His eyes filled with glowing light which expressed pride, admiration and deep affection for Diakrina. It was even better than tears!

"It is time," he said softly. And Diakrina knew the moment could no longer be delayed.

They walked side by side toward the Door of the Rose. When they reached it, once again Diakrina was entranced by its perfect beauty.

Strateia turned to her and said, "Reach toward your heart and close your eyes. Then think of the swirling rainbow of light as coming forth into your hands."

Diakrina closed her eyes and held her hands up to her heart and made the request in her mind for the light to reveal itself. Slowly the light came from within her and filled her hands.

"Now, Diakrina, take out the page of your life with one of your hands and bring them together by placing both your hands palm to palm."

This she did. The light enveloped the glowing page suspending it within the light at its very center.

Strateia then told Diakrina, "Stand at the center of the Door of the Rose and extend your hands out toward it."

Diakrina did as he said.

Strateia, taking his sword in His right hand then placed his other hand on Diakrina's head. He raised the sword to the sky and spoke in a thunderous whisper—a whisper you knew was reaching far into the sky.

"May the blessings and protection of the Living One be on you, my sister. May He keep you from all harm and danger whether it be spiritual, mental or physical. May your feet conquer everywhere you place them. And never forget to place them in the footprints going before you. This has been your primary lesson while here."

The Door of the Rose began to glow, and it began opening from its center outward. Tears were tracing down Diakrina's face but still she was full of joy.

"I declare I have fulfilled my trust, Master," said Strateia. "And Diakrina has fulfilled her trust. Please give us Your blessing."

Then the wonderful voice that comes from everywhere spoke.

"I HAVE BLESSED YOU AND I WILL BLESS YOU BOTH ALWAYS. AND NOW MY DAUGHTER, STEP THROUGH THE DOOR OF THE ROSE."

Diakrina felt Strateia's hand drop to her shoulder and give an affirming squeeze.

"I will be looking for you, my friend," she said, without looking back. And then she stepped into the door.

As she did, she heard the silver voice of Strateia whisper, "I will come."

In only a few moments she found herself lying in her bed with the sun rising, casting its first rays in through the window to her left. The rainbow of light with the glowing page was still in her hands. As she lay there looking deeply into them, they lifted and together sank into her breast.

It was at that moment she noticed the chain around her neck. She could feel the Key to the Door of Dorogon lying on her breast under her restored nightgown.

She sat partly up onto both her elbows and looked at the rays of light hitting her bed. And there on her lap, on top of the sheet which covered her, lay a perfect, red rose.

END OF
BOOK THREE

REVIEWS

"*The Other Side of Reality* is essential truth disguised as entertainment!"
— **David Russell, M.A., Founder & Director of Forever Young Counseling**
Billings, Montana

"*The Other Side of Reality* is like entering a school of philosophy and theology through the door of the imagination. Ingenious. This multi-dimensional journey into the depths of God is for ... the seeker of treasures. For years Gary Durham was my pastor. I sat spellbound as he established case after case for authenticity of the Word and the power of covenant fellowship with God. I would say he is a theological attorney who knows the Word at a level most of us would tremble to approach."
— **Pat McNab, Ph.D., Eagle's Glen Foundation, Divide, Colorado**

"I have worked and taught with Dr. Gary Durham in many different venues over the years. He is a creative thinker and a natural teacher. This wonderful story is a fresh example of his ability to share important principles through creating an entertaining and engaging story that will draw you into the characters, and before you know it, into new discoveries on your own journey."
— **Alan Scott, Former Senior Pastor, Trinity Church**
Colorado Springs, Colorado

"A riveting adventure story that bathes your mind and imagination in God's point of view. The high drama of this book took me captive much like The Lord Of The Rings. I can't wait to see this Trilogy become a movie."

— *Larry Ryan, Kingsway Foundation, Yukon, Oklahoma*

"An absolutely fascinating exploration of the deceptivity of the enemy of our souls and our ultimate victory over him in Christ! Knowing Dr. Durham as I do, I am not at all surprised at the depth, the coloring, the brilliance of his amazing insight into the reality of what we face in our spiritual journey. I highly recommend this read to anyone who seeks a broader understanding of *The Other Side of Reality*."

— *Dr. Steven Fletcher, District Superintendent Emeritus*
(and grateful friend), Church of the Nazarene

"Gary Durham has written a sensational thriller that will keep readers on the edge of their seats."

— *Dr. Stan Toler, Bestselling Author & Speaker*
Oklahoma City, Oklahoma

ABOUT THE AUTHOR

Gary L. Durham has been the Lead Pastor/Teacher of New Hope Fellowship, in Palm City, Florida for more than 20 years, and is distinguished for his captivating speaking and teaching. He is the Founder and Director of Veritas Resurgence, which focuses on educating believers through media and publishing. In the past he has served his denomination as a conference speaker, teacher, missionary and pastor and has taught in many different denominations.

He holds three earned degrees, including the Doctorate of Theology and has pursued a post-doctoral Ph.D. in Philosophy with a focus on Apologetics. He served for many years as theologian and master teacher for Freedom Ministries International, a pastoral training institute. He has been a speaker at C.S. Lewis Foundation events and a presenter at their academic forum at Oxford and Cambridge University.

In what he calls his "hobby life" he is an inventor, along with his brother Steve, and together they hold several patents worldwide in the field of electromagnetics and energy generation technology.

He has a daughter and son-in-law, Pastor David and Janet Russell, a son and daughter-in-law, Pastor Ryan and Colleen Durham, and four grandchildren, Gavin and Ethan Russell, as well as Kaia Grace and Ian Ryan Durham. He and his wife Sheryl of 52 years live in Stuart, Florida.

VERITAS RESURGENCE PUBLISHING

Other books this Trilogy:

THE OTHER SIDE OF REALITY: BOOK ONE
THE CURSE OF THE IMMORTAL FRUIT

THE OTHER SIDE OF REALITY: BOOK TWO
THE CONQUEST OF SAPIENT CASTLE

Other books available from Veritas Resurgence:

Miracle On Markel Street
Steve Morris

The Stowaway In First Class
Anthony DeSantis

The Autobiography Of Judas Iscariot
Hugh Vickery

The Ticket
Hugh Vickery